PUBLISHER'S WARNING

Readers should be advised that the consumption of the written words on the following pages could lead to nightmares, irresistible urges, spontaneous dance or ritual, and deep-seated needs to cloister oneself in a damp basement, musty library, or cavernous tomb. We urge you to bolt your doors and dim the lights, as this book is best read by antique lamp or candlelight. Should you find yourself reading this in a public setting—perhaps a lovely park bench or a crowded bus— we advise careful consideration of loud screams or gasps of horror, as they could give your fellow citizens an altogether wrong impression of you. Above all, be warned that there are some dark and twisting roads ahead, and we cannot be held responsible for what ghoulish companions you encounter—nor for what inevitably follows behind you, slinky and shuddering, as you run.

The Weiser Book of

HORROR AND
THE OCCULT

HIDDEN MAGIC, OCCULT TRUTHS,
and the Stories That Started It All

The Weiser Book of

HORROR AND THE OCCULT

Edited and Introduced by LON MILO DUQUETTE

WEISERBOOKS
San Francisco, CA / Newburyport, MA

This edition first published in 2014 by Weiser Books
Red Wheel/Weiser, LLC
With offices at:
665 Third Street, Suite 400
San Francisco, CA 94107
www.redwheelweiser.com

ISBN: 978-1-57863-572-6

Library of Congress Cataloging-in-Publication Data available upon request.

Cover design by Barb Fisher
Cover art © Symonenko Viktoriia/Shutterstock
Interior by Maureen Forys, Happenstance Type-O-Rama
Typeset in Mrs. Eaves and Futura

Printed in the United States of America.
EBM
10 9 8 7 6 5 4 3 2 1

CONTENTS

HORROR TAKES ITS TIME

Lon Milo DuQuette

The oldest and strongest emotion of mankind is fear, and the oldest and strongest kind of fear is fear of the unknown. These facts few psychologists will dispute, and their admitted truth must establish for all time the genuineness and dignity of the weirdly horrible tale as a literary form.

H.P. LOVECRAFT, *Supernatural Horror in Literature*

"Oh, my sweet summer child," Old Nan said quietly, "what do you know of fear? Fear is for the winter, my little lord, when the snows fall a hundred feet deep and the ice wind comes howling out of the north. Fear is for the long night, when the sun hides its face for years at a time, and little children are born and live and die all in darkness while the dire wolves grow gaunt and hungry, and the white walkers move through the woods."

GEORGE R.R. MARTIN, *A Game of Thrones*

Horror is the literature of the damned; a demon-child art-form— conceived in the fertile depths of subconscious hell; gestated in the lonely womb of fear and despair; brought to troubled birth by the midwife of tortured obsessions; and reared to grotesque maturity in the prison asylum of a terrified imagination. Horror, to be truly horror, must be more than a frightening story. It must be a cloistered odyssey, a claustrophobic dance with madness. Above all, horror must be a traumatic and soul-mutating spiritual experience—sublime, elegant, and terrible.

Sounds disturbing, doesn't it? I hope so. Horror *should* be disturbing. But, at first glance, classic horror seldom presents itself as the product of a disturbed mind. On the contrary, some of the best works of the genre are introduced by a narrator who seems as sane and rational as you or I—an ordinary mind which, at the moment, is merely grappling with extraordinary psychological issues with which we all can more or less identify. But beware dear reader! Your gentle empathy with the story's protagonist is a subtle poison that within a breathtakingly few paragraphs disrobes your soul and lulls you into a poppied sleep. Naked and vulnerable (and now uncertain of your own sanity), horror draws you irresistibly into the mind of the main character of a nightmare.

For me (or anyone who stubbornly refuses to grow up completely) literature doesn't get better than *that*.

I turned nine years old in July of 1957, and was enduring my second melancholy summer of exile in the uncivilized wilderness of Nebraska.[1] I realize the word "exile" probably sounds melodramatic, but I was a very melodramatic child in 1957. Nebraska was for me an alien planet, cruel and hostile.

I hadn't been *born* in Nebraska. I had been kidnapped by my own parents and taken there against my will.[2] I was a Southern California boy, and I thoroughly enjoyed my first seven years in that hip and sunny fairyland where movies were made; where rock-*n*-roll was evolving and the dreams and industries of the "Space Age" made us

---

1 I sincerely apologize to Nebraskans, past and present, who might be offended by my words, and ask the reader to please be mindful that my comments here about Nebraska and Nebraskans are merely giving voice to the private, personal, subjective, and immature observations of the high-strung and unhappy nine-year-old Lon Milo DuQuette. They do not necessarily reflect my current objective opinions of the Great State of Nebraska or her remarkable and resilient citizens. I sincerely apologize to Nebraskans, past and present, who might be offended by my words.

2 Of course I wasn't actually "kidnapped." Again, my flair for the overly dramatic is getting the best of me. (That happens, especially when writing about overly dramatic subjects like horror stories.) My family moved from Southern California to Nebraska so that my father could start a new business. I was nonetheless traumatized by the move and resisted every phase of the process.

all feel like citizens of a bright and gleaming future. The family's move to Nebraska in 1955 was in my eyes a doleful exodus back to the dark ages—a "trail of tears" from a twentieth-century beach paradise to a nineteenth-century prairie hell. Powerless to change my circumstances, I pouted and steeped in a bitter broth of self-absorbed discontentment.

I hated Nebraska. I hated Nebraskans. I hated the way they talked. I hated the way they laughed about butchering animals. I hated the way they preached about their wrathful God—a God who hated Negroes and Chinese (even though there wasn't a Negro or Chinese person within a hundred miles of our provincial town); a God who would condemn little boys to the flames of eternal torment just for the sin of *not believing* in a God who hated Negroes and Chinese. Most of all, I hated the way Nebraskans, young and old, actually took smug pride in their own lack of sophistication. They wore their ingenuousness like a badge of honor, and rudely ridiculed and bullied anyone else who *did not* also proudly clothe themselves with the same coarse robe of premeditated ignorance.

I admit this must sound terribly unkind. "Hate" is a strong and unhealthy passion, especially for a nine-year-old boy. But hate springs from *fear* (real or imagined), and in my young mind there was much to fear in Nebraska. Even as a youngster I sensed a palpable darkness; a prairie madness; a nameless evil brooding just underneath the surface of the bib overalls and cotton house dresses; a slumbering beast just waiting to be awakened by the kiss of alcohol or jealousy or greed or lust; an evil that is ever mindful that the nearest policeman is many miles (and perhaps hours) away; a black and primitive wickedness that takes poisonous root in the solitary psyche of those who toil alone in the earth from dawn to dusk, season after season, year after year; an evil that smothers in the heart all breath of human compassion or empathy for the pain and terror they inflict daily on the helpless beasts they breed for slaughter or the children they breed for labor and war; a twisted and perverse evil that feeds on guilt and self-loathing; an evil that incubates in the deafening silence of sweltering summer nights or the perpetual darkness of winter and hideously hatches like a basilisk egg into monstrous acts of rape and incest, and murder, and suicide.

The houses themselves are possessed of dark subconscious secrets—indeed, they are built upon them. Unlike the sunny and uninsulated bungalows of Southern California, Nebraska houses hide their own dungeons. Large as the footprint of the house itself, these cinder block chambers (the natives call them "basements") offer a modicum of insulation from the frozen sod of winter, and an area of damp coolness from the blistering heat of summer. Basements also provide residents a dark hole in the ground in which to cower from the whirling death clouds called tornadoes—tangible wind devils that regularly strike down from pus-green clouds and sweep across the earth, bringing grotesque death and destruction to anything and everyone in their path.

Yes. There was much for a young man to fear in Nebraska. I was lonely, depressed, and morose. One sweltering humid summer morning I became so desperately bored I did something unthinkable for a nine-year-old boy in Nebraska.

I found something to read.

That morning I lingered in my sweat-soaked bed until I knew I was alone in the house. I got up and turned on our old Raytheon television set in the living room but could only get a scattered signal of a "farm report." Like electricity and indoor toilets, television was new to rural Nebraska, and the few broadcast stations in operation were very far away. Reluctantly, I switched off the crackling television and turned my attention to the living room bookcase. I looked for something—anything—that might alleviate my ennui or titillate my idle brain.

The family library had a few things that might distract me. My father was a pretty interesting guy (a native Californian and very *un*-Nebraskan). He valued education and wanted his sons to cherish books, so he had recently purchased a new set of *World Book Encyclopedia* to display next to a few old sets of matched volumes of literature.

I figured the encyclopedia would be too much like homework, so I turned my attention to an old twenty-volume set of the *World's Greatest Literature*.[3]

At first glance *The Last of the Mohicans* looked like it might be fun, but I soon discovered it much too grown-up and difficult. I finally settled on volume 8 of the series, *Tales of Mystery and Imagination*, by Edgar Allan Poe. I opened it up and saw to my delight that it was a collection of short stories with titles that were absolutely irresistible to a miserable nine-year-old boy: "The Premature Burial," "The Masque of the Red Death," "The Tell-Tale Heart," and so on. Premature burials and red death sounded very promising indeed, but back in California I had actually seen a terrifying cartoon called "The Tell-Tale Heart" at the old Lakewood Theater. [4] I recalled that my mother became very upset with my older brother Marc for taking "little Lonnie" to see such an adult and disturbing film. I poured myself a glass of buttermilk, plopped down in the big chair by the open window, and opened the book.

Once I started to read, however, I knew I was way out of my depth. There were lots of big words, incomprehensible foreign language phrases and epigrams, and geographic references. Every other sentence seemed to make reference to some ancient legend or myth or classic poem. I was forced to actually *use* the dictionary and encyclopedia just to plod my way through the first story, "The Pit and the Pendulum." But I eventually *did* get through it, and after I closed the book I realized I had become someone else—someone I liked who could use the dictionary and encyclopedia. I learned about the horrors of the Spanish Inquisition (How delightfully evil was *that!*); I was exposed for the first time to the melodically elegant use of the English language;[5]

---

3 Spencer Press, 1936. He must have had the books since before he married Mom.

4 *The Tell-Tale Heart*, directed by Ted Parmelee, narrated by James Mason, screenplay by Bill Scott and Fred Grable. (1953; Columbia Pictures).

5 I had to read Poe so deliberately that I felt as though I was reading aloud. In my soul, Poe's voice carried the gentlest lilt of a fine Southern gentleman and the tortured desperation of my favorite actor, Vincent Price.

most importantly, I discovered I was capable of being touched by art—capable of being possessed by *passion*. My ennui lifted and was replaced by a pre-adolescent worship of the macabre and the genius and wit of its creators. This passion has yet to subside. I spent the rest of that summer with Poe . . . and the dictionary, and the *World Book Encyclopedia*.

Ironically, the same nineteenth-century-*esque* liabilities I despised about 1950s Nebraska life proved to be priceless assets of atmosphere that allowed me to conjure the perfect reading environment to savor the ecstasy of classic horror.

Horror takes its time, and to properly appreciate it you must also take your time. It has a pace, a slow, incessant rhythm—like your own heartbeat, or your own breath. After all, the great innovators of the art were writers of the Gilded Age who wrote for a nineteenth- and early twentieth-century audience.[6] Nebraska in 1957 had both her feet planted firmly in the nineteenth and early twentieth centuries. That summer morning in 1957 could have just as easily been 1857, accompanied by the same soundtrack of bucolic silence; the same light searing through the same sun-stained yellow window shades; no hint of modern objective reality, no diversions of bustling civilization; no diversions of airplanes roaring overhead, no freeways in the distance, no sirens, no television, no radio, no air-conditioner; only the white noise of a million cicadas and the hiss of my own blood running through my brain, the incessant swing of the pendulum of an ancient clock, the barking of a distant dog, the cawing of a crow, the almost imperceptible whisper of the delicate film of curtains as they billowed gently toward me like the gossamer negligée of a lovesick ghost.

This was the background music of my honeymoon with horror—playing as the honey-sweet words of Edgar Allan Poe, lugubriously woven elegant phrases from the age of gilded manners into a symphony of tortured rapture. Only had I been obliged to read the yellowing pages by the light of a whale oil lamp could my anachronistic reading experience have been more exquisitely atmospheric.

---

6 The offerings in this anthology date from 1851 to 1922.

I was so lucky.

Today most of us find it almost impossible to recapture the sepia-toned world that best conducts horror from the page to the soul. Twenty-first-century readers, spoiled by spectacular special effects of the cinema, demand instant gratification from the written word—explosive shocks and gore-splattered attacks upon the senses. We no longer allow ourselves time to refine the rapture of terror. We wolf down the junk food snacks of violence and carnage when, with just a little patience, we could leisurely savor a rich and soul-satisfying banquet of elegant horror. We are missing so much.

That summer with Poe and my newly awakened love for the written word would eventually have profound effects upon my life, the most obvious being my eventual career as a writer. Writing is not only what I do for a living, it is my art, my joy, my voice, my meditation, my prayer, my confession, my declaration of independence, my act of worship, my song of self-awareness. My profession, however, has taken many years to evolve and develop. My 1957 boyhood love affair with horror had more immediate and dramatic consequences. Simply put—*I woke up.*

Poe's narrative voice clearly revealed to me that I possessed my own narrative voice. That hot summer morning, my consciousness instantly expanded. I no longer just passively *saw* or *heard* or *smelled* or *felt* the things around me. I woke up and became consciously *aware* that I was seeing and hearing and smelling and feeling the things around me. I became at once the observer and the observed of my own movie, and like the voice-over narration in a film-noir detective story I began to tell myself the bedtime story of my own existence, and the narration continues to this moment.

Thank you, Edgar Allan Poe. Thank you, horror literature.

The genre of classic horror has also changed the world. It can be argued that horror is the mother of science fiction—and that science fiction has molded the future and touched the consciousness of countless millions of fans who now have given themselves permission to dream like gods. In its way, horror is the grandmother of theoretical mathematics, quantum physics, and the mutation of intelligence in this corner of the galaxy. But it all had to start somewhere, and the editors of this anthology have labored lovingly to pay homage to the founding fathers of art form. Some of them, like Edgar Allan Poe, or H.P. Lovecraft, or Bram Stoker, or Sir Arthur Conan Doyle, require little or no introduction. But others are perhaps less familiar to you. We have provided the briefest of biographical sketches for all our authors at the beginning of each selections, but I would like to take this opportunity to write a few extra words about three of the stars of our production who also deserve, in my opinion, to be recognized as *founding fathers* of horror:

Sir Edward Bulwer-Lytton, who I believe should be credited with establishing early in the nineteenth century the archetypal form and devices of the horror genre;

Robert W. Chambers, who late in the nineteenth century broke the space-time membrane of gothic horror and smashed open the doors of our subconscious—the same doors from which H.P. Lovecraft's primordial "Old Ones" would ooze out, forcing us to cower before our shadow souls;

and **Aleister Crowley**, a real-life, unapologetic black magician who early in the twentieth century rolled up his sleeves and did battle with those shadows to turn demons of darkness into angels of light.

Sir Edward Bulwer-Lytton (1803–1873)

Have you ever heard these phrases?

"It was a dark and stormy night . . . " or,

"The pen is mightier than the sword . . . " or,

"Pursuit of the almighty dollar"?

These familiar clichés first poured forth from the pen of Sir Edward Bulwer-Lytton, the prolific English playwright, poet, and novelist. As might be expected of a gentleman of his breeding, the noble Lord Lytton pursued these literary diversions as an amateur while he busied himself with the serious duties of serving his Queen (Victoria) as *Secretary of State for the Colonies* and a wide assortment of other stiff-collared diplomatic and political responsibilities. He published his first book of poems in 1820, and in 1828, when his semi-titillating essay on the whimsical subject of nineteenth-century *dandyism* was released, it was clear to the reading public that here was a fellow who could be wryly entertaining as well as erudite.

While his occult tales and horror stories have become favorites of lovers of the mysterious and macabre, Lytton's most publicly beloved and familiar works remain his post-biblical epic, *The Last Days of Pompeii* (1834), which has over the years captured the imagination of film-makers; and his dramatic historical fiction, *Rienzi* (1835), which Richard Wagner turned into an enduring opera. His popularity with the general public notwithstanding, Lord Lytton deserves serious recognition as one of the primary godfathers of horror. This enduring admiration attests to his skill with words, but even more impressive are his impeccable credentials among serious occultists.

Although empirical evidence is absent, Lytton is said to have been an initiate of one or more of the mysterious continental magical secret societies that obliquely claimed they were of ancient Rosicrucian origins. He was almost certainly the friend and confidant of the great French magician, Alphonse Louis Constant (Eliphas Levi, 1810-1875), the father of modern ceremonial magic.

As a young member of the Rosicrucian Order AMORC, I was instructed by my elder adepts (in no uncertain terms) that I was to read and study the *works* of *Lord Lytton*, especially his occult story *Zanoni*.[7] Written in 1842 (a full generation before the founding of Madam Blavatsky's Theosophical Society or the Hermetic Order of the Golden

---

7 Read my notes on Zanoni by purchasing an electronic copy of *Zanoni, Books One, Two, and Three*, published as digital books as part of the Magical Antiquarian Curiosity Shoppe (A Weiser Books collection!).

Dawn), the opening words of *Zanoni* can be interpreted as a Rosicrucian confession from Lord Lytton himself:

> It so chanced that some years ago, in my younger days, whether of authorship of life, I felt the desire to make myself acquainted with the true origins and tenets of the singular sect known by the name of Rosicrucians.

The plot of *Zanoni* is a darkly appealing love story that inaugurates all the genteel devices of classic horror-love that we will (a few years later) recognize in the works of Edgar Allan Poe, Robert W. Chambers, and others. But the text of *Zanoni* also reveals (to the trained eye) the language of a fellow occultist. In fact, it is clear that *Zanoni* could not possibly have been written by anyone other than a *bona fide* initiate of the mysteries. The story even makes indirect references to a magic *book*—a book that is undoubtedly the very *real* tome known to scholars today as *The Book of Abra-Melin*.[8] This landmark occult grimoire (c. 1378) would remain untranslated and unknown to the English-speaking world (or indeed anyone but the most knowledgeable and serious student of the occult) until 1888 when Golden Dawn adept S.L. MacGreggor Mathers translated fragments of the text, which he found in the Bibliotheque de l'Arsenal in Paris.

The Book of Abra-Melin is considered by many to be the Rosetta Stone of Western Magick, elevating the misunderstood superstitions of the mediaeval sorcerers to a spiritual science as sacred and viable as the self-transformational traditions of Eastern mysticism. As it would seem, His Lordship, Sir Edward Bulwer-Lytton—dandy, diplomat, and novelist—was rubbing elbows on a regular basis with very same mystics and magicians who not only knew of the book's existence but were intimately familiar with its contents and significance.

---

8 Abraham Von Worms, *The Book of Abramelin*, ed. Georg Dehn, trans. Steven Guth, foreword by Lon Milo DuQuette (Lake Worth, FL: Nicholas Hays, Inc., 2006).

It is clear to me that where secret occult mysteries and practices are concerned it was not a case of Lord Lytton gleaning his occult knowledge from nineteenth-century English Rosicrucian pretenders, but one of nineteenth-century "Rosicrucians" getting their occult knowledge from *him*!

While we heap praise on Lytton for being a founding father of *horror*, we must also credit him for helping introduce the world to the genre of *science fiction*. His 1871 novel *The Coming Race* would prove to be a breathtaking and disturbing look into the future. Unfortunately, early in the twentieth century the imaginative ideas put forth in *The Coming Race* would be seized and distorted into a monstrous vision by the madmen of Germany's Third Reich, and employed like some malevolent conjuration to invoke a great demon upon the earth in the form of the genocidal terrors of the Second World War. No horror fiction story can possibly compare to such unimaginable evil—such incalculable pain and death suffered by millions upon millions of our fellow human beings.

Of course, I am not suggesting that we blame Lord Edward Bulwer-Lytton for the genocidal horror of the Holocaust. However, we would all do well to be mindful of Lytton's own words, "The pen is mightier than the sword," and be aware of the awesome power the written word has to effect changes in human consciousness—for good or for ill.

Robert W. Chambers (1865–1933)

If H.P. Lovecraft is the *Christ of horror*, then most assuredly Robert W. Chambers was his *John the Baptist*.

Recently it was my privilege to introduce and curate the series of short stories first published in 1895 under the collective title *The King in Yellow* by Robert W. Chambers.[9] To avoid paraphrasing myself,

9 Robert W. Chambers, *Yellow Sign, An Excerpt from the King in Yellow: The King In Yellow series, Magical Antiquarian Curiosity Shoppe, A Weiser Books Collection,* Introduction by Lon Milo DuQuette (San Francisco, CA: Weiser Books, 2012).

I append a portion of my introduction below. While I refer specifically to *The King in Yellow*, my observations of Chambers' style, technique, and imagination apply also to this book's Chambers selection, "The Messenger."

Perhaps you have heard of *The King in Yellow*? No? Neither had I until a few years ago, when a filmmaker contacted me and informed me he was making a film of *The King in Yellow* and asked if I would be interested in appearing in a cameo role in the production. Before I gave him my answer (the project was later abandoned), I did a bit of digging and discovered a most remarkable treasure—a terrifying work of American horror that predates by a quarter century the first short story by H.P. Lovecraft. Indeed, *The King in Yellow* by Robert W. Chambers is arguably the archetypal inspiration for what would become an entire genre of horror fiction for which the immortal Lovecraft is ultimately credited.

Robert W. Chambers (1865-1933) is not exactly a household name, but that has not always been the case. Late in his career his romantic novels and historical fictions were wildly popular, his books best-sellers, his magazine installments eagerly awaited. For a time he was considered the most successful American literary figure of the day. Yet his later and lighter offerings, while bringing him fame and modest fortune, are forgettable bonbons when compared to the strong meat and innovative brilliance of his horror fiction. The most notable of all his work is *The King in Yellow*, a collection of short stories whose plots are loosely connected to an infamous imaginary book and play of the same title banned universally because of its ominous tendency to drive mad those who read it or came in contact with it. Indeed, the terror begins immediately, with the reader unsure whether or not madness and suicide will be the price he or she will pay for turning the page.

I was a bit disoriented when I began reading *The King in Yellow's* opening story—a dizzying effect that I'm sure Chambers intended to induce in the minds of his "gay-nineties" readers. The tale, called "The Repairer of Reputations," takes place in the science fiction "future" of a 1920s New York City, a metropolis of street names, parks, and landmarks familiar to us still today, which Chambers meticulously paints from his rich palette of images (he was, after all, a classically trained and skilled artist and designer). However, there is something disturbingly tweaked with the entire milieu of the story. It all takes place in a utopian and prosperous post-Civil War America—a blend of aristocratic republic and military dictatorship that could have easily evolved from the strange bed-fellows of the Gilded Age's contending movements: nationalistic laissez-faire capitalism and the liberal yet pragmatic ideals of social progressivism. From the opening lines, we are instantly plunged into an alternate reality where the comfortable and familiar past has been slightly altered and we are forced to confront the infinite "what ifs" of history—and in doing so calling into question the objective reality of the present.

Nestled within this surreal environment, we are introduced to a well-spoken narrator who at first seems to be a faithful servant of the truth, but who will soon give us reason to doubt both his sanity and our own. But I won't spoil that for you.

Like Lovecraft would do decades later, Chambers allows the reader's own imagination to do the heavy lifting of terror. Cassilda's Song, which serves as the epigram for the entire work, is supposedly clipped from Act I, Scene 2 of the play, *The King in Yellow*, and without burdening the reader's imagination with concrete certitudes, conjures images of strange locales and vistas not of this earth, indeed, not of this universe, and only hints of characters of unspeakable power and horror.

> *Along the shore the cloud waves break,*
> *The twin suns sink beneath the lake,*
> *The shadows lengthen*
> *In Carcosa.*
>
> *Strange is the night where black stars rise,*
> *And strange moons circle through the skies*
> *But stranger still is*
> *Lost Carcosa.*
>
> *Songs that the Hyades shall sing,*
> *Where flap the tatters of the King,*
> *Must die unheard in*
> *Dim Carcosa.*

Song of my soul, my voice is dead,
Die thou, unsung, as tears unshed
Shall dry and die in
Lost Carcosa.

Like all great works of horror, the story becomes disturbing, dark, and terrifying in direct proportion to the degree to which our own hearts and minds are disturbed, dark, and frightened.

Aleister Crowley (1875–1947)

Unlike Lord Lytton and Robert Chambers, Aleister Crowley is *not* remembered primarily for his works of fiction. Admittedly, he was a prolific poet, and in this capacity, even in his early twenties, he received a measure of critical praise and encouragement. His two novels, *Moonchild* (1917), and *Diary of a Drug Fiend* (1922), also received a modicum of critical recognition and over the years have indirectly inspired a handful of film efforts. His short stories,[10] plays, and essays (most privately published and now treasures coveted by collectors) were obviously written for an elite audience of highly educated esotericists and close associates capable of appreciating his elaborate in-jokes, pornographic allusions, and obscure references. As much as he lamented his rejection by the public, it appears he went to great lengths to openly court his own vilification.

For the reader who is completely unfamiliar with the person of Aleister Crowley I highly recommend his own *Confessions*[11] and the recent biography *Perdurabo—The Life of Aleister Crowley.*[12] I has been my pleasure and challenge to write a handful of books concerning the

---

10 Including *The Testament of Magdalen Blair,* which appears in this anthology.

11 Aleister Crowley, *The Confessions of Aleister Crowley* (1929), ed. John Symonds and Kenneth Grant (1969; repr., London and New York: Arkana, 1989).

12 Richard Kaczynski, *Perdurabo: The Life of Aleister Crowley* (Berkeley, CA: North Atlantic Books, 2010).

life and work of this remarkable man. The following brief excerpt is from my book, *Understanding Aleister Crowley's Thoth Tarot.*[13]

Paradoxes seem to define the life and career of Edward Alexander (Aleister) Crowley.[14] Yes, in many ways he was a scoundrel. There is no doubt that he wallowed shamelessly in his carefully cultivated persona as England's literary and spiritual bad-boy. At the same time he took life and himself very seriously. Among other distinctions, he was a world-class mountaineer,[15] chess master, painter, poet, sportsman, novelist, critic, and theatrical producer. He introduced America to astrology,[16] Isadora Duncan to the I Ching, Aldous Huxley to mescaline, and the poet Victor Neuberg to hiking and high magick. As an agent provocateur, writing for an English-language German propaganda newspaper in New York, he penned the outrageous and inflammatory editorials that provoked a reluctant United States Congress to enter the First World War on England's side.[17]

---

13 Lon Milo DuQuette, *Understanding Aleister Crowley's Thoth Tarot* (Boston, MA: Red Wheel/Weiser, LLC. 2003), 7-8.

14 1875-1947.

15 By 1920 Crowley still held the world record for a number of mountaineering feats, including the greatest pace uphill (4,000 feet in 83 minutes) at over 16,000 feet on Mexico's Iztaccihuatl in 1900; the first ascent of the Nevado de Toluca by a solitary climber 1901; and his 1902 assault on K2, where he spent 65 days on the Baltoro glacier.

16 Ghostwriting for Evangeline Adams, Crowley wrote the bulk of the material first published under her name, including her classic texts *Astrology: Your Place in the Sun* (1927) and *Astrology: Your Place Among the Stars* (1930). These works made "astrology" a household word in America and Europe and catapulted Adams to celebrated status as "Astrologer to Wall Street and Washington." Recently Crowley's co-authorship has been graciously acknowledged by the Adams estate and has resulted in the release of *Astrological Principles of Astrology* by Aleister Crowley and Evangeline Adams (York Beach, ME: Red Wheel/Weiser, 2001).

17 It is often forgotten that the United States was very close to entering the First World War on *Germany's* side. Much to the horror of the German Foreign Ministry, Crowley's editorials made it appear that it was Germany's intention (in fact its foreign policy) to engage in unrestricted submarine warfare against civilian shipping. Even though this was at the time an outrageous falsehood, Crowley's editorials were

During the Second World War, at the request of friend and Naval Intelligence officer Ian Fleming,[18] Crowley provided Winston Churchill with valuable insights into the superstitions and magical mindset of the leaders of the Third Reich. He also suggested to the Prime Minister, if reports can be believed, that he exploit the enemy's magical paranoia by being photographed as much as possible giving the two-fingered "V for Victory" gesture. This sign is the manual version of the magical sign of Apophis-Typhon, a powerful symbol of destruction and annihilation, that, according to magical tradition, is capable of defeating the solar energies represented by the swastika.

Astonishingly, Crowley's adventures and achievements, more than any dozen men of ambition and genius could realistically hope to garner in a lifetime, seem almost to be distractions when weighed against his monumental exploits of self-discovery. His visionary writings and his efforts to synthesize and integrate esoteric spiritual systems of East and West[19] make him one of the most fascinating cultural and religious figures of the twentieth century.

Even though Crowley did not, like Edward Bulwer-Lytton, invent the genre that would define the format and atmosphere of classic horror; even though he wasn't responsible for transforming horror into the morbid-sweet love-song of a tormented soul like Edgar Allan Poe; even though he didn't smash the dimensional boundaries of space-time to plumb new depths of psychological hell like Robert Chambers and H.P. Lovecraft; he did something none of them did. He actually lived the terrifying and ecstatic events of the real life horror-love story-adventure of his own amazing life.

---

used to create an anti-German hysteria that would eventually sweep the United States into the conflict on England's side. In a very real way, Aleister Crowley saved his beloved England using only his pen as a magical wand.

18 Ian (Lancaster) Fleming (1908-1964)—pseudonym Atticus—British journalist, secret service agent, writer, whose most famous creation was superhero James Bond, Agent 007. Crowley and Fleming were indeed friends. Copies of their correspondence still exist, some of which discuss matters of occult propaganda and the interrogation of Rudolf Hess.

19 He called his system "Scientific Illuminism." Its motto: "The Method of Science—The Aim of Religion."

Crowley is not important to us for the horror stories he wrote, but for the magnificent horror story he was.

He didn't just write about demons, and devils, and angels, vampires—he invoked them, evoked them, conjured them, battled them, conquered them; he didn't just write about the wonders and terrors of other dimensions, he willfully penetrated them, navigated them, transcended them—then he wrote about them in exacting detail.

Nearly seventy years after his death, the man who the tabloids called the "most dangerous man on earth," the man they called the "wickedest man in the world," the man who in all seriousness called himself the "Beast 666," is now receiving the academic and philosophical attention and recognition that eluded him in life.

Crowley's influence today on the literary art form of horror is incalculable. There isn't a modern writer of horror, science fiction or fantasy who has not in some fundamental way been directly or indirectly influenced by Crowley.

Crowley's dead. But his "horror" reaches from beyond the grave. Robert Chambers wrote of an accursed book and play called The King in Yellow. Supposedly, everyone who read The King in Yellow went hideously insane. I think of that and smile when I encounter people today who still fearfully hold the person of Aleister Crowley in superstitious awe.

"Is it dangerous to study Aleister Crowley?" I am still asked. Aleister Crowley was by no means perfect. He was not good with people, and often alienated those who loved him dearest. His bold explorations of human sexuality and drugs (always meticulously recorded and analyzed) are fascinating to study, but were never intended to be casually emulated. I have never encountered anyone who knew him that did not disapprove of some aspect of his character or behavior.

But he is dead. For us, only his works remain as a measure of the man, and they are currently more accessible to the general public than at any time during his life. His influence on the modern world of art, literature, religion, and philosophy is now widely acknowledged even by his most vehement critics.

But is it dangerous for some people to study Aleister Crowley? I guess I have to say "Yes." For those whose belief in a God of goodness hinges upon the reality of Devil who is equally evil—for the super-stitious, the ignorant, the lazy, the immature, the unbalanced, the mentally ill, the paranoid, the faint-hearted; for anyone who for any reason cannot or will not take responsibility for their own actions, their own lives, their own souls; for these people Aleister Crowley is still a very dangerous man.[20]

And now, dear reader, I will leave you to enjoy the works of these three masters of horror and the choir of other luminaries of the genre. I sincerely hope you enjoy your time with them and will treasure this beautifully produced book. Perhaps when you have finished reading it you'll want to put it in your family library—near the dictionary and encyclopedia. Who knows—perhaps someday some bored young man or woman will discover it on a hot summer morning.

For the time being . . . I bid you goodnight.

LON MILO DUQUETTE

---

20 From Lon Milo DuQuette, *The Magick of Aleister Crowley* (Boston, MA: Weiser Books, 2003), 8.

THE STORIES

THE HOUSE AND
THE BRAIN

by Sir Edward Bulwer Lytton

Edward Bulwer-Lytton (1803-1873) was an English author of poetry, plays, and novels. He served under Queen Victoria as Secretary of State for the Colonies from 1858-1859. Ironically, he is probably most famous for having penned the words, "It was a dark and stormy night," which have become in the rarefied school of mystery writers a cliché example of a mediocre and unimaginative way to begin a novel. Lord Lytton, however, was anything but mediocre and unimaginative. Among his many works of fiction were *The Coming Race*, which brought to the birth of the genre of science fiction literature *A Strange Story*, and *Zanoni*, whose spooky plots revealed his serious interest in (and mastery of) the occult. His story "The Haunters and the Haunted, or, The House and the Brain" was immensely popular in 1859, but was largely forgotten until the 1920s when H.P. Lovecraft made mention of it.

The Haunted and the Haunters,
Or, the House and the Brain

A friend of mine, who is a man of letters and a philosopher, said to me one day, as if between jest and earnest—"Fancy! since we last met, I have discovered a haunted house in the midst of London."

"Really haunted?—and by what?—ghosts?"

"Well, I can't answer these questions—all I know is this—six weeks ago I and my wife were in search of a furnished apartment. Passing a quiet street, we saw on the window of one of the houses a bill, 'Apartments Furnished.' The situation suited us: we entered the house—liked the rooms—engaged them by the week—and left them the third day. No power on earth could have reconciled my wife to stay longer, and I don't wonder at it."

"What did you see?"

"Excuse me—I have no desire to be ridiculed as a superstitious dreamer—nor, on the other hand, could I ask you to accept on my affirmation what you would hold to be incredible without the evidence of your own senses. Let me only say this, it was not so much what we saw or heard (in which you might fairly suppose that we were the dupes of our own excited fancy, or the victims of imposture in others) that drove us away, as it was an undefinable terror which seized both of us whenever we passed by the door of a certain unfurnished room, in which we neither saw nor heard anything. And the strangest marvel of all was, that for once in my life I agreed with my wife—silly woman though she be—and allowed, after the third night, that it was impossible to stay a fourth in that house. Accordingly, on the fourth morning, I summoned the woman who kept the house and attended on us, and told her that the rooms did not quite suit us, and we would not stay out our week. She said, dryly: 'I know why; you have stayed longer than any other lodger; few ever stayed a second night; none before you, a third. But I take it they have been very kind to you.'

"'They—who?' I asked, affecting a smile.

"'Why, they who haunt the house, whoever they are. I don't mind them; I remember them many years ago, when I lived in this house, not as a servant; but I know they will be the death of me some day. I don't care—I'm old, and must die soon, anyhow; and then I shall be with them, and in this house still.' The woman spoke with so dreary a calmness, that really it was a sort of awe that prevented my conversing with her farther. I paid for my week, and too happy were I and my wife to get off so cheaply."

"You excite my curiosity," said I; "nothing I should like better than to sleep in a haunted house. Pray give me the address of the one which you left so ignominiously."

My friend gave me the address; and when we parted, I walked straight towards the house thus indicated.

It is situated on the north side of Oxford Street, in a dull but respectable thoroughfare. I found the house shut up—no bill at the window, and no response to my knock. As I was turning away, a beer-boy, collecting pewter pots at the neighbouring areas, said to me, "Do you want anyone in that house, sir?"

"Yes, I heard it was to let."

"Let!—why, the woman who kept it is dead—has been dead these three weeks, and no one can be found to stay there, though Mr J— offered ever so much. He offered mother, who chars for him, £1 a week just to open and shut the windows, and she would not."

"Would not!—and why?"

"The house is haunted; and the old woman who kept it was found dead in her bed, with her eyes wide open. They say the devil strangled her."

"Pooh!—you speak of Mr J—. Is he the owner of the house?"

"Yes."

"Where does he live?"

"In G— Street, No. —."

"What is he?—in any business?"

"No, sir—nothing particular; a single gentleman."

I gave the pot-boy the gratuity earned by his liberal information, and proceeded to Mr J—, in G— Street, which was close by the street that boasted the haunted house. I was lucky enough to find Mr J— at home—an elderly man, with intelligent countenance and prepossessing manners.

I communicated my name and my business frankly. I said I heard the house was considered to be haunted—that I had a strong desire to examine a house with so equivocal a reputation—that I should be greatly obliged if he would allow me to hire it, though only for a night. I was willing to pay for that privilege whatever he might be inclined to ask. "Sir," said Mr J—, with great courtesy, "the house is at your service, for as short or as long a time as you please. Rent is out of the question—the obligation will be on my side should you be able to discover the cause of the strange phenomena which at present deprive it of all value. I cannot let it, for I cannot even get a servant to keep it in order or answer the door. Unluckily the house is haunted, if I may use that expression, not only by night, but by day; though at night the disturbances are of a more unpleasant and sometimes of a more alarming character.

"The poor old woman who died in it three weeks ago was a pauper whom I took out of a workhouse, for in her childhood she had been known to some of my family, and had once been in such good circumstances that she had rented that house of my uncle. She was a woman of superior education and strong mind, and was the only person I could ever induce to remain in the house. Indeed, since her death, which was sudden, and the coroner's inquest, which gave it a notoriety in the neighbourhood, I have so despaired of finding any person to take charge of it, much more a tenant, that I would willingly let it rent free for a year to anyone who would pay its rates and taxes."

"How long is it since the house acquired this sinister character?"

"That I can scarcely tell you, but very many years since. The old woman I spoke of said it was haunted when she rented it between thirty and forty years ago. The fact is that my life has been spent in the East Indies and in the civil service of the Company. I returned to England last year on inheriting the fortune of an uncle, amongst whose possessions was the house in question. I found it shut up and uninhabited. I was told that it was haunted, that no one would inhabit it. I smiled at what seemed to me so idle a story. I spent some money in repainting and roofing it—added to its old-fashioned furniture a few modern articles—advertised it, and obtained a lodger for a year. He was a colonel retired on half-pay. He came in with his family, a son and a daughter, and four or five servants: they all left the house the next day, and although they deponed that they had all seen something different, that something was equally terrible to all. I really could not in conscience sue, or even blame, the colonel for breach of agreement.

"Then I put in the old woman I have spoken of, and she was empowered to let the house in apartments. I never had one lodger who stayed more than three days. I do not tell you their stories—to no two lodgers have there been exactly the same phenomena repeated. It is better that you should judge for yourself, than enter the house with an imagination influenced by previous narratives; only be prepared to see and to hear something or other, and take whatever precautions you yourself please."

"Have you never had a curiosity yourself to pass a night in that house?"

"Yes. I passed not a night, but three hours in broad daylight alone in that house. My curiosity is not satisfied, but it is quenched. I have no desire to renew the experiment. You cannot complain, you see, sir, that I am not sufficiently candid; and unless your interest be exceedingly eager and your nerves unusually strong, I honestly add that I advise you *not* to pass a night in that house."

"My interest *is* exceedingly keen," said I, "and though only a coward will boast of his nerves in situations wholly unfamiliar to him, yet my nerves have been seasoned in such variety of danger that I have the right to rely on them—even in a haunted house."

Mr J— said very little more; he took the keys of the house out of his bureau, gave them to me,—and thanking him cordially for his frankness, and his urbane concession to my wish, I carried off my prize.

Impatient for the experiment, as soon as I reached home I summoned my confidential servant,—a young man of gay spirits, fearless temper, and as free from superstitious prejudice as anyone I could think of.

"F—," said I, "you remember in Germany how disappointed we were at not finding a ghost in that old castle, which was said to be haunted by a headless apparition? Well, I have heard of a house in London which, I have reason to hope, is decidedly haunted. I mean to sleep there to-night. From what I hear, there is no doubt that something will allow itself to be seen or to be heard—something, perhaps, excessively horrible. Do you think, if I take you with me, I may rely on your presence of mind, whatever may happen?"

"Oh, sir! pray trust me," answered F—, grinning with delight.

"Very well—then here are the keys of the house—this is the address. Go now—select for me any bedroom you please; and since the house has not been inhabited for weeks, make up a good fire—air the bed well—see, of course, that there are candles as well as fuel. Take with you my revolver and my dagger—so much for my weapons—arm yourself equally well; and if we are not a match for a dozen ghosts, we shall be but a sorry couple of Englishmen."

I was engaged for the rest of the day on business so urgent that I had not leisure to think much on the nocturnal adventure to which I had plighted my honour. I dined alone, and very late, and while dining, read, as is my habit. The volume I selected was one of Macaulay's Essays. I thought to myself that I would take the book with me; there was so much of healthfulness in the style, and practical life in the subjects, that it would serve as an antidote against the influences of superstitious fancy.

Accordingly, about half-past nine, I put the book into my pocket, and strolled leisurely towards the haunted house. I took with me a favourite dog—an exceedingly sharp, bold, and vigilant bull-terrier—a dog fond of prowling about strange ghostly corners and passages at night in search of rats—a dog of dogs for a ghost.

It was a summer night, but chilly, the sky somewhat gloomy and overcast. Still, there was a moon—faint and sickly, but still a moon—and if the clouds permitted, after midnight it would be brighter.

I reached the house, knocked, and my servant opened with a cheerful smile.

"All right, sir, and very comfortable."

"Oh!" said I, rather disappointed; "have you not seen nor heard anything remarkable?"

"Well, sir, I must own I have heard something queer."

"What?—what?"

"The sound of feet pattering behind me; and once or twice small noises like whispers close at my ear—nothing more."

"You are not at all frightened?"

"I! Not a bit of it, sir"; and the man's bold look reassured me on one point—viz. that, happen what might, he would not desert me.

We were in the hall, the street-door closed, and my attention was now drawn to my dog. He had at first ran in eagerly enough, but had sneaked back to the door, and was scratching and whining to get out. After patting him on the head, and encouraging him gently, the dog seemed to reconcile himself to the situation and followed me and F— through the house, but keeping close at my heels instead of hurrying inquisitively in advance, which was his usual and normal habit in all strange places. We first visited the subterranean apartments, the kitchen and other offices, and especially the cellars, in which last there were two or three bottles of wine still left in a bin, covered with cobwebs, and evidently, by their appearance, undisturbed for many years. It was clear that the ghosts were not wine-bibbers.

For the rest we discovered nothing of interest. There was a gloomy little backyard, with very high walls. The stones of this yard were very damp—and what with the damp, and what with the dust and smoke-grime on the pavement, our feet left a slight impression where we passed. And now appeared the first strange phenomenon witnessed by myself in this strange abode. I saw, just before me, the print of a foot suddenly form itself, as it were. I stopped, caught hold of my servant, and pointed to it. In advance of that footprint as suddenly dropped another. We both saw it. I advanced quickly to the place; the footprint kept advancing before me, a small footprint—the foot of a child: the impression was too faint thoroughly to distinguish the shape, but it seemed to us both that it was the print of a naked foot. This phenomenon ceased when we arrived at the opposite wall, nor did it repeat itself on returning.

We remounted the stairs, and entered the rooms on the ground floor, a dining parlour, a small back-parlour, and a still smaller third room that had been probably appropriated to a footman—all still as death. We then visited the drawing-rooms, which seemed fresh and new. In the front room I seated myself in an armchair. F— placed on the table the candlestick with which he had lighted us. I told him to shut the door. As he turned to do so, a chair opposite to me moved from the wall quickly and noiselessly, and dropped itself about a yard from my own chair, immediately fronting it.

"Why, this is better than the turning-tables," said I, with a half-laugh—and as I laughed, my dog put back his head and howled.

F—, coming back, had not observed the movement of the chair. He employed himself now in stilling the dog. I continued to gaze on the chair, and fancied I saw on it a pale blue misty outline of a human figure, but an outline so indistinct that I could only distrust my own vision. The dog now was quiet. "Put back that chair opposite to me," said I to F—; "put it back to the wall."

F— obeyed. "Was that you, sir?" said he, turning abruptly.

"I—what!"

"Why, something struck me. I felt it sharply on the shoulder—just here."

"No," said I. "But we have jugglers present, and though we may not discover their tricks, we shall catch *them* before they frighten *us*."

We did not stay long in the drawing-rooms—in fact, they felt so damp and so chilly that I was glad to get to the fire upstairs. We locked the doors of the drawing-rooms—a precaution which, I should observe, we had taken with all the rooms we had searched below. The bedroom my servant had selected for me was the best on the floor—a large one, with two windows fronting the street. The four-posted bed, which took up no inconsiderable space, was opposite to the fire, which burned clear and bright; a door in the wall to the left, between the bed and the window, communicated with the room which my servant appropriated to himself.

This last was a small room with a sofa-bed, and had no communication with the landing-place—no other door but that which conducted to the bedroom I was to occupy. On either side of my fireplace was a cupboard, without locks, flushed with the wall, and covered with the same dull-brown paper. We examined these cupboards—only hooks to suspend female dresses—nothing else; we sounded the walls—evidently solid—the outer walls of the building. Having finished the survey of these apartments, warmed myself a few moments, and lighted my cigar, I then, still accompanied by F—, went forth to complete my reconnoitre. In the landing-place there was another door; it was closed firmly. "Sir," said my servant in surprise, "I unlocked this door with all the others when I first came; it cannot have got locked from the inside, for it is a—"

Before he had finished his sentence the door, which neither of us then was touching, opened quietly of itself. We looked at each other a single instant. The same thought seized both—some human agency might be detected here. I rushed in first, my servant followed. A small blank dreary room without furniture—a few empty boxes and hampers in a corner—a small window—the shutters closed—not even a fireplace—no other door but that by which we had entered—no carpet on the floor, and the floor seemed very old, uneven, worm-eaten, mended here and there, as was shown by the whiter patches on the wood; but no living being, and no visible place in which a living being could have hidden. As we stood gazing around, the door by which we had entered closed as quietly as it had before opened: we were imprisoned.

For the first time I felt a creep of undefinable horror. Not so my servant. "Why, they don't think to trap us, sir; I could break that trumpery door with a kick of my foot."

"Try first if it will open to your hand," said I, shaking off the vague apprehension that had seized me, "while I open the shutters and see what is without."

I unbarred the shutters—the window looked on the little backyard I have before described; there was no ledge without—nothing but sheer descent. No man getting out of that window would have found any footing till he had fallen on the stones below.

F—, meanwhile, was vainly attempting to open the door. He now turned round to me, and asked my permission to use force. And I should here state, in justice to the servant, that, far from evincing any superstitious terrors, his nerve, composure, and even gaiety amidst circumstances so extraordinary compelled my admiration, and made me congratulate myself on having secured a companion in every way fitted to the occasion. I willingly gave him the permission he required. But though he was a remarkably strong man, his force was as idle as his milder efforts; the door did not even shake to his stoutest kick. Breathless and panting, he desisted. I then tried the door myself, equally in vain.

As I ceased from the effort, again that creep of horror came over me; but this time it was more cold and stubborn. I felt as if some strange and ghastly exhalation were rising up from the chinks of that rugged floor, and filling the atmosphere with a venomous influence hostile to human life. The door now very slowly and quietly opened as of its own accord. We precipitated ourselves into the landing-place. We both saw a large pale light—as large as the human figure, but shape-less and unsubstantial—move before us, and ascend the stairs that led from the landing into the attics. I followed the light, and my servant followed me. It entered, to the right of the landing, a small garret, of which the door stood open. I entered in the same instant. The light then collapsed into a small globule, exceedingly brilliant and vivid; rested a moment on a bed in the corner, quivered, and vanished. We approached the bed and examined it—a half-tester, such as is com-monly found in attics devoted to servants. On the drawers that stood near it we perceived an old faded silk kerchief, with the needle still left in a rent half repaired. The kerchief was covered with dust; probably it had belonged to the old woman who had last died in that house, and this might have been her sleeping-room.

I had sufficient curiosity to open the drawers; there were a few odds and ends of female dress, and two letters tied round with a nar-row ribbon of faded yellow. I took the liberty to possess myself of the letters. We found nothing else in the room worth noticing—nor did the light reappear; but we distinctly heard, as we turned to go, a pattering footfall on the floor—just before us. We went through the other attics (in all, four), the footfall still preceding us. Nothing to be seen—nothing but the footfall heard. I had the letters in my hand;

just as I was descending the stairs I distinctly felt my wrist seized, and a faint, soft effort made to draw the letters from my clasp. I only held them the more tightly, and the effort ceased.

We regained the bedchamber appropriated to myself, and I then remarked that my dog had not followed us when we had left it. He was thrusting himself close to the fire, and trembling. I was impatient to examine the letters; and while I read them, my servant opened a little box in which he had deposited the weapons I had ordered him to bring, took them out, placed them on a table close at my bed-head, and then occupied himself in soothing the dog, who, however, seemed to heed him very little.

The letters were short—they were dated; the dates exactly thirty-five years ago. They were evidently from a lover to his mistress, or a husband to some young wife. Not only the terms of expression, but a distinct reference to a former voyage indicated the writer to have been a seafarer. The spelling and handwriting were those of a man imperfectly educated, but still the language itself was forcible. In the expressions of endearment there was a kind of rough wild love; but here and there were dark unintelligible hints at some secret not of love—some secret that seemed of crime. "We ought to love each other," was one of the sentences I remember, "for how everyone else would execrate us if all was known." Again: "Don't let anyone be in the same room with you at night—you talk in your sleep." And again: "What's done can't be undone; and I tell you there's nothing against us unless the dead could come to life." Here there was underlined in a better handwriting (a female's), "They do!" At the end of the letter latest in date the same female hand had written these words: "Lost at sea the 4th of June, the same day as—"

I put down the letters, and began to muse over their contents.

Fearing, however, that the train of thought into which I fell might unsteady my nerves, I fully determined to keep my mind in a fit state to cope with whatever of marvellous the advancing night might bring forth. I roused myself—laid the letters on the table—stirred up the fire, which was still bright and cheering—and opened my volume of

Macaulay. I read quietly enough till about half-past eleven. I then threw myself dressed upon the bed, and told my servant he might retire to his own room, but must keep himself awake. I bade him leave open the door between the two rooms. Thus alone, I kept two candles burning on the table by my bed-head. I placed my watch beside the weapons, and calmly resumed my Macaulay.

Opposite to me the fire burned clear; and on the hearth-rug, seemingly asleep, lay the dog. In about twenty minutes I felt an exceedingly cold air pass by my cheek, like a sudden draught. I fancied the door to my right, communicating with the landing-place, must have got open; but no—it was closed. I then turned my glance to my left, and saw the flame of the candles violently swayed as by a wind. At the same moment the watch beside the revolver softly slid from the table—softly, softly—no visible hand—it was gone. I sprang up, seizing the revolver with the one hand, the dagger with the other; I was not willing that my weapons should share the fate of the watch. Thus armed, I looked round the floor—no sign of the watch. Three slow, loud, distinct knocks were now heard at the bed-head; my servant called out, "Is that you, sir?"

"No; be on your guard."

The dog now roused himself and sat on his haunches, his ears moving quickly backwards and forwards. He kept his eyes fixed on me with a look so strange that he concentrated all my attention on himself. Slowly he rose up, all his hair bristling, and stood perfectly rigid, and with the same wild stare. I had no time, however, to examine the dog. Presently my servant emerged from his room; and if ever I saw horror in the human face, it was then. I should not have recognised him had we met in the streets, so altered was every lineament. He passed by me quickly, saying in a whisper that seemed scarcely to come from his lips, "Run—run! it is after me!" He gained the door to the landing, pulled it open, and rushed forth. I followed him into the landing involuntarily, calling him to stop; but, without heeding me, he bounded down the stairs, clinging to the balusters, and taking several steps at a time. I heard, where I stood, the street door open—heard it again clap to. I was left alone in the haunted house.

It was but for a moment that I remained undecided whether or not to follow my servant; pride and curiosity alike forbade so dastardly a flight. I re-entered my room, closing the door after me, and proceeded cautiously into the interior chamber. I encountered nothing to justify my servant's terror. I again carefully examined the walls, to see if there were any concealed door. I could find no trace of one—not even a seam in the dull-brown paper with which the room was hung. How, then, had the Thing, whatever it was, which had so scared him, obtained ingress except through my own chamber?

I returned to my room, shut and locked the door that opened upon the interior one, and stood on the hearth, expectant and prepared. I now perceived that the dog had slunk into an angle of the wall, and was pressing himself close against it, as if literally trying to force his way into it. I approached the animal and spoke to it; the poor brute was evidently beside itself with terror. It showed all its teeth, the slaver dropping from its jaws, and would certainly have bitten me if I had touched it. It did not seem to recognise me. Whoever has seen at the Zoological Gardens a rabbit fascinated by a serpent, cowering in a corner, may form some idea of the anguish which the dog exhibited. Finding all efforts to soothe the animal in vain, and fearing that his bite might be as venomous in that state as if in the madness of hydrophobia, I left him alone, placed my weapons on the table beside the fire, seated myself, and recommenced my Macaulay.

Perhaps in order not to appear seeking credit for a courage, or rather a coolness, which the reader may conceive I exaggerate, I may be pardoned if I pause to indulge in one or two egotistical remarks.

As I hold presence of mind, or what is called courage, to be precisely proportioned to familiarity with the circumstance that lead to it, so I should say that I had been long sufficiently familiar with all experiments that appertain to the Marvellous. I had witnessed many very extraordinary phenomena in various parts of the world—phenomena that would be either totally disbelieved if I stated them, or ascribed to supernatural agencies. Now, my theory is that the Supernatural is the Impossible, and that what is called supernatural is only a something in the laws of nature of which we have been hitherto ignorant. Therefore, if a ghost rise before me, I have not the right to say, "So, then, the supernatural is possible," but rather, "So, then, the apparition of a ghost is, contrary to received opinion, within the laws of nature—*i.e.* not supernatural."

Now, in all that I had hitherto witnessed, and indeed in all the wonders which the amateurs of mystery in our age record as facts, a material living agency is always required. On the Continent you will find still magicians who assert that they can raise spirits. Assume for the moment that they assert truly, still the living material form of the magician is present; and he is the material agency by which from some constitutional peculiarities, certain strange phenomena are represented to your natural senses.

Accept again, as truthful, the tales of Spirit Manifestation in America—musical or other sounds—writings on paper, produced by no discernible hand—articles of furniture moved without apparent human agency—or the actual sight and touch of hands, to which no bodies seem to belong—still there must be found the *medium* or living being, with constitutional peculiarities capable of obtaining these signs. In fine, in all such marvels, supposing even that there is no imposture, there must be a human being like ourselves, by whom, or through whom, the effects presented to human beings are produced. It is so with the now familiar phenomena of mesmerism or electro-biology; the mind of the person operated on is affected through a material living agent. Nor, supposing it true that a mesmerised patient can respond to the will or passes of a mesmeriser a hundred miles distant, is the response less occasioned by a material being; it may be through a material fluid—call it Electric, call it Odic, call it what you will—which has the power of traversing space and passing obstacles, that the material effect is communicated from one to the other.

Hence all that I had hitherto witnessed, or expected to witness, in this strange house, I believed to be occasioned through some agency or medium as mortal as myself; and this idea necessarily prevented the awe with which those who regard as supernatural things that are not within the ordinary operations of nature, might have been impressed by the adventures of that memorable night.

As, then, it was my conjecture that all that was presented, or would be presented, to my senses, must originate in some human being gifted by constitution with the power so to present them, and having some motive so to do, I felt an interest in my theory which, in its way, was rather philosophical than superstitious. And I can sincerely say that I was in as tranquil a temper for observation as any practical experimentalist could be in awaiting the effects of some rare though perhaps perilous chemical combination. Of course, the more I kept my mind detached from fancy, the more the temper fitted for observation would be obtained; and I therefore riveted eye and thought on the strong daylight sense in the page of my Macaulay.

I now became aware that something interposed between the page and the light—the page was overshadowed; I looked up, and I saw what I shall find it very difficult, perhaps impossible, to describe.

It was a Darkness shaping itself out of the air in very undefined outline. I cannot say it was of a human form, and yet it had more resemblance to a human form, or rather shadow, than anything else. As it stood, wholly apart and distinct from the air and the light around it, its dimensions seemed gigantic, the summit nearly touching the ceiling. While I gazed, a feeling of intense cold seized me. An iceberg before me could not more have chilled me; nor could the cold of an iceberg have been more purely physical. I feel convinced that it was not the cold caused by fear. As I continued to gaze, I thought—but this I cannot say with precision—that I distinguished two eyes looking down on me from the height. One moment I seemed to distinguish them clearly, the next they seemed gone; but still two rays of a pale-blue light frequently shot through the darkness, as from the height on which I half-believed, half-doubted, that I had encountered the eyes.

I strove to speak—my voice utterly failed me; I could only think to myself, "Is this fear? it is *not* fear!" I strove to rise—in vain; I felt as if weighed down by an irresistible force. Indeed, my impression was that of an immense and overwhelming Power opposed to my volition; that sense of utter inadequacy to cope with a force beyond men's, which one may feel *physically* in a storm at sea, in a conflagration, or when confronting some terrible wild beast, or rather, perhaps, the shark of the ocean, I felt *morally*. Opposed to my will was another will, as far superior to its strength as storm, fire, and shark are superior in material force to the force of men.

And now, as this impression grew on me, now came, at last, horror—horror to a degree that no words can convey. Still I retained pride, if not courage; and in my own mind I said, "This is horror, but it is not fear; unless I fear, I cannot be harmed; my reason rejects this thing; it is an illusion—I do not fear." With a violent effort I succeeded at last in stretching out my hand towards the weapon on the table; as I did so, on the arm and shoulder I received a strange shock, and my arm fell to my side powerless. And now, to add to my horror, the light began slowly to wane from the candles—they were not, as it were, extinguished, but their flame seemed very gradually withdrawn; it was the same with the fire—the light was extracted from the fuel; in a few minutes the room was in utter darkness.

The dread that came over me, to be thus in the dark with that dark Thing, whose power was so intensely felt, brought a reaction of nerve. In fact, terror had reached that climax, that either my senses must have deserted me, or I must have burst through the spell. I did burst through it. I found voice, though the voice was a shriek. I remember that I broke forth with words like these—"I do not fear, my soul does not fear"; and at the same time I found the strength to rise. Still in that profound gloom I rushed to one of the windows—tore aside the curtain—flung open the shutters; my first thought was—light. And when I saw the moon high, clear, and calm, I felt a joy that almost compensated for the previous terror. There was the moon, there was also the light from the gas-lamps in the deserted slumberous street. I turned to look back into the room; the moon penetrated its shadow very palely and partially—but still there was light. The dark Thing, whatever it might be, was gone—except that I could yet see a dim shadow which seemed the shadow of that shade, against the opposite wall.

My eye now rested on the table, and from under the table (which was without cloth or cover—an old mahogany round table) there rose a hand, visible as far as the wrist. It was a hand, seemingly, as much of flesh and blood as my own, but the hand of an aged person—lean, wrinkled, small too—a woman's hand.

That hand very softly closed on the two letters that lay on the table: hand and letters both vanished. There then came the same three loud measured knocks I had heard at the bed-head before this extraordinary drama had commenced.

As those sounds slowly ceased, I felt the whole room vibrate sensibly; and at the far end there rose, as from the floor, sparks or globules like bubbles of light, many-coloured—green, yellow, fire-red, azure. Up and down, to and fro, hither, thither, as tiny will-o'-the-wisps, the sparks moved, slow or swift, each at its own caprice. A chair (as in the drawing-room below) was now advanced from the wall without apparent agency, and placed at the opposite side of the table. Suddenly, as forth from the chair, there grew a shape—a woman's shape. It was distinct as a shape of life—ghastly as a shape of death. The face was that of youth, with a strange mournful beauty; the throat and shoulders were bare, the rest of the form in a loose robe of cloudy white. It began sleeking its long yellow hair, which fell over its shoulders; its eyes were not turned towards me, but to the door; it seemed listening, watching, waiting. The shadow of the shade in the background grew darker; and again I thought I beheld the eyes gleaming out from the summit of the shadow—eyes fixed upon that shape.

As if from the door, though it did not open, there grew out another shape equally distinct, equally ghastly—a man's shape—a young man's. It was in the dress of the last century, or rather in a likeness of such dress; for both the male shape and the female, though defined, were evidently unsubstantial, impalpable—simulacra—phantasms; and there was something incongruous, grotesque, yet fearful, in the contrast between the elaborate finery, the courtly precision of that old-fashioned garb, with its ruffles and lace and buckles, and the corpse-like aspect and ghost-like stillness of the flitting wearer. Just as the male shape approached the female, the dark Shadow started from the wall, all three for a moment wrapped in darkness. When the pale light returned, the two phantoms were as if in the grasp of the Shadow that towered between them; and there was a bloodstain on the breast of the female; and the phantom-male was leaning on its phantom-sword, and blood seemed trickling fast from the ruffles, from the lace; and the darkness of the intermediate Shadow swallowed them up—they were gone. And again the bubbles of light shot, and sailed, and undulated, growing thicker and thicker and more wildly confused in their movements.

The closet-door to the right of the fireplace now opened, and from the aperture there came the form of a woman, aged. In her hand she held letters—the very letters over which I had seen *the* Hand close; and behind her I heard a footstep. She turned round as if to listen, then she opened the letters and seemed to read; and over her shoulder I saw a livid face, the face as of a man long drowned—bloated, bleached—seaweed tangled in its dripping hair; and at her feet lay a form as of a corpse and beside the corpse there cowered a child, a miserable, squalid child, with famine in its cheeks and fear in its eyes. And as I looked in the old woman's face, the wrinkles and lines vanished, and it became a face of youth—hard-eyed, stony, but still youth; and the Shadow darted forth, and darkened over these phantoms as it had darkened over the last.

Nothing now was left but the Shadow, and on that my eyes were intently fixed, till again eyes grew out of the Shadow—malignant, serpent eyes. And the bubbles of light again rose and fell, and in their disordered, irregular, turbulent maze, mingled with the wan moonlight. And now from these globules themselves as from the shell of an egg, monstrous things burst out; the air grew filled with them; larvae so bloodless and so hideous that I can in no way describe them except to remind the reader of the swarming life which the solar microscope brings before his eyes in a drop of water—things transparent, supple, agile, chasing each other, devouring each other—forms like nought ever beheld by the naked eye. As the shapes were without symmetry, so their movements were without order. In their very vagrancies there was no sport; they came round me and round, thicker and faster and swifter, swarming over my head, crawling over my right arm, which was outstretched in involuntary command against all evil beings.

Sometimes I felt myself touched, but not by them; invisible hands touched me. Once I felt the clutch as of cold soft fingers at my throat. I was still equally conscious that if I gave way to fear I should be in bodily peril; and I concentrated all my faculties in the single focus of resisting, stubborn will. And I turned my sight from the Shadow— above all, from those strange serpent eyes—eyes that had now become distinctly visible. For there, though in nought else around me, I was aware that there was a *will*, and a will of intense, creative, working evil, which might crush down my own.

The pale atmosphere in the room began now to redden as if in the air of some near conflagration. The larvæ grew lurid as things that live in fire. Again the room vibrated; again were heard the three measured knocks; and again all things were swallowed up in the darkness of the dark Shadow, as if out of that darkness all had come, into that darkness all returned.

As the gloom receded, the Shadow was wholly gone. Slowly as it had been withdrawn, the flame grew again into the candles on the table, again into the fuel in the grate. The whole room came once more calmly, healthfully into sight.

The two doors were still closed, the door communicating with the servants' room still locked. In the corner of the wall, into which he had so convulsively niched himself, lay the dog. I called to him—no movement; I approached—the animal was dead; his eyes protruded; his tongue out of his mouth; the froth gathered round his jaws. I took him in my arms; I brought him to the fire; I felt acute grief for the loss of my poor favourite—acute self-reproach; I accused myself of his death; I imagined he had died of fright. But what was my surprise on finding that his neck was actually broken—actually twisted out of the vertebræ. Had this been done in the dark?—must it not have been by a hand human as mine?—must there not have been a human agency all the while in that room? Good cause to suspect it. I cannot tell. I cannot do more than state the fact fairly; the reader may draw his own inference.

Another surprising circumstance—my watch was restored to the table from which it had been so mysteriously withdrawn; but it had stopped at the very moment it was so withdrawn; nor, despite all the skill of the watchmaker, has it ever gone since—that is, it will go in a strange erratic way for a few hours, and then comes to a dead stop—it is worthless.

Nothing more chanced for the rest of the night. Nor, indeed, had I long to wait before the dawn broke. Not till it was broad daylight did I quit the haunted house. Before I did so, I revisited the little blind room in which my servant and myself had been for a time imprisoned. I had a strong impression—for which I could not account—that from that room had originated the mechanism of the phenomena—if I may use the term—which had been experienced in my chamber. And though I entered it now in the clear day, with the sun peering through the filmy window, I still felt, as I stood on its floor, the creep of the horror which I had first there experienced the night before, and which had been so aggravated by what had passed in my own chamber. I could not, indeed, bear to stay more than half a minute within those walls. I descended the stairs, and again I heard the footfall before me; and when I opened the street door, I thought I could distinguish a very low laugh. I gained my own home, expecting to find my runaway servant there. But he had not presented himself; nor did I hear more of him for three days, when I received a letter from him, dated from Liverpool, to this effect:—

"Honoured Sir,—I humbly entreat your pardon, though I can scarcely hope that you will think I deserve it, unless—which Heaven forbid!—you saw what I did. I feel that it will be years before I can recover myself; and as to being fit for service, it is out of the question. I am therefore going to my brother-in-law at Melbourne. The ship sails to-morrow. Perhaps the long voyage may set me up. I do nothing now but start and tremble, and fancy It is behind me. I humbly beg you, honoured sir, to order my clothes, and whatever wages are due to me, to be sent to my mother's, at Walworth—John knows her address."

The letter ended with additional apologies, somewhat incoherent, and explanatory details as to effects that had been under the writer's charge.

This flight may perhaps warrant a suspicion that the man wished to go to Australia, and had been somehow or other fraudulently mixed up with the events of the night. I say nothing in refutation of that conjecture; rather, I suggest it as one that would seem to many persons the most probable solution of improbable occurrences. My own theory remained unshaken. I returned in the evening to the house, to bring away in a hack cab the things I had left there, with my poor dog's body. In this task I was not disturbed, nor did any incident worth note befall me, except that still, on ascending, and descending the stairs I heard the same footfall in advance. On leaving the house, I went to Mr J—'s. He was at home. I returned him the keys, told him that my curiosity was sufficiently gratified, and was about to relate quickly what had passed, when he stopped me, and said, though with much politeness, that he had no longer any interest in a mystery which none had ever solved.

I determined at least to tell him of the two letters I had read, as well as of the extraordinary manner in which they had disappeared, and I then inquired if he thought they had been addressed to the woman who had died in the house, and if there were anything in her early history which could possibly confirm the dark suspicions to which the letters gave rise. Mr J— seemed startled, and, after musing a few moments, answered, "I know but little of the woman's earlier history, except, as I before told you, that her family were known to mine. But you revive some vague reminiscences to her prejudice.

I will make inquiries, and inform you of their result. Still, even if we could admit the popular superstition that a person who had been either the perpetrator or the victim of dark crimes in life could revisit, as a restless spirit, the scene in which those crimes had been committed, I should observe that the house was infested by strange sights and sounds before the old woman died—you smile—what would you say?"

"I would say this, that I am convinced, if we could get to the bottom of these mysteries, we should find a living human agency."

"What! you believe it is all an imposture? For what object?"

"Not an imposture in the ordinary sense of the word. If suddenly I were to sink into a deep sleep, from which you could not awake me, but in that sleep could answer questions with an accuracy which I could not pretend to when awake—tell you what money you had in your pocket—nay, describe your very thoughts—it is not necessarily an imposture, any more than it is necessarily supernatural. I should be, unconsciously to myself, under a mesmeric influence, conveyed to me from a distance by a human being who had acquired power over me by previous *rapport*."

"Granting mesmerism, so far carried, to be a fact, you are right. And you would infer from this that a mesmeriser might produce the extraordinary effects you and others have witnessed over inanimate objects—fill the air with sights and sounds?"

"Or impress our senses with the belief in them—we never having been *en rapport* with the person acting on us? No. What is commonly called mesmerism could not do this; but there may be a power akin to mesmerism, and superior to it—the power that in the old days was called Magic. That such a power may extend to all inanimate objects of matter, I do not say; but if so, it would not be against nature, only a rare power in nature which might be given to constitutions with certain peculiarities, and cultivated by practice to an extraordinary degree. That such a power might extend over the dead—that is, over certain thoughts and memories that the dead may still retain—and compel, not that which ought properly to be called the *soul*, and which is far beyond human reach, but rather a phantom of what has been most earth-stained on earth, to make itself apparent to our senses—is a very ancient though obsolete theory, upon which I will hazard no opinion. But I do not conceive the power would be supernatural.

"Let me illustrate what I mean from an experiment which Paracelsus describes as not difficult, and which the author of the *Curiosities of Literature* cites as credible: A flower perishes; you burn it. Whatever were the elements of that flower while it lived are gone, dispersed, you know not whither; you can never discover nor re-collect them. But you can, by chemistry, out of the burnt dust of that flower, raise a spectrum of the flower, just as it seemed in life. It may be the same with the human being. The soul has so much escaped you as the essence or elements of the flower. Still you may make a spectrum of it. And this phantom, though in the popular superstition it is held to be the soul of the departed, must not be confounded with the true soul; it is but the eidolon of the dead form.

"Hence, like the best-attested stories of ghosts or spirits, the thing that most strikes us is the absence of what we hold to be soul—that is, of superior emancipated intelligence. They come for little or no object—they seldom speak, if they do come; they utter no ideas above that of an ordinary person on earth. These American spirit-seers have published volumes of communications in prose and verse, which they assert to be given in the names of the most illustrious dead— Shakespeare, Bacon—heaven knows whom. Those communications, taking the best, are certainly not a whit of higher order than would be communications from living persons of fair talent and education; they are wondrously inferior to what Bacon, Shakespeare, and Plato said and wrote when on earth.

"Nor, what is more notable, do they ever contain an idea that was not on the earth before. Wonderful, therefore, as such phenomena may be (granting them to be truthful), I see much that philosophy may question, nothing that it is incumbent on philosophy to deny— viz. nothing supernatural. They are but ideas conveyed somehow or other (we have not yet discovered the means) from one mortal brain to another. Whether, in so doing, tables walk of their own accord, or fiend-like shapes appear in a magic circle, or bodyless hands rise and remove material objects, or a Thing of Darkness, such as presented itself to me, freeze our blood—still am I persuaded that these are but agencies conveyed, as by electric wires, to my own brain from the brain of another. In some constitutions there is a natural chemistry, and those may produce chemic wonders—in others a natural fluid, call it electricity, and these produce electric wonders. But they differ in this from Normal Science—they are alike objectless, purposeless, puerile, frivolous. They lead on to no grand results; and therefore the world does not heed, and true sages have not cultivated them. But sure I am, that of all I saw or heard, a man, human as myself, was the remote originator; and I believe unconsciously to himself as to the exact effects produced, for this reason: no two persons, you say, have ever told you that they experienced exactly the same thing. Well, observe, no two persons ever experience exactly the same dream. If this were an ordinary imposture, the machinery would be arranged for results that would but little vary; if it were a supernatural agency permitted by the Almighty, it would surely be for some definite end.

"These phenomena belong to neither class; my persuasion is, that they originate in some brain now far distant; that that brain had no distinct volition in anything that occurred; that what does occur reflects but its devious, motley, ever-shifting, half-formed thoughts; in short, that it has been but the dreams of such a brain put into action and invested with a semisubstance. That this brain is of immense power, that it can set matter into movement, that it is malignant and destructive, I believe: some material force must have killed my dog; it might, for aught I know, have sufficed to kill myself, had I been as subjugated by terror as the dog—had my intellect or my spirit given me no countervailing resistance in my will."

"It killed your dog! that is fearful! indeed, it is strange that no animal can be induced to stay in that house; not even a cat. Rats and mice are never found in it."

"The instincts of the brute creation detect influences deadly to their existence. Man's reason has a sense less subtle, because it has a resisting power more supreme. But enough; do you comprehend my theory?"

"Yes, though imperfectly—and I accept any crotchet (pardon the word), however odd, rather than embrace at once the notion of ghosts and hobgoblins we imbibed in our nurseries. Still, to my unfortunate house the evil is the same. What on earth can I do with the house?"

"I will tell you what I would do. I am convinced from my own internal feelings that the small unfurnished room at right angles to the door of the bedroom which I occupied, forms a starting-point or receptacle for the influences which haunt the house; and I strongly advise you to have the walls opened, the floor removed—nay, the whole room pulled down. I observe that it is detached from the body of the house, built over the small back-yard, and could be removed without injury to the rest of the building."

"And you think, if I did that—"

"You would cut off the telegraph wires. Try it. I am so persuaded that I am right, that I will pay half the expense if you will allow me to direct the operations."

"Nay, I am well able to afford the cost; for the rest, allow me to write to you."

About ten days afterwards I received a letter from Mr J—, telling me that he had visited the house since I had seen him; that he had found the two letters I had described, replaced in the drawer from which I had taken them; that he had read them with misgivings like my own; that he had instituted a cautious inquiry about the woman to whom I rightly conjectured they had been written. It seemed that thirty-six years ago (a year before the date of the letters), she had married against the wish of her relatives, an American of very suspicious character; in fact, he was generally believed to have been a pirate. She herself was the daughter of very respectable tradespeople, and had served in the capacity of a nursery governess before her marriage. She had a brother, a widower, who was considered wealthy, and who had one child of about six years old. A month after the marriage, the body of this brother was found in the Thames, near London Bridge;

there seemed some marks of violence about his throat, but they were not deemed sufficient to warrant the inquest in any other verdict than that of "found drowned."

The American and his wife took charge of the little boy, the deceased brother having by his will left his sister the guardian of his only child—and in the event of the child's death, the sister inherited. The child died about six months afterwards—it was supposed to have been neglected and ill-treated. The neighbours deposed to have heard it shriek at night. The surgeon who had examined it after death, said that it was emaciated as if from want of nourishment, and the body was covered with livid bruises. It seemed that one winter night the child had sought to escape—crept out into the back-yard—tried to scale the wall—fallen back exhausted, and been found at morning on the stones in a dying state. But though there was some evidence of cruelty, there was none of murder; and the aunt and her husband had sought to palliate cruelty by alleging the exceeding stubbornness and per-versity of the child, who was declared to be half-witted. Be that as it may, at the orphan's death the aunt inherited her brother's fortune.

Before the first wedded year was out, the American quitted Eng-land abruptly, and never returned to it. He obtained a cruising ves-sel, which was lost in the Atlantic two years afterwards. The widow was left in affluence; but reverses of various kinds had befallen her: a bank broke—an investment failed—she went into a small business and became insolvent—then she entered into service, sinking lower and lower, from housekeeper down to maid-of-all-work—never long retaining a place, though nothing peculiar against her character was ever alleged. She was considered sober, honest, and peculiarly quiet in her ways; still nothing prospered with her. And so she had dropped into the workhouse, from which Mr J— had taken her, to be placed in charge of the very house which she had rented as mistress in the first year of her wedded life.

Mr J— added that he had passed an hour alone in the unfurnished room which I had urged him to destroy, and that his impressions of dread while there were so great, though he had neither heard nor seen anything, that he was eager to have the walls bared and the floors removed as I had suggested. He had engaged persons for the work, and would commence any day I would name.

The day was accordingly fixed. I repaired to the haunted house—we went into the blind dreary room, took up the skirting, and then the floors. Under the rafters, covered with rubbish, was found a trap-door, quite large enough to admit a man. It was closely nailed down, with clamps and rivets of iron. On removing these we descended into a room below, the existence of which had never been suspected. In this room there had been a window and a flue, but they had been bricked over, evidently for many years. By the help of candles we examined this place; it still retained some mouldering furniture—three chairs, an oak settle, a table—all of the fashion of about eighty years ago. There was a chest of drawers against the wall, in which we found, half-rotted away, old-fashioned articles of a man's dress, such as might have been worn eighty or a hundred years ago by a gentleman of some rank—costly steel buckles and buttons, like those yet worn in court dresses—a handsome court sword—in a waistcoat which had once been rich with gold lace, but which was now blackened and foul with damp, we found five guineas, a few silver coins, and an ivory ticket, probably for some place of entertainment long since passed away. But our main discovery was in a kind of iron safe fixed to the wall, the lock of which it cost us much trouble to get picked.

In this safe were three shelves and two small drawers. Ranged on the shelves were several small bottles of crystal, hermetically stopped. They contained colourless volatile essences, of what nature I shall say no more than that they were not poisons—phosphor and ammonia entered into some of them. There were also some very curious glass tubes, and a small pointed rod of iron, with a large lump of rock-crystal, and another of amber—also a loadstone of great power.

In one of the drawers we found a miniature portrait set in gold, and retaining the freshness of its colours most remarkably, considering the length of time it had probably been there. The portrait was

that of a man who might be somewhat advanced in middle life, perhaps forty-seven or forty-eight.

It was a most peculiar face—a most impressive face. If you could
fancy some mighty serpent transformed into man, preserving in the
human lineaments the old serpent type, you would have a better idea
of that countenance than long descriptions can convey: the width
and flatness of frontal—the tapering elegance of contour disguising
the strength of the deadly jaw—the long, large, terrible eye, glittering
and green as the emerald—and withal a certain ruthless calm, as if
from the consciousness of an immense power. The strange thing was
this—the instant I saw the miniature I recognised a startling likeness
to one of the rarest portraits in the world—the portrait of a man of a
rank only below that of royalty, who in his own day had made a considerable noise. History says little or nothing of him; but search the
correspondence of his contemporaries, and you find reference to his
wild daring, his bold profligacy, his restless spirit, his taste for the
occult sciences. While still in the meridian of life he died and was
buried, so say the chronicles, in a foreign land. He died in time to
escape the grasp of the law, for he was accused of crimes which would
have given him to the headsman.

After his death, the portraits of him, which had been numerous,
for he had been a munificent encourager of art, were bought up and
destroyed—it was supposed by his heirs, who might have been glad
could they have razed his very name from their splendid line. He had
enjoyed a vast wealth; a large portion of this was believed to have been
embezzled by a favourite astrologer or soothsayer—at all events, it had
unaccountably vanished at the time of his death. One portrait alone
of him was supposed to have escaped the general destruction; I had
seen it in the house of a collector some months before. It had made
on me a wonderful impression, as it does on all who behold it—a face
never to be forgotten; and there was that face in the miniature that lay
within my hand. True, that in the miniature the man was a few years
older than in the portrait I had seen, or than the original was even at
the time of his death. But a few years!—why, between the date in which

flourished that direful noble and the date in which the miniature was evidently painted, there was an interval of more than two centuries. While I was thus gazing, silent and wondering, Mr J— said:

"But is it possible? I have known this man."

"How—where?" I cried.

"In India. He was high in the confidence of the Rajah of —, and wellnigh drew him into a revolt which would have lost the Rajah his dominions. The man was a Frenchman—his name de V—, clever, bold, lawless. We insisted on his dismissal and banishment: it must be the same man—no two faces like his—yet this miniature seems nearly a hundred years old."

Mechanically I turned round the miniature to examine the back of it, and on the back was engraved a pentacle; in the middle of the pentacle a ladder, and the third step of the ladder was formed by the date 1765. Examining still more minutely, I detected a spring; this, on being pressed, opened the back of the miniature as a lid. Within-side the lid was engraved "Mariana to thee—Be faithful in life and in death to —." Here follows a name that I will not mention, but it was not unfamiliar to me. I had heard it spoken of by old men in my child-hood as the name borne by a dazzling charlatan, who had made a great sensation in London for a year or so, and had fled the country on the charge of a double murder within his own house—that of his mistress and his rival. I said nothing of this to Mr J—, to whom reluctantly I resigned the miniature.

We had found no difficulty in opening the first drawer within the iron safe; we found great difficulty in opening the second: it was not locked, but it resisted all efforts till we inserted in the chinks the edge of a chisel. When we had thus drawn it forth, we found a very singu-lar apparatus in the nicest order. Upon a small thin book, or rather tablet, was placed a saucer of crystal; this saucer was filled with a clear liquid—on that liquid floated a kind of compass, with a needle shift-ing rapidly round, but instead of the usual points of a compass were seven strange characters, not very unlike those used by astrologers to denote the planets. A very peculiar, but not strong nor displeasing odour, came from this drawer, which was lined with a wood that we afterwards discovered to be hazel. Whatever the cause of this odour, it produced a material effect on the nerves. We all felt it, even the two workmen who were in the room—a creeping tingling sensation from the tips of the fingers to the roots of the hair. Impatient to examine the tablet, I removed the saucer. As I did so the needle of the compass went round and round with exceeding swiftness, and I felt a shock that ran through my whole frame, so that I dropped the saucer on the floor. The liquid was spilt—the saucer was broken—the compass rolled to the end of the room—and at that instant the walls shook to and fro, as if a giant had swayed and rocked them.

The two workmen were so frightened that they ran up the ladder by which we had descended from the trap-door; but seeing that nothing more happened, they were easily induced to return.

Meanwhile I had opened the tablet: it was bound in a plain red leather, with a silver clasp; it contained but one sheet of thick vellum, and on that sheet were inscribed, within a double pentacle, words in old monkish Latin, which are literally to be translated thus:—"On all that it can reach within these walls—sentient or inanimate, living or dead—as moves the needle, so work my will! Accursed be the house, and restless be the dwellers therein."

We found no more. Mr J— burnt the tablet and its anathema. He razed to the foundations the part of the building containing the secret room with the chamber over it. He had then the courage to inhabit the house himself for a month, and a quieter, better-conditioned house could not be found in all London. Subsequently he let it to advantage, and his tenant has made no complaints.

But my story is not yet done. A few days after Mr J— had removed into the house, I paid him a visit. We were standing by the open window and conversing. A van containing some articles of furniture which he was moving from his former house was at the door. I had just urged on him my theory that all those phenomena regarded as supermundane had emanated from a human brain; adducing the charm, or rather curse, we had found and destroyed in support of my philosophy. Mr J— was observing in reply, "That even if mesmerism, or whatever analogous power it might be called, could really thus work in the absence of the operator, and produce effects so extraordinary, still could those effects continue when the operator himself was dead? and if the spell had been wrought, and, indeed, the room walled up, more than seventy years ago, the probability was, that the operator had long since departed this life"; Mr J—, I say, was thus answering, when I caught hold of his arm and pointed to the street below.

A well-dressed man had crossed from the opposite side, and was accosting the carrier in charge of the van. His face, as he stood, was exactly fronting our window. It was the face of the miniature we had discovered; it was the face of the portrait of the noble three centuries ago.

"Good Heavens!" cried Mr J—, "that is the face of de V—, and scarcely a day older than when I saw it in the Rajah's court in my youth!"

Seized by the same thought, we both hastened downstairs. I was first in the street; but the man had already gone. I caught sight of him, however, not many yards in advance, and in another moment I was by his side.

I had resolved to speak to him, but when I looked into his face I felt as if it were impossible to do so. That eye—the eye of the serpent—fixed and held me spellbound. And withal, about the man's whole person there was a dignity, an air of pride and station and superiority, that would have made anyone, habituated to the usages of the world, hesitate long before venturing upon a liberty or impertinence. And what could I say? what was it I would ask? Thus ashamed of my first impulse, I fell a few paces back, still, however, following the stranger, undecided what else to do. Meanwhile he turned the corner of the street; a plain carriage was in waiting, with a servant out of livery, dressed like a *valet-de-place*, at the carriage door. In another moment he had stepped into the carriage, and it drove off. I returned to the house. Mr J— was still at the street door. He had asked the carrier what the stranger had said to him.

"Merely asked whom that house now belonged to."

The same evening I happened to go with a friend to a place in town called the Cosmopolitan Club, a place open to men of all countries, all opinions, all degrees. One orders one's coffee, smokes one's cigar. One is always sure to meet agreeable, sometimes remarkable, persons.

I had not been two minutes in the room before I beheld at a table, conversing with an acquaintance of mine, whom I will designate by the initial G—, the man—the Original of the Miniature. He was now without his hat, and the likeness was yet more startling, only I observed that while he was conversing there was less severity in the countenance; there was even a smile, though a very quiet and very cold one. The dignity of mien I had acknowledged in the street was also more striking; a dignity akin to that which invests some prince of the East—conveying the idea of supreme indifference and habitual, indisputable, indolent, but resistless power.

G— soon after left the stranger, who then took up a scientific journal, which seemed to absorb his attention.

I drew G— aside. "Who and what is that gentleman?"

"That? Oh, a very remarkable man indeed. I met him last year amidst the caves of Petra—the scriptural Edom. He is the best Oriental scholar I know. We joined company, had an adventure with robbers, in which he showed a coolness that saved our lives; afterwards he invited me to spend a day with him in a house he had bought at Damascus—a house buried amongst almond blossoms and roses—the most beautiful thing! He had lived there for some years, quite as an Oriental, in grand style. I half suspect he is a renegade, immensely rich, very odd; by the by, a great mesmeriser. I have seen him with my own eyes produce an effect on inanimate things. If you take a letter from your pocket and throw it to the other end of the room, he will order it to come to his feet, and you will see the letter wriggle itself along the floor till it has obeyed his command. 'Pon my honour, 'tis true: I have seen him affect even the weather, disperse or collect clouds, by means of a glass tube or wand. But he does not like talking of these matters to strangers. He has only just arrived in England;

says he has not been here for a great many years; let me introduce him to you."

"Certainly! He is English, then? What is his name?"

"Oh!—a very homely one—Richards."

"And what is his birth—his family?"

"How do I know? What does it signify?—no doubt some parvenu, but rich—so infernally rich!"

G— drew me up to the stranger, and the introduction was effected. The manners of Mr Richards were not those of an adventurous traveller. Travellers are in general constitutionally gifted with high animal spirits: they are talkative, eager, imperious. Mr Richards was calm and subdued in tone, with manners which were made distant by the loftiness of punctilious courtesy—the manners of a former age. I observed that the English he spoke was not exactly of our day. I should even have said that the accent was slightly foreign. But then Mr Richards remarked that he had been little in the habit for many years of speaking in his native tongue. The conversation fell upon the changes in the aspect of London since he had last visited our metropolis. G— then glanced off to the moral changes—literary, social, political—the great men who were removed from the stage within the last twenty years—the new great men who were coming on. In all this Mr Richards evinced no interest. He had evidently read none of our living authors, and seemed scarcely acquainted by name with our younger statesmen. Once and only once he laughed; it was when G— asked him whether he had any thoughts of getting into Parliament. And the laugh was inward—sarcastic—sinister—a sneer raised into a laugh. After a few minutes G— left us to talk to some other acquaintances who had just lounged into the room, and I then said quietly:

"I have seen a miniature of you, Mr Richards, in the house you once inhabited, and perhaps built, if not wholly, at least in part, in— Street. You passed by that house this morning."

Not till I had finished did I raise my eyes to his, and then his fixed my gaze so steadfastly that I could not withdraw it—those fascinating serpent eyes. But involuntarily, and if the words that translated my thought were dragged from me, I added in a low whisper, "I have been a student in the mysteries of life and nature; of those mysteries I have known the occult professors. I have the right to speak to you thus." And I uttered a certain pass-word.

"Well," said he, dryly, "I concede the right—what would you ask?"

"To what extent human will in certain temperaments can extend?"

"To what extent can thought extend? Think, and before you draw breath you are in China!"

"True. But my thought has no power in China."

"Give it expression, and it may have: you may write down a thought which, sooner or later, may alter the whole condition of China. What is a law but a thought? Therefore thought is infinite—therefore thought has power; not in proportion to its value—a bad thought may make a bad law as potent as a good thought can make a good one."

"Yes; what you say confirms my own theory. Through invisible currents one human brain may transmit its ideas to other human brains with the same rapidity as a thought promulgated by visible means. And as thought is imperishable—as it leaves its stamp behind it in the natural world even when the thinker has passed out of this world—so the thought of the living may have power to rouse up and revive the thoughts of the dead—such as those thoughts *were in life*— though the thought of the living cannot reach the thoughts which the dead *now* may entertain. Is it not so?"

"I decline to answer, if, in my judgment, thought has the limit you would fix to it; but proceed. You have a special question you wish to put."

"Intense malignity in an intense will, engendered in a peculiar temperament, and aided by natural means within the reach of science, may produce effects like those ascribed of old to evil magic. It might thus haunt the walls of a human habitation with spectral revivals of all guilty thoughts and guilty deeds once conceived and done within those walls; all, in short, with which the evil will claims *rapport* and affinity—imperfect, incoherent, fragmentary snatches at the old dramas acted therein years ago. Thoughts thus crossing each other haphazard, as in the nightmare of a vision, growing up into phantom sights and sounds, and all serving to create horror, not because those sights and sounds are really visitations from a world without, but that they are ghastly monstrous renewals of what have been in this world itself, set into malignant play by a malignant mortal.

"And it is through the material agency of that human brain that these things would acquire even a human power—would strike as with the shock of electricity, and might kill, if the thought of the person assailed did not rise superior to the dignity of the original assailer— might kill the most powerful animal if unnerved by fear, but not injure the feeblest man, if, while his flesh crept, his mind stood out fearless. Thus, when in old stories we read of a magician rent to pieces by the fiends he had evoked—or still more, in Eastern legends, that one magician succeeds by arts in destroying another—there may be so far truth, that a material being has clothed, from its own evil propensities certain elements and fluids, usually quiescent or harmless, with awful shape and terrific force—just as the lightning that had lain hidden and innocent in the cloud becomes by natural law suddenly visible, takes a distinct shape to the eye, and can strike destruction on the object to which it is attracted."

"You are not without glimpses of a very mighty secret," said Mr Richards, composedly. "According to your view, could a mortal obtain the power you speak of, he would necessarily be a malignant and evil being."

"If the power were exercised as I have said, most malignant and most evil—though I believe in the ancient traditions that he could not injure the good. His will could only injure those with whom it has established an affinity, or over whom it forces unresisted sway. I will now imagine an example that may be within the laws of nature, yet seem wild as the fables of a bewildered monk.

"You will remember that Albertus Magnus, after describing minutely the process by which spirits may be invoked and commanded, adds emphatically that the process will instruct and avail only to the few—that a *man must be born a magician!*—that is, born with a peculiar physical temperament, as a man is born a poet. Rarely are men in whose constitution lurks this occult power of the highest order of intellect;—usually in the intellect there is some twist, perversity, or disease. But, on the other hand, they must possess, to an astonishing degree, the faculty to concentrate thought on a single object—the energic faculty that we call *will*. Therefore, though their intellect be not sound, it is exceedingly forcible for the attainment of what it desires. I will imagine such a person, pre-eminently gifted with this constitution and its concomitant forces. I will place him in the loftier grades of society. I will suppose his desires emphatically those of the sensualist—he has, therefore, a strong love of life. He is an absolute egotist—his will is concentrated in himself—he has fierce passions—he knows no enduring, no holy affections, but he can covet eagerly what for the moment he desires—he can hate implacably what opposes itself to his objects—he can commit fearful crimes, yet feel small remorse—he resorts rather to curses upon others, than to penitence for his misdeeds. Circumstances, to which his constitution guides him, lead him to a rare knowledge of the natural secrets which may serve his egotism. He is a close observer where his passions encourage observation, he is a minute calculator, not from love of truth, but where love of self sharpens his faculties—therefore he can be a man of science.

"I suppose such a being, having by experience learned the power of his arts over others, trying what may be the power of will over his own frame, and studying all that in natural philosophy may increase that power. He loves life, he dreads death; he *wills to live on*. He cannot restore himself to youth, he cannot entirely stay the progress of death, he cannot make himself immortal in the flesh and blood; but he may arrest for a time so prolonged as to appear incredible, if I said it—that hardening of the parts which constitutes old age. A year may age him no more than an hour ages another. His intense will, scientifically trained into system, operates, in short, over the wear and tear of his own frame. He lives on. That he may not seem a portent and a miracle, he *dies* from time to time, seemingly, to certain persons. Having schemed the transfer of a wealth that suffices to his wants, he disappears from one corner of the world, and contrives that his obsequies shall be celebrated. He reappears at another corner of the world, where he resides undetected, and does not revisit the scenes of his former career till all who could remember his features are no more. He would be profoundly miserable if he had affections—he has none but for himself. No good man would accept his longevity, and to no men, good or bad, would he or could he communicate its true secret. Such a man might exist; such a man as I have described I see now before me!—Duke of —, in the court of —, dividing time between lust and brawl, alchemists and wizards;—again, in the last century, charlatan and criminal, with name less noble, domiciled in the house at which you gazed to-day, and flying from the law you had outraged, none knew whither; traveller once more revisiting London, with the same earthly passions which filled your heart when races now no more walked through yonder streets; outlaw from the school of all the nobler and diviner mystics; execrable Image of Life in Death and Death in Life, I warn you back from the cities and homes of healthful men; back to the ruins of departed empires; back to the deserts of nature unredeemed!"

There answered me a whisper so musical, so potently musical, that it seemed to enter into my whole being, and subdue me despite myself. Thus it said:

"I have sought one like you for the last hundred years. Now I have found you, we part not till I know what I desire. The vision that sees through the Past, and cleaves through the veil of the Future, is in you at this hour; never before, never to come again. The vision of no puling fantastic girl, of no sick-bed somnambule, but of a strong man, with a vigorous brain. Soar and look forth!"

As he spoke I felt as if I rose out of myself upon eagle wings. All the weight seemed gone from air—roofless the room, roofless the dome of space. I was not in the body—where I knew not—but aloft over time, over earth.

Again I heard the melodious whisper,—"You say right. I have mastered great secrets by the power of Will; true, by Will and by Science I can retard the process of years: but death comes not by age alone. Can I frustrate the accidents which bring death upon the young?"

"No; every accident is a providence. Before a providence snaps every human will."

"Shall I die at last, ages and ages hence, by the slow, though inevitable, growth of time, or by the cause that I call accident?"

"By a cause you call accident."

"Is not the end still remote?" asked the whisper, with a slight tremor.

"Regarded as my life regards time, it is still remote."

"And shall I, before then, mix with the world of men as I did ere I learned these secrets, resume eager interest in their strife and their trouble—battle with ambition, and use the power of the sage to win the power that belongs to kings?"

"You will yet play a part on the earth that will fill earth with commotion and amaze. For wondrous designs have you, a wonder yourself, been permitted to live on through the centuries. All the secrets you have stored will then have their uses—all that now makes you a stranger amidst the generations will contribute then to make you their lord. As the trees and the straws are drawn into a whirlpool—as they spin round, are sucked to the deep, and again tossed aloft by the eddies, so shall races and thrones be plucked into the charm of your vortex. Awful Destroyer—but in destroying, made, against your own will, a Constructor!"

"And that date, too, is far off?"

"Far off; when it comes, think your end in this world is at hand!"

"How and what is the end? Look east, west, south, and north."

"In the north, where you never yet trod towards the point whence your instincts have warned you, there a spectre will seize you. 'Tis Death! I see a ship—it is haunted—'tis chased—it sails on. Baffled navies sail after that ship. It enters the region of ice. It passes a sky red with meteors. Two moons stand on high, over ice-reefs. I see the ship locked between white defiles—they are ice-rocks. I see the dead strew the decks—stark and livid, green mould on their limbs. All are dead but one man—it is you! But years, though so slowly they come, have then scathed you. There is the coming of age on your brow, and the will is relaxed in the cells of the brain. Still that will, though enfeebled, exceeds all that man knew before you, through the will you live on, gnawed with famine; and nature no longer obeys you in that death-spreading region; the sky is a sky of iron, and the air has iron clamps, and the ice-rocks wedge in the ship. Hark how it cracks and groans. Ice will imbed it as amber imbeds a straw. And a man has gone forth, living yet, from the ship and its dead; and he has clambered up the spikes of an iceberg, and the two moons gaze down on his form. That man is yourself; and terror is on you—terror; and terror has swallowed your will. And I see swarming up the steep ice-rock, grey grisly things. The bears of the north have scented their quarry—they come near you and nearer, shambling and rolling their bulk. And in that day every moment shall seem to you longer than the centuries through which you have passed. And heed this—after life, moments continued make the bliss or the hell of eternity."

"Hush," said the whisper; "but the day, you assure me, is far off— very far! I go back to the almond and rose of Damascus!—sleep!"

The room swam before my eyes. I became insensible. When I recovered, I found G— holding my hand and smiling. He said, "You who have always declared yourself proof against mesmerism have succumbed at last to my friend Richards."

"Where is Mr Richards?"

"Gone, when you passed into a trance—saying quietly to me, 'Your friend will not wake for an hour.'"

I asked, as collectedly as I could, where Mr Richards lodged.

"At the Trafalgar Hotel."

"Give me your arm," said I to G—; "let us call on him; I have something to say."

When we arrived at the hotel, we were told that Mr Richards had returned twenty minutes before, paid his bill, left directions with his servant (a Greek) to pack his effects and proceed to Malta by the steamer that should leave Southampton the next day. Mr Richards had merely said of his own movements that he had visits to pay in the neighbourhood of London, and it was uncertain whether he should be able to reach Southampton in time for that steamer; if not, he should follow in the next one.

The waiter asked me my name. On my informing him, he gave me a note that Mr Richards had left for me, in case I called.

The note was as follows: "I wished you to utter what was in your mind. You obeyed. I have therefore established power over you. For three months from this day you can communicate to no living man what has passed between us—you cannot even show this note to the friend by your side. During three months, silence complete as to me and mine. Do you doubt my power to lay on you this command?—try to disobey me. At the end of the third month, the spell is raised. For the rest I spare you. I shall visit your grave a year and a day after it has received you."

So ends this strange story, which I ask no one to believe. I write it down exactly three months after I received the above note. I could not write it before, nor could I show to G—, in spite of his urgent request, the note which I read under the gas-lamp by his side.

CASTING THE RUNES

by Montague Rhodes James

Montague Rhodes James has an intelligent and scientific knowledge of human nerves and feelings; and knows just how to apportion statement, imagery, and subtle suggestions in order to secure the best results with his readers.

H.P. LOVECRAFT

Such high praise from the god of modern horror is not undeserved. Montague Rhodes James (1862-1936) was, and still remains by many accounts, the undisputed master of the horror ghost story. An English academic and mediaeval scholar, he served in the position of provost at King's College, Cambridge and later Eton. He enjoyed delighting his friends and family on Christmas Eve with his contemporary, realistic ghost stories, which he read aloud while sitting next to a cozy fire. (It is likely that gin punch or brandy may have been involved.) James' style of storytelling (now known as "Jamesian") dispensed with all the Gothic clichés we might expect from a classic ghost story, and often follows the plot formula of an older scholar as protagonist and some ancient and mysterious object that summons a supernatural presence.

A James ghost story is meant to be read aloud. So if you possibly can, arrange it sit down with some friends or perhaps *your children*, get comfortable, and slowly and deliberately read aloud "Casting of Runes."

Casting the Runes

April 15th, 190-

Dear Sir,

I am requested by the Council of the—Association to return to you the draft of a paper on The Truth of Alchemy, which you have been good enough to offer to read at our forthcoming meeting, and to inform you that the Council do not see their way to including it in the programme.

> I am,
> Yours faithfully,
> —Secretary.

* * * * *

April 18th

Dear Sir,

I am sorry to say that my engagements do not permit of my affording you an interview on the subject of your proposed paper. Nor do our laws allow of your discussing the matter with a Committee of our Council, as you suggest. Please allow me to assure you that the fullest consideration was given to the draft which you submitted, and that it was not declined without having been referred to the judgment of a most competent authority. No personal question (it can hardly be necessary for me to add) can have had the slightest influence on the decision of the Council.

> Believe me (ut supra).

* * * * *

April 20th

The Secretary of the—Association begs respectfully to inform Mr Karswell that it is impossible for him to communicate the name of any person or persons to whom the draft of Mr Karswell's paper may have been submitted; and further desires to intimate that he cannot undertake to reply to any further letters on this subject.

* * * * *

"And who *is* Mr Karswell?" inquired the Secretary's wife. She had called at his office, and (perhaps unwarrantably) had picked up the last of these three letters, which the typist had just brought in.

"Why, my dear, just at present Mr Karswell is a very angry man. But I don't know much about him otherwise, except that he is a person of wealth, his address is Lufford Abbey, Warwickshire, and he's an alchemist, apparently, and wants to tell us all about it; and that's about all—except that I don't want to meet him for the next week or two. Now, if you're ready to leave this place, I am."

"What have you been doing to make him angry?" asked Mrs Secretary.

"The usual thing, my dear, the usual thing: he sent in a draft of a paper he wanted to read at the next meeting, and we referred it to Edward Dunning—almost the only man in England who knows about these things—and he said it was perfectly hopeless, so we declined it. So Karswell has been pelting me with letters ever since. The last thing he wanted was the name of the man we referred his nonsense to; you saw my answer to that. But don't you say anything about it, for goodness' sake."

"I should think not, indeed. Did I ever do such a thing? I do hope, though, he won't get to know that it was poor Mr Dunning."

"Poor Mr Dunning? I don't know why you call him that; he's a very happy man, is Dunning. Lots of hobbies and a comfortable home, and all his time to himself."

"I only meant I should be sorry for him if this man got hold of his name, and came and bothered him."

"Oh, ah! yes. I dare say he would be poor Mr Dunning then."

The Secretary and his wife were lunching out, and the friends to whose house they were bound were Warwickshire people. So Mrs Secretary had already settled it in her own mind that she would question them judiciously about Mr Karswell. But she was saved the trouble of leading up to the subject, for the hostess said to the host, before many minutes had passed, "I saw the Abbot of Lufford this morning." The host whistled. "*Did* you? What in the world brings him up to town?" "Goodness knows; he was coming out of the British Museum gate as I drove past." It was not unnatural that Mrs Secretary should inquire whether this was a real Abbot who was being spoken of. "Oh no, my dear: only a neighbour of ours in the country who bought Lufford Abbey a few years ago. His real name is Karswell." "Is he a friend of yours?" asked Mr Secretary, with a private wink to his wife. The question let loose a torrent of declamation. There was really nothing to be said for Mr Karswell. Nobody knew what he did with himself: his servants were a horrible set of people; he had invented a new religion for himself, and practised no one could tell what appalling rites; he was very easily offended, and never forgave anybody; he had a dreadful face (so the lady insisted, her husband somewhat demurring); he never did a kind action, and whatever influence he did exert was mischievous. "Do the poor man justice, dear," the husband interrupted. "You forget the treat he gave the school children." "Forget it, indeed! But I'm glad you mentioned it, because it gives an idea of the man. Now, Florence, listen to this. The first winter he was at Lufford this delightful neighbour of ours wrote to the clergyman of his parish (he's not ours, but we know him very well) and offered to show the school children some magic-lantern slides. He said he had some new kinds, which he thought would interest them. Well, the clergyman was rather surprised, because Mr Karswell had shown himself inclined to be unpleasant to the children—complaining of their trespassing, or something of the sort; but of course he accepted, and the evening was fixed, and our friend went himself to see that everything went right. He said he never had been so thankful for anything as that his own children were all prevented from being there: they were at a children's party at our house, as a matter of fact. Because this Mr Karswell had evidently set out with the intention of frightening these poor village children out of their wits, and I do believe, if he had been allowed to go on, he would actually have done so. He began with some comparatively mild things. Red Riding Hood was one, and even then, Mr Farrer said, the wolf was so dreadful that several of the smaller children had to be taken out: and he said Mr

Karswell began the story by producing a noise like a wolf howling in the distance, which was the most gruesome thing he had ever heard. All the slides he showed, Mr Farrer said, were most clever; they were absolutely realistic, and where he had got them or how he worked them he could not imagine. Well, the show went on, and the stories kept on becoming a little more terrifying each time, and the children were mesmerized into complete silence. At last he produced a series which represented a little boy passing through his own park—Lufford, I mean—in the evening. Every child in the room could recognize the place from the pictures. And this poor boy was followed, and at last pursued and overtaken, and either torn to pieces or somehow made away with, by a horrible hopping creature in white, which you saw first dodging about among the trees, and gradually it appeared more and more plainly. Mr Farrer said it gave him one of the worst nightmares he ever remembered, and what it must have meant to the children doesn't bear thinking of. Of course this was too much, and he spoke very sharply indeed to Mr Karswell, and said it couldn't go on. All *he* said was: 'Oh, you think it's time to bring our little show to an end and send them home to their beds? *Very* well!' And then, if you please, he switched on another slide, which showed a great mass of snakes, centipedes, and disgusting creatures with wings, and somehow or other he made it seem as if they were climbing out of the picture and getting in amongst the audience; and this was accompanied by a sort of dry rustling noise which sent the children nearly mad, and of course they stampeded. A good many of them were rather hurt in getting out of the room, and I don't suppose one of them closed an eye that night. There was the most dreadful trouble in the village afterwards. Of course the mothers threw a good part of the blame on poor Mr Farrer, and, if they could have got past the gates, I believe the fathers would have broken every window in the Abbey. Well, now, that's Mr Karswell: that's the Abbot of Lufford, my dear, and you can imagine how we covet *his* society."

"Yes, I think he has all the possibilities of a distinguished criminal, has Karswell," said the host. "I should be sorry for anyone who got into his bad books."

"Is he the man, or am I mixing him up with someone else?" asked the Secretary (who for some minutes had been wearing the frown of the man who is trying to recollect something). "Is he the man who brought out a *History of Witchcraft* some time back—ten years or more?"

"That's the man; do you remember the reviews of it?"

"Certainly I do; and what's equally to the point, I knew the author of the most incisive of the lot. So did you: you must remember John Harrington; he was at John's in our time."

"Oh, very well indeed, though I don't think I saw or heard anything of him between the time I went down and the day I read the account of the inquest on him."

"Inquest?" said one of the ladies. "What has happened to him?"

"Why, what happened was that he fell out of a tree and broke his neck. But the puzzle was, what could have induced him to get up there. It was a mysterious business, I must say. Here was this man—not an athletic fellow, was he? and with no eccentric twist about him that was ever noticed—walking home along a country road late in the evening— no tramps about—well known and liked in the place—and he suddenly begins to run like mad, loses his hat and stick, and finally shins up a tree—quite a difficult tree—growing in the hedgerow: a dead branch gives way, and he comes down with it and breaks his neck, and there he's found next morning with the most dreadful face of fear on him that could be imagined. It was pretty evident, of course, that he had been chased by something, and people talked of savage dogs, and beasts escaped out of menageries; but there was nothing to be made of that. That was in '89, and I believe his brother Henry (whom I remember as well at Cambridge, but *you* probably don't) has been trying to get on the track of an explanation ever since. He, of course, insists there was malice in it, but I don't know. It's difficult to see how it could have come in."

After a time the talk reverted to the *History of Witchcraft*. "Did you ever look into it?" asked the host.

"Yes, I did," said the Secretary. "I went so far as to read it."

"Was it as bad as it was made out to be?"

"Oh, in point of style and form, quite hopeless. It deserved all the pulverizing it got. But, besides that, it was an evil book. The man believed every word of what he was saying, and I'm very much mistaken if he hadn't tried the greater part of his receipts."

"Well, I only remember Harrington's review of it, and I must say if I'd been the author it would have quenched my literary ambition for good. I should never have held up my head again."

"It hasn't had that effect in the present case. But come, it's half-past three; I must be off."

On the way home the Secretary's wife said, "I do hope that horrible man won't find out that Mr Dunning had anything to do with the rejection of his paper." "I don't think there's much chance of that," said the Secretary. "Dunning won't mention it himself, for these matters are confidential, and none of us will for the same reason. Karswell won't know his name, for Dunning hasn't published anything on the same subject yet. The only danger is that Karswell might find out, if he was to ask the British Museum people who was in the habit of consulting alchemical manuscripts: I can't very well tell them not to mention Dunning, can I? It would set them talking at once. Let's hope it won't occur to him."

However, Mr Karswell was an astute man.

* * * * *

This much is in the way of prologue. On an evening rather later in the same week, Mr Edward Dunning was returning from the British Museum, where he had been engaged in research, to the comfortable house in a suburb where he lived alone, tended by two excellent women who had been long with him. There is nothing to be added by way of description of him to what we have heard already. Let us follow him as he takes his sober course homewards.

* * * * *

A train took him to within a mile or two of his house, and an electric tram a stage farther. The line ended at a point some three hundred yards from his front door. He had had enough of reading when he got into the car, and indeed the light was not such as to allow him to do more than study the advertisements on the panes of glass that faced him as he sat. As was not unnatural, the advertisements in this particular line of cars were objects of his frequent contemplation, and, with the possible exception of the brilliant and convincing dialogue between Mr Lamplough and an eminent K.C. on the subject of Pyretic Saline, none of them afforded much scope to his imagination. I am wrong: there was one at the corner of the car farthest from him which did not seem familiar. It was in blue letters on a yellow ground, and all that he could read of it was a name—John Harrington—and something like a date. It could be of no interest to him to know more; but for all that, as the car emptied, he was just curious enough to move along the seat until he could read it well. He felt to a slight extent repaid for his trouble; the advertisement was *not* of the usual type. It ran thus: "In memory of John Harrington, F.S.A., of The Laurels, Ashbrooke. Died Sept. 18th, 1889. Three months were allowed."

The car stopped. Mr Dunning, still contemplating the blue letters on the yellow ground, had to be stimulated to rise by a word from the conductor. "I beg your pardon," he said, "I was looking at that advertisement; it's a very odd one, isn't it?" The conductor read it slowly. "Well, my word," he said, "I never see that one before. Well, that is a cure, ain't it? Someone bin up to their jokes 'ere, I should think." He got out a duster and applied it, not without saliva, to the pane and then to the outside. "No," he said, returning, "that ain't no transfer; seems to me as if it was reg'lar *in* the glass, what I mean in the substance, as you may say. Don't you think so, sir?" Mr Dunning examined it and rubbed it with his glove, and agreed. "Who looks after these advertisements, and gives leave for them to be put up? I wish you would inquire. I will just take a note of the words." At this moment there came a call from the driver: "Look alive, George, time's up." "All right, all right; there's something else what's up at this end. You come and look at this 'ere glass." "What's gorn with the glass?" said the driver, approaching. "Well, and oo's 'Arrington? What's it all about?" "I was just asking who was responsible for putting the advertisements up in your cars, and saying it would be as well to make some inquiry about this one." "Well, sir, that's all done at the Company's office, that work is: it's our Mr Timms, I believe, looks into that. When we put up tonight I'll leave word, and per'aps I'll be able to tell you tomorrer if you 'appen to be coming this way."

This was all that passed that evening. Mr Dunning did just go to the trouble of looking up Ashbrooke, and found that it was in Warwickshire.

Next day he went to town again. The car (it was the same car) was too full in the morning to allow of his getting a word with the conductor: he could only be sure that the curious advertisement had been made away with. The close of the day brought a further element of mystery into the transaction. He had missed the tram, or else preferred walking home, but at a rather late hour, while he was at work in his study, one of the maids came to say that two men from the tramways was very anxious to speak to him. This was a reminder of the advertisement, which he had, he says, nearly forgotten. He had the men in—they were the conductor and driver of the car—and when the matter of refreshment had been attended to, asked what Mr Timms had had to say about the advertisement. "Well, sir, that's what we took the liberty to step round about," said the conductor. "Mr Timms 'e give William 'ere the rough side of his tongue about that: 'cordin' to 'im there warn't no advertisement of that description sent in, nor ordered, nor paid for, nor put up, nor nothink, let alone not bein' there, and we was playing the fool takin' up his time. 'Well,' I says, 'if that's the case, all I ask of you, Mr Timms,' I says, 'is to take and look at it for yourself,' I says. 'Of course if it ain't there,' I says, 'you may take and call me what you like.' 'Right,' he says, 'I will': and we went straight off. Now, I leave it to you, sir, if that ad, as we term 'em, with 'Arrington on it warn't as plain as ever you see anythink—blue letters on yeller glass, and as I says at the time, and you borne me out, reg'lar *in* the glass, because, if you remember, you recollect of me swabbing it with my duster." "To be sure I do, quite clearly—well?"

"You may say well, I don't think. Mr Timms he gets in that car with a light—no, he told William to 'old the light outside. 'Now,' he says, 'where's your precious ad. what we've 'eard so much about?' 'Ere it is,' I says, 'Mr Timms,' and I laid my 'and on it.'" The conductor paused.

"Well," said Mr Dunning, "it was gone, I suppose. Broken?"

"Broke!—not it. There warn't, if you'll believe me, no more trace of them letters—blue letters they was—on that piece o' glass, than—well, it's no good *me* talkin'. *I* never see such a thing. I leave it to William here if—but there, as I says, where's the benefit in me going on about it?"

"And what did Mr Timms say?"

"Why 'e did what I give 'im leave to—called us pretty much anythink he liked, and I don't know as I blame him so much neither. But what we thought, William and me did, was as we seen you take down a bit of a note about that—well, that letterin'—"

"I certainly did that, and I have it now. Did you wish me to speak to Mr Timms myself, and show it to him? Was that what you came in about?"

"There, didn't I say as much?" said William. "Deal with a gent if you can get on the track of one, that's my word. Now perhaps, George, you'll allow as I ain't took you very far wrong tonight."

"Very well, William, very well; no need for you to go on as if you'd 'ad to frog's-march me 'ere. I come quiet, didn't I? All the same for that, we 'adn't ought to take up your time this way, sir; but if it so 'appened you could find time to step round to the Company orfice in the morning and tell Mr Timms what you seen for yourself, we should lay under a very 'igh obligation to you for the trouble. You see it ain't bein' called—well, one thing and another, as we mind, but if they got it into their 'ead at the orfice as we seen things as warn't there, why, one thing leads to another, and where we should be a twelvemunce 'ence—well, you can understand what I mean."

Amid further elucidations of the proposition, George, conducted by William, left the room.

The incredulity of Mr Timms (who had a nodding acquaintance with Mr Dunning) was greatly modified on the following day by what the latter could tell and show him; and any bad mark that might have been attached to the names of William and George was not suffered to remain on the Company's books; but explanation there was none.

Mr Dunning's interest in the matter was kept alive by an incident of the following afternoon. He was walking from his club to the train, and he noticed some way ahead a man with a handful of leaflets such as are distributed to passers-by by agents of enterprising firms. This agent had not chosen a very crowded street for his operations: in fact, Mr Dunning did not see him get rid of a single leaflet before he himself reached the spot. One was thrust into his hand as he passed: the hand that gave it touched his, and he experienced a sort of little shock as it did so. It seemed unnaturally rough and hot. He looked in passing at the giver, but the impression he got was so unclear that, however much he tried to reckon it up subsequently, nothing would come. He was walking quickly, and as he went on glanced at the paper. It was a blue one. The name of Harrington in large capitals caught his eye. He stopped, startled, and felt for his glasses. The next instant the leaflet was twitched out of his hand by a man who hurried past, and was irrecoverably gone. He ran back a few paces, but where was the passer-by? and where the distributor?

It was in a somewhat pensive frame of mind that Mr Dunning passed on the following day into the Select Manuscript Room of the British Museum, and filled up tickets for Harley 3586, and some other volumes. After a few minutes they were brought to him, and he was settling the one he wanted first upon the desk, when he thought he heard his own name whispered behind him. He turned round hastily, and in doing so, brushed his little portfolio of loose papers on to the floor. He saw no one he recognized except one of the staff in charge of the room, who nodded to him, and he proceeded to pick up his papers. He thought he had them all, and was turning to begin work, when a stout gentleman at the table behind him, who was just rising to leave, and had collected his own belongings, touched him on the shoulder, saying, "May I give you this? I think it should be yours," and handed him a missing quire. "It is mine, thank you," said Mr Dunning. In another moment the man had left the room. Upon finishing his work for the afternoon, Mr Dunning had some conversation with the assistant in charge, and took occasion to ask who the stout gentleman was. "Oh, he's a man named Karswell," said the assistant; "he was asking me a week ago who were the great authorities on alchemy, and of course I told him you were the only one in the country. I'll see if I can catch him: he'd like to meet you, I'm sure."

"For heaven's sake don't dream of it!" said Mr Dunning, "I'm particularly anxious to avoid him."

"Oh! very well," said the assistant, "he doesn't come here often: I dare say you won't meet him."

More than once on the way home that day Mr Dunning confessed to himself that he did not look forward with his usual cheerfulness to a solitary evening. It seemed to him that something ill-defined and impalpable had stepped in between him and his fellow-men—had taken him in charge, as it were. He wanted to sit close up to his neighbours in the train and in the tram, but as luck would have it both train and car were markedly empty. The conductor George was thoughtful, and appeared to be absorbed in calculations as to the number of passengers. On arriving at his house he found Dr Watson, his medical man, on his doorstep. "I've had to upset your household arrangements, I'm sorry to say, Dunning. Both your servants *hors de combat*. In fact, I've had to send them to the Nursing Home."

"Good heavens! what's the matter?"

"It's something like ptomaine poisoning, I should think: you've not suffered yourself, I can see, or you wouldn't be walking about. I think they'll pull through all right."

"Dear, dear! Have you any idea what brought it on?" "Well, they tell me they bought some shell-fish from a hawker at their dinner-time. It's odd. I've made inquiries, but I can't find that any hawker has been to other houses in the street. I couldn't send word to you; they won't be back for a bit yet. You come and dine with me tonight, anyhow, and we can make arrangements for going on. Eight o'clock. Don't be too anxious." The solitary evening was thus obviated; at the expense of some distress and inconvenience, it is true. Mr Dunning spent the time pleasantly enough with the doctor (a rather recent settler), and returned to his lonely home at about 11.30. The night he passed is not one on which he looks back with any satisfaction. He was in bed and the light was out. He was wondering if the charwoman would come early enough to get him hot water next morning, when he heard the unmistakable sound of his study door opening. No step followed it on the passage floor, but the sound must mean mischief, for he knew that he had shut the door that evening after putting his papers away in his desk. It was rather shame than courage that induced him to slip out into the passage and lean over the banister in his night-gown, listening. No light was visible; no further sound came: only a gust of warm, or even hot air played for an instant round his shins. He went back and decided to lock himself into his room. There was more unpleasantness, however. Either an economical suburban company had decided that their light would not be required in the small hours, and had stopped working, or else something was wrong with the meter; the effect was in any case that the electric light was off. The obvious course was to find a match, and also to consult his watch: he might as well know how many hours of discomfort awaited him. So he put his hand into the well-known nook under the pillow: only, it did not get so far. What he touched was, according to his account, a mouth, with teeth, and with hair about it, and, he declares, not the mouth of a human being. I do not think it is any use to guess what he said or did; but he was in a spare room with the door locked and his ear to it before he was clearly conscious again. And there he spent the rest of a most miserable night, looking every moment for some fumbling at the door: but nothing came.

The venturing back to his own room in the morning was attended with many listenings and quiverings. The door stood open, fortunately, and the blinds were up (the servants had been out of the house before the hour of drawing them down); there was, to be short, no trace of an inhabitant. The watch, too, was in its usual place; nothing was disturbed, only the wardrobe door had swung open, in accordance with its confirmed habit. A ring at the back door now announced the charwoman, who had been ordered the night before, and nerved Mr Dunning, after letting her in, to continue his search in other parts of the house. It was equally fruitless.

The day thus begun went on dismally enough. He dared not go to the Museum: in spite of what the assistant had said, Karswell might turn up there, and Dunning felt he could not cope with a probably hostile stranger. His own house was odious; he hated sponging on the doctor. He spent some little time in a call at the Nursing Home, where he was slightly cheered by a good report of his housekeeper and maid. Towards lunch-time he betook himself to his club, again experiencing a gleam of satisfaction at seeing the Secretary of the Association. At luncheon Dunning told his friend the more material of his woes, but could not bring himself to speak of those that weighed most heavily on his spirits. "My poor dear man," said the Secretary, "what an upset! Look here: we're alone at home, absolutely. You must put up with us. Yes! no excuse: send your things in this afternoon." Dunning was unable to stand out: he was, in truth, becoming acutely anxious, as the hours went on, as to what that night might have waiting for him. He was almost happy as he hurried home to pack up.

His friends, when they had time to take stock of him, were rather shocked at his lorn appearance, and did their best to keep him up to the mark. Not altogether without success: but, when the two men were smoking alone later, Dunning became dull again. Suddenly he said, "Gayton, I believe that alchemist man knows it was I who got his paper rejected." Gayton whistled. "What makes you think that?" he said. Dunning told of his conversation with the Museum assistant, and Gayton could only agree that the guess seemed likely to be correct. "Not that I care much," Dunning went on, "only it might be a nuisance if we were to meet. He's a bad-tempered party, I imagine." Conversation dropped again; Gayton became more and more strongly impressed with the desolateness that came over Dunning's face and bearing, and finally—though with a considerable effort—he asked him point-blank whether something serious was not bothering him. Dunning gave an exclamation of relief. "I was perishing to get it off my mind," he said. "Do you know anything about a man named John Harrington?" Gayton was thoroughly startled, and at the moment could only ask why. Then the complete story of Dunning's experiences came out—what had happened in the tramcar, in his own house, and in the street, the troubling of spirit that had crept over him, and still held him; and he ended with the question he had begun with. Gayton was at a loss how to answer him. To tell the story of Harrington's end would perhaps be right; only, Dunning was in a nervous state, the story was a grim one, and he could not help asking himself whether there were not a connecting link between these two cases, in the person of Karswell. It was a difficult concession for a scientific man, but it could be eased by the phrase "hypnotic suggestion." In the end he decided that his answer tonight should be guarded; he would talk the situation over with his wife. So he said that he had known Harrington at Cambridge, and believed he had died suddenly in 1889, adding a few details about the man and his published work. He did talk over the matter with Mrs Gayton, and, as he had anticipated, she leapt at once to the conclusion which had been hovering before him. It was she who reminded him of the surviving brother, Henry Harrington, and she also who suggested that he might be got hold of by means of their hosts of the day before. "He might be a hopeless crank," objected Gayton. "That could be ascertained from the Bennetts, who knew him," Mrs Gayton retorted; and she undertook to see the Bennetts the very next day.

* * * * *

It is not necessary to tell in further detail the steps by which Henry Harrington and Dunning were brought together.

* * * * *

The next scene that does require to be narrated is a conversation that took place between the two. Dunning had told Harrington of the strange ways in which the dead man's name had been brought before him, and had said something, besides, of his own subsequent experiences. Then he had asked if Harrington was disposed, in return, to recall any of the circumstances connected with his brother's death. Harrington's surprise at what he heard can be imagined: but his reply was readily given.

"John," he said, "was in a very odd state, undeniably, from time to time, during some weeks before, though not immediately before, the catastrophe. There were several things; the principal notion he had was that he thought he was being followed. No doubt he was an impressionable man, but he never had had such fancies as this before. I cannot get it out of my mind that there was ill-will at work, and what you tell me about yourself reminds me very much of my brother. Can you think of any possible connecting link?"

"There is just one that has been taking shape vaguely in my mind. I've been told that your brother reviewed a book very severely not long before he died, and just lately I have happened to cross the path of the man who wrote that book in a way he would resent."

"Don't tell me the man was called Karswell."

"Why not? that is exactly his name."

Henry Harrington leant back. "That is final to my mind. Now I must explain further. From something he said, I feel sure that my brother John was beginning to believe—very much against his will— that Karswell was at the bottom of his trouble. I want to tell you what seems to me to have a bearing on the situation. My brother was a great musician, and used to run up to concerts in town. He came back, three months before he died, from one of these, and gave me his programme to look at—an analytical programme: he always kept them. 'I nearly missed this one,' he said. 'I suppose I must have dropped it: anyhow, I was looking for it under my seat and in my pockets and so on, and my neighbour offered me his, said "might he give it me, he had no further use for it," and he went away just afterwards. I don't know who he was—a stout, clean-shaven man. I should have been sorry to miss it; of course I could have bought another, but this cost me nothing.' At another time he told me that he had been very uncomfortable both on the way to his hotel and during the night. I piece things together now in thinking it over. Then, not very long after, he was going over these programmes, putting them in order to have them bound up, and in this particular one (which by the way I had hardly glanced at), he found quite near the beginning a strip of paper with some very odd writing on it in red and black—most carefully done—it looked to me more like Runic letters than anything else. 'Why,' he said, 'this must belong to my fat neighbour. It looks as if it might be worth returning to him; it may be a copy of something; evidently someone has taken trouble over it. How can I find his address?' We talked it over for a little and agreed that it wasn't worth advertising about, and that my brother had better look out for the man at the next concert, to which he was going very soon. The paper was lying on the book and we were both by the fire; it was a cold, windy summer evening. I suppose the door blew open, though I didn't notice it: at any rate a gust—a warm gust it was—came quite suddenly between us, took the paper and blew it straight into the fire: it was light, thin paper, and flared and went up the chimney in a single ash. 'Well,' I said, 'you can't give it back now.' He said nothing for a minute: then rather crossly, 'No, I can't; but why you should keep on saying so I don't know.' I remarked that I didn't say it more than once. 'Not more than four times, you mean,' was all he said. I remember all that very clearly, without any good reason; and now to come to the point. I don't know if you looked at that book of Karswell's which my unfortunate brother reviewed. It's not likely that you should: but I did, both before his death and after it. The first time we made game of it together. It was written in no style at all—split infinitives, and every sort of thing that makes an Oxford gorge rise. Then there was nothing that the man didn't swallow: mixing up classical myths, and stories out of the *Golden Legend* with reports of savage customs of today—all very proper, no doubt, if you know how to use them, but he didn't: he seemed to put the *Golden Legend* and the *Golden Bough* exactly on a par, and to believe both: a pitiable exhibition, in short. Well, after the misfortune, I looked over the book again. It was no better than before, but the impression which it left this time on my mind was different. I suspected—as I told you—that Karswell had borne ill-will to my brother, even that he was in some way responsible for what had happened; and now his book seemed to me to be a very sinister performance indeed. One chapter in particular struck me, in which he spoke of 'casting the Runes' on people, either for the purpose of gaining their affection or of getting them out of the way—perhaps more especially the latter: he spoke of all this in a way that really seemed to me to imply actual knowledge. I've not time to go into details, but the upshot is that I am pretty sure from information received that the civil man at the concert was Karswell: I suspect—I more than suspect—that the paper was of importance: and I do believe that if my brother had been able to give it back, he might have been alive now. Therefore, it occurs to me to ask you whether you have anything to put beside what I have told you."

By way of answer, Dunning had the episode in the Manuscript Room at the British Museum to relate.

"Then he did actually hand you some papers; have you examined them? No? because we must, if you'll allow it, look at them at once, and very carefully."

They went to the still empty house—empty, for the two servants were not yet able to return to work. Dunning's portfolio of papers was gathering dust on the writing-table. In it were the quires of small-sized scribbling paper which he used for his transcripts: and from one of these, as he took it up, there slipped and fluttered out into the room with uncanny quickness, a strip of thin light paper. The window was open, but Harrington slammed it to, just in time to intercept the paper, which he caught. "I thought so," he said; "it might be the identical thing that was given to my brother. You'll have to look out, Dunning; this may mean something quite serious for you."

A long consultation took place. The paper was narrowly examined. As Harrington had said, the characters on it were more like Runes than anything else, but not decipherable by either man, and both hesitated to copy them, for fear, as they confessed, of perpetuating whatever evil purpose they might conceal. So it has remained impossible (if I may anticipate a little) to ascertain what was conveyed in this curious message or commission. Both Dunning and Harrington are firmly convinced that it had the effect of bringing its possessors into very undesirable company. That it must be returned to the source whence it came they were agreed, and further, that the only safe and certain way was that of personal service; and here contrivance would be necessary, for Dunning was known by sight to Karswell. He must, for one thing, alter his appearance by shaving his beard. But then might not the blow fall first? Harrington thought they could time it. He knew the date of the concert at which the "black spot" had been put on his brother: it was June 18th. The death had followed on Sept. 18th. Dunning reminded him that three months had been mentioned on the inscription on the car-window. "Perhaps," he added, with a cheerless laugh, "mine may be a bill at three months too. I believe I can fix it by my diary. Yes, April 23rd was the day at the Museum; that brings us to July 23rd. Now, you know, it becomes extremely important to me to know anything you will tell me about the progress of your brother's trouble, if it is possible for you to speak of it." "Of course. Well, the sense of being watched whenever he was alone was the most distressing thing to him. After a time I took to sleeping in his room, and he was the better for that: still, he talked a great deal in his sleep. What about? Is it wise to dwell on that, at least before things are straightened out? I think not, but I can tell you this: two things came for him by post during those weeks, both with a London postmark, and addressed in a commercial hand. One was a woodcut of Bewick's, roughly torn out of the page: one which shows a moonlit road and a man walking along it, followed by an awful demon creature. Under it were written the lines out of the 'Ancient Mariner' (which I suppose the cut illustrates) about one who, having once looked round—

> walks on,
> And turns no more his head,
> Because he knows a frightful fiend
> Doth close behind him tread.

The other was a calendar, such as tradesmen often send. My brother paid no attention to this, but I looked at it after his death, and found that everything after Sept. 18 had been torn out. You may be surprised at his having gone out alone the evening he was killed, but the fact is that during the last ten days or so of his life he had been quite free from the sense of being followed or watched."

The end of the consultation was this. Harrington, who knew a neighbour of Karswell's, thought he saw a way of keeping a watch on his movements. It would be Dunning's part to be in readiness to try to cross Karswell's path at any moment, to keep the paper safe and in a place of ready access.

They parted. The next weeks were no doubt a severe strain upon Dunning's nerves: the intangible barrier which had seemed to rise about him on the day when he received the paper, gradually developed into a brooding blackness that cut him off from the means of escape to which one might have thought he might resort. No one was at hand who was likely to suggest them to him, and he seemed robbed of all initiative. He waited with inexpressible anxiety as May, June, and early July passed on, for a mandate from Harrington. But all this time Karswell remained immovable at Lufford.

At last, in less than a week before the date he had come to look upon as the end of his earthly activities, came a telegram: "Leaves Victoria by boat train Thursday night. Do not miss. I come to you to-night. Harrington."

He arrived accordingly, and they concocted plans. The train left Victoria at nine and its last stop before Dover was Croydon West. Harrington would mark down Karswell at Victoria, and look out for Dunning at Croydon, calling to him if need were by a name agreed upon. Dunning, disguised as far as might be, was to have no label or initials on any hand luggage, and must at all costs have the paper with him.

Dunning's suspense as he waited on the Croydon platform I need not attempt to describe. His sense of danger during the last days had only been sharpened by the fact that the cloud about him had perceptibly been lighter; but relief was an ominous symptom, and, if

Karswell eluded him now, hope was gone: and there were so many chances of that. The rumour of the journey might be itself a device. The twenty minutes in which he paced the platform and persecuted every porter with inquiries as to the boat train were as bitter as any he had spent. Still, the train came, and Harrington was at the window. It was important, of course, that there should be no recognition: so Dunning got in at the farther end of the corridor carriage, and only gradually made his way to the compartment where Harrington and Karswell were. He was pleased, on the whole, to see that the train was far from full.

Karswell was on the alert, but gave no sign of recognition. Dunning took the seat not immediately facing him, and attempted, vainly at first, then with increasing command of his faculties, to reckon the possibilities of making the desired transfer. Opposite to Karswell, and next to Dunning, was a heap of Karswell's coats on the seat. It would be of no use to slip the paper into these—he would not be safe, or would not feel so, unless in some way it could be proffered by him and accepted by the other. There was a handbag, open, and with papers in it. Could he manage to conceal this (so that perhaps Karswell might leave the carriage without it), and then find and give it to him? This was the plan that suggested itself. If he could only have counselled with Harrington! but that could not be. The minutes went on. More than once Karswell rose and went out into the corridor. The second time Dunning was on the point of attempting to make the bag fall off the seat, but he caught Harrington's eye, and read in it a warning.

Karswell, from the corridor, was watching: probably to see if the two men recognized each other. He returned, but was evidently restless: and, when he rose the third time, hope dawned, for something did slip off his seat and fall with hardly a sound to the floor. Karswell went out once more, and passed out of range of the corridor window. Dunning picked up what had fallen, and saw that the key was in his hands in the form of one of Cook's ticket-cases, with tickets in it. These cases have a pocket in the cover, and within very few seconds the paper of which we have heard was in the pocket of this one. To make the operation more secure, Harrington stood in the doorway of the compartment and fiddled with the blind. It was done, and done at the right time, for the train was now slowing down towards Dover.

In a moment more Karswell re-entered the compartment. As he did so, Dunning, managing, he knew not how, to suppress the tremble in his voice, handed him the ticket-case, saying, "May I give you this, sir? I believe it is yours." After a brief glance at the ticket inside, Karswell uttered the hoped-for response, "Yes, it is; much obliged to you, sir," and he placed it in his breast pocket.

Even in the few moments that remained—moments of tense anxiety, for they knew not to what a premature finding of the paper might lead—both men noticed that the carriage seemed to darken about them and to grow warmer; that Karswell was fidgety and oppressed; that he drew the heap of loose coats near to him and cast it back as if it repelled him; and that he then sat upright and glanced anxiously at both. They, with sickening anxiety, busied themselves in collecting their belongings; but they both thought that Karswell was on the point of speaking when the train stopped at Dover Town. It was natural that in the short space between town and pier they should both go into the corridor.

At the pier they got out, but so empty was the train that they were forced to linger on the platform until Karswell should have passed ahead of them with his porter on the way to the boat, and only then was it safe for them to exchange a pressure of the hand and a word of concentrated congratulation. The effect upon Dunning was to make him almost faint. Harrington made him lean up against the wall, while he himself went forward a few yards within sight of the gangway to the boat, at which Karswell had now arrived. The man at the head of it examined his ticket, and, laden with coats he passed down into the boat. Suddenly the official called after him, "You, sir, beg pardon, did the other gentleman show his ticket?" "What the devil do you mean by the other gentleman?" Karswell's snarling voice called back from the deck. The man bent over and looked at him. "The devil? Well, I don't know, I'm sure," Harrington heard him say to himself, and then aloud, "My mistake, sir; must have been your rugs! ask your pardon." And then, to a subordinate near him, "'Ad he got a dog with him, or what? Funny thing: I could 'a' swore 'e wasn't alone. Well, whatever it was, they'll 'ave to see to it aboard. She's off now. Another week and we shall be gettin' the 'oliday customers." In five minutes more there was nothing but the lessening lights of the boat, the long line of the Dover lamps, the night breeze, and the moon.

Long and long the two sat in their room at the "Lord Warden." In spite of the removal of their greatest anxiety, they were oppressed with a doubt, not of the lightest. Had they been justified in sending a man to his death, as they believed they had? Ought they not to warn him, at least? "No," said Harrington; "if he is the murderer I think him, we have done no more than is just. Still, if you think it better—but how and where can you warn him?" "He was booked to Abbeville only," said Dunning. "I saw that. If I wired to the hotels there in Joanne's Guide, 'Examine your ticket-case, Dunning,' I should feel happier. This is the 21st: he will have a day. But I am afraid he has gone into the dark." So telegrams were left at the hotel office.

It is not clear whether these reached their destination, or whether, if they did, they were understood. All that is known is that, on the afternoon of the 23rd, an English traveller, examining the front of St Wulfram's Church at Abbeville, then under extensive repair, was struck on the head and instantly killed by a stone falling from the scaffold erected round the north-western tower, there being, as was clearly proved, no workman on the scaffold at that moment: and the traveller's papers identified him as Mr Karswell.

Only one detail shall be added. At Karswell's sale a set of Bewick, sold with all faults, was acquired by Harrington. The page with the woodcut of the traveller and the demon was, as he had expected, mutilated. Also, after a judicious interval, Harrington repeated to Dunning something of what he had heard his brother say in his sleep: but it was not long before Dunning stopped him.

LUELLA MILLER

by Mary E. Wilkins Freeman

Mary E. Wilkins Freeman (1852-1930) is a rare but notable example of a nineteenth-century American woman who became commercially successful writer—fellow New Englander Louisa May Alcott being the most prominent other. Freeman's earliest works were children's stories and poems which she penned while holding down the responsible position of secretary to Oliver Wendell Holmes, Sr. Freeman's novels and stories were richly descriptive of New England life and evocative and atmospheric. When she became interested in the supernatural she melded horror with her talent for natural realism— a very successful (and distinctly American) marriage.

In 1926, just four years before her death, she became the first recipient of the William Dean Howells Medal for Distinction in Fiction from the American Academy of Arts and Letters.

Luella Miller

Close to the village street stood the one-story house in which Luella Miller, who had an evil name in the village, had dwelt. She had been dead for years, yet there were those in the village who, in spite of the clearer light which comes on a vantage-point from a long-past danger, half believed in the tale which they had heard from their childhood. In their hearts, although they scarcely would have owned it, was a survival of the wild horror and frenzied fear of their ancestors who had dwelt in the same age with Luella Miller. Young people even would stare with a shudder at the old house as they passed, and children never played around it as was their wont around an untenanted building. Not a window in the old Miller house was broken: the panes reflected the morning sunlight in patches of emerald and blue, and the latch of the sagging front door was never lifted, although no bolt secured it. Since Luella Miller had been carried out of it, the house had had no tenant except one friendless old soul who had no choice between that and the far-off shelter of the open sky. This old woman, who had survived her kindred and friends, lived in the house one week, then one morning no smoke came out of the chimney, and a body of neighbours, a score strong, entered and found her dead in her bed. There were dark whispers as to the cause of her death, and there were those who testified to an expression of fear so exalted that it showed forth the state of the departing soul upon the dead face. The old woman had been hale and hearty when she entered the house, and in seven days she was dead; it seemed that she had fallen a victim to some uncanny power. The minister talked in the pulpit with covert severity against the sin of superstition; still the belief prevailed. Not a soul in the village but would have chosen the almshouse rather than that dwelling. No vagrant, if he heard the tale, would seek shelter beneath that old roof, unhallowed by nearly half a century of superstitious fear.

There was only one person in the village who had actually known Luella Miller. That person was a woman well over eighty, but a marvel of vitality and unextinct youth. Straight as an arrow, with the spring of one recently let loose from the bow of life, she moved about the streets, and she always went to church, rain or shine. She had never married, and had lived alone for years in a house across the road from Luella Miller's.

This woman had none of the garrulousness of age, but never in all her life had she ever held her tongue for any will save her own, and she never spared the truth when she essayed to present it. She it was who bore testimony to the life, evil, though possibly wittingly or designedly so, of Luella Miller, and to her personal appearance. When this old woman spoke—and she had the gift of description, although her thoughts were clothed in the rude vernacular of her native village—one could seem to see Luella Miller as she had really looked. According to this woman, Lydia Anderson by name, Luella Miller had been a beauty of a type rather unusual in New England. She had been a slight, pliant sort of creature, as ready with a strong yielding to fate and as unbreakable as a willow. She had glimmering lengths of straight, fair hair, which she wore softly looped round a long, lovely face. She had blue eyes full of soft pleading, little slender, clinging hands, and a wonderful grace of motion and attitude.

"Luella Miller used to sit in a way nobody else could if they sat up and studied a week of Sundays," said Lydia Anderson, "and it was a sight to see her walk. If one of them willows over there on the edge of the brook could start up and get its roots free of the ground, and move off, it would go just the way Luella Miller used to. She had a green shot silk she used to wear, too, and a hat with green ribbon streamers, and a lace veil blowing across her face and out sideways, and a green ribbon flyin' from her waist. That was what she came out bride in when she married Erastus Miller. Her name before she was married was Hill. There was always a sight of "l's" in her name, married or single. Erastus Miller was good lookin', too, better lookin' than Luella. Sometimes I used to think that Luella wa'n't so handsome after all. Erastus just about worshiped her. I used to know him pretty well. He lived next door to me, and we went to school together. Folks used to say he was waitin' on me, but he wa'n't. I never thought he was except once or twice when he said things that some girls might have suspected meant somethin'. That was before Luella came here to teach the district school. It was funny how she came to get it, for folks said she hadn't any education, and that one of the big girls, Lottie Henderson, used to do all the teachin' for her, while she sat back and did embroidery work on a cambric pocket-handkerchief. Lottie Henderson was a real smart girl, a splendid scholar, and she just set her eyes by Luella, as all the girls did. Lottie would have made a real smart woman, but she died when Luella had been here about a year—just faded away and died: nobody knew what ailed her. She dragged herself to that schoolhouse and helped Luella teach till the very last minute. The committee all knew how Luella didn't do much of the work herself, but they winked at it. It wa'n't long after Lottie died that Erastus married her. I always thought he hurried it up because she wa'n't fit to teach. One of the big boys used to help her after Lottie died, but he hadn't much government, and the school didn't do very well, and Luella might have had to give it up, for the committee couldn't have shut their eyes to things much longer. The boy that helped her was a real honest, innocent sort of fellow, and he was a good scholar, too. Folks said he overstudied, and that was the reason he was took crazy the year after Luella married, but I don't know. And I don't know what made Erastus Miller go into consumption of the blood the year after he was married: consumption wa'n't in his family. He just grew weaker and weaker, and went almost bent double when he tried to wait on Luella, and he spoke feeble, like an old man. He worked terrible hard till the last trying to save up a little to leave Luella. I've seen him out in the worst storms on a wood-sled— he used to cut and sell wood—and he was hunched up on top lookin' more dead than alive. Once I couldn't stand it: I went over and helped him pitch some wood on the cart—I was always strong in my arms. I wouldn't stop for all he told me to, and I guess he was glad enough for the help. That was only a week before he died. He fell on the kitchen floor while he was gettin' breakfast. He always got the breakfast and let Luella lay abed. He did all the sweepin' and the washin' and the ironin' and most of the cookin'. He couldn't bear to have Luella lift her finger, and she let him do for her. She lived like a queen for all the work she did. She didn't even do her sewin'. She said it made her shoulder ache to sew, and poor Erastus's sister Lily used to do all her sewin'. She wa'n't able to, either; she was never strong in her back, but she did it beautifully. She had to, to suit Luella, she was so dreadful particular. I never saw anythin' like the fagottin' and hemstitchin' that Lily Miller did for Luella. She made all Luella's weddin' outfit, and that green silk dress, after Maria Babbit cut it. Maria she cut it for nothin', and she did a lot more cuttin' and fittin' for nothin' for Luella, too. Lily Miller went to live with Luella after Erastus died. She gave up her home, though she was real attached to it and wa'n't a mite afraid to stay alone. She rented it and she went to live with Luella right away after the funeral."

Then this old woman, Lydia Anderson, who remembered Luella Miller, would go on to relate the story of Lily Miller. It seemed that on the removal of Lily Miller to the house of her dead brother, to live with his widow, the village people first began to talk. This Lily Miller had been hardly past her first youth, and a most robust and blooming woman, rosy-cheeked, with curls of strong, black hair over-shadowing round, candid temples and bright dark eyes. It was not six months after she had taken up her residence with her sister-in-law that her rosy colour faded and her pretty curves became wan hollows. White shadows began to show in the black rings of her hair, and the light died out of her eyes, her features sharpened, and there were pathetic lines at her mouth, which yet wore always an expression of utter sweetness and even happiness. She was devoted to her sister; there was no doubt that she loved her with her whole heart, and was perfectly content in her service. It was her sole anxiety lest she should die and leave her alone.

"The way Lily Miller used to talk about Luella was enough to make you mad and enough to make you cry," said Lydia Anderson. "I've been in there sometimes toward the last when she was too feeble to cook and carried her some blanc-mange or custard—somethin' I thought she might relish, and she'd thank me, and when I asked her how she was, say she felt better than she did yesterday, and asked me if I didn't think she looked better, dreadful pitiful, and say poor Luella had an awful time takin' care of her and doin' the work—she wa'n't strong enough to do anythin'—when all the time Luella wa'n't liftin' her finger and poor Lily didn't get any care except what the neighbours gave her, and Luella eat up everythin' that was carried in for Lily. I had it real straight that she did. Luella used to just sit and cry and do nothin'. She did act real fond of Lily, and she pined away considerable, too. There was those that thought she'd go into a decline herself. But after Lily died, her Aunt Abby Mixter came, and then Luella picked up and grew as fat and rosy as ever. But poor Aunt Abby begun to droop just the way Lily had, and I guess somebody wrote to her married daughter, Mrs. Sam Abbot, who lived in Barre, for she wrote her mother that she must leave right away and come and make her a visit, but Aunt Abby wouldn't go. I can see her now. She was a real good-lookin' woman, tall and large, with a big, square face and a high forehead that looked of itself kind of benevolent and good. She just tended out on Luella as if she had been a baby, and when her married daughter sent for her she wouldn't stir one inch. She'd always thought a lot of her daughter, too, but she said Luella needed her and her married daughter didn't. Her daughter kept writin' and writin', but it didn't do any good. Finally she came, and when she saw how bad her mother looked, she broke down and cried and all but went on her knees to have her come away. She spoke her mind out to Luella, too. She told her that she'd killed her husband and everybody that had anythin' to do with her, and she'd thank her to leave her mother alone. Luella went into hysterics, and Aunt Abby was so frightened that she called me after her daughter went. Mrs. Sam Abbot she went away fairly cryin' out loud in the buggy, the neighbours heard her, and well she might, for she never saw her mother again alive. I went in that night when Aunt Abby called for me, standin' in the door with her little green-checked shawl over her head. I can see her now. 'Do come over here, Miss Anderson,' she sung out, kind of gasping for breath. I didn't stop for anythin'. I put over as fast as I could, and when I got there, there was Luella laughin' and cryin' all together, and Aunt Abby trying to hush her, and all the time she herself was white as a sheet and shakin' so she could hardly stand. 'For the land sakes, Mrs. Mixter,' says I, 'you look worse than she does. You ain't fit to be up out of your bed.'

"'Oh, there ain't anythin' the matter with me,' says she. Then she went on talkin' to Luella. 'There, there, don't, don't, poor little lamb,' says she. 'Aunt Abby is here. She ain't goin' away and leave you. Don't, poor little lamb.'

"'Do leave her with me, Mrs. Mixter, and you get back to bed,' says I, for Aunt Abby had been layin' down considerable lately, though somehow she contrived to do the work.

"'I'm well enough,' says she. 'Don't you think she had better have the doctor, Miss Anderson?'

"'The doctor,' says I, 'I think YOU had better have the doctor. I think you need him much worse than some folks I could mention.' And I looked right straight at Luella Miller laughin' and cryin' and goin' on as if she was the centre of all creation. All the time she was actin' so—seemed as if she was too sick to sense anythin'—she was keepin' a sharp lookout as to how we took it out of the corner of one eye. I see her. You could never cheat me about Luella Miller. Finally I got real mad and I run home and I got a bottle of valerian I had, and I poured some boilin' hot water on a handful of catnip, and I mixed up that catnip tea with most half a wineglass of valerian, and I went with it over to Luella's. I marched right up to Luella, a-holdin' out that cup, all smokin'. 'Now,' says I, 'Luella Miller, 'YOU SWALLER THIS!'

"'What is—what is it, oh, what is it?' she sort of screeches out. Then she goes off a-laughin' enough to kill.

"'Poor lamb, poor little lamb,' says Aunt Abby, standin' over her, all kind of tottery, and tryin' to bathe her head with camphor.

"'YOU SWALLER THIS RIGHT DOWN,' says I. And I didn't waste any ceremony. I just took hold of Luella Miller's chin and I tipped her head back, and I caught her mouth open with laughin', and I clapped that cup to her lips, and I fairly hollered at her: 'Swaller, swaller, swaller!' and she gulped it right down. She had to, and I guess it did her good. Anyhow, she stopped cryin' and laughin' and let me put her to bed, and she went to sleep like a baby inside of half an hour. That was more than poor Aunt Abby did. She lay awake all that night and I stayed with her, though she tried not to have me; said she wa'n't sick enough for watchers. But I stayed, and I made some good cornmeal gruel and I fed her a teaspoon every little while all night long. It seemed to me as if she was jest dyin' from bein' all wore out. In the mornin' as soon as it was light I run over to the Bisbees and sent Johnny Bisbee for the doctor. I told him to tell the doctor to hurry, and he come pretty quick. Poor Aunt Abby didn't seem to know much of anythin' when he got there. You couldn't hardly tell she breathed, she was so used up. When the doctor had gone, Luella came into the room lookin' like a baby in her ruffled nightgown. I can see her now. Her eyes were as blue and her face all pink and white like a blossom, and she looked at Aunt Abby in the bed sort of innocent and surprised. 'Why,' says she, 'Aunt Abby ain't got up yet?'

"'No, she ain't,' says I, pretty short.

"'I thought I didn't smell the coffee,' says Luella.

"'Coffee,' says I. 'I guess if you have coffee this mornin' you'll make it yourself.'

"'I never made the coffee in all my life,' says she, dreadful astonished. 'Erastus always made the coffee as long as he lived, and then Lily she made it, and then Aunt Abby made it. I don't believe I CAN make the coffee, Miss Anderson.'

"'You can make it or go without, jest as you please,' says I.

"'Ain't Aunt Abby goin' to get up?' says she.

"'I guess she won't get up,' says I, 'sick as she is.' I was gettin' madder and madder. There was somethin' about that little pink-and-white thing standin' there and talkin' about coffee, when she had killed so many better folks than she was, and had jest killed another, that made me feel 'most as if I wished somebody would up and kill her before she had a chance to do any more harm.

"'Is Aunt Abby sick?' says Luella, as if she was sort of aggrieved and injured.

"'Yes,' says I, 'she's sick, and she's goin' to die, and then you'll be left alone, and you'll have to do for yourself and wait on yourself, or do without things.' I don't know but I was sort of hard, but it was the truth, and if I was any harder than Luella Miller had been I'll give up. I ain't never been sorry that I said it. Well, Luella, she up and had hysterics again at that, and I jest let her have 'em. All I did was to bundle her into the room on the other side of the entry where Aunt Abby couldn't hear her, if she wa'n't past it—I don't know but she was—and set her down hard in a chair and told her not to come back into the other room, and she minded. She had her hysterics in there till she got tired. When she found out that nobody was comin' to coddle her and do for her she stopped. At least I suppose she did. I had all I could do with poor Aunt Abby tryin' to keep the breath of life in her. The doctor had told me that she was dreadful low, and give me some very strong medicine to give to her in drops real often, and told me real particular about the nourishment. Well, I did as he told me real faithful till she wa'n't able to swaller any longer. Then I had her daughter sent for. I had begun to realize that she wouldn't last any time at all. I hadn't realized it before, though I spoke to Luella the way I did. The doctor he came, and Mrs. Sam Abbot, but when she got there it was too late; her mother was dead. Aunt Abby's daughter just give one look at her mother layin' there, then she turned sort of sharp and sudden and looked at me.

"'Where is she?' says she, and I knew she meant Luella.

"'She's out in the kitchen,' says I. 'She's too nervous to see folks die. She's afraid it will make her sick.'

"The Doctor he speaks up then. He was a young man. Old Doctor Park had died the year before, and this was a young fellow just out of college. 'Mrs. Miller is not strong,' says he, kind of severe, 'and she is quite right in not agitating herself.'

"'You are another, young man; she's got her pretty claw on you,' thinks I, but I didn't say anythin' to him. I just said over to Mrs. Sam Abbot that Luella was in the kitchen, and Mrs. Sam Abbot she went out there, and I went, too, and I never heard anythin' like the way she talked to Luella Miller. I felt pretty hard to Luella myself, but this was more than I ever would have dared to say. Luella she was too scared to go into hysterics. She jest flopped. She seemed to jest shrink away to nothin' in that kitchen chair, with Mrs. Sam Abbot standin' over her and talkin' and tellin' her the truth. I guess the truth was most too much for her and no mistake, because Luella presently actually did faint away, and there wa'n't any sham about it, the way I always suspected there was about them hysterics. She fainted dead away and we had to lay her flat on the floor, and the Doctor he came runnin' out and he said somethin' about a weak heart dreadful fierce to Mrs.

Sam Abbot, but she wa'n't a mite scared. She faced him jest as white as even Luella was layin' there lookin' like death and the Doctor feelin' of her pulse.

"'Weak heart,' says she, 'weak heart; weak fiddlesticks! There ain't nothin' weak about that woman. She's got strength enough to hang onto other folks till she kills 'em. Weak? It was my poor mother that was weak: this woman killed her as sure as if she had taken a knife to her.'

"But the Doctor he didn't pay much attention. He was bendin' over Luella layin' there with her yellow hair all streamin' and her pretty pink-and-white face all pale, and her blue eyes like stars gone out, and he was holdin' onto her hand and smoothin' her forehead, and tellin' me to get the brandy in Aunt Abby's room, and I was sure as I wanted to be that Luella had got somebody else to hang onto, now Aunt Abby was gone, and I thought of poor Erastus Miller, and I sort of pitied the poor young Doctor, led away by a pretty face, and I made up my mind I'd see what I could do.

"I waited till Aunt Abby had been dead and buried about a month, and the Doctor was goin' to see Luella steady and folks were beginnin' to talk; then one evenin', when I knew the Doctor had been called out of town and wouldn't be round, I went over to Luella's. I found her all dressed up in a blue muslin with white polka dots on it, and her hair curled jest as pretty, and there wa'n't a young girl in the place could compare with her. There was somethin' about Luella Miller seemed to draw the heart right out of you, but she didn't draw it out of ME. She was settin' rocking in the chair by her sittin'-room window, and Maria Brown had gone home. Maria Brown had been in to help her, or rather to do the work, for Luella wa'n't helped when she didn't do anythin'. Maria Brown was real capable and she didn't have any ties; she wa'n't married, and lived alone, so she'd offered. I couldn't see why she should do the work any more than Luella; she wa'n't any too strong; but she seemed to think she could and Luella seemed to think so, too, so she went over and did all the work—washed, and ironed, and baked, while Luella sat and rocked. Maria didn't live long afterward. She began to fade away just the same fashion the others had. Well, she was warned, but she acted real mad when folks said anythin': said Luella was a poor, abused woman, too delicate to help herself, and they'd ought to be ashamed, and if she died helpin' them that couldn't help themselves she would—and she did.

"'I s'pose Maria has gone home,' says I to Luella, when I had gone in and sat down opposite her.

"'Yes, Maria went half an hour ago, after she had got supper and washed the dishes,' says Luella, in her pretty way.

"'I suppose she has got a lot of work to do in her own house to-night,' says I, kind of bitter, but that was all thrown away on Luella Miller. It seemed to her right that other folks that wa'n't any better able than she was herself should wait on her, and she couldn't get it through her head that anybody should think it WA'N'T right.

"'Yes,' says Luella, real sweet and pretty, 'yes, she said she had to do her washin' to-night. She has let it go for a fortnight along of comin' over here.'

"'Why don't she stay home and do her washin' instead of comin' over here and doin' YOUR work, when you are just as well able, and enough sight more so, than she is to do it?' says I.

"Then Luella she looked at me like a baby who has a rattle shook at it. She sort of laughed as innocent as you please. 'Oh, I can't do the work myself, Miss Anderson,' says she. 'I never did. Maria HAS to do it.'

"Then I spoke out: 'Has to do it I' says I. 'Has to do it!' She don't have to do it, either. Maria Brown has her own home and enough to live on. She ain't beholden to you to come over here and slave for you and kill herself.'

"Luella she jest set and stared at me for all the world like a doll-baby that was so abused that it was comin' to life.

"'Yes,' says I, 'she's killin' herself. She's goin' to die just the way Erastus did, and Lily, and your Aunt Abby. You're killin' her jest as you did them. I don't know what there is about you, but you seem to bring a curse,' says I. 'You kill everybody that is fool enough to care anythin' about you and do for you.'

"She stared at me and she was pretty pale.

"'And Maria ain't the only one you're goin' to kill,' says I. 'You're goin' to kill Doctor Malcom before you're done with him.'

"Then a red colour came flamin' all over her face. 'I ain't goin' to kill him, either,' says she, and she begun to cry.

"'Yes, you BE!' says I. Then I spoke as I had never spoke before. You see, I felt it on account of Erastus. I told her that she hadn't any business to think of another man after she'd been married to one that had died for her: that she was a dreadful woman; and she was, that's true enough, but sometimes I have wondered lately if she knew it—if she wa'n't like a baby with scissors in its hand cuttin' everybody without knowin' what it was doin'.

"Luella she kept gettin' paler and paler, and she never took her eyes off my face. There was somethin' awful about the way she looked at me and never spoke one word. After awhile I quit talkin' and I went home. I watched that night, but her lamp went out before nine o'clock, and when Doctor Malcom came drivin' past and sort of slowed up he see there wa'n't any light and he drove along. I saw her sort of shy out of meetin' the next Sunday, too, so he shouldn't go home with her, and I begun to think mebbe she did have some conscience after all. It was only a week after that that Maria Brown died—sort of sudden at the last, though everybody had seen it was comin'. Well, then there was a good deal of feelin' and pretty dark whispers. Folks said the days of witchcraft had come again, and they were pretty shy of Luella. She acted sort of offish to the Doctor and he didn't go there, and there wa'n't anybody to do anythin' for her. I don't know how she DID get along. I wouldn't go in there and offer to help her—not because I was afraid of dyin' like the rest, but I thought she was just as well able to do her own work as I was to do it for her, and I thought it was about time that she did it and stopped killin' other folks. But it wa'n't very long before folks began to say that Luella herself was goin' into a decline jest the way her husband, and Lily, and Aunt Abby and the others had, and I saw myself that she looked pretty bad. I used to see her goin' past from the store with a bundle as if she could hardly crawl, but I remembered how Erastus used to wait and 'tend when he couldn't hardly put one foot before the other, and I didn't go out to help her.

"But at last one afternoon I saw the Doctor come drivin' up like mad with his medicine chest, and Mrs. Babbit came in after supper and said that Luella was real sick.

"'I'd offer to go in and nurse her,' says she, 'but I've got my children to consider, and mebbe it ain't true what they say, but it's queer how many folks that have done for her have died.'

"I didn't say anythin', but I considered how she had been Erastus's wife and how he had set his eyes by her, and I made up my mind to go in the next mornin', unless she was better, and see what I could do; but the next mornin' I see her at the window, and pretty soon she came steppin' out as spry as you please, and a little while afterward Mrs. Babbit came in and told me that the Doctor had got a girl from out of town, a Sarah Jones, to come there, and she said she was pretty sure that the Doctor was goin' to marry Luella.

"I saw him kiss her in the door that night myself, and I knew it was true. The woman came that afternoon, and the way she flew around was a caution. I don't believe Luella had swept since Maria died. She swept and dusted, and washed and ironed; wet clothes and dusters and carpets were flyin' over there all day, and every time Luella set her foot out when the Doctor wa'n't there there was that Sarah Jones helpin' of her up and down the steps, as if she hadn't learned to walk.

"Well, everybody knew that Luella and the Doctor were goin' to be married, but it wa'n't long before they began to talk about his lookin' so poorly, jest as they had about the others; and they talked about Sarah Jones, too.

"Well, the Doctor did die, and he wanted to be married first, so as to leave what little he had to Luella, but he died before the minister could get there, and Sarah Jones died a week afterward.

"Well, that wound up everything for Luella Miller. Not another soul in the whole town would lift a finger for her. There got to be a sort of panic. Then she began to droop in good earnest. She used to have to go to the store herself, for Mrs. Babbit was afraid to let Tommy go for her, and I've seen her goin' past and stoppin' every two or three steps to rest. Well, I stood it as long as I could, but one day I see her comin' with her arms full and stoppin' to lean against the Babbit fence, and I run out and took her bundles and carried them to her house. Then I went home and never spoke one word to her though she called after me dreadful kind of pitiful. Well, that night I was taken sick with a chill, and I was sick as I wanted to be for two weeks. Mrs. Babbit had seen me run out to help Luella and she came in and told me I was goin' to die on account of it. I didn't know whether I was or not, but I considered I had done right by Erastus's wife.

"That last two weeks Luella she had a dreadful hard time, I guess. She was pretty sick, and as near as I could make out nobody dared go near her. I don't know as she was really needin' anythin' very much, for there was enough to eat in her house and it was warm weather, and she made out to cook a little flour gruel every day, I know, but I guess she had a hard time, she that had been so petted and done for all her life.

"When I got so I could go out, I went over there one morning. Mrs. Babbit had just come in to say she hadn't seen any smoke and she didn't know but it was somebody's duty to go in, but she couldn't help thinkin' of her children, and I got right up, though I hadn't been out of the house for two weeks, and I went in there, and Luella she was layin' on the bed, and she was dyin'.

"She lasted all that day and into the night. But I sat there after the new doctor had gone away. Nobody else dared to go there. It was about midnight that I left her for a minute to run home and get some medicine I had been takin', for I begun to feel rather bad.

"It was a full moon that night, and just as I started out of my door to cross the street back to Luella's, I stopped short, for I saw something."

Lydia Anderson at this juncture always said with a certain defiance that she did not expect to be believed, and then proceeded in a hushed voice:

"I saw what I saw, and I know I saw it, and I will swear on my death bed that I saw it. I saw Luella Miller and Erastus Miller, and Lily, and Aunt Abby, and Maria, and the Doctor, and Sarah, all goin' out of her door, and all but Luella shone white in the moonlight, and they were all helpin' her along till she seemed to fairly fly in the midst of them. Then it all disappeared. I stood a minute with my heart poundin', then I went over there. I thought of goin' for Mrs. Babbit, but I thought she'd be afraid. So I went alone, though I knew what had happened. Luella was layin' real peaceful, dead on her bed."

This was the story that the old woman, Lydia Anderson, told, but the sequel was told by the people who survived her, and this is the tale which has become folklore in the village.

Lydia Anderson died when she was eighty-seven. She had continued wonderfully hale and hearty for one of her years until about two weeks before her death.

One bright moonlight evening she was sitting beside a window in her parlour when she made a sudden exclamation, and was out of the house and across the street before the neighbour who was taking care of her could stop her. She followed as fast as possible and found Lydia Anderson stretched on the ground before the door of Luella Miller's deserted house, and she was quite dead.

The next night there was a red gleam of fire athwart the moonlight and the old house of Luella Miller was burned to the ground. Nothing is now left of it except a few old cellar stones and a lilac bush, and in summer a helpless trail of morning glories among the weeds, which might be considered emblematic of Luella herself.

AN INHABITANT
OF CARCOSA

by Ambrose Bierce

CHRISTIAN, n. One who believes that the New Testament is a divinely inspired book admirably suited to the spiritual needs of his neighbor. One who follows the teachings of Christ in so far as they are not inconsistent with a life of sin.

AMBROSE BIERCE, *The Devil's Dictionary*

Ambrose Gwinnet Bierce (1842-1913? 1914? or ?) was a brilliant journalist and writer of short stories, fables, and satire. The reason we don't have definitive date for the death of Ambrose Gwinnet Bierce is because quite frankly nobody knows when or how he died. He left his comfortable (and now historic) home in Washington, D.C. in October of 1913 (he was seventy-one years old at the time) and by December had crossed into Mexico and joined Pancho Villa's army to get a good look at the Mexican Revolution. That's the last we hear of him.

The works of Ambrose Bierce are not usually associated with the horror genre. However, because he is such a singularly unique fixture in nineteenth-century American literature (not to mention his breathtaking penchant for being shockingly frank, even macabre) he offers us no better category in which to place him. It is almost certain that his fictional alternate realities and speculations on future events were enjoyed by the founding fathers of horror, especially Robert W. Chambers, whose terrible mythological *King in Yellow* kingdom of Carcosa—its landmarks and characters—are lifted directly from Bierce's story, "The Inhabitant of Carcosa." I encourage the reader who is not familiar with Bierce to do a little homework. I will go so far as to promise that if you enjoy Mark Twain, you will love Ambrose Bierce. His life story is an adventure no novelist could invent.

An Inhabitant of Carcosa

For there be divers sorts of death—some wherein the body remaineth; and in some it vanisheth quite away with the spirit. This commonly occurreth only in solitude (such is God's will) and, none seeing the end, we say the man is lost, or gone on a long journey—which indeed he hath; but sometimes it hath happened in sight of many, as abundant testimony showeth. In one kind of death the spirit also dieth, and this it hath been known to do while yet the body was in vigor for many years. Sometimes, as is veritably attested, it dieth with the body, but after a season is raised up again in that place where the body did decay.

Pondering these words of Hali (whom God rest) and questioning their full meaning, as one who, having an intimation, yet doubts if there be not something behind, other than that which he has discerned, I noted not whither I had strayed until a sudden chill wind striking my face revived in me a sense of my surroundings. I observed with astonishment that everything seemed unfamiliar. On every side of me stretched a bleak and desolate expanse of plain, covered with a tall overgrowth of sere grass, which rustled and whistled in the autumn wind with heaven knows what mysterious and disquieting suggestion. Protruded at long intervals above it, stood strangely shaped and somber-colored rocks, which seemed to have an understanding with one another and to exchange looks of uncomfortable significance, as if they had reared their heads to watch the issue of some foreseen event. A few blasted trees here and there appeared as leaders in this malevolent conspiracy of silent expectation.

The day, I thought, must be far advanced, though the sun was invisible; and although sensible that the air was raw and chill my consciousness of that fact was rather mental than physical—I had no feeling of discomfort. Over all the dismal landscape a canopy of low, lead-colored clouds hung like a visible curse. In all this there were a menace and a portent—a hint of evil, an intimation of doom. Bird, beast, or insect there was none. The wind sighed in the bare branches of the dead trees and the gray grass bent to whisper its dread secret to the earth; but no other sound nor motion broke the awful repose of that dismal place.

I observed in the herbage a number of weather-worn stones, evidently shaped with tools. They were broken, covered with moss and half sunken in the earth. Some lay prostrate, some leaned at various angles, none was vertical. They were obviously headstones of graves, though the graves themselves no longer existed as either mounds or depressions; the years had leveled all. Scattered here and there, more massive blocks showed where some pompous tomb or ambitious monument had once flung its feeble defiance at oblivion. So old seemed these relics, these vestiges of vanity and memorials of affection and piety, so battered and worn and stained—so neglected, deserted, forgotten the place, that I could not help thinking myself the discoverer of the burial-ground of a prehistoric race of men whose very name was long extinct.

Filled with these reflections, I was for some time heedless of the sequence of my own experiences, but soon I thought, "How came I hither?" A moment's reflection seemed to make this all clear and explain at the same time, though in a disquieting way, the singular character with which my fancy had invested all that I saw or heard. I was ill. I remembered now that I had been prostrated by a sudden fever, and that my family had told me that in my periods of delirium I had constantly cried out for liberty and air, and had been held in bed to prevent my escape out-of-doors. Now I had eluded the vigilance of my attendants and had wandered hither to—to where? I could not conjecture. Clearly I was at a considerable distance from the city where I dwelt—the ancient and famous city of Carcosa.

No signs of human life were anywhere visible nor audible; no rising smoke, no watch-dog's bark, no lowing of cattle, no shouts of children at play—nothing but that dismal burial-place, with its air of mystery and dread, due to my own disordered brain. Was I not becoming again delirious, there beyond human aid? Was it not indeed all an illusion of my madness? I called aloud the names of my wives and sons, reached out my hands in search of theirs, even as I walked among the crumbling stones and in the withered grass.

A noise behind me caused me to turn about. A wild animal—a lynx—was approaching. The thought came to me: If I break down here in the desert—if the fever return and I fail, this beast will be at my throat. I sprang toward it, shouting. It trotted tranquilly by within a hand's breadth of me and disappeared behind a rock.

A moment later a man's head appeared to rise out of the ground a short distance away. He was ascending the farther slope of a low hill whose crest was hardly to be distinguished from the general level. His whole figure soon came into view against the background of gray cloud. He was half naked, half clad in skins. His hair was unkempt, his beard long and ragged. In one hand he carried a bow and arrow; the other held a blazing torch with a long trail of black smoke. He walked slowly and with caution, as if he feared falling into some open grave concealed by the tall grass. This strange apparition surprised but did not alarm, and taking such a course as to intercept him I met him almost face to face, accosting him with the familiar salutation, "God keep you."

He gave no heed, nor did he arrest his pace.

"Good stranger," I continued, "I am ill and lost. Direct me, I beseech you, to Carcosa."

The man broke into a barbarous chant in an unknown tongue, passing on and away.

An owl on the branch of a decayed tree hooted dismally and was answered by another in the distance. Looking upward, I saw through a sudden rift in the clouds Aldebaran and the Hyades! In all this there was a hint of night—the lynx, the man with the torch, the owl. Yet I saw—I saw even the stars in absence of the darkness. I saw, but was apparently not seen nor heard. Under what awful spell did I exist?

I seated myself at the root of a great tree, seriously to consider what it were best to do. That I was mad I could no longer doubt, yet recognized a ground of doubt in the conviction. Of fever I had no trace. I had, withal, a sense of exhilaration and vigor altogether unknown to me—a feeling of mental and physical exaltation. My senses seemed all alert; I could feel the air as a ponderous substance; I could hear the silence.

A great root of the giant tree against whose trunk I leaned as I sat held enclosed in its grasp a slab of stone, a part of which protruded into a recess formed by another root. The stone was thus partly protected from the weather, though greatly decomposed. Its edges were worn round, its corners eaten away, its surface deeply furrowed and scaled. Glittering particles of mica were visible in the earth about it—vestiges of its decomposition. This stone had apparently marked the grave out of which the tree had sprung ages ago. The tree's exacting roots had robbed the grave and made the stone a prisoner.

A sudden wind pushed some dry leaves and twigs from the uppermost face of the stone; I saw the low-relief letters of an inscription and bent to read it. God in Heaven! my name in full!—the date of my birth!—the date of my death!

A level shaft of light illuminated the whole side of the tree as I sprang to my feet in terror. The sun was rising in the rosy east. I stood between the tree and his broad red disk—no shadow darkened the trunk!

A chorus of howling wolves saluted the dawn. I saw them sitting on their haunches, singly and in groups, on the summits of irregular mounds and tumuli filling a half of my desert prospect and extending to the horizon. And then I knew that these were ruins of the ancient and famous city of Carcosa.

Such are the facts imparted to the medium Bayrolles by the spirit Hoseib Alar Robardin.

NO. 252 RUE M. LE PRINCE

by Ralph Adams Cram

. . . the eminent architect and medievalist Ralph Adams Cram achieves a memorably potent degree of vague regional horror through subtleties of atmosphere and description.

H.P. LOVECRAFT

Ralph Adams Cram was an architectural genius of near divine stature. His passion and specialty was Gothic revival churches, cathedrals, monasteries, chapels, courthouses, government buildings, and college and university edifices; but he was equally the pioneering master of the Art Deco style that dominated the latter half of his life.

In 1887, while studying architecture in Rome, he experienced dramatic spiritual epiphany while attending a Christmas Eve Mass. He became a zealous convert to the Anglo-Catholicism and for the rest of his life identified himself as a "High Church Anglican." His passion for the faith coupled with his almost superhuman output of churches earned him his own liturgical Feast Day (December 16th) in the Calendar of Saints of the Episcopal Church in America.

Despite his patently orthodox credentials and leanings, he secretly harbored a love and fascination for the magical arts, and quietly wrote some of the finest occult fiction ever penned. "No. 252 Rue M. le Prince" was the first story in his classic 1895 collection of short stories *Black Spirits and White—a Book of Ghost Stories.*

Black spirits and white, red spirits and gray, mingle, mingle, mingle, ye that mingle may.

No. 252 Rue M. le Prince

When in May, 1886, I found myself at last in Paris, I naturally determined to throw myself on the charity of an old chum of mine, Eugene Marie d'Ardeche, who had forsaken Boston a year or more ago on receiving word of the death of an aunt who had left him such property as she possessed. I fancy this windfall surprised him not a little, for the relations between the aunt and nephew had never been cordial, judging from Eugene's remarks touching the lady, who was, it seems, a more or less wicked and witch-like old person, with a penchant for black magic, at least such was the common report.

Why she should leave all her property to d'Ardeche, no one could tell, unless it was that she felt his rather hobbledehoy tendencies towards Buddhism and occultism might some day lead him to her own unhallowed height of questionable illumination. To be sure d'Ardeche reviled her as a bad old woman, being himself in that state of enthusiastic exaltation which sometimes accompanies a boyish fancy for occultism; but in spite of his distant and repellent attitude, Mlle. Blaye de Tartas made him her sole heir, to the violent wrath of a questionable old party known to infamy as the Sar Torrevieja, the "King of the Sorcerers." This malevolent old portent, whose gray and crafty face was often seen in the Rue M. le Prince during the life of Mlle. de Tartas had, it seems, fully expected to enjoy her small wealth after her death; and when it appeared that she had left him only the contents of the gloomy old house in the Quartier Latin, giving the house itself and all else of which she died possessed to her nephew in America, the Sar proceeded to remove everything from the place, and then to curse it elaborately and comprehensively, together with all those who should ever dwell therein.

Whereupon he disappeared.

This final episode was the last word I received from Eugene, but I knew the number of the house, 252 Rue M. le Prince. So, after a day or two given to a first cursory survey of Paris, I started across the Seine to find Eugene and compel him to do the honors of the city.

Every one who knows the Latin Quarter knows the Rue M. le Prince, running up the hill towards the Garden of the Luxembourg. It is full of queer houses and odd corners,—or was in '86,—and certainly No. 252 was, when I found it, quite as queer as any. It was nothing but a doorway, a black arch of old stone between and under two new houses painted yellow. The effect of this bit of seventeenth-century masonry, with its dirty old doors, and rusty broken lantern sticking gaunt and grim out over the narrow sidewalk, was, in its frame of fresh plaster, sinister in the extreme.

I wondered if I had made a mistake in the number; it was quite evident that no one lived behind those cobwebs. I went into the doorway of one of the new hotels and interviewed the concierge.

No, M. d'Ardeche did not live there, though to be sure he owned the mansion; he himself resided in Meudon, in the country house of the late Mlle. de Tartas. Would Monsieur like the number and the street?

Monsieur would like them extremely, so I took the card that the concierge wrote for me, and forthwith started for the river, in order that I might take a steamboat for Meudon. By one of those coincidences which happen so often, being quite inexplicable, I had not gone twenty paces down the street before I ran directly into the arms of Eugene d'Ardeche. In three minutes we were sitting in the queer little garden of the Chien Bleu, drinking vermouth and absinthe, and talking it all over.

"You do not live in your aunt's house?" I said at last, interrogatively.

"No, but if this sort of thing keeps on I shall have to. I like Meudon much better, and the house is perfect, all furnished, and nothing in it newer than the last century. You must come out with me to-night and see it. I have got a jolly room fixed up for my Buddha. But there is something wrong with this house opposite. I can't keep a tenant in it,—not four days. I have had three, all within six months, but the stories have gone around and a man would as soon think of hiring the Cour des Comptes to live in as No. 252. It is notorious. The fact is, it is haunted the worst way."

I laughed and ordered more vermouth.

"That is all right. It is haunted all the same, or enough to keep it empty, and the funny part is that no one knows *how* it is haunted. Nothing is ever seen, nothing heard. As far as I can find out, people just have the horrors there, and have them so bad they have to go to the hospital afterwards. I have one ex-tenant in the Bicêtre now. So the house stands empty, and as it covers considerable ground and is taxed for a lot, I don't know what to do about it. I think I'll either give it to that child of sin, Torrevieja, or else go and live in it myself. I shouldn't mind the ghosts, I am sure."

"Did you ever stay there?"

"No, but I have always intended to, and in fact I came up here to-day to see a couple of rake-hell fellows I know, Fargeau and Duchesne, doctors in the Clinical Hospital beyond here, up by the Parc Mont Souris. They promised that they would spend the night with me some time in my aunt's house,—which is called around here, you must know, 'la Bouche d'Enfer,'—and I thought perhaps they would make it this week, if they can get off duty. Come up with me while I see them, and then we can go across the river to Véfour's and have some luncheon, you can get your things at the Chatham, and we will go out to Meudon, where of course you will spend the night with me."

The plan suited me perfectly, so we went up to the hospital, found Fargeau, who declared that he and Duchesne were ready for anything, the nearer the real "bouche d'enfer" the better; that the following Thursday they would both be off duty for the night, and that on that day they would join in an attempt to outwit the devil and clear up the mystery of No. 252.

"Does M. l'Américain go with us?" asked Fargeau.

"Why of course," I replied, "I intend to go, and you must not refuse me, d'Ardeche; I decline to be put off. Here is a chance for you to do the honors of your city in a manner which is faultless. Show me a real live ghost, and I will forgive Paris for having lost the Jardin Mabille."

So it was settled.

Later we went down to Meudon and ate dinner in the terrace room of the villa, which was all that d'Ardeche had said, and more, so utterly was its atmosphere that of the seventeenth century. At dinner Eugene told me more about his late aunt, and the queer goings on in the old house.

Mlle. Blaye lived, it seems, all alone, except for one female servant of her own age; a severe, taciturn creature, with massive Breton features and a Breton tongue, whenever she vouchsafed to use it. No one ever was seen to enter the door of No. 252 except Jeanne the servant and the Sar Torrevieja, the latter coming constantly from none knew whither, and always entering, *never leaving*. Indeed, the neighbors, who for eleven years had watched the old sorcerer sidle crab-wise up to the bell almost every day, declared vociferously that *never* had he been seen to leave the house. Once, when they decided to keep absolute guard, the watcher, none other than Maître Garceau of the Chien Bleu, after keeping his eyes fixed on the door from ten o'clock one morning when the Sar arrived until four in the afternoon, during which time the door was unopened (he knew this, for had he not gummed a ten-centime stamp over the joint and was not the stamp unbroken) nearly fell down when the sinister figure of Torrevieja slid wickedly by him with a dry "Pardon, Monsieur!" and disappeared again through the black doorway.

This was curious, for No. 252 was entirely surrounded by houses, its only windows opening on a courtyard into which no eye could look from the hôtels of the Rue M. le Prince and the Rue de l'Ecole, and the mystery was one of the choice possessions of the Latin Quarter.

Once a year the austerity of the place was broken, and the denizens of the whole quarter stood open-mouthed watching many carriages drive up to No. 252, many of them private, not a few with crests on the door panels, from all of them descending veiled female figures and men with coat collars turned up. Then followed curious sounds of music from within, and those whose houses joined the blank walls of No. 252 became for the moment popular, for by placing the ear against the wall strange music could distinctly be heard, and the sound of monotonous chanting voices now and then. By dawn the last guest would have departed, and for another year the hotel of Mlle. de Tartas was ominously silent.

Eugene declared that he believed it was a celebration of "Walpurgisnacht," and certainly appearances favored such a fancy.

"A queer thing about the whole affair is," he said, "the fact that every one in the street swears that about a month ago, while I was out in Concarneau for a visit, the music and voices were heard again, just as when my revered aunt was in the flesh. The house was perfectly empty, as I tell you, so it is quite possible that the good people were enjoying an hallucination."

I must acknowledge that these stories did not reassure me; in fact, as Thursday came near, I began to regret a little my determination to spend the night in the house. I was too vain to back down, however, and the perfect coolness of the two doctors, who ran down Tuesday to Meudon to make a few arrangements, caused me to swear that I would die of fright before I would flinch. I suppose I believed more or less in ghosts, I am sure now that I am older I believe in them, there are in fact few things I can *not* believe. Two or three inexplicable things had happened to me, and, although this was before my adventure with Rendel in Pæstum, I had a strong predisposition to believe some things that I could not explain, wherein I was out of sympathy with the age.

Well, to come to the memorable night of the twelfth of June, we had made our preparations, and after depositing a big bag inside the doors of No. 252, went across to the Chien Bleu, where Fargeau and Duchesne turned up promptly, and we sat down to the best dinner Père Garceau could create.

I remember I hardly felt that the conversation was in good taste. It began with various stories of Indian fakirs and Oriental jugglery, matters in which Eugene was curiously well read, swerved to the horrors of the great Sepoy mutiny, and thus to reminiscences of the dissecting-room. By this time we had drunk more or less, and Duchesne launched into a photographic and Zolaesque account of the only time (as he said) when he was possessed of the panic of fear; namely, one night many years ago, when he was locked by accident into the dissecting-room of the Loucine, together with several cadavers of a rather unpleasant nature. I ventured to protest mildly against the choice of subjects, the result being a perfect carnival of horrors, so that when we finally drank our last *crème de cacao* and started for "la Bouche d'Enfer," my nerves were in a somewhat rocky condition.

It was just ten o'clock when we came into the street. A hot dead wind drifted in great puffs through the city, and ragged masses of vapor swept the purple sky; an unsavory night altogether, one of those nights of hopeless lassitude when one feels, if one is at home, like doing nothing but drink mint juleps and smoke cigarettes.

Eugene opened the creaking door, and tried to light one of the lanterns; but the gusty wind blew out every match, and we finally had to close the outer doors before we could get a light. At last we had all the lanterns going, and I began to look around curiously. We were in a long, vaulted passage, partly carriageway, partly footpath, perfectly bare but for the street refuse which had drifted in with eddying winds. Beyond lay the courtyard, a curious place rendered more curious still by the fitful moonlight and the flashing of four dark lanterns. The place had evidently been once a most noble palace. Opposite rose the oldest portion, a three-story wall of the time of Francis I., with a great wisteria vine covering half. The wings on either side were more modern, seventeenth century, and ugly, while towards the street was nothing but a flat unbroken wall.

The great bare court, littered with bits of paper blown in by the wind, fragments of packing cases, and straw, mysterious with flashing lights and flaunting shadows, while low masses of torn vapor drifted overhead, hiding, then revealing the stars, and all in absolute silence, not even the sounds of the streets entering this prison-like place, was weird and uncanny in the extreme. I must confess that already I began to feel a slight disposition towards the horrors, but with that curious inconsequence which so often happens in the case of those who are deliberately growing scared, I could think of nothing more reassuring than those delicious verses of Lewis Carroll's:—

"Just the place for a Snark! I have said it twice, That alone should encourage the crew. Just the place for a Snark! I have said it thrice, What I tell you three times is true,"—which kept repeating themselves over and over in my brain with feverish insistence.

Even the medical students had stopped their chaffing, and were studying the surroundings gravely.

"There is one thing certain," said Fargeau, "*anything* might have happened here without the slightest chance of discovery. Did ever you see such a perfect place for lawlessness?"

"And *anything* might happen here now, with the same certainty of impunity," continued Duchesne, lighting his pipe, the snap of the match making us all start. "D'Ardeche, your lamented relative was certainly well fixed; she had full scope here for her traditional experiments in demonology."

"Curse me if I don't believe that those same traditions were more or less founded on fact," said Eugene. "I never saw this court under these conditions before, but I could believe anything now. What's that!"

"Nothing but a door slamming," said Duchesne, loudly.

"Well, I wish doors wouldn't slam in houses that have been empty eleven months."

"It is irritating," and Duchesne slipped his arm through mine; "but we must take things as they come. Remember we have to deal not only with the spectral lumber left here by your scarlet aunt, but as well with the supererogatory curse of that hell-cat Torrevieja. Come on! let's get inside before the hour arrives for the sheeted dead to squeak and gibber in these lonely halls. Light your pipes, your tobacco is a sure protection against 'your whoreson dead bodies'; light up and move on."

We opened the hall door and entered a vaulted stone vestibule, full of dust, and cobwebby.

"There is nothing on this floor," said Eugene, "except servants' rooms and offices, and I don't believe there is anything wrong with them. I never heard that there was, any way. Let's go up stairs."

So far as we could see, the house was apparently perfectly uninteresting inside, all eighteenth-century work, the façade of the main building being, with the vestibule, the only portion of the Francis I. work.

"The place was burned during the Terror," said Eugene, "for my great-uncle, from whom Mlle. de Tartas inherited it, was a good and true Royalist; he went to Spain after the Revolution, and did not come back until the accession of Charles X., when he restored the house, and then died, enormously old. This explains why it is all so new."

The old Spanish sorcerer to whom Mlle. de Tartas had left her personal property had done his work thoroughly. The house was absolutely empty, even the wardrobes and bookcases built in had been carried away; we went through room after room, finding all absolutely dismantled, only the windows and doors with their casings, the parquet floors, and the florid Renaissance mantels remaining.

"I feel better," remarked Fargeau. "The house may be haunted, but it don't look it, certainly; it is the most respectable place imaginable."

"Just you wait," replied Eugene. "These are only the state apartments, which my aunt seldom used, except, perhaps, on her annual 'Walpurgisnacht.' Come up stairs and I will show you a better *mise en scène*."

On this floor, the rooms fronting the court, the sleeping-rooms, were quite small,—("They are the bad rooms all the same," said Eugene,)—four of them, all just as ordinary in appearance as those below. A corridor ran behind them connecting with the wing corridor, and from this opened a door, unlike any of the other doors in that it was covered with green baize, somewhat moth-eaten. Eugene selected a key from the bunch he carried, unlocked the door, and with some difficulty forced it to swing inward; it was as heavy as the door of a safe.

"We are now," he said, "on the very threshold of hell itself; these rooms in here were my scarlet aunt's unholy of unholies. I never let them with the rest of the house, but keep them as a curiosity. I only wish Torrevieja had kept out; as it was, he looted them, as he did the rest of the house, and nothing is left but the walls and ceiling and floor. They are something, however, and may suggest what the former condition must have been. Tremble and enter."

The first apartment was a kind of anteroom, a cube of perhaps twenty feet each way, without windows, and with no doors except that by which we entered and another to the right. Walls, floor, and ceiling were covered with a black lacquer, brilliantly polished, that flashed the light of our lanterns in a thousand intricate reflections. It was like the inside of an enormous Japanese box, and about as empty. From this we passed to another room, and here we nearly dropped our lanterns. The room was circular, thirty feet or so in diameter, covered by a hemispherical dome; walls and ceiling were dark blue, spotted with gold stars; and reaching from floor to floor across the dome stretched a colossal figure in red lacquer of a nude woman kneeling, her legs reaching out along the floor on either side, her head touching the lintel of the door through which we had entered, her arms forming its sides, with the fore arms extended and stretching along the walls until they met the long feet. The most astounding, misshapen, absolutely terrifying thing, I think, I ever saw. From the navel hung a great white object, like the traditional roe's egg of the Arabian Nights. The floor was of red lacquer, and in it was inlaid a pentagram the size of the room, made of wide strips of brass. In the centre of this pentagram was a circular disk of black stone, slightly saucer-shaped, with a small outlet in the middle.

The effect of the room was simply crushing, with this gigantic red figure crouched over it all, the staring eyes fixed on one, no matter what his position. None of us spoke, so oppressive was the whole thing.

The third room was like the first in dimensions, but instead of being black it was entirely sheathed with plates of brass, walls, ceiling, and floor,—tarnished now, and turning green, but still brilliant under the lantern light. In the middle stood an oblong altar of porphyry, its longer dimensions on the axis of the suite of rooms, and at one end, opposite the range of doors, a pedestal of black basalt.

This was all. Three rooms, stranger than these, even in their emptiness, it would be hard to imagine. In Egypt, in India, they would not be entirely out of place, but here in Paris, in a commonplace *hotel*, in the Rue M. le Prince, they were incredible.

We retraced our steps, Eugene closed the iron door with its baize covering, and we went into one of the front chambers and sat down, looking at each other.

"Nice party, your aunt," said Fargeau. "Nice old party, with amiable tastes; I am glad we are not to spend the night in *those* rooms."

"What do you suppose she did there?" inquired Duchesne. "I know more or less about black art, but that series of rooms is too much for me."

"My impression is," said d'Ardeche, "that the brazen room was a kind of sanctuary containing some image or other on the basalt base, while the stone in front was really an altar,—what the nature of the sacrifice might be I don't even guess. The round room may have been used for invocations and incantations. The pentagram looks like it. Any way it is all just about as queer and *fin de siècle* as I can well imagine. Look here, it is nearly twelve, let's dispose of ourselves, if we are going to hunt this thing down."

The four chambers on this floor of the old house were those said to be haunted, the wings being quite innocent, and, so far as we knew, the floors below. It was arranged that we should each occupy a room, leaving the doors open with the lights burning, and at the slightest cry or knock we were all to rush at once to the room from which the warning sound might come. There was no communication between the rooms to be sure, but, as the doors all opened into the corridor, every sound was plainly audible.

The last room fell to me, and I looked it over carefully.

It seemed innocent enough, a commonplace, square, rather lofty Parisian sleeping-room, finished in wood painted white, with a small marble mantel, a dusty floor of inlaid maple and cherry, walls hung with an ordinary French paper, apparently quite new, and two deeply embrasured windows looking out on the court.

I opened the swinging sash with some trouble, and sat down in the window seat with my lantern beside me trained on the only door, which gave on the corridor.

The wind had gone down, and it was very still without,—still and hot. The masses of luminous vapor were gathering thickly overhead, no longer urged by the gusty wind. The great masses of rank wisteria leaves, with here and there a second blossoming of purple flowers, hung dead over the window in the sluggish air. Across the roofs I could hear the sound of a belated *fiacre* in the streets below. I filled my pipe again and waited.

For a time the voices of the men in the other rooms were a companionship, and at first I shouted to them now and then, but my voice echoed rather unpleasantly through the long corridors, and had a suggestive way of reverberating around the left wing beside me, and coming out at a broken window at its extremity like the voice of another man. I soon gave up my attempts at conversation, and devoted myself to the task of keeping awake.

It was not easy; why did I eat that lettuce salad at Père Garceau's? I should have known better. It was making me irresistibly sleepy, and wakefulness was absolutely necessary. It was certainly gratifying to know that I could sleep, that my courage was by me to that extent, but in the interests of science I must keep awake. But almost never, it seemed, had sleep looked so desirable. Half a hundred times, nearly, I would doze for an instant, only to awake with a start, and find my pipe gone out. Nor did the exertion of relighting it pull me together. I struck my match mechanically, and with the first puff dropped off again. It was most vexing. I got up and walked around the room. It was most annoying. My cramped position had almost put both my legs to sleep. I could hardly stand. I felt numb, as though with cold. There was no longer any sound from the other rooms, nor from without. I sank down in my window seat. How dark it was growing! I turned up the lantern. That pipe again, how obstinately it kept going out! and my last match was gone. The lantern, too, was *that* going out? I lifted my hand to turn it up again. It felt like lead, and fell beside me.

Then I awoke,—absolutely. I remembered the story of "The Haunters and the Haunted." *This* was the Horror. I tried to rise, to cry out. My body was like lead, my tongue was paralyzed. I could hardly move my eyes. And the light was going out. There was no question about that. Darker and darker yet; little by little the pattern of the paper was swallowed up in the advancing night. A prickling numbness gathered in every nerve, my right arm slipped without feeling from my lap to my side, and I could not raise it,—it swung helpless. A thin, keen humming began in my head, like the cicadas on a hillside in September. The darkness was coming fast.

Yes, this was it. Something was subjecting me, body and mind, to slow paralysis. Physically I was already dead. If I could only hold my mind, my consciousness, I might still be safe, but could I? Could I resist the mad horror of this silence, the deepening dark, the creeping numbness? I knew that, like the man in the ghost story, my only safety lay here.

It had come at last. My body was dead, I could no longer move my eyes. They were fixed in that last look on the place where the door had been, now only a deepening of the dark.

Utter night: the last flicker of the lantern was gone. I sat and waited; my mind was still keen, but how long would it last? There was a limit even to the endurance of the utter panic of fear.

Then the end began. In the velvet blackness came two white eyes, milky, opalescent, small, far away,—awful eyes, like a dead dream. More beautiful than I can describe, the flakes of white flame moving from the perimeter inward, disappearing in the centre, like a never ending flow of opal water into a circular tunnel. I could not have moved my eyes had I possessed the power: they devoured the fearful, beautiful things that grew slowly, slowly larger, fixed on me, advancing, growing more beautiful, the white flakes of light sweeping more swiftly into the blazing vortices, the awful fascination deepening in its insane intensity as the white, vibrating eyes grew nearer, larger.

Like a hideous and implacable engine of death the eyes of the unknown Horror swelled and expanded until they were close before me, enormous, terrible, and I felt a slow, cold, wet breath propelled with mechanical regularity against my face, enveloping me in its fetid mist, in its charnel-house deadliness.

With ordinary fear goes always a physical terror, but with me in the presence of this unspeakable Thing was only the utter and awful terror of the mind, the mad fear of a prolonged and ghostly nightmare. Again and again I tried to shriek, to make some noise, but physically I was utterly dead. I could only feel myself go mad with the terror of hideous death. The eyes were close on me,—their movement so swift that they seemed to be but palpitating flames, the dead breath was around me like the depths of the deepest sea.

Suddenly a wet, icy mouth, like that of a dead cuttle-fish, shapeless, jelly-like, fell over mine. The horror began slowly to draw my life from me, but, as enormous and shuddering folds of palpitating jelly swept sinuously around me, my will came back, my body awoke with the reaction of final fear, and I closed with the nameless death that enfolded me.

What was it that I was fighting? My arms sunk through the unresisting mass that was turning me to ice. Moment by moment new folds of cold jelly swept round me, crushing me with the force of Titans. I fought to wrest my mouth from this awful Thing that sealed it, but, if ever I succeeded and caught a single breath, the wet, sucking mass closed over my face again before I could cry out. I think I fought for hours, desperately, insanely, in a silence that was more hideous than any sound,—fought until I felt final death at hand, until the memory of all my life rushed over me like a flood, until I no longer had strength to wrench my face from that hellish succubus, until with a last mechanical struggle I fell and yielded to death.

Then I heard a voice say, "If he is dead, I can never forgive myself; I was to blame."

Another replied, "He is not dead, I know we can save him if only we reach the hospital in time. Drive like hell, *cocher*! twenty francs for you, if you get there in three minutes."

Then there was night again, and nothingness, until I suddenly awoke and stared around. I lay in a hospital ward, very white and sunny, some yellow *fleurs-de-lis* stood beside the head of the pallet, and a tall sister of mercy sat by my side.

To tell the story in a few words, I was in the Hotel Dieu, where the men had taken me that fearful night of the twelfth of June. I asked for Fargeau or Duchesne, and by and by the latter came, and sitting beside the bed told me all that I did not know.

It seems that they had sat, each in his room, hour after hour, hearing nothing, very much bored, and disappointed. Soon after two o'clock Fargeau, who was in the next room, called to me to ask if I was awake. I gave no reply, and, after shouting once or twice, he took his lantern and came to investigate. The door was locked on the inside! He instantly called d'Ardeche and Duchesne, and together they hurled themselves against the door. It resisted. Within they could hear irregular footsteps dashing here and there, with heavy breathing. Although frozen with terror, they fought to destroy the door and finally succeeded by using a great slab of marble that formed the shelf of the mantel in Fargeau's room. As the door crashed in, they were suddenly hurled back against the walls of the corridor, as though by an explosion, the lanterns were extinguished, and they found themselves in utter silence and darkness.

As soon as they recovered from the shock, they leaped into the room and fell over my body in the middle of the floor. They lighted one of the lanterns, and saw the strangest sight that can be imagined. The floor and walls to the height of about six feet were running with something that seemed like stagnant water, thick, glutinous, sickening. As for me, I was drenched with the same cursed liquid. The odor of musk was nauseating. They dragged me away, stripped off my clothing, wrapped me in their coats, and hurried to the hospital, thinking me perhaps dead. Soon after sunrise d'Ardeche left the hospital, being assured that I was in a fair way to recovery, with time, and with Fargeau went up to examine by daylight the traces of the adventure that was so nearly fatal. They were too late. Fire engines were coming down the street as they passed the Académie. A neighbor rushed up to d'Ardeche: "O Monsieur! what misfortune, yet what fortune! It is true *la Bouche d'Enfer*—I beg pardon, the residence of the lamented Mlle. de Tartas,—was burned, but not wholly, only the ancient building. The wings were saved, and for that great credit is due the brave firemen. Monsieur will remember them, no doubt."

It was quite true. Whether a forgotten lantern, overturned in the excitement, had done the work, or whether the origin of the fire was more supernatural, it was certain that "the Mouth of Hell" was no more. A last engine was pumping slowly as d'Ardeche came up; half a dozen limp, and one distended, hose stretched through the *porte cochère*, and within only the façade of Francis I. remained, draped still with the black stems of the wisteria. Beyond lay a great vacancy, where thin smoke was rising slowly. Every floor was gone, and the strange halls of Mlle. Blaye de Tartas were only a memory.

With d'Ardeche I visited the place last year, but in the stead of the ancient walls was then only a new and ordinary building, fresh and respectable; yet the wonderful stories of the old *Bouche d'Enfer* still lingered in the quarter, and will hold there, I do not doubt, until the Day of Judgment.

THE TESTAMENT OF MAGDALEN BLAIR

by Aleister Crowley

Ralph Adams Cram might be honored with a Feast Day in the liturgical calendar of the Anglican Church, but Aleister Crowley (1875-1947) is worshipped by thousands of devotees throughout the world as the Prophet of the magical religion/philosophy Thelema, and Logos of the Aeon of Horus.

It is impossible to acknowledge even a fraction of the highlights of the life of this larger-than-life personage. Even if we were to focus exclusively on his literary output—his poetry, his essays, his magazine articles, his reviews, his novels, his short stories, his plays—we would soon run out of space allotted us for the production of this book. Even if we were to rashly judge that he was a mad, wicked scoundrel and con-man, we would still be forced to conclude by the sheer weight of evidence that he was the most magnificently brilliant madman-wicked-scoundrel con-man to appear on earth since the Apostle Paul.

If "The Testament of Magdalen Blair" is to be your first taste of Crowley, I respectfully suggest that you keep in mind the most exquisitely delicious delicacies are often an acquired taste, but a taste well worth cultivating.

The Testament of Magdalen Blair

Part One

In my third term at Newnham I was already Professor Blair's favourite pupil. Later, he wasted a great deal of time praising my slight figure and my piquant face, with its big round grey eyes and their long black lashes; but the first attraction was my singular gift. Few men, and, I believe, no other women, could approach me on one of the most priceless qualifications for scientific study, the faculty of apprehending minute differences. My memory was poor, extraordinarily so; I had the utmost trouble to enter Cambridge at all. But I could adjust a micrometer better than either students or professor, and read a vernier with an accuracy to which none of them could even aspire. To this I added a faculty of subconscious calculation which was really uncanny. If I were engaged in keeping a solution between (say) 70° and 80° I had no need to watch the thermometer. Automatically I became aware that the mercury was close to the limit, and would go over from my other work and adjust the Bunsen without a thought.

More remarkable still, if any object were placed on my bench without my knowledge and then removed, I could, if asked within a few minutes, describe the object roughly, especially distinguishing the shape of its base and the degree of its opacity to heat and light. From these data I could make a pretty good guess at what the object was.

This faculty of mine was repeatedly tested, and always with success. Extreme sensitiveness to minute degrees of heat was its obvious cause.

I was also a singularly good thought-reader, even at this time. The other girls feared me absolutely. They need not have done so; I had neither ambition nor energy to make use of any of my powers. Even now, when I bring to mankind this message of a doom so appalling that at the age of twenty-four I am a shrivelled, blasted, withered wreck, I am supremely weary, supremely indifferent.

I have the heart of a child and the consciousness of Satan, the lethargy of I know not what disease; and yet, thank—oh! there can be no God!—the resolution to warn mankind to follow my example, and then to explode a dynamite cartridge in my mouth.

I

In my third year at Newnham I spent four hours of every day at Professor Blair's house. All other work was neglected, gone through mechanically, if at all. This came about gradually, as the result of an accident.

The chemical laboratory has two rooms, one small and capable of being darkened. On this occasion (the May term of my second year) this room was in use. It was the first week of June, and extremely fine. The door was shut. Within was a girl, alone, experimenting with the galvanometer.

I was absorbed in my own work. Quite without warning I looked up. "Quick," said I, "Gladys is going to faint." Every one in the room stared at me. I took a dozen steps towards the door, when the fall of a heavy body sent the laboratory into hysterics.

It was only the heat and confined atmosphere, and Gladys should not have come to work that day at all, but she was easily revived, and then the demonstrator acquiesced in the anarchy that followed. "How did she know?" was the universal query; for that I knew was evident. Ada Brown (Athanasia contra mundum) pooh-poohed the whole affair; Margaret Letchmere thought I must have heard something; perhaps a cry inaudible to the others, owing to their occupied attention; Doris Leslie spoke of second sight, and Amy Gore of "sympathy." All the theories, taken together, went round the clock of conjecture. Professor Blair came in at the most excited part of the discussion, calmed the room in two minutes, elicited the facts in five, and took me off to dine with him. "I believe it's this human thermopile affair of yours," he said. "Do you mind if we try a few parlour tricks after dinner?" His aunt, who kept house for him, protested in vain, and was appointed Grand Superintendent in Ordinary of my five senses.

My hearing was first tested, and found normal, or thereabouts. I was then blindfolded, and the aunt (by excess of precaution) stationed between me and the Professor. I found that I could describe even small movements that he made, so long as he was between me and the western window, not at all when he moved round to other quarters. This is in conformity with the "Thermopile" theory; it was contradicted completely on other occasions. The results (in short) were very remarkable and very puzzling; we wasted two precious hours in futile theorizing. In the event, the aunt (cowed by a formidable frown) invited me to spend the Long Vacation in Cornwall.

During these months the Professor and I assiduously worked to discover exactly the nature and limit of my powers. The result, in a sense, was nil.

For one thing, these powers kept on "breaking out in a new place." I seemed to do all I did by perception of minute differences; but then it seemed as if I had all sorts of different apparatus. "One down, t'other come on," said Professor Blair.

Those who have never made scientific experiments cannot conceive how numerous and subtle are the sources of error, even in the simplest matters. In so obscure and novel a field of research no result is trustworthy until it has been verified a thousand times. In our field we discovered no constants, all variables.

Although we had hundreds of facts any one of which seemed capable of overthrowing all accepted theories of the means of communication between mind and mind, we had nothing, absolutely nothing, which we could use as the basis of a new theory.

It is naturally impossible to give even an outline of the course of our research. Twenty-eight closely written note books referring to the first period are at the disposal of my executors.

II

In the middle of the day, in my third year, my father was dangerously ill. I bicycled over to Peterborough at once, never thinking of my work. (My father is a canon of Peter-borough Cathedral.) On the third day I received a telegram from Professor Blair, "Will you be my wife?" I had never realized myself as a woman, or him as a man, till that moment, and in that moment I knew that I loved him and had always loved him. It was a case of what one might call "Love at first absence." My father recovered rapidly; I returned to Cambridge; we were married during the May week, and went immediately to Switzerland. I beg to be spared any recital of so sacred a period of my life; but I must record one fact.

We were sitting in a garden by Lago Maggiore after a delightful tramp from Chamounix over the Col du Geant to Courmayeur, and thence to Aosta, and so by degrees to Pallanza. Arthur rose, apparently struck by some idea, and began to walk up and down the terrace. I was quite suddenly impelled to turn my head to assure myself of his presence.

This may seem nothing to you who read, unless you have true imagination. But think of yourself talking to a friend in full light, and suddenly leaning forward to touch him. "Arthur!" I cried, "Arthur!"

The distress in my tone brought him running to my side. "What is it, Magdalen?" he cried, anxiety in every word.

I closed my eyes. "Make gestures!" said I. (He was directly between me and the sun.)

He obeyed, wondering.

"You are—you are—" I stammered, "No! I don't know what you are doing. I am blind!"

He sawed his arm up and down. Useless; I had become absolutely insensitive. We repeated a dozen experiments that night. All failed.

We concealed our disappointment, and it did not cloud our love. The sympathy between us grew even subtler and stronger, but only as it grows between all men and women who love with their whole hearts, and love unselfishly.

III

We returned to Cambridge in October, and Arthur threw himself vigorously into the new year's work. Then I fell ill, and the hope we had indulged was disappointed. Worse, the course of the illness revealed a condition which demanded the most complete series of operations which a woman can endure. Not only the past hope, but all future hope, was annihilated.

It was during my convalescence that the most remarkable incident of my life took place.

I was in great pain one afternoon, and wished to see the doctor. The nurse went to the study to telephone for him.

"Nurse!" I said, as she returned, "don't lie to me. He's not gone to Royston; he's got cancer, and is too upset to come."

"Whatever next?" said the nurse. "It's right he can't come, and I was going to tell you he had gone to Royston; but I never heard nothing about no cancer."

This was true; she had not been told. But the next morning we heard that my "intuition" was correct.

As soon as I was well enough, we began our experiments again. My powers had returned, and in triple force.

Arthur explained my "intuition" as follows: "The doctor (when you last saw him) did not know consciously that he had cancer; but subconsciously Nature gave warning. You read this subconsciously, and it sprang into your consciousness when you read on the nurse's face that he was ill."

This, far-fetched as it may seem, at least avoids the shallow theories about "telepathy."

From this time my powers constantly increased. I could read my husband's thoughts from imperceptible movements of his face as easily as a trained deaf-mute can sometimes read the speech of a distant man from the movements of his lips. Gradually as we worked, day by day, I found my grasp of detail ever fuller. It is not only that I could read emotions; I could tell whether he was thinking 3465822 or 3456822. In the year following my illness, we made 436 experiments of this kind, each extending over several hours; in all 9363, with only 122 failures, and these all, without exception, partial.

The year following, our experiments were extended to a reading of his dreams. In this I proved equally successful. My practice was to leave the room before he woke, write down the dream that he had dreamt, and await him at the breakfast table, where he would compare his record with mine.

Invariably they were identical, with this exception, that my record was always much fuller than his. He would nearly always, however, purport to remember the details supplied by me; but this detail has (I think) no real scientific value.

But what does it all matter, when I think of the horror impending?

IV

That my only means of discovering Arthur's thought was by muscle-reading became more than doubtful during the third year of our marriage. We practised "telepathy" unashamed. We excluded the "muscle-reader" and the "super-auditor" and the "human thermopile" by elaborate precautions; yet still I was able to read every thought of his mind. On our holiday in North Wales at Easter one year we separated for a week, at the end of that week he to be on the leeward, I on the windward side of Tryfan, at the appointed hour, he there to open and read to himself a sealed packet given him by "some stranger met at Pen-y-Pass during the week." The experiment was entirely successful; I reproduced every word of the document. If the "telepathy" is to be vitiated, it is on the theory that I had previously met the "stranger" and read from him what he would write in such circumstances! Surely direct communication of mind with mind is an easier theory!

Had I known in what all this was to culminate, I suppose I should have gone mad. Thrice fortunate that I can warn humanity of what awaits each one. The greatest benefactor of his race will be he who discovers an explosive indefinitely swifter and more devastating than dynamite. If I could only trust myself to prepare Chloride of Nitrogen in sufficient quantity . . .

V

Arthur became listless and indifferent. The perfection of love that had been our marriage failed without warning, and yet by imperceptible gradations. My awakening to the fact was, however, altogether sudden. It was one summer evening; we were paddling on the Cam. One of Arthur's pupils, also in a Canadian canoe, challenged us to a race. At Magdalen Bridge we were a length ahead—suddenly I heard my husband's thought. It was the most hideous and horrible laugh that it is possible to conceive. No devil could laugh so. I screamed, and dropped my paddle. Both the men thought me ill. I assured myself that it was not the laugh of some townee on the bridge, distorted by my over-sensitive organization. I said no more; Arthur looked grave. At night he asked abruptly after a long period of brooding, "Was that my thought?" I could only stammer that I did not know.

Incidentally he complained of fatigue, and the listlessness, which before had seemed nothing to me, assumed a ghastly shape. There was something in him that was not he! The indifference had appeared transitory; I now became aware of it as constant and increasing. I was at this time twenty-three years old. You wonder that I write with such serious attitude of mind. I sometimes think that I have never had any thoughts of my own; that I have always been reading the thoughts of another, or perhaps of Nature. I seem only to have been a woman in those first few months of marriage.

VI

The six months following held for me nothing out of the ordinary, save that six or seven times I had dreams, vivid and terrible. Arthur had no share in these. Yet I knew, I cannot say how, that they were his dreams and not mine; or rather that they were in his subconscious waking self, for one occurred in the afternoon, when he was out shooting, and not in the least asleep.

The last of them occurred towards the end of the October term. He was lecturing as usual, I was at home, lethargic after a too heavy breakfast following a wakeful night. I saw suddenly a picture of the lecture-room, enormously greater than in reality, so that it filled all space; and in the rostrum, bulging over it in all directions, was a vast, deadly pale devil with a face which was a blasphemy on Arthur's. The evil joy of it was indescribable. So wan and bloated, its lips so loose and bloodless; fold after fold of its belly flopping over the rostrum and pushing the students out of the ball, it leered unspeakably. Then dribbled from its mouth these words; "Ladies and gentlemen, the course is finished. You may go home." I cannot hope even to suggest the wickedness and filth of these simple expressions. Then, raising its voice to a grating scream, it yelled:

"White of egg! White of egg! White of egg!" again and again for twenty minutes. The effect on me was shocking. It was as if I had a vision of Hell.

Arthur found me in a very hysterical condition, but soon soothed me. "Do you know," he said at dinner, "I believe I have got a devilish bad chill?"

It was the first time I had known him to complain of his health. In six years he had not had as much as a headache.

I told him my "dream" when we were in bed, and he seemed unusually grave, as if he understood where I had failed in its interpretation. In the morning he was feverish; I made him stay in bed and sent for the doctor. The same afternoon I learnt that Arthur was seriously ill, had been ill, indeed, for months. The doctor called it Bright's disease.

VII

I said "the last of the dreams." For the next year we travelled, and tried various treatments. My powers remained excellent, but I received none of the subconscious horrors. With few fluctuations, he grew steadily worse; daily he became more listless, more indifferent, more depressed. Our experiments were necessarily curtailed. Only one problem exercised him, the problem of his personality. He began to wonder who he was. I do not mean that he suffered from delusions, I mean that the problem of the true Ego took hold of his imagination. One perfect summer night at Contrexeville he was feeling much better; the symptoms had (temporarily) disappeared almost entirely under the treatment of a very skillful doctor at that Spa, a Dr. Barbezieux, a most kind and thoughtful man.

"I am going to try," said Arthur, "to penetrate myself. Am I an animal, and is the world without a purpose? Or am I a soul in a body?

Or am I, one and indivisible in some incredible sense, a spark of the infinite light of God? I am going to think inwards; I shall possibly go into some form of trance, unintelligible to myself. You may be able to interpret it." The experiment had lasted about half-an-hour when he sat up gasping with effort.

"I have seen nothing, heard nothing," I said. "Not one thought has passed from you to me." But at that very moment what had been in his mind flashed into mine.

"It is a blind abyss," I told him, "and there hangs in it a vulture vaster than the whole starry system."

"Yes," he said, "that was it. But that was not all. I could not get beyond it. I shall try again."

He tried. Again I was cut off from his thought, although his face was twitching so that one might have said that any one might read his mind.

"I have been looking in the wrong place," said he suddenly, but very quietly and without moving. "The thing I want lies at the base of the spine."

This time I saw. In a blue heaven was coiled an infinite snake of gold and green, with four eyes of fire, black fire and red, that darted rays in every direction; held within its coils was a great multitude of laughing children. And even as I looked, all this was blotted out. Crawling rivers of blood spread over the heaven, of blood purulent with nameless forms—mangy dogs with their bowels dragging behind them; creatures half elephant, half beetle; things that were but a ghastly bloodshot eye, set about with leathery tentacles; women whose skins heaved and bubbled like boiling sulphur, giving off clouds that condensed into a thousand other shapes, more hideous than their mother; these were the least of the denizens of these hateful rivers. The most were things impossible to name or to describe.

I was brought back from the vision by the stertorous and strangling breath of Arthur, who had been seized with a convulsion.

From this he never really rallied. The dim sight grew dimmer, the speech slower and thicker, the headaches more persistent and acute.

Torpor succeeded to his old splendid energy and activity; his days became continual lethargy ever deepening towards coma. Convulsions now and then alarmed me for his immediate danger.

Sometimes his breath came hard and hissing like a snake in anger; towards the end it assumed the Cheyne-Strokes type in bursts of ever increasing duration and severity.

In all this, however, he was still himself; the horror that was and yet was not himself did not peer from behind the veil.

"So long as I am consciously myself," he said in one of his rare fits of brightness, "I can communicate to you what I am consciously thinking; as soon as this conscious ego is absorbed, you get the subconscious thought which I fear—oh how I fear!—is the greater and truer part of me. You have brought unguessed explanations from the world of sleep; you are the one woman in the world—perhaps there may never be another—who has such an opportunity to study the phenomena of death."

He charged me earnestly to suppress my grief, to concentrate wholly on the thoughts that passed through his mind when he could no longer express them, and also on those of his subconsciousness when coma inhibited consciousness.

It is this experiment that I now force myself to narrate. The prologue has been long; it has been necessary to put the facts before mankind in a simple way so that they may seize the opportunity of the proper kind of suicide. I beg my readers most earnestly not to doubt my statements; the notes, of our experiments, left in my will to the greatest thinker now living, Professor von Buehle, will make clear the truth of my relation, and the great and terrible necessity of immediate, drastic action.

Part Two

The stunning physical fact of my husband's illness was the immense prostration. So strong a body, as too often the convulsions gave proof; such inertia with it! He would lie all day like a log; then without warning or apparent cause the convulsions would begin. Arthur's steady scientific brain stood it well; it was only two days before his death that delirium began. I was not with him, worn out as I was, and yet utterly unable to sleep, the doctor had insisted on my taking a long motor drive. In the fresh air I slumbered. I awoke to hear an unfamiliar voice saying in my ear. "Now for the fun of the fair!" There was no one there. Quick on its heels followed my husband's voice as I had long since known and loved it, clear, strong, resonant, measured: "Get this down right; it is very important. I am passing into the power of the subconsciousness. I may not be able to speak to you again. But I am here; I am not to be touched by all that I may suffer; I can always think; you can always read my—" The voice broke off sharply to inquire, "But will it ever end?" as if some one had spoken to it. And then I heard the laugh. The laugh that I had heard by Magdalen Bridge was heavenly music beside that! The face of Calvin (even) as he gloated over the burning of Servetus would have turned pitiful had he heard it, so perfectly did it express the quintessence of damnation.

Now then my husband's thought seemed to have changed places with the other. It was below, within, withdrawn. I said to myself, "He is dead!"

Then came Arthur's thought, "I had better pretend to be mad. It will save her, perhaps; and it will be a change. I shall pretend I have killed her with an axe. Damn it! I hope she is not listening." I was now thoroughly awake, and told the driver to get home quickly. "I hope she is killed in the motor; I hope she is smashed into a million pieces. O God! Hear my one prayer! Let an Anarchist throw a bomb and smash Magdalen into a million pieces! Especially the brain! And the brain first. O God! my first and last prayer; smash Magdalen into a million pieces!"

The horror of this thought was my conviction—then and now—that it represented perfect sanity and coherence of thought. For I dreaded utterly to think what such words might imply.

At the door of the sick-room I was met by the male nurse, who asked me not to enter. Uncontrollably, I asked, "Is he dead?" and though Arthur lay absolutely senseless on the bed I read the answering thought "Dead!" silently pronounced in such tones of mockery, horror, cynicism and despair as I never thought to hear. There was a something or somebody who suffered infinitely, and yet who gloated infinitely upon that very suffering. And that something was a veil between me and Arthur.

The hissing breath recommenced; Arthur seemed to be trying to express himself—the self I knew. He managed to articulate feebly, "Is that the police? Let me get out of the house! The police are coming for me. I killed Magdalen with an axe." The symptoms of delirium began to appear. "I killed Magdalen" he muttered a dozen times, then changing to "Magdalen with" again and again; the voice low, slow, thick, yet reiterated. Then suddenly, quite clear and loud, attempting to rise in the bed: "I smashed Magdalen into a million pieces with an axe." After a moment's pause: "a million is not very many now-a-days." From this—which I now see to have been the speech of a sane Arthur—he dropped again into delirium. "A million pieces," "a cool million," "a million million million million million million" and so on; then abruptly: "Fanny's dog's dead."

I cannot explain the last sentence to my readers; I may, however, remark that it meant everything to me. I burst into tears. At that moment I caught Arthur's thought, "You ought to be busy with the note-book, not crying." I resolutely dried my eyes, took courage, and began to write.

I

The doctor came in at this moment and begged me to go and rest. "You are only distressing yourself, Mrs. Blair," he said, "and needlessly, for he is absolutely unconscious and suffers nothing." A pause. "My God! why do you look at me like that?" he exclaimed, frightened out of his wits. I think my face had caught something of that devil's, something of that sneer, that loathing, that mire of contempt and stark despair.

I sank back into myself, ashamed already that mere knowledge—and such mean vile knowledge—should so puff one up with hideous pride. No wonder Satan fell! I began to understand all the old legends, and far more—I told Doctor Kershaw that I was carrying out Arthur's last wishes. He raised no further opposition; but I saw him sign to the male nurse to keep an eye on me.

The sick man's finger beckoned us. He could not speak; he traced circles on the counterpane. The doctor (with characteristic intelligence) having counted the circles, nodded, and said: "Yes it is nearly seven o'clock. Time for your medicine, eh?"

"No," I explained, "he means that he is in the seventh circle of Dante's Hell."

At that instant he entered on a period of noisy delirium. Wild and prolonged howls burst from his throat; he was being chewed unceasingly by "Dis"; each howl signaled the meeting of the monster's teeth. I explained this to the doctor. "No," said he, "he is perfectly unconscious.

"Well," said I, "he will howl about eighty times more."

Doctor Kershaw looked at me curiously, but began to count. My calculation was correct. He turned to me, "Are you a woman?"

"No," said I. "I am my husband's colleague."

"I think it is suggestion. You have hypnotized him?" "Never; but I can read his thoughts."

"Yes, I remember now; I read a very remarkable paper on Mind, two years ago." "That was child's play. But let me go on with my work."

He gave some final instructions to the nurse, and went out.

The suffering of Arthur was at this time unspeakable. Chewed as he was into a mere pulp that passed over the tongue of "Dis," each bleeding fragment kept its own identity and his.

The papillae of the tongue were serpents, and each one gnashed its poisoned teeth upon that fodder.

And yet, though the sensorium of Arthur was absolutely unimpaired, indeed hyperaesthetic, his consciousness of pain seemed to depend upon the opening of the mouth. As it closed in mastication, oblivion fell upon him like a thunderbolt. A merciful oblivion? Oh! what a master stroke of cruelty! Again and again he woke from nothing to a hell of agony, of pure ecstasy of agony, until he understood that this would continue for all his life, the alternation was but systole and diastole; the throb of his envenomed pulse, the reflection in consciousness of his blood-beat. I became conscious of his intense longing for death to end the torture.

The blood circulated ever slower and more painfully; I could feel him hoping for the end.

This dreadful rose-dawn suddenly greyed and sickened with doubt. Hope sank to its nadir; fear rose like a dragon, with leaden wings. Suppose, thought he, that after all death does not end me!

I cannot express this conception. It is not that the heart sank, it had no whither to sink; it knew itself immortal, and immortal in a realm of unimagined pain and terror, unlighted by one glimpse of any other light than that pale glare of hate and of pestilence. This thought took shape in these words:

I AM THAT I AM.

One cannot say that the blasphemy added to the horror; rather it was the essence of the horror. It was the gnashing of the teeth of a damned soul.

II

The demon-shape, which I now clearly recognise as that which had figured in my last "dream" at Cambridge, seemed to gulp. At that instant a convulsion shook the dying man and a coughing eructation took the "demon." Instantly the whole theory dawned on me, that this "demon" was an imaginary personification of the disease. Now at once I understood demonology, from Bodin and Weirus to the modems, without a flaw. But was it imaginary or was it real? Real enough to swallow up the "sane" thought!

At that instant the old Arthur reappeared. "I am not the monster! I am Arthur Blair, of Fettes and Trinity. I have passed through a paroxysm."

The sick man stirred feebly. A portion of his brain had shaken off the poison for the moment, and was working furiously against time.

"I am going to die.

"The consolation of death is Religion. "There is no use for Religion in life.

"How many atheists have I not known sign the articles for the sake of fellowships and livings! Religion in life is either an amusement and a soporific, or a sham and a swindle.

"I was brought up a Presbyterian.

"How easily I drifted into the English Church! And now where is God?

"Where is the Lamb of God?

"Where is the Saviour?

"Where is the Comforter?

"Why was I not saved from that devil?"

"Is he going to eat me again? To absorb me into him? O fate inconceivably hideous! It is quite clear to me—I hope you've got it down, Magdalen!—that the demon is made of all those that have died of Bright's disease. There must be different ones for each disease. I thought I once caught sight of a coughing bog of bloody slime.

"Let me pray."

A frenzied appeal to the Creator followed. Sincere as it was, it would read like irreverence in print.

And then there came the cold-drawn horror of stark blasphemy against this God—who would not answer. Followed the bleak black agony of the conviction—the absolute certitude—"There is no God!" combined with a wave of frenzied wrath against the people who had so glibly assured him that there was, an almost maniac hope that they would suffer more than he, if it were possible.

(Poor Arthur! He had not yet brushed the bloom off Suffering's grape; he was to drink its fiercest distillation to the dregs.)

"No!"thought he, "perhaps I lack their 'faith.'

"Perhaps if I could really persuade myself of God and Christ—perhaps if I could deceive myself, could make believe-—"

Such a thought is to surrender one's honesty, to abdicate one's reason. It marked the final futile struggle of his will.

The demon caught and crunched him, and the noisy delirium began anew.

My flesh and blood rebelled. Taken with a deathly vomit, I rushed from the room, and resolutely, for a whole hour, diverted my sensorium from thought . I had always found that the slightest trace of tobacco smoke in a room greatly disturbed my power. On this occasion I puffed cigarette after cigarette with excellent effect. I knew nothing of what had been going on.

III

Arthur, stung by the venomous chyle, was tossing in that vast arched belly, which resembled the dome of hell, churned in its bubbling slime. I felt that he was not only disintegrated mechanically, but chemically, that his being was loosened more and more into parts, that these were being absorbed into new and hateful things, but that (worst of all) Arthur stood immune from all, behind it, unimpaired, memory and reason ever more acute as ever new and ghastlier experience informed them. It seemed to me as if some mystic state were super-added to the torment; for while he was not, emphatically not, this tortured mass of consciousness, yet that was he. There are always at least two of us! The one who feels and the one who knows are not radically one person. This double personality is enormously accentuated at death..

Another point was that the time-sense, which with men is usually so reliable—especially in my own case—was decidedly deranged, if not abrogated altogether.

We all judge of the lapse of time in relation to our daily habits or some similar standard. The conviction of immortality must naturally destroy all values for this sense. If I am immortal, what is the difference between a long time and a short time? A thousand years and a day are obviously the same thing from the point of view of "for ever."

There is a sub-conscious clock in us, a clock wound up by the experience of the race to go for seventy years or so. Five minutes is a very long time to us if we are waiting for an omnibus, an age if we are waiting for a lover, nothing at all if we are pleasantly engaged or sleeping.[21]

We think of seven years as a long time in connection with penal servitude; as a negligibly small period in dealing with geology.

But, given immortality, the age of the stellar system itself is nothing.

This conviction had not fully impregnated the consciousness of Arthur; it hung over him like a threat, while the intensification of that consciousness, its liberation from the sense of time natural to life, caused each act of the demon to appear of vast duration, although the intervals between the howls of the body on the bed were very short. Each pang of torture or suspense was born, rose to its crest, and died to be reborn again through what seemed countless aeons.

Still more was this the case in the process of his assimilation by the "demon." The coma of the dying man was a phenomenon altogether out of time. The conditions of "digestion" were new to Arthur, he had no reason to suppose, no data from which to calculate the distance of, an end. It is impossible to do more than sketch this process; as he was absorbed, so did his consciousness expand into that of the "demon"; he became one with all its hunger and corruption. Yet always did lie suffer as himself in his own person the tearing asunder of his finest molecules; and this was confirmed by a most filthy humiliation of that part of him that was rejected.

---

21 It is one of the greatest cruelties of nature that all painful or depressing emotions seem to lengthen time; pleasant thoughts and exalted moods make time fly. Thus, in summing up a life from an outside standpoint, it would seem that, supposing pleasure and pain to have occupied equal periods, the impression would be that pain was enormously greater than pleasure. This may be controverted. Virgil writes: "Forsitan haec olim meminisse juvabit," and there is at least one modern writer thoroughly conversant with pessimism who is very optimistic. But the new facts which I here submit overthrow the whole argument; they cast a sword of infinite weight on that petty trembling scale.

I shall not attempt to describe the final process; suffice it that the demoniac consciousness drew away; he was but the excrement of the demon, and as that excrement he was flung filthily further into the abyss of blackness and of night whose name is death.

I rose with ashen cheeks. I stammered; "He is dead." The male nurse bent over the body. "Yes!" he echoed, "he is dead." And it seemed as if the whole Universe gathered itself into one ghastly laugh of hate and horror. "Dead!"

IV

I resumed my seat. I felt that I must know that all was well, that death had ended all. Woe to humanity! The consciousness of Arthur was more alive than ever. It was the black fear of falling, a dumb ecstasy of changeless fear. There were no waves upon that sea of shame, no troubling of those accursed Waters by any thought. There was no hope of any ground to that abyss, no thought that it might stop. So tireless was that fall that even acceleration was absent; it was constant and level as the fall of a star. There was not even a feeling of pace; infinitely fast as it must be, judging from the peculiar dread which it inspired, it was yet infinitely slow, having regard to the infinitude of the abyss.

I took measures not to be disturbed by the duties that men—how foolishly!—pay to the dead; and I took refuge in a cigarette.

It was now for the first time, strangely enough, that I began to consider the possibility of helping him.

I analysed the position. It must be his thought, or I could not read it. I had no reason to conjecture that any other thoughts could reach me. He must be alive in the true sense of the word; it was he and not another that was the prey of this fear ineffable. Of this fear it was evident that there must be a physical basis in the constitution of his brain and body. All the other phenomena had been shown to correspond exactly with a physical condition; it was the reflection in a consciousness from which human limitation had fallen away, of things actually taking place in the body.

It was a false interpretation perhaps; but it was his interpretation; and it was that which caused suffering so beyond all that poets have ever dreamt of the infernal.

I am ashamed to say that my first thought was of the Catholic Church and its masses for the repose of the dead. I went to the Cathedral, revolving as I went all that had ever been said—the superstitions of a hundred savage tribes. At bottom I could find no difference between their barbarous rites and those of Christianity. However that might be, I was baffled. The priests refused to pray for the soul of a heretic.

I hurried back to the house, resumed my vigil. There was no change, except a deepening of the fear, an intensification of the loneliness, a more utter absorption in the shame. I could but hope that in the ultimate stagnation of all vital forces, death would become final, hell merged into annihilation.

This started a train of thought which ended in a determination to hasten the process. I thought of blowing out the brains, remembered that I had no means of doing so. I thought of freezing the body, imagined a story for the nurse, reflected that no cold could excite in his soul aught icier than that illimitable void of black.

I thought of telling the doctor that he had wished to bequeath his body to the surgeons, that he had been afraid of being buried alive, anything that might induce him to remove the brain. At that moment I looked into the mirror. I saw that I must not speak. My hair was white, my face drawn, my eyes wild and bloodshot.

In utter helplessness and misery I flung myself on the couch in the study, and puffed greedily at cigarettes. The relief was so immense that my sense of loyalty and duty had a hard fight to get me to resume the task. The mingling of horror, curiosity, and excitement must have aided.

I threw away my fifth cigarette, and returned to the death chamber.

V

Before I had sat at the table ten minutes a change burst out with startling suddenness. At one point in the void the blackness gathered, concentrated, sprang into an evil flame that gushed aimlessly forth from nowhere into nowhere.

This was accompanied by the most noxious stench.

It was gone before I could realize it. As lightning precedes thunder, it was followed by a hideous clamour that I can only describe as the cry of a machine in pain.

This recurred constantly for an hour and five minutes, then ceased as suddenly as it began. Arthur still fell.

It was succeeded after the lapse of five hours by another paroxysm of the same kind, but fiercer and more continuous. Another silence followed, age upon age of fear and loneliness and shame.

About midnight there appeared a grey ocean of bowels below the falling soul. This ocean seemed to be limitless. It fell headlong into it, and the splash awakened it to a new consciousness of things.

This sea, though infinitely cold, was boiling like tubercles. Itself a more or less homogeneous slime, the stench of which is beyond all human conception (human language is singularly deficient in words that describe smell and taste; we always refer our sensations to things generally known) it constantly budded into greenish boils with angry red craters, whose jagged edges were of a livid white; and from these issued pus formed of all things known of man—each one distorted, degraded, blasphemed.[22]

Things innocent, things happy, things holy! Every one unspeakably deified, loathsome, sickening! During the vigil of the day following I recognized one group. I saw Italy. First the Italy of the Map, a booted leg. But this leg changed rapidly through myriad phases.

---

22 This is my general complaint, and that of all research students on the one hand and imaginative writers on the other. We can only express a new idea by combining two or more old ideas, or by the use of metaphor; just so any number can be formed from two others. James Hinton had undoubtedly a perfectly crisp, simple, and concise idea of the "fourth dimension of space"; he found the utmost difficulty in conveying it to others, even when they were advanced mathematicians. It is (I believe) the greatest factor that militates against human progress that great men assume that they will be understood by others.

It was in turn the leg of every beast and bird, and in every case each leg was suffering with all diseases from leprosy and elephantiasis to scrofula and syphilis. There was also the consciousness that this was inalienably and for ever part of Arthur.

Then Italy itself, in every detail foul. Then I myself, seen as every woman that has ever been, each one with every disease and torture that Nature and man have plotted in their hellish brains, each ended with a death, a death like Arthur's, whose infinite pangs were added to his own, recognized and accepted as his own.

The same with our child that never was. All children of all nations, incredibly aborted, deformed, tortured, torn in pieces, abused by every foulness that the imagination of an arch-devil could devise.

And so for every thought. I realized that the putrefactive changes in the dead man's brain were setting in motion every memory of his, and smearing them with hell's own paint.

I timed one thought, despite its myriad million details, each one clear, vivid and prolonged, it occupied but three seconds of earthly time. I considered the incalculable array of the thoughts in his well-furnished mind; I saw that thousands of years would not exhaust them.

But, perhaps, when the brain was destroyed beyond recognition of its component parts. We have always casually assumed that consciousness depends upon a proper flow of blood in the vessels of the brain; we have never stopped to think whether the records might not be excited in some other manner. And yet we know how tumour of the brain begets hallucinations. Consciousness works strangely; the least disturbance of the blood supply, and it goes out like a candle, or else takes monstrous forms.

Here was the overwhelming truth; in death man lives again, and lives for ever. Yet we might have thought of it; the phantasmagoria of life which throng the mind of a drowning man might have suggested something of the sort to any man with a sympathetic and active imagination.

Worse even than the thoughts themselves was the apprehension of the thoughts ere they arose. Carbuncles, boils, ulcers, cancers, there is no equivalent for these pustules of the bowels of hell, into whose seething convulsions Arthur sank, deeper, ever deeper.

The magnitude of this experience is not to be apprehended by the human mind as we know it. I was convinced that an end must come, for me, with the cremation of the body. I was infinitely glad that he had directed this to be done. But for him, end and beginning seemed to have no meaning. Through it all I seemed to hear the real Arthur's thought. "Though all this is I, yet it is only an accident of me; I stand behind it all, immune, eternal."

It must not be supposed that this in any way detracted from the intensity of the suffering. Rather it added to it. To be loathsome is less than to be linked to loathsomeness. To plunge into impurity is to become deadened to disgust. But to do so and yet remain pure—every vileness adds a pang. Think of Madonna imprisoned in a body of a prostitute, and compelled to acknowledge "This is I," while never losing her abhorrence. Not only immured in hell, but compelled to partake of its sacraments; not only high priest at its agape, but begetter and manifestor of its cult; a Christ nauseated at the kiss of Judas, and yet aware that the treachery was his own.

VI

As the putrefaction of the brain advanced, the bursting of the pustules occasionally overlapped, with the result that the confusion and exaggeration of madness with all its poignancy was super added to the simpler hell. One might have thought that any confusion would have been a welcome relief to a lucidity so appalling; but this was not so. The torture was infused with a shattering sense of alarm.

The images rose up threatening, disappeared only by blasting themselves into pultaceous coprolite which was, as it were, the main body of the army which composed Arthur. Deeper and deeper as he dropped the phenomena grew constantly in every sense. Now they were a jungle in which the obscurity and terror of the whole gradually overshadowed even the abhorrence due to every part.

The madness of the living is a thing so abominable and fearful as to chill every human heart with horror; it is less than nothing in comparison with the madness of the dead!

A further complication now arose, in the destruction irrevocable and complete of that compensating mechanism of the brain, which is the basis of the sense of time. Hideously distorted and deformed as it had been in the derangement of the brain like a shapeless jelly shooting out, of a sudden, vast, unsuspected tentacles, the destruction of it cut a thousandfold deeper. The sense of consecution itself was destroyed; things sequent appeared as things superposed or concurrent spatially; a new dimension unfolded; a new destruction of all limitation exposed a new and unfathomable abyss.

To all the rest was added the bewilderment and fear which earthly agoraphobia faintly shadows forth; and at the same time the close immurement weighted upon him, since from infinitude there can be no escape.

Add to this the hopelessness of the monotony of the situation. Infinitely as the phenomena were varied, they were yet recognised as essentially the same. All human tasks are lightened by the certainty that they must end. Even our joys would be intolerable were we convinced that they must endure, through irksomeness and disgust, through weariness and satiety, even for ever and for evermore. In this inhuman, this praeterdiabolic inferno was a wearisome repetition, a harping on the same hateful discord, a continuous nagging whose intervals afforded no relief, only a suspense brimming with the anticipation of some fresh terror.

For hours which were to him eternities this stage continued as each cell that held the record of a memory underwent the degenerative changes which awoke it into hyperbromic purulence.

VII

The minute bacterial corruption now assumed a gross chemistry. The gases of putrefaction forming in the brain and interpenetrating it were represented in his consciousness by the denizens of the pustules becoming formless and impersonal—Arthur had not yet fathomed the abyss.

Creeping, winding, embracing, the Universe enfolded him, violated him with a nameless and intimate contamination, involved his being in a more suffocating terror.

Now and again it drowned that consciousness in a gulf which his thought could not express to me; and indeed the first and least of his torments is utterly beyond human expression.

It was a woe ever expanded, ever intensified, by each vial of wrath. Memory increased, and understanding grew; the imagination had equally got rid of limit.

What this means who can tell? The human mind cannot really appreciate numbers beyond a score or so; it can deal with numbers by ratiocination, it cannot apprehend them by direct impression. It requires a highly trained intelligence to distinguish between fifteen and sixteen matches on a plate without counting them. In death this limitation is entirely removed. Of the infinite content of the Universe every item was separately realized. The brain of Arthur had become equal in power to that attributed by theologians to the Creator; yet of executive power there was no seed. The impotence of man before circumstance was in him magnified indefinitely, yet without loss of detail or of mass. He understood that The Many was The One without losing or fusing the conception of either. He was God, but a God irretrievably damned; a being infinite, yet limited by the nature of things, and that nature solely compact of loathliness.

VIII

I have little doubt that the cremation of my husband's body cut short a process which in the normally buried man continues until no trace of organic substance remains.

The first kiss of the furnace awoke an activity so violent and so vivid that all the past paled in its lurid light.

The quenchless agony of the pang is not to be described; if alleviation there were, it was but the exultation of feeling that this was final.

Not only time, but all expansions of time, all monsters of time's womb were to be annihilated; even the ego might hope some end.

The ego is the "worm that dieth not," and existence the "fire that is not quenched." Yet in this universal pyre, in this barathrum of liquid lava, jetted from the volcanoes of the infinite, this "lake of fire that is reserved for the devil and his angels," might not one at last touch bottom? Ah! but time was no more, neither any eidolon thereof.

The shell was consumed; the gases of the body, combined and recombined, flamed off, free from organic form.

Where was Arthur?

His brain, his individuality, his life, were utterly destroyed. As separate things, yes: Arthur had entered the universal consciousness.

And I heard this utterance; or rather this is my translation into English of a single thought whose synthesis is "Woe."

Substance is called spirit or matter.

Spirit and matter are one, indivisible, eternal, indestructible. Infinite and eternal change!

Infinite and eternal pain!

No absolute; no truth, no beauty, no idea, nothing but the whirl-winds of form, unresting, unappeasable.

Eternal hunger! Eternal wart Change and pain infinite and increasing.

There is no individuality but in illusion. And the illusion is change and pain, and its destruction is change and pain, and its new segregation from the infinite and eternal is change and pain; and substance infinite and eternal is change and pain unspeakable.

Beyond thought, which is change and pain, lies being, which is change and pain.

These were the last words intelligible; they lapsed into the eternal moan, Woe! Woe! Woe! Woe! Woe! Woe! Woe! in unceasing monotony that rings always in my ears if I let my thought fall from the height of activity, listen to the voice of my sensorium.

In my sleep I am partially protected, and I keep a lamp constantly alight to burn tobacco in the room; yet too often my dreams throb with that reiterated Woe! Woe! Woe! Woe! Woe! Woe! Woe!

IX

The final stage is clearly enough inevitable, unless we believe the Buddhist theories, which I am somewhat inclined to do, as their theory of the Universe is precisely confirmed in every detail by the facts here set down. But it is one thing to recognise a disease, another to discover a remedy. Frankly my whole being revolts from their methods, and I had rather acquiesce in the ultimate destiny and achieve it as quickly as may be. My earnest preoccupation is to avoid the preliminary tortures, and I am convinced that the explosion of a dynamite cartridge in the mouth is the most practicable method of effecting this. There is just the possibility that if all thinking minds, all "spiritual beings," were thus destroyed, and especially if all organic life could be annihilated, the Universe might cease to be, since (as Bishop Berkeley has shown) it can only exist in some thinking mind. And there is really no evidence (in spite of Berkeley) for the existence of any extra-human consciousness. Matter in itself may think, in a sense, but its monotony of woe is less awful than its abomination, the building up of high and holy things only to drag them through infamy and terror to the old abyss.

I shall consequently cause this record to be widely distributed. The note-books of my work with Arthur (Vols. I-ccxiv) will be edited by Professor von Buehle, whose marvellous mind may perhaps discover some escape from the destiny which menaces mankind. Everything is in order in these notebooks; and I am free to die, for I can endure no more, and above all things I dread the onset of illness, and the possibility of natural or accidental death.

Notes

I am glad to have the opportunity of publishing, in a medium so widely read by the medical profession, the MS. of the widow of the late Professor Blair.

Her mind undoubtedly became unhinged through grief at her husband's death; the medical man who attended him in his last illness grew alarmed at her condition, and had her watched. She tried (fruitlessly) to purchase dynamite at several shops, but on her going to the laboratory of her late husband, and attempting to manufacture Chloride of Nitrogen, obviously for the purpose of suicide, she was seized, certified insane, and placed in my care.

The case is most unusual in several respects.

I have never known her inaccurate in any statement of verifiable fact.

She can undoubtedly read thoughts in an astonishing manner. In particular, she is actually useful to me by her ability to foretell attacks of acute insanity in my patients. Some hours before they occur she can predict them to a minute. On an early occasion my disbelief in her power led to the dangerous wounding of one of my attendants.

She combines a fixed determination of suicide (in the extraordinary manner described by her) with an intense fear of death. She smokes uninterruptedly, and I am obliged to allow her to fumigate her room at night with the same drug.

She is certainly only twenty-four years old, and any competent judge would with equal certainty declare her sixty.

Professor von Buehle, to whom the notebooks were sent, addressed to me a long and urgent telegram, begging her release on condition that she would promise not to commit suicide, but go to work with him in Bonn. I have yet to learn, however, that German professors, however eminent, have any voice in the management of a private asylum in England, and I am certain that the Lunacy

Commissioners will uphold me in my refusal to consider the question.

It will then be clearly understood that this document is published with all reserve as the lucubration of a very peculiar, perhaps unique, type of insanity.

V. ENGLISH, M.D.

THE MESSENGER

by Robert W. Chambers

As I wrote in the Introduction, If H.P. Lovecraft is the Christ of horror, then most assuredly Robert W. Chambers (1865-1933) was his John the Baptist. It is ironic that as influential as Chambers would become to the horror and science fiction genre, he was even more celebrated during his life for his popular novels, short stories, war adventure stories, and romantic fictions. He was a formally trained artist whose illustrations graced the pages of *Life*, *Truth*, and *Vogue* magazines. But, it is his innovative and imaginative works of horror that have made him one the brightest stars in the firmament of horror.

Little gray messenger,
Robed like painted Death,
Your robe is dust.
Whom do you seek
Among lilies and closed buds
At dusk?
Among lilies and closed buds
At dusk,
Whom do you seek,
Little gray messenger,
Robed in the awful panoply
Of painted Death?
All-wise,
Hast thou seen all there is to see with thy two eyes?
Dost thou know all there is to know, and so,
Omniscient,
Darest thou still to say thy brother lies?

R.W.C., 1897

The Messenger

I

"The bullet entered here," said Max Fortin, and he placed his middle finger over a smooth hole exactly in the center of the forehead.

I sat down upon a mound of dry seaweed and unslung my fowling piece.

The little chemist cautiously felt the edges of the shot-hole, first with his middle finger, and then with his thumb.

"Let me see the skull again," said I.

Max Fortin picked it up from the sod.

"It's like all the others," he repeated, wiping his glasses on his handkerchief. "I thought you might care to see one of the skulls, so I brought this over from the gravel pit. The men from Bannalec are digging yet. They ought to stop."

"How many skulls are there altogether?" I inquired.

"They found thirty-eight skulls; there are thirty-nine noted in the list. They lie piled up in the gravel pit on the edge of Le Bihan's wheat field. The men are at work yet. Le Bihan is going to stop them."

"Let's go over," said I; and I picked up my gun and started across the cliffs, Portin on one side, Môme on the other.

"Who has the list?" I asked, lighting my pipe. "You say there is a list?"

"The list was found rolled up in a brass cylinder," said the chemist. He added: "You should not smoke here. You know that if a single spark drifted into the wheat—"

"Ah, but I have a cover to my pipe," said I, smiling.

Fortin watched me as I closed the pepper-box arrangement over the glowing bowl of the pipe. Then he continued:

"The list was made out on thick yellow paper; the brass tube has preserved it. It is as fresh to-day as it was in 1760. You shall see it."

"Is that the date?"

"The list is dated 'April, 1760.' The Brigadier Durand has it. It is not written in French."

"Not written in French!" I exclaimed.

"No," replied Fortin solemnly, "it is written in Breton."

"But," I protested, "the Breton language was never written or printed in 1760."

"Except by priests," said the chemist.

"I have heard of but one priest who ever wrote the Breton language," I began.

Fortin stole a glance at my face.

"You mean—the Black Priest?" he asked.

I nodded.

Fortin opened his mouth to speak again, hesitated, and finally shut his teeth obstinately over the wheat stem that he was chewing.

"And the Black Priest?" I suggested encouragingly. But I knew it was useless; for it is easier to move the stars from their courses than to make an obstinate Breton talk. We walked on for a minute or two in silence.

"Where is the Brigadier Durand?" I asked, motioning Môme to come out of the wheat, which he was trampling as though it were heather. As I spoke we came in sight of the farther edge of the wheat field and the dark, wet mass of cliffs beyond.

"Durand is down there—you can see him; he stands just behind the mayor of St. Gildas."

"I see," said I; and we struck straight down, following a sun-baked cattle path across the heather.

When we reached the edge of the wheat field, Le Bihan, the mayor of St. Gildas, called to me, and I tucked my gun under my arm and skirted the wheat to where he stood.

"Thirty-eight skulls," he said in his thin, high-pitched voice; "there is but one more, and I am opposed to further search. I suppose Fortin told you?"

I shook hands with him, and returned the salute of the Brigadier Durand.

"I am opposed to further search," repeated Le Bihan, nervously picking at the mass of silver buttons which covered the front of his velvet and broadcloth jacket like a breastplate of scale armor.

Durand pursed up his lips, twisted his tremendous mustache, and hooked his thumbs in his saber belt.

"As for me," he said, "I am in favor of further search."

"Further search for what—for the thirty-ninth skull?" I asked.

Le Bihan nodded. Durand frowned at the sunlit sea, rocking like a bowl of molten gold from the cliffs to the horizon. I followed his eyes. On the dark glistening cliffs, silhouetted against the glare of the sea, sat a cormorant, black, motionless, its horrible head raised toward heaven.

"Where is that list, Durand?" I asked.

The gendarme rummaged in his despatch pouch and produced a brass cylinder about a foot long. Very gravely he unscrewed the head and dumped out a scroll of thick yellow paper closely covered with writing on both sides. At a nod from Le Bihan he handed me the scroll. But I could make nothing of the coarse writing, now faded to a dull brown.

"Come, come, Le Bihan," I said impatiently, "translate it, won't you? You and Max Fortin make a lot of mystery out of nothing, it seems."

Le Bihan went to the edge of the pit where the three Bannalec men were digging, gave an order or two in Breton, and turned to me.

As I came to the edge of the pit the Bannalec men were removing a square piece of sailcloth from what appeared to be a pile of cobblestones.

"Look!" said Le Bihan shrilly. I looked. The pile below was a heap of skulls. After a moment I clambered down the gravel sides of the pit and walked over to the men of Bannalec. They saluted me gravely, leaning on their picks and shovels, and wiping their sweating faces with sunburned hands.

"How many?" said I in Breton.

"Thirty-eight," they replied.

I glanced around. Beyond the heap of skulls lay two piles of human bones. Beside these was a mound of broken, rusted bits of iron and steel. Looking closer, I saw that this mound was composed of rusty bayonets, saber blades, scythe blades, with here and there a tarnished buckle attached to a bit of leather hard as iron.

I picked up a couple of buttons and a belt plate. The buttons bore the royal arms of England; the belt plate was emblazoned with the English arms and also with the number "27."

"I have heard my grandfather speak of the terrible English regiment, the 27th Foot, which landed and stormed the fort up there," said one of the Bannalec men.

"Oh!" said I; "then these are the bones of English soldiers?"

"Yes," said the men of Bannalec.

Le Bihan was calling to me from the edge of the pit above, and I handed the belt plate and buttons to the men and climbed the side of the excavation.

"Well," said I, trying to prevent Môme from leaping up and licking my face as I emerged from the pit, "I suppose you know what these bones are. What are you going to do with them?"

"There was a man," said Le Bihan angrily, "an Englishman, who passed here in a dog-cart on his way to Quimper about an hour ago, and what do you suppose he wished to do?"

"Buy the relics?" I asked, smiling.

"Exactly—the pig!" piped the mayor of St. Gildas. "Jean Marie Tregunc, who found the bones, was standing there where Max Fortin stands, and do you know what he answered? He spat upon the ground, and said: 'Pig of an Englishman, do you take me for a desecrator of graves?'"

I knew Tregunc, a sober, blue-eyed Breton, who lived from one year's end to the other without being able to afford a single bit of meat for a meal.

"How much did the Englishman offer Tregunc?" I asked.

"Two hundred francs for the skulls alone."

I thought of the relic hunters and the relic buyers on the battle-fields of our civil war.

"Seventeen hundred and sixty is long ago," I said.

"Respect for the dead can never die," said Fortin.

"And the English soldiers came here to kill your fathers and burn your homes," I continued.

"They were murderers and thieves, but—they are dead," said Tregunc, coming up from the beach below, his long sea rake balanced on his dripping jersey.

"How much do you earn every year, Jean Marie?" I asked, turning to shake hands with him.

"Two hundred and twenty francs, monsieur."

"Forty-five dollars a year," I said. "Bah! you are worth more, Jean. Will you take care of my garden for me? My wife wished me to ask you. I think it would be worth one hundred francs a month to you and to me. Come on, Le Bihan—come along, Fortin—and you, Durand. I want somebody to translate that list into French for me."

Tregunc stood gazing at me, his blue eyes dilated.

"You may begin at once," I said, smiling, "if the salary suits you?"

"It suits," said Tregunc, fumbling for his pipe in a silly way that annoyed Le Bihan.

"Then go and begin your work," cried the mayor impatiently; and Tregunc started across the moors toward St. Gildas, taking off his velvet-ribboned cap to me and gripping his sea rake very hard.

"You offer him more than my salary," said the mayor, after a moment's contemplation of his silver buttons.

"Pooh!" said I, "what do you do for your salary except play dominoes with Max Portin at the Groix Inn?"

Le Bihan turned red, but Durand rattled his saber and winked at Max Fortin, and I slipped my arm through the arm of the sulky magistrate, laughing.

"There's a shady spot under the cliff," I said; "come on, Le Bihan, and read me what is in the scroll."

In a few moments we reached the shadow of the cliff, and I threw myself upon the turf, chin on hand, to listen.

The gendarme, Durand, also sat down, twisting his mustache into needlelike points. Fortin leaned against the cliff, polishing his glasses and examining us with vague, near-sighted eyes; and Le Bihan, the mayor, planted himself in our midst, rolling up the scroll and tucking it under his arm.

"First of all," he began in a shrill voice, "I am going to light my pipe, and while lighting it I shall tell you what I have heard about the attack on the fort yonder. My father told me; his father told him."

He jerked his head in the direction of the ruined fort, a small, square stone structure on the sea cliff, now nothing but crumbling walls. Then he slowly produced a tobacco pouch, a bit of flint and tinder, and a long-stemmed pipe fitted with a microscopical bowl of baked clay. To fill such a pipe requires ten minutes' close attention. To smoke it to a finish takes but four puffs. It is very Breton, this Breton pipe. It is the crystallization of everything Breton.

"Go on," said I, lighting a cigarette.

"The fort," said the mayor, "was built by Louis XIV, and was dismantled twice by the English. Louis XV restored it in 1730. In 1760 it was carried by assault by the English. They came across from the island of Groix—three shiploads, and they stormed the fort and sacked St. Julien yonder, and they started to burn St. Gildas—you can see the marks of their bullets on my house yet; but the men of Bannalec and the men of Lorient fell upon them with pike and scythe and blunderbuss, and those who did not run away lie there below in the gravel pit now—thirty-eight of them."

"And the thirty-ninth skull?" I asked, finishing my cigarette.

The mayor had succeeded in filling his pipe, and now he began to put his tobacco pouch away.

"The thirty-ninth skull," he mumbled, holding the pipe stem between his defective teeth—"the thirty-ninth skull is no business of mine. I have told the Bannalec men to cease digging."

"But what is—whose is the missing skull?" I persisted curiously.

The mayor was busy trying to strike a spark to his tinder. Presently he set it aglow, applied it to his pipe, took the prescribed four puffs, knocked the ashes out of the bowl, and gravely replaced the pipe in his pocket.

"The missing skull?" he asked.

"Yes," said I, impatiently.

The mayor slowly unrolled the scroll and began to read, translating from the Breton into French. And this is what he read:

On the Cliffs of St. Gildas,
April 13, 1760.

On this day, by order of the Count of Soisic, general in chief of the Breton forces now lying in Kerselec Forest, the bodies of thirty-eight English soldiers of the 27th, 50th, and 72nd regiments of Foot were buried in this spot, together with their arms and equipments.

The mayor paused and glanced at me reflectively.

"Go on, Le Bihan," I said.

"With them," continued the mayor, turning the scroll and reading on the other side, "was buried the body of that vile traitor who betrayed the fort to the English. The manner of his death was as follows: By order of the most noble Count of Soisic, the traitor was first branded upon the forehead with the brand of an arrowhead. The iron burned through the flesh and was pressed heavily so that the brand should even burn into the bone of the skull. The traitor was then led out and bidden to kneel. He admitted having guided the English from the island of Groix. Although a priest and a Frenchman, he had violated his priestly office to aid him in discovering the password to the fort. This password he extorted during confession from a young Breton girl who was in the habit of rowing across from the island of Groix to visit her husband in the fort. When the fort fell, this young girl, crazed by the death of her husband, sought the Count of Soisic and told how the priest had forced her to confess to him all she knew about the fort. The priest was arrested at St. Gildas as he was about to cross the river to Lorient. When arrested he cursed the girl, Marie Trevec—"

"What!" I exclaimed, "Marie Trevec!"

"Marie Trevec," repeated Le Bihan; "the priest cursed Marie Trevec, and all her family and descendants. He was shot as he knelt, having a mask of leather over his face, because the Bretons who composed the squad of execution refused to fire at a priest unless his face was concealed. The priest was l'Abbé Sorgue, commonly known as the Black Priest on account of his dark face and swarthy eyebrows. He was buried with a stake through his heart."

Le Bihan paused, hesitated, looked at me, and handed the manuscript back to Durand. The gendarme took it and slipped it into the brass cylinder.

"So," said I, "the thirty-ninth skull is the skull of the Black Priest."

"Yes," said Fortin. "I hope they won't find it."

"I have forbidden them to proceed," said the mayor querulously. "You heard me, Max Fortin."

I rose and picked up my gun. Môme came and pushed his head into my hand.

"That's a fine dog," observed Durand, also rising.

"Why don't you wish to find his skull?" I asked Le Bihan. "It would be curious to see whether the arrow brand really burned into the bone."

"There is something in that scroll that I didn't read to you," said the mayor grimly. "Do you wish to know what it is?"

"Of course," I replied in surprise.

"Give me the scroll again, Durand," he said; then he read from the bottom: "I, l'Abbé Sorgue, forced to write the above by my executioners, have written it in my own blood; and with it I leave my curse. My curse on St. Gildas, on Marie Trevec, and on her descendants. I will come back to St. Gildas when my remains are disturbed. Woe to that Englishman whom my branded skull shall touch!"

"What rot!" I said. "Do you believe it was really written in his own blood?"

"I am going to test it," said Fortin, "at the request of Monsieur le Maire. I am not anxious for the job, however."

"See," said Le Bihan, holding out the scroll to me, "it is signed, 'L'Abbé Sorgue.'"

I glanced curiously over the paper.

"It must be the Black Priest," I said. "He was the only man who wrote in the Breton language. This is a wonderfully interesting discovery, for now, at last, the mystery of the Black Priest's disappearance is cleared up. You will, of course, send this scroll to Paris, Le Bihan?"

"No," said the mayor obstinately, "it shall be buried in the pit below where the rest of the Black Priest lies."

I looked at him and recognized that argument would be useless. But still I said, "It will be a loss to history, Monsieur Le Bihan."

"All the worse for history, then," said the enlightened Mayor of St. Gildas.

We had sauntered back to the gravel pit while speaking. The men of Bannalec were carrying the bones of the English soldiers toward the St. Gildas cemetery, on the cliffs to the east, where already a knot of white-coiffed women stood in attitudes of prayer; and I saw the somber robe of a priest among the crosses of the little graveyard.

"They were thieves and assassins; they are dead now," muttered Max Fortin.

"Respect the dead," repeated the Mayor of St. Gildas, looking after the Bannalec men.

"It was written in that scroll that Marie Trevec, of Groix Island, was cursed by the priest—she and her descendants," I said, touching Le Bihan on the arm. "There was a Marie Trevec who married an Yves Trevec of St. Gildas—"

"It is the same," said Le Bihan, looking at me obliquely.

"Oh!" said I; "then they were ancestors of my wife."

"Do you fear the curse?" asked Le Bihan.

"What?" I laughed.

"There was the case of the Purple Emperor," said Max Fortin timidly.

Startled for a moment, I faced him, then shrugged my shoulders and kicked at a smooth bit of rock which lay near the edge of the pit, almost embedded in gravel.

"Do you suppose the Purple-Emperor drank himself crazy because he was descended from Marie Trevec?" I asked contemptuously.

"Of course not," said Max Fortin hastily.

"Of course not," piped the mayor. "I only—Hellow! what's that you're kicking?"

"What?" said I, glancing down, at the same time involuntarily giving another kick. The smooth bit of rock dislodged itself and rolled out of the loosened gravel at my feet.

"The thirty-ninth skull!" I exclaimed. "By jingo, it's the noddle of the Black Priest! See! there is the arrowhead branded on the front!"

The mayor stepped back. Max Fortin also retreated. There was a pause, during which I looked at them, and they looked anywhere but at me.

"I don't like it," said the mayor at last, in a husky, high voice. "I don't like it! The scroll says he will come back to St. Gildas when his remains are disturbed. I—I don't like it, Monsieur Darrel—"

"Bosh!" said I; "the poor wicked devil is where he can't get out. For Heaven's sake, Le Bihan, what is this stuff you are talking in the year of grace 1896?"

The mayor gave me a look.

"And he says 'Englishman.' You are an Englishman, Monsieur Darrel," he announced.

"You know better. You know I'm an American."

"It's all the same," said the Mayor of St. Gildas, obstinately.

"No, it isn't!" I answered, much exasperated, and deliberately pushed the skull till it rolled into the bottom of the gravel pit below.

"Cover it up," said I; "bury the scroll with it too, if you insist, but I think you ought to send it to Paris. Don't look so gloomy, Fortin, unless you believe in werewolves and ghosts. Hey! what the—what the devil's the matter with you, anyway? What are you staring at, Le Bihan?"

"Come, come," muttered the mayor in a low, tremulous voice, "it's time we got out of this. Did you see? Did you see, Fortin?"

"I saw," whispered Max Fortin, pallid with fright.

The two men were almost running across the sunny pasture now, and I hastened after them, demanding to know what was the matter.

"Matter!" chattered the mayor, gasping with exasperation and terror. "The skull is rolling up hill again," and he burst into a terrified gallop, Max Fortin followed close behind.

I watched them stampeding across the pasture, then turned toward the gravel pit, mystified, incredulous. The skull was lying on the edge of the pit, exactly where it had been before I pushed it over the edge. For a second I stared at it; a singular chilly feeling crept up my spinal column, and I turned and walked away, sweat starting from the root of every hair on my head. Before I had gone twenty paces the absurdity of the whole thing struck me. I halted, hot with shame and annoyance, and retraced my steps.

There lay the skull.

"I rolled a stone down instead of the skull," I muttered to myself. Then with the butt of my gun I pushed the skull over the edge of the pit and watched it roll to the bottom; and as it struck the bottom of the pit, Môme, my dog, suddenly whipped his tail between his legs, whimpered, and made off across the moor.

"Môme!" I shouted, angry and astonished; but the dog only fled the faster, and I ceased calling from sheer surprise.

"What the mischief is the matter with that dog!" I thought. He had never before played me such a trick.

Mechanically I glanced into the pit, but I could not see the skull. I looked down. The skull lay at my feet again, touching them.

"Good heavens!" I stammered, and struck at it blindly with my gunstock. The ghastly thing flew into the air, whirling over and over, and rolled again down the sides of the pit to the bottom. Breathlessly I stared at it, then, confused and scarcely comprehending, I stepped back from the pit, still facing it, one, ten, twenty paces, my eyes almost starting from my head, as though I expected to see the thing roll up from the bottom of the pit under my very gaze. At last I turned my back to the pit and strode out across the gorse-covered moorland toward my home. As I reached the road that winds from St. Gildas to St. Julien I gave one hasty glance at the pit over my shoulder. The sun shone hot on the sod about the excavation. There was something white and bare and round on the turf at the edge of the pit. It might have been a stone; there were plenty of them lying about.

II

When I entered my garden I saw Môme sprawling on the stone door-step. He eyed me sideways and flopped his tail.

"Are you not mortified, you idiot dog?" I said, looking about the upper windows for Lys.

Môme rolled over on his back and raised one deprecating forepaw, as though to ward off calamity.

"Don't act as though I was in the habit of beating you to death," I said, disgusted. I had never in my life raised whip to the brute. "But you are a fool dog," I continued. "No, you needn't come to be babied and wept over; Lys can do that, if she insists, but I am ashamed of you, and you can go to the devil."

Môme slunk off into the house, and I followed, mounting directly to my wife's boudoir. It was empty.

"Where has she gone?" I said, looking hard at Môme, who had followed me. "Oh! I see you don't know. Don't pretend you do. Come off that lounge! Do you think Lys wants tan-colored hairs all over her lounge?"

I rang the bell for Catherine and Fine, but they didn't know where "madame" had gone; so I went into my room, bathed, exchanged my somewhat grimy shooting clothes for a suit of warm, soft knicker-bockers, and, after lingering some extra moments over my toilet—for I was particular, now that I had married Lys—I went down to the garden and took a chair out under the fig-trees.

"Where can she be?" I wondered, Môme came sneaking out to be comforted, and I forgave him for Lys's sake, whereupon he frisked.

"You bounding cur," said I, "now what on earth started you off across the moor? If you do it again I'll push you along with a charge of dust shot."

As yet I had scarcely dared think about the ghastly hallucination of which I had been a victim, but now I faced it squarely, flushing a little with mortification at the thought of my hasty retreat from the gravel pit.

"To think," I said aloud, "that those old woman's tales of Max Fortin and Le Bihan should have actually made me see what didn't exist at all! I lost my nerve like a schoolboy in a dark bedroom." For I knew now that I had mistaken a round stone for a skull each time, and had pushed a couple of big pebbles into the pit instead of the skull itself.

"By jingo!" said I, "I'm nervous; my liver must be in a devil of a condition if I see such things when I'm awake! Lys will know what to give me."

I felt mortified and irritated and sulky, and thought disgustedly of Le Bihan and Max Fortin.

But after a while I ceased speculating, dismissed the mayor, the chemist, and the skull from my mind, and smoked pensively, watching the sun low dipping in the western ocean. As the twilight fell for a moment over ocean and moorland, a wistful, restless happiness filled my heart, the happiness that all men know—all men who have loved.

Slowly the purple mist crept out over the sea; the cliffs darkened; the forest was shrouded.

Suddenly the sky above burned with the afterglow, and the world was alight again.

Cloud after cloud caught the rose dye; the cliffs were tinted with it; moor and pasture, heather and forest burned and pulsated with the gentle flush. I saw the gulls turning and tossing above the sand bar, their snowy wings tipped with pink; I saw the sea swallows sheering the surface of the still river, stained to its placid depths with warm reflections of the clouds. The twitter of drowsy hedge birds broke out in the stillness; a salmon rolled its shining side above tidewater.

The interminable monotone of the ocean intensified the silence. I sat motionless, holding my breath as one who listens to the first low rumor of an organ. All at once the pure whistle of a nightingale cut the silence, and the first moonbeam silvered the wastes of mist-hung waters.

I raised my head.

Lys stood before me in the garden.

When we had kissed each other, we linked arms and moved up and down the gravel walks, watching the moonbeams sparkle on the sand bar as the tide ebbed and ebbed. The broad beds of white pinks about us were atremble with hovering white moths; the October roses hung all abloom, perfuming the salt wind.

"Sweetheart," I said, "where is Yvonne? Has she promised to spend Christmas with us?"

"Yes, Dick; she drove me down from Plougat this afternoon. She sent her love to you. I am not jealous. What did you shoot?"

"A hare and four partridges. They are in the gun room. I told Catherine not to touch them until you had seen them."

Now I suppose I knew that Lys could not be particularly enthusiastic over game or guns; but she pretended she was, and always scornfully denied that it was for my sake and not for the pure love of sport. So she dragged me off to inspect the rather meager game bag, and she paid me pretty compliments, and gave a little cry of delight and pity as I lifted the enormous hare out of the sack by his ears.

"He'll eat no more of our lettuce," I said attempting to justify the assassination.

"Unhappy little bunny—and what a beauty! O Dick, you are a splendid shot, are you not?"

I evaded the question and hauled out a partridge.

"Poor little dead things'" said Lys in a whisper; "it seems a pity—doesn't it, Dick? But then you are so clever—"

"We'll have them broiled," I said guardedly, "tell Catherine."

Catherine came in to take away the game, and presently 'Fine Lelocard, Lys's maid, announced dinner, and Lys tripped away to her boudoir.

I stood an instant contemplating her blissfully, thinking, "My boy, you're the happiest fellow in the world—you're in love with your wife"

I walked into the dining-room, beamed at the plates, walked out again; met Tregunc in the hallway, beamed on him; glanced into the kitchen, beamed at Catherine, and went up stairs, still beaming.

Before I could knock at Lys's door it opened, and Lys came hastily out. When she saw me she gave a little cry of relief, and nestled close to my breast.

"There is something peering in at my window," she said.

"What!" I cried angrily.

"A man, I think, disguised as a priest, and he has a mask on. He must have climbed up by the bay tree."

I was down the stairs and out of doors in no time. The moonlit garden was absolutely deserted. Tregunc came up, and together we searched the hedge and shrubbery around the house and out to the road.

"Jean Marie," said I at length, "loose my bulldog—he knows you—and take your supper on the porch where you can watch. My wife says the fellow is disguised as a priest, and wears a mask."

Tregunc showed his white teeth in a smile. "He will not care to venture in here again, I think, Monsieur Darrel."

I went back and found Lys seated quietly at the table.

"The soup is ready, dear," she said. "Don't worry; it was only some foolish lout from Bannalec. No one in St. Gildas or St. Julien would do such a thing."

I was too much exasperated to reply at first, but Lys treated it as a stupid joke, and after a while I began to look at it in that light.

Lys told me about Yvonne, and reminded me of my promise to have Herbert Stuart down to meet her.

"You wicked diplomat!" I protested. "Herbert is in Paris, and hard at work for the Salon."

"Don't you think he might spare a week to flirt with the prettiest girl in Finistere?" inquired Lys innocently.

"Prettiest girl! Not much!" I said.

"Who is, then?" urged Lys.

I laughed a trifle sheepishly.

"I suppose you mean me, Dick," said Lys, coloring up.

"Now I bore you, don't I?"

"Bore me? Ah, no, Dick."

After coffee and cigarettes were served I spoke about Tregunc, and Lys approved.

"Poor Jean! He will be glad, won't he? What a dear fellow you are!"

"Nonsense," said I; "we need a gardener; you said so yourself, Lys."

But Lys leaned over and kissed me, and then bent down and hugged Môme—who whistled through his nose in sentimental appreciation.

"I am a very happy woman," said Lys.

"Môme was a very bad dog to-day," I observed.

"Poor Môme!" said Lys, smiling.

When dinner was over and Môme lay snoring before the blaze—for the October nights are often chilly in Finistere—Lys curled up in the chimney corner with her embroidery, and gave me a swift glance from under her dropping lashes.

"You look like a schoolgirl, Lys," I said teasingly. "I don't believe you are sixteen yet."

She pushed back her heavy burnished hair thoughtfully. Her wrist was as white as surf foam.

"Have we been married four years? I don't believe it," I said.

She gave me another swift glance and touched the embroidery on her knee, smiling faintly.

"I see," said I, also smiling at the embroidered garment. "Do you think it will fit?"

"Fit?" repeated Lys. Then she laughed

"And," I persisted, "are you perfectly sure that you—er—we shall need it?"

"Perfectly," said Lys. A delicate color touched her cheeks and neck. She held up the little garment, all fluffy with misty lace and wrought with quaint embroidery.

"It is very gorgeous," said I; "don't use your eyes too much, dearest. May I smoke a pipe?"

"Of course," she said selecting a skein of pale blue silk.

For a while I sat and smoked in silence, watching her slender fingers among the tinted silks and thread of gold.

Presently she spoke: "What did you say your crest is, Dick?"

"My crest? Oh, something or other rampant on a something or other—"

"Dick!"

"Dearest?"

"Don't be flippant."

"But I really forget. It's an ordinary crest; everybody in New York has them. No family should be without 'em."

"You are disagreeable, Dick. Send Josephine upstairs for my album."

"Are you going to put that crest on the—the—whatever it is?"

"I am; and my own crest, too."

I thought of the Purple Emperor and wondered a little.

"You didn't know I had one, did you?" she smiled.

"What is it?" I replied evasively.

"You shall see. Ring for Josephine."

I rang, and, when 'Fine appeared, Lys gave her some orders in a low voice, and Josephine trotted away, bobbing her white-coiffed head with a "Bien, Madame!"

After a few minutes she returned, bearing a tattered, musty volume, from which the gold and blue had mostly disappeared.

I took the book in my hands and examined the ancient emblazoned covers.

"Lilies!" I exclaimed.

"Fleur-de-lis," said my wife demurely.

"Oh!" said I, astonished, and opened the book.

"You have never before seen this book?" asked Lys, with a touch of malice in her eyes.

"You know I haven't. Hello! What's this? Oho! So there should be a de before Trevec? Lys de Trevec? Then why in the world did the Purple Emperor—"

"Dick!" cried Lys.

"All right," said I. "Shall I read about the Sieur de Trevec who rode to Saladin's tent alone to seek for medicine for St. Louise? Or shall I read about—what is it? Oh, here it is, all down in black and white—about the Marquis de Trevec who drowned himself before Alva's eyes rather than surrender the banner of the fleur-de-lis to Spain? It's all written here. But, dear, how about that soldier named Trevec who was killed in the old fort on the cliff yonder?"

"He dropped the de, and the Trevecs since then have been Republicans," said Lys—"all except me."

"That's quite right," said I; "it is time that we Republicans should agree upon some feudal system. My dear, I drink to the king!" and I raised my wine glass and looked at Lys.

"To the king," said Lys, flushing. She smoothed out the tiny garment on her knees; she touched the glass with her lips; her eyes were very sweet. I drained the glass to the king.

After a silence I said: "I will tell the king stories. His majesty shall be amused."

"His majesty," repeated Lys softly.

"Or hers," I laughed. "Who knows?"

"Who knows?" murmured Lys; with a gentle sigh.

"I know some stories about Jack the Giant-Killer," I announced. "Do you, Lys?"

"I? No, not about a giant-killer, but I know all about the werewolf, and Jeanne-la-Flamme, and the Man in Purple Tatters, and—O dear me, I know lots more."

"You are very wise," said I. "I shall teach his majesty, English."

"And I Breton," cried Lys jealously.

"I shall bring playthings to the king," said I—"big green lizards from the gorse, little gray mullets to swim in glass globes, baby rabbits from the forest of Kerselec—"

"And I," said Lys, "will bring the first primrose, the first branch of aubepine, the first jonquil, to the king—my king."

"Our king," said I; and there was peace in Finistere.

I lay back, idly turning the leaves of the curious old volume.

"I am looking," said I, "for the crest."

"The crest, dear? It is a priest's head with an arrow-shaped mark on the forehead, on a field—"

I sat up and stared at my wife.

"Dick, whatever is the matter?" she smiled. "The story is there in that book. Do you care to read it? No? Shall I tell it to you? Well, then: It happened in the third crusade. There was a monk whom men called the Black Priest. He turned apostate, and sold himself to the enemies of Christ. A Sieur de Trevec burst into the Saracen camp, at the head of only one hundred lances, and carried the Black Priest away out of the very midst of their army."

"So that is how you come by the crest," I said quietly; but I thought of the branded skull in the gravel pit, and wondered.

"Yes," said Lys. "The Sieur de Trevec cut the Black Priest's head off, but first he branded him with an arrow mark on the forehead. The book says it was a pious action, and the Sieur de Trevec got great merit by it. But I think it was cruel, the branding," she sighed.

"Did you ever hear of any other Black Priest?"

"Yes. There was one in the last century, here in St. Gildas. He cast a white shadow in the sun. He wrote in the Breton language. Chronicles, too, I believe. I never saw them. His name was the same as that of the old chronicler, and of the other priest, Jacques Sorgue. Some said he was a lineal descendant of the traitor. Of course the first Black Priest was bad enough for anything. But if he did have a child, it need not have been the ancestor of the last Jacques Sorgue. They say he was so good he was not allowed to die, but was caught up to heaven one day," added Lys, with believing eyes.

I smiled.

"But he disappeared," persisted Lys.

"I'm afraid his journey was in another direction," I said jestingly, and thoughtlessly told her the story of the morning. I had utterly forgotten the masked man at her window, but before I finished I remembered him fast enough, and realized what I had done as I saw her face whiten.

"Lys," I urged tenderly, "that was only some clumsy clown's trick. You said so yourself. You are not superstitious, my dear?"

Her eyes were on mine. She slowly drew the little gold cross from her bosom and kissed it. But her lips trembled as they pressed the symbol of faith.

III

About nine o'clock the next morning I walked into the Groix Inn and sat down at the long discolored oaken table, nodding good-day to Marianne Bruyere, who in turn bobbed her white coiffe at me.

"My clever Bannalec maid," said I, "what is good for a stirrup-cup at the Groix Inn?"

"Schist?" she inquired in Breton.

"With a dash of red wine, then," I replied.

She brought the delicious Quimperle cider, and I poured a little Bordeaux into it. Marianne watched me with laughing black eyes.

"What makes your cheeks so red, Marianne?" I asked. "Has Jean Marie been here?"

"We are to be married, Monsieur Darrel," she laughed.

"Ah! Since when has Jean Marie Tregunc lost his head?"

"His head? Oh, Monsieur Darrel—his heart, you mean!"

"So I do," said I. "Jean Marie is a practical fellow."

"It is all due to your kindness—" began the girl, but I raised my hand and held up the glass.

"It's due to himself. To your happiness, Marianne"; and I took a hearty draught of the schist. "Now," said I, "tell me where I can find Le Bihan and Max Fortin."

"Monsieur Le Bihan and Monsieur Fortin are above in the broad room. I believe they are examining the Red Admiral's effects."

"To send them to Paris? Oh, I know. May I go up, Marianne?"

"And God go with you," smiled the girl.

When I knocked at the door of the broad room above little Max Fortin opened it. Dust covered his spectacles and nose; his hat, with the tiny velvet ribbons fluttering, was all awry.

"Come in, Monsieur Darrel," he said; "the mayor and I are packing up the effects of the Purple Emperor and of the poor Red Admiral."

"The collections?" I asked, entering the room. "You must be very careful in packing those butterfly cases; the slightest jar might break wings and antennas, you know."

Le Bihan shook hands with me and pointed to the great pile of boxes.

"They're all cork lined," he said, "but Fortin and I are putting felt around each box. The Entomological Society of Paris pays the freight."

The combined collection of the Red Admiral and the Purple Emperor made a magnificent display.

I lifted and inspected case after case set with gorgeous butterflies and moths, each specimen carefully labelled with the name in Latin. There were cases filled with crimson tiger moths all aflame with color; cases devoted to the common yellow butterflies; symphonies in orange and pale yellow; cases of soft gray and dun-colored sphinx moths; and cases of grayish nettle-bed butterflies of the numerous family of Vanessa.

All alone in a great case by itself was pinned the purple emperor, the Apatura Iris, that fatal specimen that had given the Purple Emperor his name and quietus.

I remembered the butterfly, and stood looking at it with bent eyebrows.

Le Bihan glanced up from the floor where he was nailing down the lid of a box full of cases.

"It is settled, then," said he, "that madame, your wife, gives the Purple Emperor's entire Collection to the city of Paris?"

I nodded.

"Without accepting anything for it?"

"It is a gift," I said.

"Including the purple emperor there in the case? That butterfly is worth a great deal of money," persisted Le Bihan.

"You don't suppose that we would wish to sell that specimen, do you?" I answered a trifle sharply.

"If I were you I should destroy it," said the mayor in his high-pitched voice.

"That would be nonsense," said I, "like your burying the brass cylinder and scroll yesterday."

"It was not nonsense," said Le Bihan doggedly, "and I should prefer not to discuss the subject of the scroll."

I looked at Max Portin, who immediately avoided my eyes.

"You are a pair of superstitious old women," said I, digging my hands into my pockets; "you swallow every nursery tale that is invented."

"What of it?" said Le Bihan sulkily; "there's more truth than lies in most of 'em."

"Oh!" I sneered, "does the Mayor of St. Gildas and St. Julien believe in the loup-garou?"

"No, not in the loup-garou."

"In what, then—Jeanne-la-Flamme?"

"That," said Le Bihan with conviction, "is history."

"The devil it is!" said I; "and perhaps, Monsieur the mayor, your faith in giants is unimpaired?"

"There were giants—everybody knows it," growled Max Fortin.

"And you a chemist!" I observed scornfully.

"Listen, Monsieur Darrel," squeaked Le Bihan; "you know yourself that the Purple Emperor was a scientific man. Now suppose I should tell you that he always refused to include in his collection a Death's Messenger?"

"A what?" I exclaimed.

"You know what I mean—that moth that flies by night; some call it the Death's Head, but in St. Gildas we call it 'Death's Messenger.'"

"Oh!" said I, "you mean that big sphinx moth that is commonly known as the 'death's-head moth.' Why the mischief should the people here call it death's messenger?"

"For hundreds of years it has been known as death's messenger in St. Gildas," said Max Fortin. "Even Froissart speaks of it in his commentaries on Jacques Sorgue's *Chronicles*. The book is in your library."

"Sorgue? And who was Jacques Sorgue? I never read his book."

"Jacques Sorgue was the son of some unfrocked priest—I forget. It was during the crusades."

"Good Heavens!" I burst out, "I've been hearing of nothing but crusades and priests and death and sorcery ever since I kicked that skull into the gravel pit, and I am tired of it, I tell you frankly. One would think we lived in the dark ages. Do you know what year of our Lord it is, Le Bihan?"

"Eighteen hundred and ninety-six," replied the mayor.

"And yet you two hulking men are afraid of a death's-head moth."

"I don't care to have one fly into the window," said Max Fortin; "it means evil to the house and the people in it."

"God alone knows why he marked one of his creatures with a yellow death's head on the back," observed Le Bihan piously, "but I take it that he meant it as a warning; and I propose to profit by it," he added triumphantly.

"See here, Le Bihan," I said; "by a stretch of imagination one can make out a skull on the thorax of a certain big sphinx moth. What of it?"

"It is a bad thing to touch," said the mayor wagging his head.

"It squeaks when handled," added Max Fortin.

"Some creatures squeak all the time," I observed, looking hard at Le Bihan.

"Pigs," added the mayor.

"Yes, and asses," I replied. "Listen, Le Bihan: do you mean to tell me that you saw that skull roll uphill yesterday?"

The mayor shut his mouth tightly and picked up his hammer.

"Don't be obstinate," I said; "I asked you a question."

"And I refuse to answer," snapped Le Bihan. "Fortin saw what I saw; let him talk about it."

I looked searchingly at the little chemist.

"I don't say that I saw it actually roll up out of the pit, all by itself," said Fortin with a shiver, "but—but then, how did it come up out of the pit, if it didn't roll up all by itself?"

"It didn't come up at all; that was a yellow cobblestone that you mistook for the skull again," I replied. "You were nervous, Max."

"A—a very curious cobblestone, Monsieur Darrel," said Fortin.

"I also was a victim to the same hallucination," I continued, "and I regret to say that I took the trouble to roll two innocent cobblestones into the gravel pit, imagining each time that it was the skull I was rolling."

"It was," observed Le Bihan with a morose shrug.

"It just shows," said I, ignoring the mayor's remark, "how easy it is to fix up a train of coincidences so that the result seems to savor of the supernatural. Now, last night my wife imagined that she saw a priest in a mask peer in at her window—"

Fortin and Le Bihan scrambled hastily from their knees, dropping hammer and nails.

"W-h-a-t—what's that?" demanded the mayor.

I repeated what I had said. Max Fortin turned livid.

"My God!" muttered Le Bihan, "the Black Priest is in St. Gildas!"

"D-don't you—you know the old prophecy?" stammered Fortin; "Froissart quotes it from Jacques Sorgue:

> When the Black Priest rises from the dead,
> St. Gildas folk shall shriek in bed;
> When the Black Priest rises from his grave,
> May the good God St. Gildas save!

"Aristide Le Bihan," I said angrily, "and you, Max Fortin, I've got enough of this nonsense! Some foolish lout from Bannalec has been in St. Gildas playing tricks to frighten old fools like you. If you have nothing better to talk about than nursery legends I'll wait until you come to your senses. Good-morning." And I walked out, more disturbed than I cared to acknowledge to myself.

The day had become misty and overcast. Heavy, wet clouds hung in the east. I heard the surf thundering against the cliffs, and the gray gulls squealed as they tossed and turned high in the sky. The tide was creeping across the river sands, higher, higher, and I saw the seaweed floating on the beach, and the lancons springing from the foam, silvery threadlike flashes in the gloom. Curlew were flying up the river in twos and threes; the timid sea swallows skimmed across the moors toward some quiet, lonely pool, safe from the coming tempest. In every hedge field birds were gathering, huddling together, twittering restlessly.

When I reached the cliffs I sat down, resting my chin on my clenched hands. Already a vast curtain of rain, sweeping across the ocean miles away, hid the island of Groix. To the east, behind the white semaphore on the hills, black clouds crowded up over the horizon. After a little the thunder boomed, dull, distant, and slender skeins of lightning unraveled across the crest of the coming storm. Under the cliff at my feet the surf rushed foaming over the shore, and the lancons jumped and skipped and quivered until they seemed to be but the reflections of the meshed lightning.

I turned to the east. It was raining over Groix, it was raining at Sainte Barbe, it was raining now at the semaphore. High in the storm whirl a few gulls pitched; a nearer cloud trailed veils of rain in its wake; the sky was spattered with lightning; the thunder boomed.

As I rose to go, a cold raindrop fell upon the back of my hand, and another, and yet another on my face. I gave a last glance at the sea, where the waves were bursting into strange white shapes that seemed to fling out menacing arms toward me. Then something moved on the cliff, something black as the black rock it clutched—a filthy cormorant, craning its hideous head at the sky.

Slowly I plodded homeward across the somber moorland, where the gorse stems glimmered with a dull metallic green, and the heather, no longer violet and purple, hung drenched and dun-colored among the dreary rocks. The wet turf creaked under my heavy boots, the black-thorn scraped and grated against knee and elbow. Over all lay a strange light, pallid, ghastly, where the sea spray whirled across the landscape and drove into my face until it grew numb with the cold.

In broad bands, rank after rank, billow on billow, the rain burst out across the endless moors, and yet there was no wind to drive it at such a pace.

Lys stood at the door as I turned into the garden, motioning me to hasten; and then for the first time I became conscious that I was soaked to the skin.

"However in the world did you come to stay out when such a storm threatened?" she said. "Oh, you are dripping! Go quickly and change; I have laid your warm underwear on the bed, Dick."

I kissed my wife, and went upstairs to change my dripping clothes for something more comfortable.

When I returned to the morning room there was a driftwood fire on the hearth, and Lys sat in the chimney corner embroidering.

"Catherine tells me that the fishing fleet from Lorient is out. Do you think they are in danger, dear?" asked Lys, raising her blue eyes to mine as I entered.

"There is no wind, and there will be no sea," said I, looking out of the window. Far across the moor I could see the black cliffs looming in the mist.

"How it rains!" murmured Lys; "come to the fire, Dick."

I threw myself on the fur rug, my hands in my pockets, my head on Lys's knees.

"Tell me a story," I said. "I feel like a boy of ten."

Lys raised a finger to her scarlet lips. I always waited for her to do that.

"Will you be very still, then?" she said.

"Still as death."

"Death," echoed a voice, very softly.

"Did you speak, Lys?" I asked, turning so that I could see her face.

"No; did you, Dick?"

"Who said 'death'?" I asked, startled.

"Death," echoed a voice, softly.

I sprang up and looked about. Lys rose too, her needles and embroidery falling to the floor. She seemed about to faint, leaning heavily on me, and I led her to the window and opened it a little way to give her air. As I did so the chain lightning split the zenith, the thunder crashed, and a sheet of rain swept into the room, driving with it something that fluttered—something that flapped, and squeaked, and beat upon the rug with soft, moist wings.

We bent over it together, Lys clinging to me, and we saw that it was a death's-head moth drenched with rain.

The dark day passed slowly as we sat beside the fire, hand in hand, her head against my breast, speaking of sorrow and mystery and death. For Lys believed that there were things on earth that none might understand, things that must be nameless forever and ever, until God rolls up the scroll of life and all is ended. We spoke of hope and fear and faith, and the mystery of the saints; we spoke of the beginning and the end, of the shadow of sin, of omens, and of love. The moth still lay on the floor quivering its somber wings in the warmth of the fire, the skull and ribs clearly etched upon its neck and body.

"If it is a messenger of death to this house," I said, "why should we fear, Lys?"

"Death should be welcome to those who love God," murmured Lys, and she drew the cross from her breast and kissed it.

"The moth might die if I threw it out into the storm," I said after a silence.

"Let it remain," sighed Lys.

Late that night my wife lay sleeping, and I sat beside her bed and read in the Chronicle of Jacques Sorgue. I shaded the candle, but Lys grew restless, and finally I took the book down into the morning room, where the ashes of the fire rustled and whitened on the hearth.

The death's-head moth lay on the rug before the fire where I had left it. At first I thought it was dead, but when I looked closer I saw a lambent fire in its amber eyes. The straight white shadow it cast across the floor wavered as the candle flickered.

The pages of the Chronicle of Jacques Sorgue were damp and sticky; the illuminated gold and blue initials left flakes of azure and gilt where my hand brushed them.

"It is not paper at all; it is thin parchment," I said to myself; and I held the discolored page close to the candle flame and read, translating laboriously:

"I, Jacques Sorgue, saw all these things. And I saw the Black Mass celebrated in the chapel of St. Gildas-on-the-Cliff. And it was said by the Abbé Sorgue, my kinsman: for which deadly sin the apostate priest was seized by the most noble Marquis of Plougastel and by him condemned to be burned with hot irons, until his seared soul quit its body and fly to its master the devil. But when the Black Priest lay in the crypt of Plougastel, his master Satan came at night and set him free, and carried him across land and sea to Mahmoud, which is Soldan or Saladin. And I, Jacques Sorgue, traveling afterward by sea, beheld with my own eyes my kinsman, the Black Priest of St. Gildas, borne along in the air upon a vast black wing, which was the wing of his master Satan. And this was seen also by two men of the crew."

I turned the page. The wings of the moth on the floor began to quiver. I read on and on, my eyes blurring under the shifting candle flame. I read of battles and of saints, and I learned how the Great Soldan made his pact with Satan, and then I came to the Sieur de Trevec, and read how he seized the Black Priest in the midst of Saladin's tents and carried him away and cut off his head first branding him on the forehead. "And before he suffered," said the Chronicle, "he cursed the Sieur de Trevec and his descendants, and he said he would surely return to St. Gildas. 'For the violence you do to me, I will do violence to you. For the evil I suffer at your hands, I will work evil on you and your descendants. Woe to your children, Sieur de Trevec!'" There was a whirr, a beating of strong wings, and my candle flashed up as in a sudden breeze. A humming filled the room; the great moth darted hither and thither, beating, buzzing, on ceiling and wall. I flung down my book and stepped forward. Now it lay fluttering upon the window sill, and for a moment I had it under my hand, but the thing squeaked and I shrank back. Then suddenly it darted across the candle flame; the light flared and went out, and at the same moment a shadow moved in the darkness outside. I raised my eyes to the window. A masked face was peering in at me.

Quick as thought I whipped out my revolver and fired every cartridge, but the face advanced beyond the window, the glass melting away before it like mist, and through the smoke of my revolver I saw something creep swiftly into the room. Then I tried to cry out, but the thing was at my throat, and I fell backward among the ashes of the hearth.

When my eyes unclosed I was lying on the hearth, my head among the cold ashes. Slowly I got on my knees, rose painfully, and groped my way to a chair. On the floor lay my revolver, shining in the pale light of early morning. My mind clearing by degrees, I looked, shuddering, at the window. The glass was unbroken. I stooped stiffly, picked up my revolver and opened the cylinder. Every cartridge had been fired. Mechanically I closed the cylinder and placed the revolver in my pocket. The book, the Chronicles of Jacques Sorgue, lay on the table beside me, and as I started to close it I glanced at the page. It was all splashed with rain, and the lettering had run, so that the page was merely a confused blur of gold and red and black. As I stumbled toward the door I cast a fearful glance over my shoulder. The death's-head moth crawled shivering on the rug.

IV

The sun was about three hours high. I must have slept, for I was aroused by the sudden gallop of horses under our window. People were shouting and calling in the road. I sprang up and opened the sash. Le Bihan was there, an image of helplessness, and Max Fortin stood beside him polishing his glasses. Some gendarmes had just arrived from Quimperle, and I could hear them around the corner of the house, stamping, and rattling their sabres and carbines, as they led their horses into my stable.

Lys sat up, murmuring half-sleepy, half-anxious questions.

"I don't know," I answered. "I am going out to see what it means."

"It is like the day they came to arrest you," Lys said, giving me a troubled look. But I kissed her and laughed at her until she smiled too. Then I flung on coat and cap and hurried down the stairs.

The first person I saw standing in the road was the Brigadier Durand.

"Hello!" said I, "have you come to arrest me again? What the devil is all this fuss about, anyway?"

"We were telegraphed for an hour ago," said Durand briskly, "and for a sufficient reason, I think. Look there, Monsieur Darrel!"

He pointed to the ground almost under my feet.

"Good heavens!" I cried, "where did that puddle of blood come from?"

"That's what I want to know, Monsieur Darrel. Max Fortin found it at daybreak. See, it's splashed all over the grass, too. A trail of it leads into your garden, across the flower beds to your very window, the one that opens from the morning room. There is another trail leading from this spot across the road to the cliffs, then to the gravel pit, and thence across the moor to the forest of Kerselec. We are going to mount in a minute and search the bosquets. Will you join us? Bon Dieu! but the fellow bled like an ox. Max Fortin says it's human blood, or I should not have believed it."

The little chemist of Quimperle came up at that moment, rubbing his glasses with a colored handkerchief.

"Yes, it is human blood," he said, "but one thing puzzles me: the corpuscles are yellow. I never saw any human blood before with yellow corpuscles. But your English Doctor Thompson asserts that he has—"

"Well, it's human blood, anyway—isn't it?" insisted Durand, impatiently.

"Ye-es," admitted Max Fortin.

"Then it's my business to trail it," said the big gendarme, and he called his men and gave the order to mount.

"Did you hear anything last night?" asked Durand of me.

"I heard the rain. I wonder the rain did not wash away these traces."

"They must have come after the rain ceased. See this thick splash, how it lies over and weighs down the wet grass blades. Pah!"

It was a heavy, evil-looking clot, and I stepped back from it, my throat closing in disgust.

"My theory," said the brigadier, "is this: Some of those Biribi fishermen, probably the Icelanders, got an extra glass of cognac into their hides and quarreled on the road. Some of them were slashed, and staggered to your house. But there is only one trail, and yet—and yet, how could all that blood come from only one person? Well, the wounded man, let us say, staggered first to your house and then back here, and he wandered off, drunk and dying, God knows where. That's my theory."

"A very good one," said I calmly. "And you are going to trail him?"

"Yes."

"When?"

"At once. Will you come?"

"Not now. I'll gallop over by-and-bye. You are going to the edge of the Kerselec forest?"

"Yes; you will hear us calling. Are you coming, Max Fortin? And you, Le Bihan? Good; take the dog-cart."

The big gendarme tramped around the corner to the stable and presently returned mounted on a strong gray horse, his sabre shone on his saddle; his pale yellow and white facings were spotless. The little crowd of white-coiffed women with their children fell back as Durand touched spurs and clattered away followed by his two troopers. Soon after Le Bihan and Max Fortin also departed in the mayor's dingy dog-cart.

"Are you coming?" piped Le Bihan shrilly.

"In a quarter of an hour," I replied, and went back to the house.

When I opened the door of the morning room the death's-head moth was beating its strong wings against the window. For a second I hesitated, then walked over and opened the sash. The creature fluttered out, whirred over the flower beds a moment, then darted across the moorland toward the sea. I called the servants together and questioned them. Josephine, Catherine, Jean Marie Tregunc, not one of them had heard the slightest disturbance during the night. Then I told Jean Marie to saddle my horse, and while I was speaking Lys came down.

"Dearest," I began, going to her.

"You must tell me everything you know, Dick," she interrupted, looking me earnestly in the face.

"But there is nothing to tell—only a drunken brawl, and some one wounded."

"And you are going to ride—where, Dick?"

"Well, over to the edge of Kerselec forest. Durand and the mayor, and Max Fortin, have gone on, following a—a trail."

"What trail?"

"Some blood."

"Where did they find it?"

"Out in the road there." Lys crossed herself.

"Does it come near our house?"

"Yes."

"How near?"

"It comes up to the morning room window," said I, giving in.

Her hand on my arm grew heavy. "I dreamed last night—"

"So did I—" but I thought of the empty cartridges in my revolver, and stopped.

"I dreamed that you were in great danger, and I could not move hand or foot to save you; but you had your revolver, and I called out to you to fire—"

"I did fire!" I cried excitedly.

"You—you fired?"

I took her in my arms. "My darling," I said "something strange has happened—something that I cannot understand as yet. But, of course, there is an explanation. Last night I thought I fired at the Black Priest."

"Ah!" gasped Lys.

"Is that what you dreamed?"

"Yes, yes, that was it! I begged you to fire—"

"And I did."

Her heart was beating against my breast. I held her close in silence.

"Dick," she said at length, "perhaps you killed the—the thing."

"If it was human I did not miss," I answered grimly. "And it was human," I went on, pulling myself together, ashamed of having so nearly gone to pieces. "Of course it was human! The whole affair is plain enough. Not a drunken brawl, as Durand thinks; it was a drunken lout's practical joke, for which he has suffered. I suppose I must have filled him pretty full of bullets, and he has crawled away to die in Kerselec forest. It's a terrible affair; I'm sorry I fired so hastily; but that idiot Le Bihan and Max Fortin have been working on my nerves till I am as hysterical as a schoolgirl," I ended angrily.

"You fired—but the window glass was not shattered," said Lys in a low voice.

"Well, the window was open, then. And as for the—the rest—I've got nervous indigestion, and a doctor will settle the Black Priest for me, Lys."

I glanced out of the window at Tregunc waiting with my horse at the gate.

"Dearest, I think I had better go to join Durand and the others."

"I will go, too."

"Oh, no!"

"Yes, Dick."

"Don't, Lys."

"I shall suffer every moment you are away."

"The ride is too fatiguing, and we can't tell what unpleasant sight you may come upon. Lys, you don't really think there is anything supernatural in this affair?"

"Dick," she answered gently, "I am a Bretonne." With both arms around my neck, my wife said, "Death is the gift of God. I do not fear it when we are together. But alone—oh, my husband, I should fear a God who could take you away from me!"

We kissed each other soberly, simply, like two children. Then Lys hurried away to change her gown, and I paced up and down the garden waiting for her.

She came, drawing on her slender gauntlets. I swung her into the saddle, gave a hasty order to Jean Marie, and mounted.

Now, to quail under thoughts of terror on a morning like this, with Lys in the saddle beside me, no matter what had happened or might happen was impossible. Moreover, Môme came sneaking after us. I asked Tregunc to catch him, for I was afraid he might be brained by our horses' hoofs if he followed, but the wily puppy dodged and bolted after Lys, who was trotting along the highroad. "Never mind," I thought; "if he's hit he'll live, for he has no brains to lose."

Lys was waiting for me in the road beside the Shrine of Our Lady of St. Gildas when I joined her. She crossed herself, I doffed my cap, then we shook out our bridles and galloped toward the forest of Kerselec.

We said very little as we rode. I always loved to watch Lys in the saddle. Her exquisite figure and lovely face were the incarnation of youth and grace; her curling hair glistened like threaded gold.

Out of the corner of my eye I saw the spoiled puppy Môme come bounding cheerfully alongside, oblivious of our horses' heels. Our road swung close to the cliffs. A filthy cormorant rose from the black rocks and flapped heavily across our path. Lys's horse reared, but she pulled him down, and pointed at the bird with her riding crop.

"I see," said I; "it seems to be going our way. Curious to see a cormorant in a forest, isn't it?"

"It is a bad sign," said Lys. "You know the Morbihan proverb: 'When the cormorant turns from the sea, Death laughs in the forest, and wise woodsmen build boats.'"

"I wish," said I sincerely, "that there were fewer proverbs in Brittany."

We were in sight of the forest now; across the gorse I could see the sparkle of gendarmes' trappings, and the glitter of Le Bihan's silver-buttoned jacket. The hedge was low and we took it without difficulty, and trotted across the moor to where Le Bihan and Durand stood gesticulating.

They bowed ceremoniously to Lys as we rode up.

"The trail is horrible—it is a river," said the mayor in his squeaky voice. "Monsieur Darrel, I think perhaps madame would scarcely care to come any nearer."

Lys drew bridle and looked at me.

"It is horrible!" said Durand, walking up beside me; "it looks as though a bleeding regiment had passed this way. The trail winds and winds about here in the thickets; we lose it at times, but we always find it again. I can't understand how one man—no, nor twenty—could bleed like that!"

A halloo, answered by another, sounded from the depths of the forest.

"It's my men; they are following the trail," muttered the brigadier. "God alone knows what is at the end!"

"Shall we gallop back, Lys?" I asked.

"No; let us ride along the western edge of the woods and dismount. The sun is so hot now, and I should like to rest for a moment," she said.

"The western forest is clear of anything disagreeable," said Durand.

"Very well," I answered; "call me, Le Bihan, if you find anything."

Lys wheeled her mare, and I followed across the springy heather, Môme trotting cheerfully in the rear.

We entered the sunny woods about a quarter of a kilometer from where we left Durand. I took Lys from her horse, flung both bridles over a limb, and, giving my wife my arm, aided her to a flat mossy rock which overhung a shallow brook gurgling among the beech trees. Lys sat down and drew off her gauntlets. Môme pushed his head into her lap, received an undeserved caress, and came doubtfully toward me. I was weak enough to condone his offense, but I made him lie down at my feet, greatly to his disgust.

I rested my head on Lys's knees, looking up at the sky through the crossed branches of the trees.

"I suppose I have killed him," I said. "It shocks me terribly, Lys."

"You could not have known, dear. He may have been a robber, and—if—not—did—have you ever fired your revolver since that day four years ago when the Red Admiral's son tried to kill you? But I know you have not."

"No," said I, wondering. "It's a fact, I have not. Why?"

"And don't you remember that I asked you to let me load it for you the day when Yves went off, swearing to kill you and his father?"

"Yes, I do remember. Well?"

"Well, I—I took the cartridges first to St. Gildas chapel and dipped them in holy water. You must not laugh, Dick," said Lys gently, laying her cool hands on my lips.

"Laugh, my darling!"

Overhead the October sky was pale amethyst, and the sunlight burned like orange flame through the yellow leaves of beech and oak. Gnats and midges danced and wavered overhead; a spider dropped from a twig halfway to the ground and hung suspended on the end of his gossamer thread.

"Are you sleepy, dear?" asked Lys, bending over me.

"I am—a little; I scarcely slept two hours last night," I answered.

"You may sleep, if you wish," said Lys, and touched my eyes caressingly.

"Is my head heavy on your knees?"

"No, Dick."

I was already in a half doze; still I heard the brook babbling under the beeches and the humming of forest flies overhead. Presently even these were stilled.

The next thing I knew I was sitting bolt upright, my ears ringing with a scream, and I saw Lys cowering beside me, covering her white face with both hands.

As I sprang to my feet she cried again and clung to my knees. I saw my dog rush growling into a thicket, then I heard him whimper, and he came backing out, whining, ears flat, tail down. I stooped and disengaged Lys's hand.

"Don't go, Dick!" she cried. "O God, it's the Black Priest!"

In a moment I had leaped across the brook and pushed my way into the thicket. It was empty. I stared about me; I scanned every tree trunk, every bush. Suddenly I saw him. He was seated on a fallen log, his head resting in his hands, his rusty black robe gathered around him. For a moment my hair stirred under my cap; sweat started on forehead and cheek bone; then I recovered my reason, and understood that the man was human and was probably wounded to death. Ay, to death; for there at my feet, lay the wet trail of blood, over leaves and stones, down into the little hollow, across to the figure in black resting silently under the trees.

I saw that he could not escape even if he had the strength, for before him, almost at his very feet, lay a deep, shining swamp.

As I stepped forward my foot broke a twig. At the sound the figure started a little, then its head fell forward again. Its face was masked. Walking up to the man, I bade him tell where he was wounded. Durand and the others broke through the thicket at the same moment and hurried to my side.

"Who are you who hide a masked face in a priest's robe?" said the gendarme loudly.

There was no answer.

"See—see the stiff blood all over his robe," muttered Le Bihan to Fortin.

"He will not speak," said I.

"He may be too badly wounded," whispered Le Bihan.

"I saw him raise his head," I said, "my wife saw him creep up here."

Durand stepped forward and touched the figure.

"Speak!" he said.

"Speak!" quavered Fortin.

Durand waited a moment, then with a sudden upward movement he stripped off the mask and threw back the man's head. We were looking into the eye sockets of a skull. Durand stood rigid; the mayor shrieked. The skeleton burst out from its rotting robes and collapsed on the ground before us. From between the staring ribs and the grinning teeth spurted a torrent of black blood, showering the shrinking grasses; then the thing shuddered, and fell over into the black ooze of the bog. Little bubbles of iridescent air appeared from the mud; the bones were slowly engulfed, and, as the last fragments sank out of sight, up from the depths and along the bank crept a creature, shiny, shivering, quivering its wings.

It was a death's-head moth.

I wish I had time to tell you how Lys outgrew superstitions—for she never knew the truth about the affair, and she never will know, since she has promised not to read this book. I wish I might tell you about the king and his coronation, and how the coronation robe fitted. I wish that I were able to write how Yvonne and Herbert Stuart rode to a boar hunt in Quimperle, and how the hounds raced the quarry right through the town, overturning three gendarmes, the notary, and an old woman. But I am becoming garrulous and Lys is calling me to come and hear the king say that he is sleepy. And his highness shall not be kept waiting.

The King's Cradle Song

Seal with a seal of gold
The scroll of a life unrolled;
Swathe him deep in his purple stole;
Ashes of diamonds, crystalled coal,
Drops of gold in each scented fold.
Crimson wings of the Little Death,
Stir his hair with your silken breath;
Flaming wings of sins to be,
Splendid pinions of prophecy,
Smother his eyes with hues and dyes,
While the white moon spins and the winds arise,
And the stars drip through the skies.
Wave, O wings of the Little Death!
Seal his sight and stifle his breath,
Cover his breast with the gemmed shroud pressed;
From north to north, from west to west,
Wave, O wings of the Little Death!
Till the white moon reels in the cracking skies,
And the ghosts of God arise.

THE RING OF THOTH

by Sir Arthur Conan Doyle

Creator of the immortal Sherlock Holmes, Sir Arthur Conan Doyle (1859-1930) needs no introduction. He was an exuberantly prolific writer who churned out a seemly endless variety of masterpieces (mystery, science fiction, horror, romance, poetry, historical fictions, non-fiction and fantasy). He was an occultist whose interest in magic and Theosophy injected real substance into his subjects and characters. It has often been suggested that he was a member of the great nineteenth-century magical society, the Hermetic Order of the Golden Dawn, but that is not the case. He was nominated for membership and had initially given his permission to process his nomination, but evidence shows he withdrew his permission and was not officially associated with the organization.

The Ring of Thoth

Mr. John Vansittart Smith, F.R.S., of 147-A Gower Street, was a man whose energy of purpose and clearness of thought might have placed him in the very first rank of scientific observers. He was the victim, however, of a universal ambition which prompted him to aim at distinction in many subjects rather than preeminence in one.

In his early days he had shown an aptitude for zoology and for botany which caused his friends to look upon him as a second Darwin, but when a professorship was almost within his reach he had suddenly discontinued his studies and turned his whole attention to chemistry. Here his researches upon the spectra of the metals had won him his fellowship in the Royal Society; but again he played the coquette with his subject, and after a year's absence from the laboratory he joined the Oriental Society, and delivered a paper on the Hieroglyphic and Demotic inscriptions of El Kab, thus giving a crowning example both of the versatility and of the inconstancy of his talents.

The most fickle of wooers, however, is apt to be caught at last, and so it was with John Vansittart Smith. The more he burrowed his way into Egyptology the more impressed he became by the vast field which it opened to the inquirer, and by the extreme importance of a subject which promised to throw a light upon the first germs of human civilisation and the origin of the greater part of our arts and sciences. So struck was Mr. Smith that he straightway married an Egyptological young lady who had written upon the sixth dynasty, and having thus secured a sound base of operations he set himself to collect materials for a work which should unite the research of Lepsius and the ingenuity of Champollion. The preparation of this magnum opus entailed many hurried visits to the magnificent Egyptian collections of the Louvre, upon the last of which, no longer ago than the middle of last October, he became involved in a most strange and noteworthy adventure.

The trains had been slow and the Channel had been rough, so that the student arrived in Paris in a somewhat befogged and feverish condition. On reaching the Hotel de France, in the Rue Laffitte, he had thrown himself upon a sofa for a couple of hours, but finding that he was unable to sleep, he determined, in spite of his fatigue, to make his way to the Louvre, settle the point which he had come to decide, and take the evening train back to Dieppe. Having come to this conclusion, he donned his greatcoat, for it was a raw rainy day, and made his way across the Boulevard des Italiens and down the Avenue de l'Opera. Once in the Louvre he was on familiar ground, and he speedily made his way to the collection of papyri which it was his intention to consult.

The warmest admirers of John Vansittart Smith could hardly claim for him that he was a handsome man. His high-beaked nose and prominent chin had something of the same acute and incisive character which distinguished his intellect. He held his head in a birdlike fashion, and birdlike, too, was the pecking motion with which, in conversation, he threw out his objections and retorts. As he stood, with the high collar of his greatcoat raised to his ears, he might have seen from the reflection in the glass-case before him that his appearance was a singular one. Yet it came upon him as a sudden jar when an English voice behind him exclaimed in very audible tones, "What a queer-looking mortal!"

The student had a large amount of petty vanity in his composition which manifested itself by an ostentatious and overdone disregard of all personal considerations. He straightened his lips and looked rigidly at the roll of papyrus, while his heart filled with bitterness against the whole race of travelling Britons.

"Yes," said another voice, "he really is an extraordinary fellow."

"Do you know," said the first speaker, "one could almost believe that by the continual contemplation of mummies the chap has become half a mummy himself?"

"He has certainly an Egyptian cast of countenance," said the other.

John Vansittart Smith spun round upon his heel with the intention of shaming his countrymen by a corrosive remark or two. To his surprise and relief, the two young fellows who had been conversing had their shoulders turned towards him, and were gazing at one of the Louvre attendants who was polishing some brass-work at the other side of the room.

"Carter will be waiting for us at the Palais Royal," said one tourist to the other, glancing at his watch, and they clattered away, leaving the student to his labours.

"I wonder what these chatterers call an Egyptian cast of countenance," thought John Vansittart Smith, and he moved his position slightly in order to catch a glimpse of the man's face. He started as his eyes fell upon it. It was indeed the very face with which his studies had made him familiar. The regular statuesque features, broad brow, well-rounded chin, and dusky complexion were the exact counterpart of the innumerable statues, mummy-cases, and pictures which adorned the walls of the apartment.

The thing was beyond all coincidence. The man must be an Egyptian.

The national angularity of the shoulders and narrowness of the hips were alone sufficient to identify him.

John Vansittart Smith shuffled towards the attendant with some intention of addressing him. He was not light of touch in conversation, and found it difficult to strike the happy mean between the brusqueness of the superior and the geniality of the equal. As he came nearer, the man presented his side face to him, but kept his gaze still bent upon his work. Vansittart Smith, fixing his eyes upon the fellow's skin, was conscious of a sudden impression that there was something inhuman and preternatural about its appearance. Over the temple and cheek-bone it was as glazed and as shiny as varnished parchment. There was no suggestion of pores. One could not fancy a drop of moisture upon that arid surface. From brow to chin, however, it was cross-hatched by a million delicate wrinkles, which shot and interlaced as though Nature in some Maori mood had tried how wild and intricate a pattern she could devise.

"Ou est la collection de Memphis?" asked the student, with the awkward air of a man who is devising a question merely for the purpose of opening a conversation.

"C'est la," replied the man brusquely, nodding his head at the other side of the room.

"Vous etes un Egyptien, n'est-ce pas?" asked the Englishman.

The attendant looked up and turned his strange dark eyes upon his questioner. They were vitreous, with a misty dry shininess, such as Smith had never seen in a human head before. As he gazed into them he saw some strong emotion gather in their depths, which rose and deepened until it broke into a look of something akin both to horror and to hatred.

"Non, monsieur; je suis Fransais." The man turned abruptly and bent low over his polishing. The student gazed at him for a moment in astonishment, and then turning to a chair in a retired corner behind one of the doors he proceeded to make notes of his researches among the papyri. His thoughts, however refused to return into their natural groove. They would run upon the enigmatical attendant with the sphinx-like face and the parchment skin.

"Where have I seen such eyes?" said Vansittart Smith to himself. "There is something saurian about them, something reptilian. There's the membrana nictitans of the snakes," he mused, bethinking himself of his zoological studies. "It gives a shiny effect. But there was something more here. There was a sense of power, of wisdom—so I read them—and of weariness, utter weariness, and ineffable despair. It may be all imagination, but I never had so strong an impression. By Jove, I must have another look at them!" He rose and paced round the Egyptian rooms, but the man who had excited his curiosity had disappeared.

The student sat down again in his quiet corner, and continued to work at his notes. He had gained the information which he required from the papyri, and it only remained to write it down while it was still fresh in his memory. For a time his pencil travelled rapidly over the paper, but soon the lines became less level, the words more blurred, and finally the pencil tinkled down upon the floor, and the head of the student dropped heavily forward upon his chest.

Tired out by his journey, he slept so soundly in his lonely post behind the door that neither the clanking civil guard, nor the footsteps of sightseers, nor even the loud hoarse bell which gives the signal for closing, were sufficient to arouse him.

Twilight deepened into darkness, the bustle from the Rue de Rivoli waxed and then waned, distant Notre Dame clanged out the hour of midnight, and still the dark and lonely figure sat silently in the shadow. It was not until close upon one in the morning that, with a sudden gasp and an intaking of the breath, Vansittart Smith returned to consciousness. For a moment it flashed upon him that he had dropped asleep in his study-chair at home. The moon was shining fitfully through the unshuttered window, however, and, as his eye ran along the lines of mummies and the endless array of polished cases, he remembered clearly where he was and how he came there. The student was not a nervous man. He possessed that love of a novel situation which is peculiar to his race. Stretching out his cramped limbs, he looked at his watch, and burst into a chuckle as he observed the hour. The episode would make an admirable anecdote to be introduced into his next paper as a relief to the graver and heavier speculations. He was a little cold, but wide awake and much refreshed. It was no wonder that the guardians had overlooked him, for the door threw its heavy black shadow right across him.

The complete silence was impressive. Neither outside nor inside was there a creak or a murmur. He was alone with the dead men of a dead civilisation. What though the outer city reeked of the garish nineteenth century! In all this chamber there was scarce an article, from the shrivelled ear of wheat to the pigment-box of the painter, which had not held its own against four thousand years. Here was the flotsam and jetsam washed up by the great ocean of time from that far-off empire. From stately Thebes, from lordly Luxor, from the great temples of Heliopolis, from a hundred rifled tombs, these relics had been brought. The student glanced round at the long silent figures who flickered vaguely up through the gloom, at the busy toilers who were now so restful, and he fell into a reverent and thoughtful mood. An unwonted sense of his own youth and insignificance came over him. Leaning back in his chair, he gazed dreamily down the long vista of rooms, all silvery with the moonshine, which extend through the whole wing of the widespread building. His eyes fell upon the yellow glare of a distant lamp.

John Vansittart Smith sat up on his chair with his nerves all on edge. The light was advancing slowly towards him, pausing from time to time, and then coming jerkily onwards. The bearer moved noiselessly. In the utter silence there was no suspicion of the pat of a footfall. An idea of robbers entered the Englishman's head. He snuggled up further into the corner. The light was two rooms off. Now it was in the next chamber, and still there was no sound. With something approaching to a thrill of fear the student observed a face, floating in the air as it were, behind the flare of the lamp. The figure was wrapped in shadow, but the light fell full upon the strange eager face. There was no mistaking the metallic glistening eyes and the cadaverous skin. It was the attendant with whom he had conversed.

Vansittart Smith's first impulse was to come forward and address him. A few words of explanation would set the matter clear, and lead doubtless to his being conducted to some side door from which he might make his way to his hotel. As the man entered the chamber, however, there was something so stealthy in his movements, and so furtive in his expression, that the Englishman altered his intention. This was clearly no ordinary official walking the rounds. The fellow wore felt-soled slippers, stepped with a rising chest, and glanced quickly from left to right, while his hurried gasping breathing thrilled the flame of his lamp. Vansittart Smith crouched silently back into the corner and watched him keenly, convinced that his errand was one of secret and probably sinister import.

There was no hesitation in the other's movements. He stepped lightly and swiftly across to one of the great cases, and, drawing a key from his pocket, he unlocked it. From the upper shelf he pulled down a mummy, which he bore away with him, and laid it with much care and solicitude upon the ground. By it he placed his lamp, and then squatting down beside it in Eastern fashion he began with long quivering fingers to undo the cerecloths and bandages which girt it round. As the crackling rolls of linen peeled off one after the other, a strong aromatic odour filled the chamber, and fragments of scented wood and of spices pattered down upon the marble floor.

It was clear to John Vansittart Smith that this mummy had never been unswathed before. The operation interested him keenly. He thrilled all over with curiosity, and his birdlike head protruded further and further from behind the door. When, however, the last roll had been removed from the four-thousand-year-old head, it was all that he could do to stifle an outcry of amazement. First, a cascade of long, black, glossy tresses poured over the workman's hands and arms. A second turn of the bandage revealed a low, white forehead, with a pair of delicately arched eyebrows. A third uncovered a pair of bright, deeply fringed eyes, and a straight, well-cut nose, while a fourth and last showed a sweet, full, sensitive mouth, and a beautifully curved chin. The whole face was one of extraordinary loveliness, save for the one blemish that in the centre of the forehead there was a single irregular, coffee-coloured splotch. It was a triumph of the embalmer's art. Vansittart Smith's eyes grew larger and larger as he gazed upon it, and he chirruped in his throat with satisfaction.

Its effect upon the Egyptologist was as nothing, however, compared with that which it produced upon the strange attendant. He threw his hands up into the air, burst into a harsh clatter of words, and then, hurling himself down upon the ground beside the mummy, he threw his arms round her, and kissed her repeatedly upon the lips and brow. "Ma petite!" he groaned in French. "Ma pauvre petite!" His voice broke with emotion, and his innumerable wrinkles quivered and writhed, but the student observed in the lamplight that his shining eyes were still as dry and tearless as two beads of steel. For some minutes he lay, with a twitching face, crooning and moaning over the beautiful head. Then he broke into a sudden smile, said some words in an unknown tongue, and sprang to his feet with the vigorous air of one who has braced himself for an effort.

In the centre of the room there was a large circular case which contained, as the student had frequently remarked, a magnificent collection of early Egyptian rings and precious stones. To this the attendant strode, and, unlocking it, he threw it open. On the ledge at the side he placed his lamp, and beside it a small earthenware jar which he had drawn from his pocket. He then took a handful of rings from the case, and with a most serious and anxious face he proceeded to smear each in turn with some liquid substance from the earthen pot, holding them to the light as he did so. He was clearly disappointed with the first lot, for he threw them petulantly back into the case, and drew out some more. One of these, a massive ring with a large crystal set in it, he seized and eagerly tested with the contents of the jar. Instantly he uttered a cry of joy, and threw out his arms in a wild gesture which upset the pot and sent the liquid streaming across the floor to the very feet of the Englishman. The attendant drew a red handkerchief from his bosom, and, mopping up the mess, he followed it into the corner, where in a moment he found himself face to face with his observer.

"Excuse me," said John Vansittart Smith, with all imaginable politeness; "I have been unfortunate enough to fall asleep behind this door."

"And you have been watching me?" the other asked in English, with a most venomous look on his corpse-like face.

The student was a man of veracity. "I confess," said he, "that I have noticed your movements, and that they have aroused my curiosity and interest in the highest degree."

The man drew a long flamboyant-bladed knife from his bosom. "You have had a very narrow escape," he said; "had I seen you ten minutes ago, I should have driven this through your heart. As it is, if you touch me or interfere with me in any way you are a dead man."

"I have no wish to interfere with you," the student answered. "My presence here is entirely accidental. All I ask is that you will have the extreme kindness to show me out through some side door." He spoke with great suavity, for the man was still pressing the tip of his dagger against the palm of his left hand, as though to assure himself of its sharpness, while his face preserved its malignant expression.

"If I thought—" said he. "But no, perhaps it is as well. What is your name?"

The Englishman gave it.

"Vansittart Smith," the other repeated. "Are you the same Vansittart Smith who gave a paper in London upon El Kab? I saw a report of it. Your knowledge of the subject is contemptible."

"Sir!" cried the Egyptologist.

"Yet it is superior to that of many who make even greater pretensions. The whole keystone of our old life in Egypt was not the inscriptions or monuments of which you make so much, but was our hermetic philosophy and mystic knowledge, of which you say little or nothing."

"Our old life!" repeated the scholar, wide-eyed; and then suddenly, "Good God, look at the mummy's face!"

The strange man turned and flashed his light upon the dead woman, uttering a long doleful cry as he did so. The action of the air had already undone all the art of the embalmer. The skin had fallen away, the eyes had sunk inwards, the discoloured lips had writhed away from the yellow teeth, and the brown mark upon the forehead alone showed that it was indeed the same face which had shown such youth and beauty a few short minutes before.

The man flapped his hands together in grief and horror. Then mastering himself by a strong effort he turned his hard eyes once more upon the Englishman.

"It does not matter," he said, in a shaking voice. "It does not really matter. I came here to-night with the fixed determination to do something. It is now done. All else is as nothing. I have found my quest. The old curse is broken. I can rejoin her. What matter about her inanimate shell so long as her spirit is awaiting me at the other side of the veil!"

"These are wild words," said Vansittart Smith. He was becoming more and more convinced that he had to do with a madman.

"Time presses, and I must go," continued the other. "The moment is at hand for which I have waited this weary time. But I must show you out first. Come with me."

Taking up the lamp, he turned from the disordered chamber, and led the student swiftly through the long series of the Egyptian, Assyrian, and Persian apartments. At the end of the latter he pushed open a small door let into the wall and descended a winding stone stair. The Englishman felt the cold fresh air of the night upon his brow. There was a door opposite him which appeared to communicate with the street. To the right of this another door stood ajar, throwing a spurt of yellow light across the passage. "Come in here!" said the attendant shortly.

Vansittart Smith hesitated. He had hoped that he had come to the end of his adventure. Yet his curiosity was strong within him. He could not leave the matter unsolved, so he followed his strange companion into the lighted chamber.

It was a small room, such as is devoted to a concierge. A wood fire sparkled in the grate. At one side stood a truckle bed, and at the other a coarse wooden chair, with a round table in the centre, which bore the remains of a meal. As the visitor's eye glanced round he could not but remark with an ever-recurring thrill that all the small details of the room were of the most quaint design and antique workmanship. The candlesticks, the vases upon the chimney-piece, the fire-irons, the ornaments upon the walls, were all such as he had been wont to associate with the remote past. The gnarled heavy-eyed man sat himself down upon the edge of the bed, and motioned his guest into the chair.

"There may be design in this," he said, still speaking excellent English. "It may be decreed that I should leave some account behind as a warning to all rash mortals who would set their wits up against workings of Nature. I leave it with you. Make such use as you will of it. I speak to you now with my feet upon the threshold of the other world.

"I am, as you surmised, an Egyptian—not one of the down-trodden race of slaves who now inhabit the Delta of the Nile, but a survivor of that fiercer and harder people who tamed the Hebrew, drove the Ethiopian back into the southern deserts, and built those mighty works which have been the envy and the wonder of all after generations. It was in the reign of Tuthmosis, sixteen hundred years before the birth of Christ, that I first saw the light. You shrink away from me. Wait, and you will see that I am more to be pitied than to be feared.

"My name was Sosra. My father had been the chief priest of Osiris in the great temple of Abaris, which stood in those days upon the Bubastic branch of the Nile. I was brought up in the temple and was trained in all those mystic arts which are spoken of in your own Bible. I was an apt pupil. Before I was sixteen I had learned all which the wisest priest could teach me. From that time on I studied Nature's secrets for myself, and shared my knowledge with no man.

"Of all the questions which attracted me there were none over which I laboured so long as over those which concern themselves with the nature of life. I probed deeply into the vital principle. The aim of medicine had been to drive away disease when it appeared. It seemed to me that a method might be devised which should so fortify the body as to prevent weakness or death from ever taking hold of it. It is useless that I should recount my researches. You would scarce comprehend them if I did. They were carried out partly upon animals, partly upon slaves, and partly on myself. Suffice it that their result was to furnish me with a substance which, when injected into the blood, would endow the body with strength to resist the effects of time, of violence, or of disease. It would not indeed confer immortality, but its potency would endure for many thousands of years. I used it upon a cat, and afterwards drugged the creature with the most deadly poisons. That cat is alive in Lower Egypt at the present moment. There was nothing of mystery or magic in the matter. It was simply a chemical discovery, which may well be made again.

"Love of life runs high in the young. It seemed to me that I had broken away from all human care now that I had abolished pain and driven death to such a distance. With a light heart I poured the accursed stuff into my veins. Then I looked round for some one whom I could benefit. There was a young priest of Thoth, Parmes by name, who had won my goodwill by his earnest nature and his devotion to his studies. To him I whispered my secret, and at his request I injected him with my elixir. I should now, I reflected, never be without a companion of the same age as myself.

"After this grand discovery I relaxed my studies to some extent, but Parmes continued his with redoubled energy. Every day I could see him working with his flasks and his distiller in the Temple of Thoth, but he said little to me as to the result of his labours. For my own part, I used to walk through the city and look around me with exultation as I reflected that all this was destined to pass away, and that only I should remain. The people would bow to me as they passed me, for the fame of my knowledge had gone abroad.

"There was war at this time, and the Great King had sent down his soldiers to the eastern boundary to drive away the Hyksos. A Governor, too, was sent to Abaris, that he might hold it for the King. I had heard much of the beauty of the daughter of this Governor, but one day as I walked out with Parmes we met her, borne upon the shoulders of her slaves. I was struck with love as with lightning. My heart went out from me. I could have thrown myself beneath the feet of her bearers. This was my woman. Life without her was impossible. I swore by the head of Horus that she should be mine. I swore it to the Priest of Thoth. He turned away from me with a brow which was as black as midnight.

"There is no need to tell you of our wooing. She came to love me even as I loved her. I learned that Parmes had seen her before I did, and had shown her that he too loved her, but I could smile at his passion, for I knew that her heart was mine. The white plague had come upon the city and many were stricken, but I laid my hands upon the sick and nursed them without fear or scathe. She marvelled at my daring. Then I told her my secret, and begged her that she would let me use my art upon her.

"'Your flower shall then be unwithered, Atma,' I said. 'Other things may pass away, but you and I, and our great love for each other, shall outlive the tomb of King Chefru.'

"But she was full of timid, maidenly objections. 'Was it right?' she asked, 'was it not a thwarting of the will of the gods? If the great Osiris had wished that our years should be so long, would he not himself have brought it about?'

"With fond and loving words I overcame her doubts, and yet she hesitated. It was a great question, she said. She would think it over for this one night. In the morning I should know her resolution. Surely one night was not too much to ask. She wished to pray to Isis for help in her decision.

"With a sinking heart and a sad foreboding of evil I left her with her tirewomen. In the morning, when the early sacrifice was over, I hurried to her house. A frightened slave met me upon the steps. Her mistress was ill, she said, very ill. In a frenzy I broke my way through the attendants, and rushed through hall and corridor to my Atma's chamber. She lay upon her couch, her head high upon the pillow, with a pallid face and a glazed eye. On her forehead there blazed a single angry purple patch. I knew that hell-mark of old. It was the scar of the white plague, the sign-manual of death.

"Why should I speak of that terrible time? For months I was mad, fevered, delirious, and yet I could not die. Never did an Arab thirst after the sweet wells as I longed after death. Could poison or steel have shortened the thread of my existence, I should soon have rejoined my love in the land with the narrow portal. I tried, but it was of no avail. The accursed influence was too strong upon me. One night as I lay upon my couch, weak and weary, Parmes, the priest of Thoth, came to my chamber. He stood in the circle of the lamplight, and he looked down upon me with eyes which were bright with a mad joy.

"'Why did you let the maiden die?' he asked; 'why did you not strengthen her as you strengthened me?'

"'I was too late,' I answered. 'But I had forgot. You also loved her. You are my fellow in misfortune. Is it not terrible to think of the centuries which must pass ere we look upon her again? Fools, fools, that we were to take death to be our enemy!'

"'You may say that,' he cried with a wild laugh; 'the words come well from your lips. For me they have no meaning.'

"'What mean you?' I cried, raising myself upon my elbow. 'Surely, friend, this grief has turned your brain.' His face was aflame with joy, and he writhed and shook like one who hath a devil.

"'Do you know whither I go?' he asked.

"'Nay,' I answered, 'I cannot tell.'

"'I go to her,' said he. 'She lies embalmed in the further tomb by the double palm-tree beyond the city wall.'

"'Why do you go there?' I asked.

"'To die!' he shrieked, 'to die! I am not bound by earthen fetters.'

"'But the elixir is in your blood,' I cried.

"'I can defy it,' said he; 'I have found a stronger principle which will destroy it. It is working in my veins at this moment, and in an hour I shall be a dead man. I shall join her, and you shall remain behind.'

"As I looked upon him I could see that he spoke words of truth. The light in his eye told me that he was indeed beyond the power of the elixir.

"'You will teach me!' I cried.

"'Never!' he answered.

"'I implore you, by the wisdom of Thoth, by the majesty of Anubis!'

"'It is useless,' he said coldly.

"'Then I will find it out,' I cried.

"'You cannot,' he answered; 'it came to me by chance. There is one ingredient which you can never get. Save that which is in the ring of Thoth, none will ever more be made.

"'In the ring of Thoth!' I repeated; 'where then is the ring of Thoth?'

"'That also you shall never know,' he answered. 'You won her love. Who has won in the end? I leave you to your sordid earth life. My chains are broken. I must go!' He turned upon his heel and fled from the chamber. In the morning came the news that the Priest of Thoth was dead.

"My days after that were spent in study. I must find this subtle poison which was strong enough to undo the elixir. From early dawn to midnight I bent over the test-tube and the furnace. Above all, I collected the papyri and the chemical flasks of the Priest of Thoth. Alas! they taught me little. Here and there some hint or stray expression would raise hope in my bosom, but no good ever came of it. Still, month after month, I struggled on. When my heart grew faint I would make my way to the tomb by the palm-trees. There, standing by the dead casket from which the jewel had been rifled, I would feel her sweet presence, and would whisper to her that I would rejoin her if mortal wit could solve the riddle.

"Parmes had said that his discovery was connected with the ring of Thoth. I had some remembrance of the trinket. It was a large and weighty circlet, made, not of gold, but of a rarer and heavier metal brought from the mines of Mount Harbal. Platinum, you call it. The ring had, I remembered, a hollow crystal set in it, in which some few drops of liquid might be stored. Now, the secret of Parmes could not have to do with the metal alone, for there were many rings of that metal in the Temple. Was it not more likely that he had stored his precious poison within the cavity of the crystal? I had scarce come to this conclusion before, in hunting through his papers, I came upon one which told me that it was indeed so, and that there was still some of the liquid unused.

"But how to find the ring? It was not upon him when he was stripped for the embalmer. Of that I made sure. Neither was it among his private effects. In vain I searched every room that he had entered, every box, and vase, and chattel that he had owned. I sifted the very sand of the desert in the places where he had been wont to walk; but, do what I would, I could come upon no traces of the ring of Thoth. Yet it may be that my labours would have overcome all obstacles had it not been for a new and unlooked-for misfortune.

"A great war had been waged against the Hyksos, and the Captains of the Great King had been cut off in the desert, with all their bowmen and horsemen. The shepherd tribes were upon us like the locusts in a dry year. From the wilderness of Shur to the great bitter lake there was blood by day and fire by night. Abaris was the bulwark of Egypt, but we could not keep the savages back. The city fell. The Governor and the soldiers were put to the sword, and I, with many more, was led away into captivity.

"For years and years I tended cattle in the great plains by the Euphrates. My master died, and his son grew old, but I was still as far from death as ever. At last I escaped upon a swift camel, and made my way back to Egypt. The Hyksos had settled in the land which they had conquered, and their own King ruled over the country Abaris had been torn down, the city had been burned, and of the great Temple there was nothing left save an unsightly mound. Everywhere the tombs had been rifled and the monuments destroyed. Of my Atma's grave no sign was left. It was buried in the sands of the desert, and the palm-trees which marked the spot had long disappeared. The papers of Parmes and the remains of the Temple of Thoth were either destroyed or scattered far and wide over the deserts of Syria. All search after them was vain.

"From that time I gave up all hope of ever finding the ring or discovering the subtle drug. I set myself to live as patiently as might be until the effect of the elixir should wear away. How can you understand how terrible a thing time is, you who have experience only of the narrow course which lies between the cradle and the grave! I know it to my cost, I who have floated down the whole stream of history. I was old when Ilium fell. I was very old when Herodotus came to Memphis. I was bowed down with years when the new gospel came upon earth. Yet you see me much as other men are, with the cursed elixir still sweetening my blood, and guarding me against that which I would court. Now at last, at last I have come to the end of it!

"I have travelled in all lands and I have dwelt with all nations. Every tongue is the same to me. I learned them all to help pass the weary time. I need not tell you how slowly they drifted by, the long dawn of modern civilisation, the dreary middle years, the dark times of barbarism. They are all behind me now, I have never looked with the eyes of love upon another woman. Atma knows that I have been constant to her.

"It was my custom to read all that the scholars had to say upon Ancient Egypt. I have been in many positions, sometimes affluent, sometimes poor, but I have always found enough to enable me to buy the journals which deal with such matters. Some nine months ago I was in San Francisco, when I read an account of some discoveries made in the neighbourhood of Abaris. My heart leapt into my mouth as I read it. It said that the excavator had busied himself in exploring some tombs recently unearthed. In one there had been found an unopened mummy with an inscription upon the outer case setting forth that it contained the body of the daughter of the Governor of the city in the days of Tuthmosis. It added that on removing the outer case there had been exposed a large platinum ring set with a crystal, which had been laid upon the breast of the embalmed woman. This, then was where Parmes had hid the ring of Thoth. He might well say that it was safe, for no Egyptian would ever stain his soul by moving even the outer case of a buried friend.

"That very night I set off from San Francisco, and in a few weeks I found myself once more at Abaris, if a few sand-heaps and crumbling walls may retain the name of the great city. I hurried to the Frenchmen who were digging there and asked them for the ring. They replied that both the ring and the mummy had been sent to the Boulak Museum at Cairo. To Boulak I went, but only to be told that Mariette Bey had claimed them and had shipped them to the Louvre. I followed them, and there at last, in the Egyptian chamber, I came, after close upon four thousand years, upon the remains of my Atma, and upon the ring for which I had sought so long.

"But how was I to lay hands upon them? How was I to have them for my very own? It chanced that the office of attendant was vacant. I went to the Director. I convinced him that I knew much about Egypt. In my eagerness I said too much. He remarked that a Professor's chair would suit me better than a seat in the Conciergerie. I knew more, he said, than he did. It was only by blundering, and letting him think that he had over-estimated my knowledge, that I prevailed upon him to let me move the few effects which I have retained into this chamber. It is my first and my last night here.

"Such is my story, Mr. Vansittart Smith. I need not say more to a man of your perception. By a strange chance you have this night looked upon the face of the woman whom I loved in those far-off days. There were many rings with crystals in the case, and I had to test for the platinum to be sure of the one which I wanted. A glance at the crystal has shown me that the liquid is indeed within it, and that I shall at last be able to shake off that accursed health which has been worse to me than the foulest disease. I have nothing more to say to you. I have unburdened myself. You may tell my story or you may withhold it at your pleasure. The choice rests with you. I owe you some amends, for you have had a narrow escape of your life this night. I was a desperate man, and not to be baulked in my purpose. Had I seen you before the thing was done, I might have put it beyond your power to oppose me or to raise an alarm. This is the door. It leads into the Rue de Rivoli. Good night!"

The Englishman glanced back. For a moment the lean figure of Sosra the Egyptian stood framed in the narrow doorway. The next the door had slammed, and the heavy rasping of a bolt broke on the silent night.

It was on the second day after his return to London that Mr. John Vansittart Smith saw the following concise narrative in the Paris correspondence of the Times:—

"Curious Occurrence in the Louvre.—Yesterday morning a strange discovery was made in the principal Egyptian Chamber. The ouvriers who are employed to clean out the rooms in the morning found one of the attendants lying dead upon the floor with his arms round one of the mummies. So close was his embrace that it was only with the utmost difficulty that they were separated. One of the cases containing valuable rings had been opened and rifled. The authorities are of opinion that the man was bearing away the mummy with some idea of selling it to a private collector, but that he was struck down in the very act by long-standing disease of the heart. It is said that he was a man of uncertain age and eccentric habits, without any living relations to mourn over his dramatic and untimely end."

A DREAM OF RED HANDS

by Bram Stoker

The name Bram Stoker (1847-1912) will forever be associated with *Dracula* and the world of vampires. Even though he never actually visited Transylvania, he was indeed inspired by legends and traditions taken very seriously by inhabitants of Eastern Europe. It is likely, however, that Stoker's real inspiration for the Dracula was the character and nuances of his boss, actor, and theatrical director and producer Sir Henry Irving. Stoker was for years Irving's personal assistant and helped direct the activities of London's famed Lyceum Theatre. Like Arthur Conan Doyle, it was rumored that Stoker was a member of the magical society the Hermetic Order the Golden Dawn, but no evidence has ever been produced to support this claim.

A Dream of Red Hands

The first opinion given to me regarding Jacob Settle was a simple descriptive statement, "He's a down-in-the-mouth chap," but I found that it embodied the thoughts and ideas of all his fellow-workmen. There was in the phrase a certain easy tolerance, an absence of positive feeling of any kind, rather than any complete opinion, which marked pretty accurately the man's place in public esteem. Still, there was some dissimilarity between this and his appearance which unconsciously set me thinking, and by degrees, as I saw more of the place and the workmen, I came to have a special interest in him. He was, I found, for ever doing kindnesses, not involving money expenses beyond his humble means, but in the manifold ways of forethought and forbearance and self-repression which are of the truer charities of life. Women and children trusted him implicitly, though, strangely enough, he rather shunned them, except when anyone was sick, and then he made his appearance to help if he could, timidly and awkwardly. He led a very solitary life, keeping house by himself in a tiny cottage, or rather hut, of one room, far on the edge of the moorland. His existence seemed so sad and solitary that I wished to cheer it up, and for the purpose took the occasion when we had both been sitting up with a child, injured by me through accident, to offer to lend him books. He gladly accepted, and as we parted in the grey of the dawn I felt that something of mutual confidence had been established between us.

The books were always most carefully and punctually returned, and in time Jacob Settle and I became quite friends. Once or twice as I crossed the moorland on Sundays I looked in on him; but on such occasions he was shy and ill at ease so that I felt diffident about calling to see him. He would never under any circumstances come into my own lodgings.

One Sunday afternoon, I was coming back from a long walk beyond the moor, and as I passed Settle's cottage stopped at the door to say "How do you do?" to him. As the door was shut, I thought that he was out, and merely knocked for form's sake, or through habit, not expecting to get any answer. To my surprise, I heard a feeble voice from within, though what was said I could not hear. I entered at once, and found Jacob lying half-dressed upon his bed. He was as pale as death, and the sweat was simply rolling off his face. His hands were unconsciously gripping the bedclothes as a drowning man holds on to whatever he may grasp. As I came in he half arose, with a wild, hunted look in his eyes, which were wide open and staring, as though something of horror had come before him; but when he recognised me he sank back on the couch with a smothered sob of relief and closed his eyes. I stood by him for a while, quite a minute or two, while he gasped. Then he opened his eyes and looked at me, but with such a despairing, woeful expression that, as I am a living man, I would have rather seen that frozen look of horror. I sat down beside him and asked after his health. For a while he would not answer me except to say that he was not ill; but then, after scrutinising me closely, he half arose on his elbow and said:

"I thank you kindly, sir, but I'm simply telling you the truth. I am not ill, as men call it, though God knows whether there be not worse sicknesses than doctors know of. I'll tell you, as you are so kind, but I trust that you won't even mention such a thing to a living soul, for it might work me more and greater woe. I am suffering from a bad dream."

"A bad dream!" I said, hoping to cheer him; "but dreams pass away with the light—even with waking." There I stopped, for before he spoke I saw the answer in his desolate look round the little place.

"No! No! That's all well for people that live in comfort and with those they love around them. It is a thousand times worse for those who live alone and have to do so. What cheer is there for me, waking here in the silence of the night, with the wide moor around me full of voices and full of faces that make my waking a worse dream than my sleep? Ah, young sir, you have no past that can send its legions to people the darkness and the empty space, and I pray the good God that you may never have!" As he spoke, there was such an almost irresistible gravity of conviction in his manner that I abandoned my remonstrance about his solitary life. I felt that I was in the presence of some secret influence which I could not fathom. To my relief, for I knew not what to say, he went on:

"Two nights past have I dreamed it. It was hard enough the first night, but I came through it. Last night the expectation was in itself almost worse than the dream—until the dream came, and then it swept away every remembrance of lesser pain. I stayed awake till just before the dawn, and then it came again, and ever since I have been in such an agony as I am sure the dying feel, and with it all the dread of tonight." Before he had got to the end of the sentence my mind was made up, and I felt that I could speak to him more cheerfully.

"Try and get to sleep early tonight—in fact, before the evening has passed away. The sleep will refresh you, and I promise you there will not be any bad dreams after tonight." He shook his head hopelessly, so I sat a little longer and then left him.

When I got home I made my arrangements for the night, for I had made up my mind to share Jacob Settle's lonely vigil in his cottage on the moor. I judged that if he got to sleep before sunset he would wake well before midnight, and so, just as the bells of the city were striking eleven, I stood opposite his door armed with a bag, in which were my supper, an extra large flask, a couple of candles, and a book. The moonlight was bright, and flooded the whole moor, till it was almost as light as day; but ever and anon black clouds drove across the sky, and made a darkness which by comparison seemed almost tangible. I opened the door softly, and entered without waking Jacob, who lay asleep with his white face upward. He was still, and again bathed in sweat. I tried to imagine what visions were passing before those closed eyes which could bring with them the misery and woe which were stamped on the face, but fancy failed me, and I waited for the awakening. It came suddenly, and in a fashion which touched me to the quick, for the hollow groan that broke from the man's white lips as he half arose and sank back was manifestly the realisation or completion of some train of thought which had gone before.

"If this be dreaming," said I to myself, "then it must be based on some very terrible reality. What can have been that unhappy fact that he spoke of?"

While I thus spoke, he realised that I was with him. It struck me as strange that he had no period of that doubt as to whether dream or reality surrounded him which commonly marks an expected environment of waking men. With a positive cry of joy, he seized my hand and held it in his two wet, trembling hands, as a frightened child clings on to someone whom it loves. I tried to soothe him:

"There, there! it is all right. I have come to stay with you tonight, and together we will try to fight this evil dream." He let go my hand suddenly, and sank back on his bed and covered his eyes with his hands.

"Fight it?—the evil dream! Ah! no, sir, no! No mortal power can fight that dream, for it comes from God—and is burned in here;" and he beat upon his forehead. Then he went on:

"It is the same dream, ever the same, and yet it grows in its power to torture me every time it comes."

"What is the dream?" I asked, thinking that the speaking of it might give him some relief, but he shrank away from me, and after a long pause said:

"No, I had better not tell it. It may not come again."

There was manifestly something to conceal from me—something that lay behind the dream, so I answered:

"All right. I hope you have seen the last of it. But if it should come again, you will tell me, will you not? I ask, not out of curiosity, but because I think it may relieve you to speak." He answered with what I thought was almost an undue amount of solemnity:

"If it comes again, I shall tell you all."

Then I tried to get his mind away from the subject to more mundane things, so I produced supper, and made him share it with me, including the contents of the flask. After a little he braced up, and when I lit my cigar, having given him another, we smoked a full hour, and talked of many things. Little by little the comfort of his body stole over his mind, and I could see sleep laying her gentle hands on his eyelids. He felt it, too, and told me that now he felt all right, and I might safely leave him; but I told him that, right or wrong, I was going to see in the daylight. So I lit my other candle, and began to read as he fell asleep.

By degrees I got interested in my book, so interested that presently I was startled by its dropping out of my hands. I looked and saw that Jacob was still asleep, and I was rejoiced to see that there was on his face a look of unwonted happiness, while his lips seemed to move with unspoken words. Then I turned to my work again, and again woke, but this time to feel chilled to my very marrow by hearing the voice from the bed beside me:

"Not with those red hands! Never! never!" On looking at him, I found that he was still asleep. He woke, however, in an instant, and did not seem surprised to see me; there was again that strange apathy as to his surroundings. Then I said:

"Settle, tell me your dream. You may speak freely, for I shall hold your confidence sacred. While we both live I shall never mention what you may choose to tell me."

He replied:

"I said I would; but I had better tell you first what goes before the dream, that you may understand. I was a schoolmaster when I was a very young man; it was only a parish school in a little village in the West Country. No need to mention any names. Better not. I was engaged to be married to a young girl whom I loved and almost reverenced. It was the old story. While we were waiting for the time when we could afford to set up house together, another man came along. He was nearly as young as I was, and handsome, and a gentleman, with all a gentleman's attractive ways for a woman of our class. He would go fishing, and she would meet him while I was at my work in school. I reasoned with her and implored her to give him up. I offered to get married at once and go away and begin the world in a strange country; but she would not listen to anything I could say, and I could see that she was infatuated with him. Then I took it on myself to meet the man and ask him to deal well with the girl, for I thought he might mean honestly by her, so that there might be no talk or chance of talk on the part of others. I went where I should meet him with none by, and we met!" Here Jacob Settle had to pause, for something seemed to rise in his throat, and he almost gasped for breath. Then he went on:

"Sir, as God is above us, there was no selfish thought in my heart that day, I loved my pretty Mabel too well to be content with a part of her love, and I had thought of my own unhappiness too often not to have come to realise that, whatever might come to her, my hope was gone. He was insolent to me—you, sir, who are a gentleman, cannot know, perhaps, how galling can be the insolence of one who is above you in station—but I bore with that. I implored him to deal well with the girl, for what might be only a pastime of an idle hour with him might be the breaking of her heart. For I never had a thought of her truth, or that the worst of harm could come to her—it was only the unhappiness to her heart I feared. But when I asked him when he intended to marry her his laughter galled me so that I lost my temper and told him that I would not stand by and see her life made unhappy. Then he grew angry too, and in his anger said such cruel things of her that then and there I swore he should not live to do her harm. God knows how it came about, for in such moments of passion it is hard to remember the steps from a word to a blow, but I found myself standing over his dead body, with my hands crimson with the blood that welled from his torn throat. We were alone and he was a stranger, with none of his kin to seek for him and murder does not always out— not all at once. His bones may be whitening still, for all I know, in the pool of the river where I left him. No one suspected his absence, or why it was, except my poor Mabel, and she dared not speak. But it was all in vain, for when I came back again after an absence of months—for I could not live in the place—I learned that her shame had come and that she had died in it. Hitherto I had been borne up by the thought that my ill deed had saved her future, but now, when I learned that I had been too late, and that my poor love was smirched with that man's sin, I fled away with the sense of my useless guilt upon me more heavily than I could bear. Ah! sir, you that have not done such a sin don't know what it is to carry it with you. You may think that custom makes it easy to you, but it is not so. It grows and grows with every hour, till it becomes intolerable, and with it growing, too, the feeling that you must for ever stand outside Heaven. You don't know what that means, and I pray God that you never may. Ordinary men, to whom all things are possible, don't often, if ever, think of Heaven. It is a name, and nothing more, and they are content to wait and let things be, but to those who are doomed to be shut out for ever you cannot think what it means, you cannot guess or measure the terrible endless longing to see the gates opened, and to be able to join the white figures within.

"And this brings me to my dream. It seemed that the portal was before me, with great gates of massive steel with bars of the thickness of a mast, rising to the very clouds, and so close that between them was just a glimpse of a crystal grotto, on whose shining walls were figured many white-clad forms with faces radiant with joy. When I stood before the gate my heart and my soul were so full of rapture and longing that I forgot. And there stood at the gate two mighty angels with sweeping wings, and, oh! so stern of countenance. They held each in one hand a flaming sword, and in the other the latchet, which moved to and fro at their lightest touch. Nearer were figures all draped in black, with heads covered so that only the eyes were seen, and they handed to each who came white garments such as the angels wear. A low murmur came that told that all should put on their own robes, and without soil, or the angels would not pass them in, but would smite them down with the flaming swords. I was eager to don my own garment, and hurriedly threw it over me and stepped swiftly to the gate; but it moved not, and the angels, loosing the latchet, pointed to my dress, I looked down, and was aghast, for the whole robe was smeared with blood. My hands were red; they glittered with the blood that dripped from them as on that day by the river bank. And then the angels raised their flaming swords to smite me down, and the horror was complete—I awoke. Again, and again, and again, that awful dream comes to me. I never learn from the experience, I never remember, but at the beginning the hope is ever there to make the end more appalling; and I know that the dream does not come out of the common darkness where the dreams abide, but that it is sent from God as a punishment! Never, never shall I be able to pass the gate, for the soil on the angel garments must ever come from these bloody hands!"

I listened as in a spell as Jacob Settle spoke. There was something so far away in the tone of his voice—something so dreamy and mystic in the eyes that looked as if through me at some spirit beyond—something so lofty in his very diction and in such marked contrast to his workworn clothes and his poor surroundings that I wondered if the whole thing were not a dream.

We were both silent for a long time. I kept looking at the man before me in growing wonderment. Now that his confession had been made, his soul, which had been crushed to the very earth, seemed to leap back again to uprightness with some resilient force. I suppose I ought to have been horrified with his story, but, strange to say, I was not. It certainly is not pleasant to be made the recipient of the confidence of a murderer, but this poor fellow seemed to have had, not only so much provocation, but so much self-denying purpose in his deed of blood that I did not feel called upon to pass judgment upon him. My purpose was to comfort, so I spoke out with what calmness I could, for my heart was beating fast and heavily:

"You need not despair, Jacob Settle. God is very good, and His mercy is great. Live on and work on in the hope that some day you may feel that you have atoned for the past." Here I paused, for I could see that deep, natural sleep this time, was creeping upon him. "Go to sleep," I said; "I shall watch with you here and we shall have no more evil dreams tonight."

He made an effort to pull himself together, and answered:

"I don't know how to thank you for your goodness to me this night, but I think you had best leave me now. I'll try and sleep this out; I feel a weight off my mind since I have told you all. If there's anything of the man left in me, I must try and fight out life alone."

"I'll go tonight, as you wish it," I said; "but take my advice, and do not live in such a solitary way. Go among men and women; live among them. Share their joys and sorrows, and it will help you to forget. This solitude will make you melancholy mad."

"I will!" he answered, half unconsciously, for sleep was overmastering him.

I turned to go, and he looked after me. When I had touched the latch I dropped it, and, coming back to the bed, held out my hand. He grasped it with both his as he rose to a sitting posture, and I said my goodnight, trying to cheer him:

"Heart, man, heart! There is work in the world for you to do, Jacob Settle. You can wear those white robes yet and pass through that gate of steel!"

Then I left him.

A week after I found his cottage deserted, and on asking at the works was told that he had "gone north," no one exactly knew whither.

Two years afterwards, I was staying for a few days with my friend Dr. Munro in Glasgow. He was a busy man, and could not spare much time for going about with me, so I spent my days in excursions to the Trossachs and Loch Katrine and down the Clyde. On the second last evening of my stay I came back somewhat later than I had arranged, but found that my host was late too. The maid told me that he had been sent for to the hospital—a case of accident at the gas-works, and the dinner was postponed an hour; so telling her I would stroll down to find her master and walk back with him, I went out. At the hospital I found him washing his hands preparatory to starting for home. Casually, I asked him what his case was.

"Oh, the usual thing! A rotten rope and men's lives of no account. Two men were working in a gasometer, when the rope that held their scaffolding broke. It must have occurred just before the dinner hour, for no one noticed their absence till the men had returned. There was about seven feet of water in the gasometer, so they had a hard fight for it, poor fellows. However, one of them was alive, just alive, but we have had a hard job to pull him through. It seems that he owes his life to his mate, for I have never heard of greater heroism. They swam together while their strength lasted, but at the end they were so done up that even the lights above, and the men slung with ropes, coming down to help them, could not keep them up. But one of them stood on the bottom and held up his comrade over his head, and those few breaths made all the difference between life and death. They were a shocking sight when they were taken out, for that water is like a purple dye with the gas and the tar. The man upstairs looked as if he had been washed in blood. Ugh!"

"And the other?"

"Oh, he's worse still. But he must have been a very noble fellow. That struggle under the water must have been fearful; one can see that by the way the blood has been drawn from the extremities. It makes the idea of the *Stigmata* possible to look at him. Resolution like this could, you would think, do anything in the world. Ay! it might almost unbar the gates of Heaven. Look here, old man, it is not a very pleasant sight, especially just before dinner, but you are a writer, and this is an odd case. Here is something you would not like to miss, for in all human probability you will never see anything like it again." While he was speaking he had brought me into the mortuary of the hospital.

On the bier lay a body covered with a white sheet, which was wrapped close round it.

"Looks like a chrysalis, don't it? I say, Jack, if there be anything in the old myth that a soul is typified by a butterfly, well, then the one that this chrysalis sent forth was a very noble specimen and took all the sunlight on its wings. See here!" He uncovered the face. Horrible, indeed, it looked, as though stained with blood. But I knew him at once, Jacob Settle! My friend pulled the winding sheet further down.

The hands were crossed on the purple breast as they had been reverently placed by some tender-hearted person. As I saw them my heart throbbed with a great exultation, for the memory of his harrowing dream rushed across my mind. There was no stain now on those poor, brave hands, for they were blanched white as snow.

And somehow as I looked I felt that the evil dream was all over. That noble soul had won a way through the gate at last. The white robe had now no stain from the hands that had put it on.

LIGEIA

by Edgar Allan Poe

No introduction to Edgar Allan Poe (1809-1849) could be adequate or worthy. Master of mystery and macabre, inventor of "detective fiction," poet, critic, star of the Romantic Movement, Poe in his forty short and tragic years was a god of American literature.

Ligeia

And the will therein lieth, which dieth not. Who knoweth the mystery of the will, with its vigor? For God is but a great will pervading all things by nature of its intentness. Man doth not yield himself to the angels, nor unto death utterly, save only through the weakness of his feeble will.

JOSEPH GLANVILL

I cannot, for my soul, remember how, when, or even precisely where, I first became acquainted with the lady Ligeia. Long years have since elapsed, and my memory is feeble through much suffering. Or, perhaps, I cannot *now* bring these points to mind, because, in truth, the character of my beloved, her rare learning, her singular yet placid cast of beauty, and the thrilling and enthralling eloquence of her low musical language, made their way into my heart by paces so steadily and stealthily progressive, that they have been unnoticed and unknown. Yet I believe that I met her first and most frequently in some large, old, decaying city near the Rhine. Of her family—I have surely heard her speak. That it is of a remotely ancient date cannot be doubted. Ligeia! Ligeia! Buried in studies of a nature more than all else adapted to deaden impressions of the outward world, it is by that sweet word alone—by Ligeia—that I bring before mine eyes in fancy the image of her who is no more. And now, while I write, a recollection flashes upon me that I have *never known* the paternal name of her who was my friend and my bethrothed, and who became the partner of my studies, and finally the wife of my bosom. Was it a playful charge on the part of my Ligeia? or was it a test of my strength of affection, that I should institute no inquiries upon this point? or was it rather a caprice of my own—a wildly romantic offering on the shrine of the most passionate devotion? I but indistinctly recall the fact itself—what wonder that I have utterly forgotten the circumstances which originated or attended it? And, indeed, if ever that spirit which is entitled *Romance*—if ever she, the wan misty-winged *Ashtophet* of idolatrous Egypt, presided, as they tell, over marriages ill-omened, then most surely she presided over mine.

There is one dear topic, however, on which my memory fails me not. It is the *person* of Ligeia. In stature she was tall, somewhat slender, and, in her latter days, even emaciated. I would in vain attempt to portray the majesty, the quiet ease of her demeanor, or the incomprehensible lightness and elasticity of her footfall. She came and departed as a shadow. I was never made aware of her entrance into my closed study, save by the dear music of her low sweet voice, as she placed her marble hand upon my shoulder. In beauty of face no maiden ever equaled her. It was the radiance of an opium-dream—an airy and spirit-lifting vision more wildly divine than the phantasies which hovered about the slumbering souls of the daughters of Delos. Yet her features were not of that regular mold which we have been falsely taught to worship in the classical labors of the heathen. "There is no exquisite beauty," says Bacon, Lord Verulam, speaking truly of all the forms and *genera* of beauty, "without some *strangeness* in the proportion." Yet, although I saw that the features of Ligeia were not of a classic regularity—although I perceived that her loveliness was indeed "exquisite," and felt that there was much of "strangeness" pervading it, yet I have tried in vain to detect the irregularity and to trace home my own perception of "the strange." I examined the contour of the lofty and pale forehead—it was faultless—how cold indeed that word when applied to a majesty so divine!—the skin rivaling the purest ivory, the commanding extent and repose, the gentle prominence of the regions above the temples; and then the raven-black, the glossy, the luxuriant, and naturally-curling tresses, setting forth the full force of the Homeric epithet, "hyacinthine!" I looked at the delicate outlines of the nose—and nowhere but in the graceful medallions of the Hebrews had I beheld a similar perfection. There were the same luxurious smoothness of surface, the same scarcely perceptible tendency to the aquiline, the same harmoniously curved nostrils speaking the free spirit. I regarded the sweet mouth. Here was indeed the triumph of all things heavenly—the magnificent turn of the short upper lip—the soft, voluptuous slumber of the under—the dimples which sported, and the color which spoke—the teeth glancing back, with a brilliancy almost startling, every ray of the holy light which fell upon them in her serene and placid yet most exultingly radiant of all smiles. I scrutinized the formation of the chin—and, here, too, I found the gentleness of breadth, the softness and the majesty, the fullness and the spirituality, of the Greek—the contour which the god Apollo revealed but in a dream, to Cleomenes, the son of the Athenian. And then I peered into the large eyes of Ligeia.

For eyes we have no models in the remotely antique. It might have been, too, that in these eyes of my beloved lay the secret to which Lord Verulam alludes. They were, I must believe, far larger than the ordinary eyes of our own race. They were even fuller than the fullest of the gazelle eyes of the tribe of the valley of Nourjahad. Yet it was only at intervals—in moments of intense excitement—that this peculiarity became more than slightly noticeable in Ligeia. And at such moments was her beauty—in my heated fancy thus it appeared perhaps—the beauty of beings either above or apart from the earth— the beauty of the fabulous Houri of the Turk. The hue of the orbs was the most brilliant of black, and, far over them, hung jetty lashes of great length. The brows, slightly irregular in outline, had the same tint. The "strangeness," however, which I found in the eyes was of a nature distinct from the formation, or the color, or the brilliancy of the features, and must, after all, be referred to the *expression*. Ah, word of no meaning! behind whose vast latitude of mere sound we intrench our ignorance of so much of the spiritual. The expression of the eyes of Ligeia! How for long hours have I pondered upon it! How have I, through the whole of a midsummer night, struggled to fathom it! What was it—that something more profound than the well of Democritus—which lay far within the pupils of my beloved? What *was* it? I was possessed with a passion to discover. Those eyes! those large, those shining, those divine orbs! they became to me twin stars of Leda, and I to them devoutest of astrologers.

There is no point, among the many incomprehensible anomalies of the science of mind, more thrillingly exciting than the fact—never, I believe, noticed in the schools—than in our endeavors to recall to memory something long forgotten, we often find ourselves *upon the very verge* of remembrance, without being able, in the end, to remember. And thus how frequently, in my intense scrutiny of Ligeia's eyes, have I felt approaching the full knowledge of their expression—felt it approaching—yet not quite be mine—and so at length entirely depart! And (strange, oh, strangest mystery of all!) I found, in the commonest objects of the universe, a circle of analogies to that expression. I mean to say that, subsequently to the period when Ligeia's beauty passed into my spirit, there dwelling as in a shrine, I derived, from many existences in the material world, a sentiment such as I felt always around, within me, by her large and luminous orbs. Yet not the more could I define that sentiment, or analyze, or even steadily view it. I recognized it, let me repeat, sometimes in the survey of a rapidly growing vine— in the contemplation of a moth, a butterfly, a chrysalis, a stream of running water. I have felt it in the ocean—in the falling of a meteor. I have felt it in the glances of unusually aged people. And there are one or two stars in heaven (one especially, a star of the sixth magnitude, double and changeable, to be found near the large star in Lyra) in a telescopic scrutiny of which I have been made aware of the feeling. I have been filled with it by certain sounds from stringed instruments, and not unfrequently by passages from books. Among innumerable other instances, I well remember something in a volume of Joseph

Glanvill, which (perhaps merely from its quaintness—who shall say?) never failed to inspire me with the sentiment: "And the will therein lieth, which dieth not. Who knoweth the mysteries of the will, with its vigor? For God is but a great will pervading all things by nature of its intentness. Man doth not yield him to the angels, nor unto death utterly, save only through the weakness of his feeble will."

Length of years and subsequent reflection have enabled me to trace, indeed, some remote connection between this passage in the English moralist and a portion of the character of Ligeia. An *intensity* in thought, action, or speech was possibly, in her, a result, or at least an index, of that gigantic volition which, during our long intercourse, failed to give other and more immediate evidence of its existence. Of all the women whom I have ever known, she, the outwardly calm, the ever-placid Ligeia, was the most violently a prey to the tumultuous vultures of stern passion. And of such passion I could form no estimate, save by the miraculous expansion of those eyes which at once so delighted and appalled me,—by the almost magical melody, modulation, distinctness, and placidity of her very low voice,—and by the fierce energy (rendered doubly effective by contrast with her manner of utterance) of the wild words which she habitually uttered.

I have spoken of the learning of Ligeia: it was immense—such as I have never known in woman. In the classical tongues was she deeply proficient, and as far as my own acquaintance extended in regard to the modern dialects of Europe, I have never known her at fault. Indeed upon any theme of the most admired because simply the most abstruse of the boasted erudition of the Academy, have I *ever* found Ligeia at fault? How singularly—how thrillingly, this one point in the nature of my wife has forced itself, at this late period only, upon my attention! I said her knowledge was such as I have never known in woman—but where breathes the man who has traversed, and successfully, *all* the wide areas of moral, physical, and mathematical science? I saw not then what I now clearly perceive that the acquisitions of Ligeia were gigantic, were astounding; yet I was sufficiently aware of her infinite supremacy to resign myself, with a child-like confidence, to her guidance through the chaotic world of metaphysical investigation at which I was most busily occupied during the earlier years of our marriage. With how vast a triumph—with how vivid a delight—with how much of all that is ethereal in hope did I *feel*, as she bent over me in studies but little sought—but less known,—that delicious vista by slow degrees expanding before me, down whose long, gorgeous, and all untrodden path, I might at length pass onward to the goal of a wisdom too divinely precious not to be forbidden.

How poignant, then, must have been the grief with which, after some years, I beheld my well-grounded expectations take wings to themselves and fly away! Without Ligeia I was but as a child groping benighted. Her presence, her readings alone, rendered vividly luminous the many mysteries of the transcendentalism in which we were immersed. Wanting the radiant luster of her eyes, letters, lambent and golden, grew duller than Saturnian lead. And now those eyes shone less and less frequently upon the pages over which I pored. Ligeia grew ill. The wild eyes blazed with a too—too glorious effulgence; the pale fingers became of the transparent waxen hue of the grave; and the blue veins upon the lofty forehead swelled and sank impetuously with the tides of the most gentle emotion. I saw that she must die—and I struggled desperately in spirit with the grim Azrael. And the struggles of the passionate wife were, to my astonishment, even more energetic than my own. There had been much in her stern nature to impress me with the belief that, to her, death would have come without its terrors; but not so. Words are impotent to convey any just idea of the fierceness of resistance with which she wrestled with the Shadow. I groaned in anguish at the pitiable spectacle. I would have soothed—I would have reasoned; but in the intensity of her wild desire for life—for life—*but* for life—solace and reason were alike the uttermost of folly. Yet not until the last instance, amid the most convulsive writhings of her fierce spirit, was shaken the external placidity of her demeanor. Her voice grew more gentle—grew more low—yet I would not wish to dwell upon the wild meaning of the quietly uttered words. My brain reeled as I hearkened, entranced, to a melody more than mortal—to assumptions and aspirations which mortality had never before known.

That she loved me I should not have doubted; and I might have been easily aware that, in a bosom such as hers, love would have reigned no ordinary passion. But in death only was I fully impressed with the strength of her affection. For long hours, detaining my hand, would she pour out before me the overflowing of a heart whose more than passionate devotion amounted to idolatry. How had I deserved to be so blessed by such confessions?—how had I deserved to be so cursed with the removal of my beloved in the hour of my making them? But upon this subject I cannot bear to dilate. Let me say only, that in Ligeia's more than womanly abandonment to a love, alas! all unmerited, all unworthily bestowed, I at length, recognized the principle of her longing, with so wildly earnest a desire, for the life which was now fleeing so rapidly away. It is this wild longing—it is this eager vehemence of desire for life—*but* for life—that I have no power to portray—no utterance capable of expressing.

At high noon of the night in which she departed, beckoning me, peremptorily, to her side, she bade me repeat certain verses composed by herself not many days before. I obeyed her. They were these:—

> Lo! 'tis a gala night
> Within the lonesome latter years!
> An angel throng, bewinged, bedight
> In veils, and drowned in tears,
> Sit in a theatre, to see
> A play of hopes and fears,
> While the orchestra breathes fitfully
> The music of the spheres.
> Mimes, in the form of God on high,
> Mutter and mumble low,
> And hither and thither fly;
> Mere puppets they, who come and go
> At bidding of vast formless things
> That shift the scenery to and fro,
> Flapping from out their condor wings
> Invisible Wo!

That motley drama!—oh, be sure
It shall not be forgot!
With its Phantom chased for evermore
By a crowd that seize it not,
Through a circle that ever returneth in
To the self-same spot;
And much of Madness, and more of Sin
And Horror, the soul of the plot!
But see, amid the mimic rout,
A crawling shape intrude!
A blood-red thing that writhes from out
The scenic solitude!
It writhes!—it writhes!—with mortal pangs
The mimes become its food,
And the seraphs sob at vermin fangs
In human gore imbued.
Out—out are the lights—out all:
And over each quivering form,
The curtain, a funeral pall,
Comes down with the rush of a storm—
And the angels, all pallid and wan,
Uprising, unveiling, affirm
That the play is the tragedy, "Man,"
And its hero, the conqueror Worm.

"O God!" half shrieked Ligeia, leaping to her feet and extending
her arms aloft with a spasmodic movement, as I made an end of these
lines—"O God! O Divine Father!—shall these things be undeviatingly
so?—shall this conqueror be not once conquered? Are we not part and
parcel in Thee? Who—who knoweth the mysteries of the will with its
vigor? Man doth not yield him to the angels, *nor unto death utterly*, save
only through the weakness of his feeble will."

And now, as if exhausted with emotion, she suffered her white
arms to fall, and returned solemnly to her bed of death. And as she
breathed her last sighs, there came mingled with them a low murmur
from her lips. I bent to them my ear, and distinguished, again, the
concluding words of the passage in Glanvill: "*Man doth not yield him to the
angels, nor unto death utterly, save only through the weakness of his feeble will.*"

She died: and I, crushed into the very dust with sorrow, could no longer endure the lonely desolation of my dwelling in the dim and decaying city by the Rhine. I had no lack of what the world calls wealth. Ligeia had brought me far more, very far more, than ordinarily falls to the lot of mortals. After a few months, therefore, of weary and aimless wandering, I purchased and put in some repair, an abbey, which I shall not name, in one of the wildest and least frequented portions of fair England. The gloomy and dreary grandeur of the building, the almost savage aspect of the domain, the many melancholy and time-honored memories connected with both, had much in unison with the feelings of utter abandonment which had driven me into that remote and unsocial region of the country. Yet although the external abbey, with its verdant decay hanging about it, suffered but little alteration, I gave way, with a child-like perversity, and perchance with a faint hope of alleviating my sorrows, to a display of more than regal magnificence within. For such follies, even in childhood, I had imbibed a taste, and now they came back to me as if in the dotage of grief. Alas, I feel how much even of incipient madness might have been discovered in the gorgeous and fantastic draperies, in the solemn carvings of Egypt, in the wild cornices and furniture, in the Bedlam patterns of the carpets of tufted gold! I had become a bounden slave in the trammels of opium, and my labors and my orders had taken a coloring from my dreams. But these absurdities I must not pause to detail. Let me speak only of that one chamber, ever accursed, whither, in a moment of mental alienation, I led from the altar as my bride—as the successor of the unforgotten Ligeia—the fair-haired and blue-eyed Lady Rowena Trevanion, of Tremaine.

There is no individual portion of the architecture and decoration of that bridal chamber which is not visibly before me. Where were the souls of the haughty family of the bride, when, through thirst of gold, they permitted to pass the threshold of an apartment *so* bedecked, a maiden and a daughter so beloved? I have said, that I minutely remember the details of the chamber—yet I am sadly forgetful on topics of deep moment; and here there was no system, no keeping, in the fantastic display to take hold upon the memory. The room lay in a high turret of the castellated abbey, was pentagonal in shape, and of capacious size. Occupying the whole southern face of the pentagonal was the sole window—an immense sheet of unbroken glass from Venice—a single pane, and tinted of a leaden hue, so that the rays of either the sun or moon passing through it, fell with a ghastly luster on the objects within. Over the upper portion of this huge window extended the trellis-work of an aged vine, which clambered up the massy walls of the turret. The ceiling, of gloomy-looking oak, was excessively lofty, vaulted, and elaborately fretted with the wildest and most grotesque specimens of a semi-Gothic, semi-Druidical device. From out the most central recess of this melancholy vaulting, depended, by a single chain of gold with long links, a huge censer of the same metal, Saracenic in pattern, and with many perforations so contrived that there writhed in and out of them, as if endued with a serpent vitality, a continual succession of parti-colored fires.

Some few ottomans and golden candelabra, of Eastern figure, were in various stations about; and there was the couch, too—the bridal couch—of an Indian model, and low, and sculptured of solid ebony, with a pall-like canopy above. In each of the angles of the chamber stood on end a gigantic sarcophagus of black granite, from the tombs of the kings over against Luxor, with their aged lids full of immemorial sculpture. But in the draping of the apartment lay, alas! the chief phantasy of all. The lofty walls, gigantic in height— even unproportionably so—were hung from summit to foot, in vast folds, with a heavy and massive-looking tapestry—tapestry of a material which was found alike as a carpet on the floor, as a covering for the ottomans and the ebony bed, as a canopy for the bed, and as the gorgeous volutes of the curtains which partially shaded the window. The material was the richest cloth of gold. It was spotted all over, at irregular intervals, with arabesque figures, about a foot in diameter, and wrought upon the cloth in patterns of the most jetty black. But these figures partook of the true character of the arabesque only when regarded from a single point of view. By a contrivance now common, and indeed traceable to a very remote period of antiquity, they were made changeable in aspect. To one entering the room, they bore the appearance of simple monstrosities; but upon a farther advance, this appearance gradually departed; and, step by step, as the visitor moved his station in the chamber, he saw himself surrounded by an endless succession of the ghastly forms which belong to the superstition of the Norman, or arise in the guilty slumbers of the monk. The phantasmagoric effect was vastly heightened by the artificial introduction of a strong continual current of wind behind the draperies—giving a hideous and uneasy animation to the whole.

In halls such as these—in a bridal chamber such as this—I passed, with the Lady of Tremaine, the unhallowed hours of the first month of our marriage—passed them with but little disquietude. That my wife dreaded the fierce moodiness of my temper—that she shunned me, and loved me but little—I could not help perceiving; but it gave me rather pleasure than otherwise. I loathed her with a hatred belonging more to demon than to man. My memory flew back (oh, with what intensity of regret!) to Ligeia, the beloved, the august, the beautiful, the entombed. I reveled in recollections of her purity, of her wisdom, of her lofty—her ethereal nature, of her passionate, her idolatrous love. Now, then, did my spirit fully and freely burn with more than all the fires of her own. In the excitement of my opium dreams (for I was habitually fettered in the shackles of the drug), I would call aloud upon her name, during the silence of the night, or among the sheltered recesses of the glens by day, as if, through the wild eagerness, the solemn passion, the consuming ardor of my longing for the departed, I could restore her to the pathways she had abandoned—ah, *could* it be forever?—upon the earth.

About the commencement of the second month of the marriage, the Lady Rowena was attacked with sudden illness, from which her recovery was slow. The fever which consumed her rendered her nights uneasy; and in her perturbed state of half-slumber, she spoke of sounds, and of motions, in and about the chamber of the turret, which I concluded had no origin save in the distemper of her fancy, or perhaps in the phantasmagoric influences of the chamber itself. She became at length convalescent—finally, well. Yet but a second more violent disorder again threw her upon a bed of suffering; and from this attack her frame, at all times feeble, never altogether recovered. Her illnesses were, after this epoch, of alarming character, and of more alarming recurrence, defying alike the knowledge and the great exertions of her physicians. With the increase of the chronic disease, which had thus, apparently, taken too sure hold upon her constitution to be eradicated by human means, I could not fail to observe a similar increase in the nervous irritation of her temperament, and in her excitability by trivial causes of fear. She spoke again, and now more frequently and pertinaciously, of the sounds—of the slight sounds—and of the unusual motions among the tapestries, to which she had formerly alluded.

One night, near the closing in of September, she pressed this distressing subject with more than usual emphasis upon my attention. She had just awakened from an unquiet slumber, and I had been watching, with feelings half of anxiety, half of vague terror, the workings of her emaciated countenance. I sat by the side of her ebony bed, upon one of the ottomans of India. She partly arose, and spoke, in an earnest low whisper, of sounds which she *then* heard, but which I could not hear—of motions which she *then* saw, but which I could not perceive. The wind was rushing hurriedly behind the tapestries, and I wished to show her (what, let me confess it, I could not *all* believe) that those almost inarticulate breathings, and those very gentle variations of the figures upon the wall, were but the natural effects of that customary rushing of the wind. But a deadly pallor, overspreading her face, had proved to me that my exertions to reassure her would be fruitless. She appeared to be fainting, and no attendants were within call. I remembered where was deposited a decanter of light wine which had been ordered by her physicians, and hastened across the chamber to procure it. But, as I stepped beneath the light of the censer, two circumstances of a startling nature attracted my attention. I had felt that some palpable although invisible object had passed lightly by my person; and I saw that there lay upon the golden carpet, in the very middle of the rich luster thrown from the censer, a shadow—a faint, indefinite shadow of angelic aspect—such as might be fancied for the shadow of a shade. But I was wild with the excitement of an immoderate dose of opium, and heeded these things but little, nor spoke of them to Rowena. Having found the wine, I recrossed the chamber, and poured out a gobletful, which I held to the lips of the fainting lady. She had now partially recovered, however, and took the vessel herself, while I sank upon an ottoman near me, with my eyes fastened upon her person. It was then that I became distinctly aware of a gentle footfall upon the carpet, and near the couch; and in a second thereafter, as Rowena was in the act of raising the wine to her lips, I saw, or may have dreamed that I saw, fall within the goblet, as if from some invisible spring in the atmosphere of the room, three or four large drops of a brilliant and ruby colored fluid. If this I saw—not so Rowena. She swallowed the wine unhesitatingly, and I forebore to speak to her of a circumstance which must, after all, I considered, have been but the suggestion of a vivid imagination, rendered mor-bidly active by the terror of the lady, by the opium, and by the hour.

Yet I cannot conceal it from my own perception that, immediately subsequent to the fall of the ruby drops, a rapid change for the worse took place in the disorder of my wife; so that, on the third subsequent night, the hands of her menials prepared her for the tomb, and on the fourth, I sat alone, with her shrouded body, in that fantastic chamber which had received her as my bride. Wild visions, opium-engendered, flitted, shadow-like, before me. I gazed with unquiet eye upon the sarcophagi in the angles of the room, upon the varying figures of the drapery, and upon the writhing of the parti-colored fires in the censer overhead. My eyes then fell, as I called to mind the circum-stances of a former night, to the spot beneath the glare of the censer where I had seen the faint traces of the shadow. It was there, however, no longer; and breathing with greater freedom, I turned my glances to the pallid and rigid figure upon the bed. Then rushed upon me a thousand memories of Ligeia—and then came back upon my heart,

with the turbulent violence of a flood, the whole of that unutterable woe with which I had regarded *her* thus enshrouded. The night
waned; and still, with a bosom full of bitter thoughts of the one only
and supremely beloved, I remained gazing upon the body of Rowena.

It might have been midnight, or perhaps earlier, or later, for
I had taken no note of time, when a sob, low, gentle, but very distinct, startled me from my reverie. I *felt* that it came from the bed
of ebony—the bed of death. I listened in an agony of superstitious
terror—but there was no repetition of the sound. I strained my vision
to detect any motion in the corpse—but there was not the slightest
perceptible. Yet I could not have been deceived. I *had* heard the noise,
however faint, and my soul was awakened within me. I resolutely
and perseveringly kept my attention riveted upon the body. Many
minutes elapsed before any circumstance occurred tending to throw
light upon the mystery. At length it became evident that a slight,
a very feeble, and barely noticeable tinge of color had flushed up
within the cheeks, and along the sunken small veins of the eyelids.
Through a species of unutterable horror and awe, for which the
language of mortality has no sufficiently energetic expression, I felt
my heart cease to beat, my limbs grow rigid where I sat. Yet a sense
of duty finally operated to restore my self-possession. I could no
longer doubt that we had been precipitate in our preparations—that
Rowena still lived. It was necessary that some immediate exertion
be made; yet the turret was altogether apart from the portion of the
abbey tenanted by the servants—there were none within call—I had
no means of summoning them to my aid without leaving the room
for many minutes—and this I could not venture to do. I therefore
struggled alone in my endeavors to call back the spirit still hovering.
In a short period it was certain, however, that a relapse had taken
place; the color disappeared from both eyelid and cheek, leaving
a wanness even more than that of marble; the lips became doubly
shriveled and pinched up in the ghastly expression of death; a repul-
sive clamminess and coldness overspread rapidly the surface of the
body; and all the usual rigorous stiffness immediately supervened.

I fell back with a shudder upon the couch from which I had been so startlingly aroused, and again gave myself up to passionate waking visions of Ligeia.

An hour thus elapsed, when (could it be possible?) I was a second time aware of some vague sound issuing from the region of the bed. I listened—in extremity of horror. The sound came again—it was a sigh. Rushing to the corpse, I saw—distinctly saw—a tremor upon the lips. In a minute afterward they relaxed, disclosing a bright line of the pearly teeth. Amazement now struggled in my bosom with the profound awe which had hitherto reigned there alone. I felt that my vision grew dim, that my reason wandered; and it was only by a violent effort that I at length succeeded in nerving myself to the task which duty thus once more had pointed out. There was now a partial glow upon the forehead and upon the cheek and throat; a perceptible warmth pervaded the whole frame; there was even a slight pulsation at the heart. The lady *lived*; and with redoubled ardor I betook myself to the task of restoration. I chafed and bathed the temples and the hands and used every exertion which experience, and no little medical reading, could suggest. But in vain. Suddenly, the color fled, the pulsation ceased, the lips resumed the expression of the dead, and, in an instant afterward, the whole body took upon itself the icy chilliness, the livid hue, the intense rigidity, the sunken outline, and all the loathsome peculiarities of that which has been, for many days, a tenant of the tomb.

And again I sunk into visions of Ligeia—and again (what marvel that I shudder while I write?), *again* there reached my ears a low sob from the region of the ebony bed. But why shall I minutely detail the unspeakable horrors of that night? Why shall I pause to relate how, time after time, until near the period of the gray dawn, this hideous drama of revivification was repeated; how each terrific relapse was only into a sterner and apparently more irredeemable death; how each agony wore the aspect of a struggle with some invisible foe; and how each struggle was succeeded by I know not what of wild change in the personal appearance of the corpse? Let me hurry to a conclusion.

The greater part of the fearful night had worn away, and she who had been dead once again stirred—and now more vigorously than hitherto, although arousing from a dissolution more appalling in its utter hopelessness than any. I had long ceased to struggle or to move, and remained sitting rigidly upon the ottoman, a helpless prey to a whirl of violent emotions, of which extreme awe was perhaps the least terrible, the least consuming. The corpse, I repeat, stirred, and now more vigorously than before. The hues of life flushed up with unwonted energy into the countenance—the limbs relaxed—and, save that the eyelids were yet pressed heavily together, and that the bandages and draperies of the grave still imparted their charnel character to the figure, I might have dreamed that Rowena had indeed shaken off, utterly, the fetters of Death. But if this idea was not, even then, altogether adopted, I could at least doubt no longer, when, arising from the bed, tottering, with feeble steps, with closed eyes, and with the manner of one bewildered in a dream, the thing that was enshrouded advanced boldly and palpably into the middle of the apartment.

I trembled not—I stirred not—for a crowd of unutterable fancies connected with the air, the stature, the demeanor, of the figure, rushing hurriedly through my brain, had paralyzed—had chilled me into stone. I stirred not—but gazed upon the apparition. There was a mad disorder in my thoughts—a tumult unappeasable. Could it, indeed, be the *living* Rowena who confronted me? Could it, indeed, be Rowena *at all*—the fair-haired, the blue-eyed Lady Rowena Trevanion of Tremaine? Why, *why* should I doubt it? The bandage lay heavily about the mouth—but then might it not be the mouth of the breathing Lady of Tremaine? And the cheeks—there were the roses as in her noon of life—yes, these might indeed be the fair cheeks of the living Lady of Tremaine. And the chin, with its dimples, as in health, might it not be hers?—but *had she then grown taller since her malady?* What inexpressible madness seized me with that thought? One bound, and I had reached her feet! Shrinking from my touch, she let fall from her head, unloosened, the ghastly cerements which had confined it, and there streamed forth into the rushing atmosphere of the chamber huge masses of long and disheveled hair; *it was blacker than the raven wings of midnight.* And now slowly opened *the eyes* of the figure which stood before me. "Here then, at least," I shrieked aloud, "can I never—can I never be mistaken—these are the full, and the black, and the wild eyes—of my lost love—of the Lady—of the LADY LIGEIA."

AT THE HOME OF POE

by Frank Belknap Long, Jr.

In his seventy-plus years of writing, Frank Belknap Long (1901-1994) garnered more than his share of awards, foremost of which being the World Fantasy Award for Life Achievement (1978), the Horror Writers Association's Bram Stoker Award for Lifetime Achievement (1987), and the First Fandom Hall of Fame Award (1977). His prodigious output of works included comic books, non-fiction, fantasy, science fiction, gothic romance, horror, and fantasy.

At the Home of Poe

A Poem in Prose

To H. P. Lovecraft

The home of Poe! It is like a fairy dwelling, a gnomic palace built of the aether of dreams. It is tiny and delicate and lovely, and replete with memories of sere leaves in November and of lilies in April. It is a castle of vanished hopes, of dimly-remembered dreams, of sad memories older than the deluge. The dead years circle slowly and solemnly around its low white walls, and clothe it in a mystic veil of unseen tears. And many marvellous stories could this quaint little old house tell, many weird and cryptic stories of him of the Raven hair, and high, pallid brow, and sad, sweet face, and melancholy mien; and of the beloved Virginia, that sweet child of a thousand magic visions, child of the lonesome, pale-gray latter years, child of the soft and happy South. And how the dreamer of the spheres must have loved this strange little house. Every night the hollow boards of its porch must have echoed to his footfall, and every morn the great rising sun must have sent its rays through the little window, and bathed the lovely tresses of the dream-child in mystical yellow. And perhaps there was laughter within the walls of that house—laughter and merriment and singing. But we know that the Evil One came at last, the grim humourless spectre who loves not beauty, and is not of this world. And we know that the house of youth and of love became a house of death, and that memories bitter as the tears of a beautiful woman assailed the dreamer within. And at last he himself left that house of mourning and sought solace among the stars. But the house remains a vision out of a magical book; a thing seen darkly as in a looking-glass; but lovely beyond the dreams of mortals, and ineffably sad.

THE ALCHEMIST

by H.P. Lovecraft

The undisputed father of modern horror, the shy and reclusive Howard Phillips Lovecraft (1890-1937) received little exposure or acclaim during his lifetime, but his immortality has been mightily thrust upon him posthumously. He is without question one of the most influential writers of the twentieth century. In Lovecraft the genre of horror reached a zenith that in many respects has yet to be seriously surpassed. Mental illness seemed to run in the family at the Lovecraft home, a factor that played (at least in some measure) a role in his fears and obsessions. For many of us horror would not be nearly so horrifying without the terrifying madness of H.P. Lovecraft.

This story was written in his early career, when he was the tender age of sixteen or seventeen.

The Alchemist

High up, crowning the grassy summit of a swelling mound whose sides are wooded near the base with the gnarled trees of the primeval forest, stands the old chateau of my ancestors. For centuries its lofty battlements have frowned down upon the wild and rugged country-side about, serving as a home and stronghold for the proud house whose honoured line is older even than the moss-grown castle walls. These ancient turrets, stained by the storms of generations and crumbling under the slow yet mighty pressure of time, formed in the ages of feudalism one of the most dreaded and formidable fortresses in all France. From its machicolated parapets and mounted battlements Barons, Counts, and even Kings had been defied, yet never had its spacious halls resounded to the footstep of the invader.

But since those glorious years all is changed. A poverty but little above the level of dire want, together with a pride of name that forbids its alleviation by the pursuits of commercial life, have prevented the scions of our line from maintaining their estates in pristine splendour; and the falling stones of the walls, the overgrown vegetation in the parks, the dry and dusty moat, the ill-paved courtyards, and toppling towers without, as well as the sagging floors, the worm-eaten wainscots, and the faded tapestries within, all tell a gloomy tale of fallen grandeur. As the ages passed, first one, then another of the four great turrets were left to ruin, until at last but a single tower housed the sadly reduced descendants of the once mighty lords of the estate.

It was in one of the vast and gloomy chambers of this remaining tower that I, Antoine, last of the unhappy and accursed Comtes de C—, first saw the light of day, ninety long years ago. Within these walls, and amongst the dark and shadowy forests, the wild ravines and grottoes of the hillside below, were spent the first years of my troubled life. My parents I never knew. My father had been killed at the age of thirty-two, a month before I was born, by the fall of a stone somehow dislodged from one of the deserted parapets of the castle, and my mother having died at my birth, my care and education devolved solely upon one remaining servitor, an old and trusted man of considerable intelligence, whose name I remember as Pierre. I was an only child, and the lack of companionship which this fact entailed upon me was augmented by the strange care exercised by my aged guardian in excluding me from the society of the peasant children whose abodes were scattered here and there upon the plains that surround the base of the hill. At the time, Pierre said that this restriction was imposed upon me because my noble birth placed me above association with such plebeian company. Now I know that its real object was to keep from my ears the idle tales of the dread curse upon our line, that were nightly told and magnified by the simple tenantry as they conversed in hushed accents in the glow of their cottage hearths.

Thus isolated, and thrown upon my own resources, I spent the hours of my childhood in poring over the ancient tomes that filled the shadow-haunted library of the chateau, and in roaming without aim or purpose through the perpetual dusk of the spectral wood that clothes the sides of the hill near its foot. It was perhaps an effect of such surroundings that my mind early acquired a shade of melancholy. Those studies and pursuits which partake of the dark and occult in nature most strongly claimed my attention.

Of my own race I was permitted to learn singularly little, yet what small knowledge of it I was able to gain, seemed to depress me much. Perhaps it was at first only the manifest reluctance of my old preceptor to discuss with me my paternal ancestry that gave rise to the terror which I ever felt at the mention of my great house, yet as I grew out of childhood, I was able to piece together disconnected fragments of discourse, let slip from the unwilling tongue which had begun to falter in approaching senility, that had a sort of relation to a certain circumstance which I had always deemed strange, but which now became dimly terrible. The circumstance to which I allude is the early age at which all the Comtes of my line had met their end. Whilst I had hitherto considered this but a natural attribute of a family of short-lived men, I afterward pondered long upon these premature deaths, and began to connect them with the wanderings of the old man, who often spoke of a curse which for centuries had prevented the lives of the holders of my title from much exceeding the span of thirty-two years. Upon my twenty-first birthday, the aged Pierre gave to me a family document which he said had for many generations been handed down from father to son, and continued by each possessor. Its contents were of the most startling nature, and its perusal confirmed the gravest of my apprehensions. At this time, my belief in the supernatural was firm and deep-seated, else I should have dismissed with scorn the incredible narrative unfolded before my eyes.

The paper carried me back to the days of the thirteenth century, when the old castle in which I sat had been a feared and impregnable fortress. It told of a certain ancient man who had once dwelt on our estates, a person of no small accomplishments, though little above the rank of peasant; by name, Michel, usually designated by the surname of Mauvais, the Evil, on account of his sinister reputation. He had studied beyond the custom of his kind, seeking such things as the Philosopher's Stone, or the Elixir of Eternal Life, and was reputed wise in the terrible secrets of Black Magic and Alchemy. Michel Mauvais had one son, named Charles, a youth as proficient as himself in the hidden arts, and who had therefore been called Le Sorcier, or the Wizard. This pair, shunned by all honest folk, were suspected of the most hideous practices. Old Michel was said to have burnt his wife alive as a sacrifice to the Devil, and the unaccountable disappearances of many small peasant children were laid at the dreaded door of these two. Yet through the dark natures of the father and the son ran one redeeming ray of humanity; the evil old man loved his offspring with fierce intensity, whilst the youth had for his parent a more than filial affection.

One night the castle on the hill was thrown into the wildest confusion by the vanishment of young Godfrey, son to Henri, the Comte. A searching party, headed by the frantic father, invaded the cottage of the sorcerers and there came upon old Michel Mauvais, busy over a huge and violently boiling cauldron. Without certain cause, in the ungoverned madness of fury and despair, the Comte laid hands on the aged wizard, and ere he released his murderous hold his victim was no more. Meanwhile joyful servants were proclaiming aloud the finding of young Godfrey in a distant and unused chamber of the great edifice, telling too late that poor Michel had been killed in vain. As the Comte and his associates turned away from the lowly abode of the alchemists, the form of Charles Le Sorcier appeared through the trees. The excited chatter of the menials standing about told him what had occurred, yet he seemed at first unmoved at his father's fate. Then, slowly advancing to meet the Comte, he pronounced in dull yet terrible accents the curse that ever afterward haunted the house of C—.

"May ne'er a noble of thy murd'rous line Survive to reach a greater age than thine!" spake he, when, suddenly leaping backwards into the black wood, he drew from his tunic a phial of colourless liquid which he threw in the face of his father's slayer as he disappeared behind the inky curtain of the night. The Comte died without utterance, and was buried the next day, but little more than two and thirty years from the hour of his birth. No trace of the assassin could be found, though relentless bands of peasants scoured the neighboring woods and the meadow-land around the hill.

Thus time and the want of a reminder dulled the memory of the curse in the minds of the late Comte's family, so that when Godfrey, innocent cause of the whole tragedy and now bearing the title, was killed by an arrow whilst hunting, at the age of thirty-two, there were no thoughts save those of grief at his demise. But when, years afterward, the next young Comte, Robert by name, was found dead in a nearby field from no apparent cause, the peasants told in whispers that their seigneur had but lately passed his thirty-second birthday when surprised by early death. Louis, son to Robert, was found drowned in the moat at the same fateful age, and thus down through the centuries ran the ominous chronicle; Henris, Roberts, Antoines, and Armands snatched from happy and virtuous lives when a little below the age of their unfortunate ancestor at his murder.

That I had left at most but eleven years of further existence was made certain to me by the words which I read. My life, previously held at small value, now became dearer to me each day, as I delved deeper and deeper into the mysteries of the hidden world of black magic. Isolated as I was, modern science had produced no impression upon me, and I laboured as in the Middle Ages, as wrapt as had been old Michel and young Charles themselves in the acquisition of demonological and alchemical learning. Yet read as I might, in no manner could I account for the strange curse upon my line. In unusually rational moments, I would even go so far as to seek a natural explanation, attributing the early deaths of my ancestors to the sinister Charles Le Sorcier and his heirs; yet having found upon careful inquiry that there were no known descendants of the alchemist, I would fall back to my occult studies, and once more endeavour to find a spell that would release my house from its terrible burden. Upon one thing I was absolutely resolved. I should never wed, for since no other branches of my family were in existence, I might thus end the curse with myself.

As I drew near the age of thirty, old Pierre was called to the land beyond. Alone I buried him beneath the stones of the courtyard about which he had loved to wander in life. Thus was I left to ponder on myself as the only human creature within the great fortress, and in my utter solitude my mind began to cease its vain protest against the impending doom, to become almost reconciled to the fate which so many of my ancestors had met. Much of my time was now occupied in the exploration of the ruined and abandoned halls and towers of the old chateau, which in youth fear had caused me to shun, and some of which old Pierre had once told me had not been trodden by human foot for over four centuries. Strange and awsome were many of the objects I encountered. Furniture, covered by the dust of ages and crumbling with the rot of long dampness met my eyes. Cobwebs in a profusion never before seen by me were spun everywhere, and huge bats flapped their bony and uncanny wings on all sides of the other-wise untenanted gloom.

Of my exact age, even down to days and hours, I kept a most care-ful record, for each movement of the pendulum of the massive clock in the library tolled off so much more of my doomed existence. At length I approached that time which I had so long viewed with appre-hension. Since most of my ancestors had been seized some little while before they reached the exact age of the Comte Henri at his end, I was every moment on the watch for the coming of the unknown death. In what strange form the curse should overtake me, I knew not; but I was resolved at least that it should not find me a cowardly or a passive victim. With new vigour I applied myself to my examination of the old chateau and its contents.

It was upon one of the longest of all my excursions of discovery in the deserted portion of the castle, less than a week before that fatal hour which I felt must mark the utmost limit of my stay on earth, beyond which I could have not even the slightest hope of continuing to draw breath, that I came upon the culminating event of my whole life. I had spent the better part of the morning in climbing up and down half ruined staircases in one of the most dilapidated of the ancient turrets. As the afternoon progressed, I sought the lower levels, descending into what appeared to be either a mediaeval place of confinement, or a more recently excavated storehouse for gunpowder. As I slowly traversed the nitre-encrusted passageway at the foot of the last staircase, the paving became very damp, and soon I saw by the light of my flickering torch that a blank, water-stained wall impeded my journey. Turning to retrace my steps, my eye fell upon a small trap-door with a ring, which lay directly beneath my feet. Pausing, I succeeded with difficulty in raising it, whereupon there was revealed a black aperture, exhaling noxious fumes which caused my torch to sputter, and disclosing in the unsteady glare the top of a flight of stone steps. As soon as the torch, which I lowered into the repellent depths, burned freely and steadily, I commenced my descent. The steps were many, and led to a narrow stone-flagged passage which I knew must be far underground. This passage proved of great length, and terminated in a massive oaken door, dripping with the moisture of the place, and stoutly resisting all my attempts to open it. Ceasing after a time my efforts in this direction, I had proceeded back some distance toward the steps, when there suddenly fell to my experience one of the most profound and maddening shocks capable of reception by the human mind. Without warning, I heard the heavy door behind me creak slowly open upon its rusted hinges. My immediate sensations are incapable of analysis. To be confronted in a place as thoroughly deserted as I had deemed the old castle with evidence of the presence of man or spirit, produced in my brain a horror of the most acute description. When at last I turned and faced the seat of the sound, my eyes must have started from their orbits at the sight that they beheld. There in the ancient Gothic doorway stood a human figure. It was that of a man clad in a skull-cap and long mediaeval tunic of dark colour. His long hair and flowing beard were of a terrible and intense black hue, and of incredible profusion.

His forehead, high beyond the usual dimensions; his cheeks, deep sunken and heavily lined with wrinkles; and his hands, long, claw-like and gnarled, were of such a deathly, marble-like whiteness as I have never elsewhere seen in man. His figure, lean to the proportions of a skeleton, was strangely bent and almost lost within the voluminous folds of his peculiar garment. But strangest of all were his eyes; twin caves of abysmal blackness; profound in expression of understanding, yet inhuman in degree of wickedness. These were now fixed upon me, piercing my soul with their hatred, and rooting me to the spot whereon I stood. At last the figure spoke in a rumbling voice that chilled me through with its dull hollowness and latent malevolence. The language in which the discourse was clothed was that debased form of Latin in use amongst the more learned men of the Middle Ages, and made familiar to me by my prolonged researches into the works of the old alchemists and demonologists. The apparition spoke of the curse which had hovered over my house, told me of my coming end, dwelt on the wrong perpetrated by my ancestor against old Michel Mauvais, and gloated over the revenge of Charles Le Sorcier. He told me how the young Charles had escaped into the night, returning in after years to kill Godfrey the heir with an arrow just as he approached the age which had been his father's at his assassination; how he had secretly returned to the estate and established himself, unknown, in the even then deserted subterranean chamber whose doorway now framed the hideous narrator; how he had seized Robert, son of Godfrey, in a field, forced poison down his throat and left him to die at the age of thirty-two, thus maintaining the foul provisions of his vengeful curse. At this point I was left to imagine the solution of the greatest mystery of all, how the curse had been fulfilled since that time when Charles Le Sorcier must in the course of nature have died, for the man digressed into an account of the deep alchemical studies of the two wizards, father and son, speaking most particularly of the researches of Charles Le Sorcier concerning the elixir which should grant to him who partook of it eternal life and youth.

His enthusiasm had seemed for the moment to remove from his terrible eyes the hatred that had at first so haunted them, but suddenly the fiendish glare returned, and with a shocking sound like the hissing of a serpent, the stranger raised a glass phial with the evident intent of ending my life as had Charles Le Sorcier, six hundred years before, ended that of my ancestor. Prompted by some preserving instinct of self-defense, I broke through the spell that had hitherto held me immovable, and flung my now dying torch at the creature who menaced my existence. I heard the phial break harmlessly against the stones of the passage as the tunic of the strange man caught fire and lit the horrid scene with a ghastly radiance. The shriek of fright and impotent malice emitted by the would-be assassin proved too much for my already shaken nerves, and I fell prone upon the slimy floor in a total faint.

When at last my senses returned, all was frightfully dark, and my mind remembering what had occurred, shrank from the idea of beholding more; yet curiosity overmastered all. Who, I asked myself, was this man of evil, and how came he within the castle walls? Why should he seek to avenge the death of poor Michel Mauvais, and how had the curse been carried on through all the long centuries since the time of Charles Le Sorcier? The dread of years was lifted off my shoulders, for I knew that he whom I had felled was the source of all my danger from the curse; and now that I was free, I burned with the desire to learn more of the sinister thing which had haunted my line for centuries, and made of my own youth one long-continued nightmare. Determined upon further exploration, I felt in my pockets for flint and steel, and lit the unused torch which I had with me. First of all, the new light revealed the distorted and blackened form of the mysterious stranger. The hideous eyes were now closed. Disliking the sight, I turned away and entered the chamber beyond the Gothic door. Here I found what seemed much like an alchemist's laboratory. In one corner was an immense pile of a shining yellow metal that sparkled gorgeously in the light of the torch. It may have been gold, but I did not pause to examine it, for I was strangely affected by that which I had undergone. At the farther end of the apartment was an opening leading out into one of the many wild ravines of the dark hillside forest. Filled with wonder, yet now realizing how the man had obtained access to the chateau, I proceeded to return. I had intended to pass by the remains of the stranger with averted face, but as I approached the body, I seemed to hear emanating from it a faint sound, as though life were not yet wholly extinct. Aghast, I turned to examine the charred and shrivelled figure on the floor.

Then all at once the horrible eyes, blacker even than the seared face in which they were set, opened wide with an expression which I was unable to interpret. The cracked lips tried to frame words which I could not well understand. Once I caught the name of Charles Le Sorcier, and again I fancied that the words "years" and "curse" issued from the twisted mouth. Still I was at a loss to gather the purport of his disconnected speech. At my evident ignorance of his meaning, the pitchy eyes once more flashed malevolently at me, until, helpless as I saw my opponent to be, I trembled as I watched him.

Suddenly the wretch, animated with his last burst of strength, raised his hideous head from the damp and sunken pavement. Then, as I remained, paralyzed with fear, he found his voice and in his dying breath screamed forth those words which have ever afterward haunted my days and my nights. "Fool," he shrieked, "can you not guess my secret? Have you no brain whereby you may recognize the will which has through six long centuries fulfilled the dreadful curse upon your house? Have I not told you of the great elixir of eternal life? Know you not how the secret of Alchemy was solved? I tell you, it is I! I! I! that have lived for six hundred years to maintain my revenge, FOR I AM CHARLES LE SORCIER!"

DICKON THE DEVIL

by Joseph Sheridan Le Fanu

Grandson of Irish playwright Alicia Sheridan LeFanu and grand-nephew of the equally celebrated playwright Richard Brinsley Sheridan, Joseph Le Fanu (1814-1873) carved out (in his lifetime) his own immortal place as a founding father of horror (although he would have probably preferred we use the term "Dark Romanticism.") His specialty: the ghost story. A singular characteristic of a La Fanu tale obliges the reader to speculate that there are hidden supernatural forces at work even if it is likely there is a reasonable and rational explanation to the mystery. "Dickon the Devil" is a jewel-box sampling of La Fanu's lush and descriptive style.

Dickon the Devil

About thirty years ago I was selected by two rich old maids to visit a property in that part of Lancashire which lies near the famous forest of Pendle, with which Mr. Ainsworth's "Lancashire Witches" has made us so pleasantly familiar. My business was to make partition of a small property, including a house and demesne to which they had, a long time before, succeeded as coheiresses.

The last forty miles of my journey I was obliged to post, chiefly by cross-roads, little known, and less frequented, and presenting scenery often extremely interesting and pretty. The picturesqueness of the landscape was enhanced by the season, the beginning of September, at which I was travelling.

I had never been in this part of the world before; I am told it is now a great deal less wild, and, consequently, less beautiful.

At the inn where I had stopped for a relay of horses and some dinner—for it was then past five o'clock—I found the host, a hale old fellow of five-and-sixty, as he told me, a man of easy and garrulous benevolence, willing to accommodate his guests with any amount of talk, which the slightest tap sufficed to set flowing, on any subject you pleased.

I was curious to learn something about Barwyke, which was the name of the demesne and house I was going to. As there was no inn within some miles of it, I had written to the steward to put me up there, the best way he could, for a night.

The host of the "Three Nuns," which was the sign under which he entertained wayfarers, had not a great deal to tell. It was twenty years, or more, since old Squire Bowes died, and no one had lived in the Hall ever since, except the gardener and his wife.

"Tom Wyndsour will be as old a man as myself; but he's a bit taller, and not so much in flesh, quite," said the fat innkeeper.

"But there were stories about the house," I repeated, "that, they said, prevented tenants from coming into it?"

"Old wives' tales; many years ago, that will be, sir; I forget 'em; I forget 'em all. Oh yes, there always will be, when a house is left so; foolish folk will always be talkin'; but I han't heard a word about it this twenty year."

It was vain trying to pump him; the old landlord of the "Three Nuns," for some reason, did not choose to tell tales of Barwyke Hall, if he really did, as I suspected, remember them.

I paid my reckoning, and resumed my journey, well pleased with the good cheer of that old-world inn, but a little disappointed.

We had been driving for more than an hour, when we began to cross a wild common; and I knew that, this passed, a quarter of an hour would bring me to the door of Barwyke Hall.

The peat and furze were pretty soon left behind; we were again in the wooded scenery that I enjoyed so much, so entirely natural and pretty, and so little disturbed by traffic of any kind. I was looking from the chaise-window, and soon detected the object of which, for some time, my eye had been in search. Barwyke Hall was a large, quaint house, of that cage-work fashion known as "black-and-white," in which the bars and angles of an oak framework contrast, black as ebony, with the white plaster that overspreads the masonry built into its interstices. This steep-roofed Elizabethan house stood in the midst of park-like grounds of no great extent, but rendered imposing by the noble stature of the old trees that now cast their lengthening shadows eastward over the sward, from the declining sun.

The park-wall was gray with age, and in many places laden with ivy. In deep gray shadow, that contrasted with the dim fires of evening reflected on the foliage above it, in a gentle hollow, stretched a lake that looked cold and black, and seemed, as it were, to skulk from observation with a guilty knowledge.

I had forgot that there was a lake at Barwyke; but the moment this caught my eye, like the cold polish of a snake in the shadow, my instinct seemed to recognize something dangerous, and I knew that the lake was connected, I could not remember how, with the story I had heard of this place in my boyhood.

I drove up a grass-grown avenue, under the boughs of these noble trees, whose foliage, dyed in autumnal red and yellow, returned the beams of the western sun gorgeously.

We drew up at the door. I got out, and had a good look at the front of the house; it was a large and melancholy mansion, with signs of long neglect upon it; great wooden shutters, in the old fashion, were barred, outside, across the windows; grass, and even nettles, were growing thick on the courtyard, and a thin moss streaked the timber beams; the plaster was discolored by time and weather, and bore great russet and yellow stains. The gloom was increased by several grand old trees that crowded close about the house.

I mounted the steps, and looked round; the dark lake lay near me now, a little to the left. It was not large; it may have covered some ten or twelve acres; but it added to the melancholy of the scene. Near the centre of it was a small island, with two old ash-trees, leaning toward each other, their pensive images reflected in the stirless water. The only cheery influence of this scene of antiquity, solitude, and neglect was that the house and landscape were warmed with the ruddy western beams. I knocked, and my summons resounded hollow and ungenial in my ear; and the bell, from far away, returned a deep-mouthed and surly ring, as if it resented being roused from a score years' slumber.

A light-limbed, jolly-looking old fellow, in a barracan jacket and gaiters, with a smirk of welcome, and a very sharp, red nose, that seemed to promise good cheer, opened the door with a promptitude that indicated a hospitable expectation of my arrival.

There was but little light in the hall, and that little lost itself in darkness in the background. It was very spacious and lofty, with a gallery running round it, which, when the door was open, was visible at two or three points. Almost in the dark my new acquaintance led me across this wide hall into the room destined for my reception. It was spacious, and wainscoted up to the ceiling. The furniture of this capacious chamber was old-fashioned and clumsy. There were curtains still to the windows, and a piece of Turkey carpet lay upon the floor; those windows were two in number, looking out, through the trunks of the trees close to the house, upon the lake. It needed all the fire, and all the pleasant associations of my entertainer's red nose, to light up this melancholy chamber. A door at its farther end admitted to the room that was prepared for my sleeping apartment. It was wainscoted, like the other. It had a four-post bed, with heavy tapestry curtains, and in other respects was furnished in the same old-world and ponderous style as the other room. Its window, like those of that apartment, looked out upon the lake.

Sombre and sad as these rooms were, they were yet scrupulously clean. I had nothing to complain of; but the effect was rather dispiriting. Having given some directions about supper—a pleasant incident to look forward to—and made a rapid toilet, I called on my friend with the gaiters and red nose (Tom Wyndsour), whose occupation was that of a "bailiff," or under-steward, of the property, to accompany me, as we had still an hour or so of sun and twilight, in a walk over the grounds.

It was a sweet autumn evening, and my guide, a hardy old fellow, strode at a pace that tasked me to keep up with.

Among clumps of trees at the northern boundary of the demesne we lighted upon the little antique parish church. I was looking down upon it, from an eminence, and the park-wall interposed; but a little way down was a stile affording access to the road, and by this we approached the iron gate of the churchyard. I saw the church door open; the sexton was replacing his pick, shovel, and spade, with which he had just been digging a grave in the churchyard, in their little repository under the stone stair of the tower. He was a polite, shrewd little hunchback, who was very happy to show me over the church. Among the monuments was one that interested me; it was erected to commemorate the very Squire Bowes from whom my two old maids had inherited the house and estate of Barwyke. It spoke of him in terms of grandiloquent eulogy, and informed the Christian reader that he had died, in the bosom of the Church of England, at the age of seventy-one.

I read this inscription by the parting beams of the setting sun, which disappeared behind the horizon just as we passed out from under the porch.

"Twenty years since the Squire died," said I, reflecting, as I loitered still in the churchyard.

"Ay, sir; 'twill be twenty year the ninth o' last month."

"And a very good old gentleman?"

"Good-natured enough, and an easy gentleman he was, sir; I don't think while he lived he ever hurt a fly," acquiesced Tom Wyndsour. "It ain't always easy sayin' what's in 'em, though, and what they may take or turn to afterward; and some o' them sort, I think, goes mad."

"You don't think he was out of his mind?" I asked.

"He? La! no; not he, sir; a bit lazy, mayhap, like other old fellows; but a knew devilish well what he was about."

Tom Wyndsour's account was a little enigmatical; but, like old Squire Bowes, I was "a bit lazy" that evening, and asked no more questions about him.

We got over the stile upon the narrow road that skirts the churchyard. It is overhung by elms more than a hundred years old, and in the twilight, which now prevailed, was growing very dark. As side-by-side we walked along this road, hemmed in by two loose stone-like walls, something running toward us in a zig-zag line passed us at a wild pace, with a sound like a frightened laugh or a shudder, and I saw, as it passed, that it was a human figure. I may confess, now, that I was a little startled. The dress of this figure was, in part, white: I know I mistook it at first for a white horse coming down the road at a gallop. Tom Wyndsour turned about and looked after the retreating figure.

"He'll be on his travels to-night," he said, in a low tone. "Easy served with a bed, *that* lad be; six foot o' dry peat or heath, or a nook in a dry ditch. That lad hasn't slept once in a house this twenty year, and never will while grass grows."

"Is he mad?" I asked.

"Something that way, sir; he's an idiot, an awpy; we call him 'Dickon the devil,' because the devil's almost the only word that's ever in his mouth."

It struck me that this idiot was in some way connected with the story of old Squire Bowes.

"Queer things are told of him, I dare say?" I suggested.

"More or less, sir; more or less. Queer stories, some."

"Twenty years since he slept in a house? That's about the time the Squire died," I continued.

"So it will be, sir; not very long after."

"You must tell me all about that, Tom, to-night, when I can hear it comfortably, after supper."

Tom did not seem to like my invitation; and looking straight before him as we trudged on, he said:

"You see, sir, the house has been quiet, and nout's been troubling folk inside the walls or out, all round the woods of Barwyke, this ten year, or more; and my old woman, down there, is clear against talking about such matters, and thinks it best—and so do I—to let sleepin' dogs be."

He dropped his voice toward the close of the sentence, and nodded significantly.

We soon reached a point where he unlocked a wicket in the park wall, by which we entered the grounds of Barwyke once more.

The twilight deepening over the landscape, the huge and solemn trees, and the distant outline of the haunted house, exercised a sombre influence on me, which, together with the fatigue of a day of travel, and the brisk walk we had had, disinclined me to interrupt the silence in which my companion now indulged.

A certain air of comparative comfort, on our arrival, in great measure dissipated the gloom that was stealing over me. Although it was by no means a cold night, I was very glad to see some wood blazing in the grate; and a pair of candles aiding the light of the fire, made the room look cheerful. A small table, with a very white cloth, and preparations for supper, was also a very agreeable object.

I should have liked very well, under these influences, to have listened to Tom Wyndsour's story; but after supper I grew too sleepy to attempt to lead him to the subject; and after yawning for a time, I found there was no use in contending against my drowsiness, so I betook myself to my bedroom, and by ten o'clock was fast asleep.

What interruption I experienced that night I shall tell you presently. It was not much, but it was very odd.

By next night I had completed my work at Barwyke. From early morning till then I was so incessantly occupied and hard-worked, that I had no time to think over the singular occurrence to which I have just referred. Behold me, however, at length once more seated at my little supper-table, having ended a comfortable meal. It had been a sultry day, and I had thrown one of the large windows up as high as it would go. I was sitting near it, with my brandy and water at my elbow, looking out into the dark. There was no moon, and the trees that are grouped about the house make the darkness round it supernaturally profound on such nights.

"Tom," said I, so soon as the jug of hot punch I had supplied him with began to exercise its genial and communicative influence; "you must tell me who beside your wife and you and myself slept in the house last night."

Tom, sitting near the door, set down his tumbler, and looked at me askance, while you might count seven, without speaking a word.

"Who else slept in the house?" he repeated, very deliberately. "Not a living soul, sir;" and he looked hard at me, still evidently expecting something more.

"That *is* very odd," I said, returning his stare, and feeling really a little odd. "You are sure *you* were not in my room last night?"

"Not till I came to call you, sir, this morning; I can make oath of that."

"Well," said I, "there was some one there, *I* can make oath of that. I was so tired I could not make up my mind to get up; but I was waked by a sound that I thought was some one flinging down the two tin boxes in which my papers were locked up violently on the floor. I heard a slow step on the ground, and there was light in the room, although I remembered having put out my candle. I thought it must have been you, who had come in for my clothes, and upset the boxes by accident. Whoever it was, he went out, and the light with him. I was about to settle again, when, the curtain being a little open at the foot of the bed, I saw a light on the wall opposite; such as a candle from outside would cast if the door were very cautiously opening. I started up in the bed, drew the side curtain, and saw that the door *was* opening, and admitting light from outside. It is close, you know, to the head of the bed. A hand was holding on the edge of the door and pushing it open; not a bit like yours; a very singular hand. Let me look at yours."

He extended it for my inspection.

"Oh no; there's nothing wrong with your hand. This was differently shaped; fatter; and the middle finger was stunted, and shorter than the rest, looking as if it had once been broken, and the nail was crooked like a claw. I called out, "Who's there?" and the light and the hand were withdrawn, and I saw and heard no more of my visitor."

"So sure as you're a living man, that was him!" exclaimed Tom Wyndsour, his very nose growing pale, and his eyes almost starting out of his head.

"Who?" I asked.

"Old Squire Bowes; 'twas *his* hand you saw; the Lord a' mercy on us!" answered Tom. "The broken finger, and the nail bent like a hoop. Well for you, sir, he didn't come back when you called, that time. You came here about them Miss Dymock's business, and he never meant they should have a foot o' ground in Barwyke; and he was making a will to give it away quite different, when death took him short. He never was uncivil to no one; but he couldn't abide them ladies. My mind misgave me when I heard 'twas about their business you were coming; and now you see how it is; he'll be at his old tricks again!"

With some pressure, and a little more punch, I induced Tom Wyndsour to explain his mysterious allusions by recounting the occurrences which followed the old Squire's death.

"Squire Bowes, of Barwyke, died without making a will, as you know," said Tom. "And all the folk round were sorry; that is to say, sir, as sorry as folk will be for an old man that has seen a long tale of years, and has no right to grumble that death has knocked an hour too soon at his door. The Squire was well liked; he was never in a passion, or said a hard word; and he would not hurt a fly; and that made what happened after his decease the more surprising.

"The first thing these ladies did, when they got the property, was to buy stock for the park.

"It was not wise, in any case, to graze the land on their own account. But they little knew all they had to contend with.

"Before long something went wrong with the cattle; first one, and then another, took sick and died, and so on, till the loss began to grow heavy. Then, queer stories, little by little, began to be told. It was said, first by one, then by another, that Squire Bowes was seen, about evening time, walking, just as he used to do when he was alive, among the old trees, leaning on his stick; and, sometimes, when he came up with the cattle, he would stop and lay his hand kindly like on the back of one of them; and that one was sure to fall sick next day, and die soon after.

"No one ever met him in the park, or in the woods, or ever saw him, except a good distance off. But they knew his gait and his figure well, and the clothes he used to wear; and they could tell the beast he laid his hand on by its color—white, dun, or black; and that beast was sure to sicken and die. The neighbors grew shy of taking the path over the park; and no one liked to walk in the woods, or come inside the bounds of Barwyke; and the cattle went on sickening and dying, as before.

"At that time there was one Thomas Pyke; he had been a groom to the old Squire; and he was in care of the place, and was the only one that used to sleep in the house.

"Tom was vexed, hearing these stories; which he did not believe the half on 'em; and more especial as he could not get man or boy to herd the cattle; all being afeared. So he wrote to Matlock, in Derbyshire, for his brother, Richard Pyke, a clever lad, and one that knew nout o' the story of the old Squire walking.

"Dick came; and the cattle was better; folk said they could still see the old Squire, sometimes, walking, as before, in openings of the wood, with his stick in his hand; but he was shy of coming nigh the cattle, whatever his reason might be, since Dickon Pyke came; and he used to stand a long bit off, looking at them, with no more stir in him than a trunk o' one of the old trees, for an hour at a time, till the shape melted away, little by little, like the smoke of a fire that burns out.

"Tom Pyke and his brother Dickon, being the only living souls in the house, lay in the big bed in the servants' room, the house being fast barred and locked, one night in November.

"Tom was lying next the wall, and, he told me, as wide awake as ever he was at noonday. His brother Dickon lay outside, and was sound asleep.

"Well, as Tom lay thinking, with his eyes turned toward the door, it opens slowly, and who should come in but old Squire Bowes, his face lookin' as dead as he was in his coffin.

"Tom's very breath left his body; he could not take his eyes off him; and he felt the hair rising up on his head.

"The Squire came to the side of the bed, and put his arms under Dickon, and lifted the boy—in a dead sleep all the time—and carried him out so, at the door.

"Such was the appearance, to Tom Pyke's eyes, and he was ready to swear to it, anywhere.

"When this happened, the light, wherever it came from, all on a sudden went out, and Tom could not see his own hand before him.

"More dead than alive, he lay till daylight.

"Sure enough his brother Dickon was gone. No sign of him could he discover about the house; and with some trouble he got a couple of the neighbors to help him to search the woods and grounds. Not a sign of him anywhere.

"At last one of them thought of the island in the lake; the little boat was moored to the old post at the water's edge. In they got, though with small hope of finding him there. Find him, nevertheless, they did, sitting under the big ash-tree, quite out of his wits; and to all their questions he answered nothing but one cry—'Bowes, the devil! See him; see him; Bowes, the devil!' An idiot they found him; and so he will be till God sets all things right. No one could ever get him to sleep under roof-tree more. He wanders from house to house while daylight lasts; and no one cares to lock the harmless creature in the workhouse. And folk would rather not meet him after nightfall, for they think where he is there may be worse things near."

A silence followed Tom's story. He and I were alone in that large room; I was sitting near the open window, looking into the dark night air. I fancied I saw something white move across it; and I heard a sound like low talking, that swelled into a discordant shriek—"Hoo-oo-oo! Bowes, the devil! Over your shoulder. Hoo-oo-oo! ha! ha! ha!" I started up, and saw, by the light of the candle with which Tom strode to the window, the wild eyes and blighted face of the idiot, as, with a sudden change of mood, he drew off, whispering and tittering to himself, and holding up his long fingers, and looking at them as if they were lighted at the tips like a "hand of glory."

Tom pulled down the window. The story and its epilogue were over. I confessed I was rather glad when I heard the sound of the horses' hoofs on the courtyard, a few minutes later; and still gladder when, having bidden Tom a kind farewell, I had left the neglected house of Barwyke a mile behind me.

THE WHITE PEOPLE
by Arthur Machen

Born Arthur Llewelyn Jones (he would later adopt his wife's maiden name, Machen, to acquire an inheritance) in Caerleon, Monmouthshire (Gwent) Wales, Arthur Machen (1863-1947) is one of the most colorful and interesting figures in English literature. In his eventful life, he played the part of essayist, novelist, war correspondent, magician, philosopher, actor, and critic. He had much in common with another of our authors, Aleister Crowley. Both were occultists with a passion for magic, alchemy, and the darker side of the human psyche. Both were for a time members of the Hermetic Order of the Golden Dawn, and colleagues of one of the Order's most illustrious adepts, Arthur Edward Waite.

Machen's story "The White People" is a subtle masterpiece of the most horrific kind, published in 1904 and often described as the greatest of all short horror stories.

Prologue

"Sorcery and sanctity," said Ambrose, "these are the only realities. Each is an ecstasy, a withdrawal from the common life."

Cotgrave listened, interested. He had been brought by a friend to this mouldering house in a northern suburb, through an old garden to the room where Ambrose the recluse dozed and dreamed over his books.

"Yes," he went on, "magic is justified of her children. There are many, I think, who eat dry crusts and drink water, with a joy infinitely sharper than anything within the experience of the 'practical' epicure."

"You are speaking of the saints?"

"Yes, and of the sinners, too. I think you are falling into the very general error of confining the spiritual world to the supremely good; but the supremely wicked, necessarily, have their portion in it. The merely carnal, sensual man can no more be a great sinner than he can be a great saint. Most of us are just indifferent, mixed-up creatures; we muddle through the world without realizing the meaning and the inner sense of things, and, consequently, our wickedness and our goodness are alike second-rate, unimportant."

"And you think the great sinner, then, will be an ascetic, as well as the great saint?"

"Great people of all kinds forsake the imperfect copies and go to the perfect originals. I have no doubt but that many of the very highest among the saints have never done a 'good action' (using the words in their ordinary sense). And, on the other hand, there have been those who have sounded the very depths of sin, who all their lives have never done an 'ill deed.'"

He went out of the room for a moment, and Cotgrave, in high delight, turned to his friend and thanked him for the introduction.

"He's grand," he said. "I never saw that kind of lunatic before."

Ambrose returned with more whisky and helped the two men in a liberal manner. He abused the teetotal sect with ferocity, as he handed the seltzer, and pouring out a glass of water for himself, was about to resume his monologue, when Cotgrave broke in—

"I can't stand it, you know," he said, "your paradoxes are too monstrous. A man may be a great sinner and yet never do anything sinful! Come!"

"You're quite wrong," said Ambrose. "I never make paradoxes; I wish I could. I merely said that a man may have an exquisite taste in Romanée Conti, and yet never have even smelt four ale. That's all, and it's more like a truism than a paradox, isn't it? Your surprise at my remark is due to the fact that you haven't realized what sin is. Oh, yes, there is a sort of connexion between Sin with the capital letter, and actions which are commonly called sinful: with murder, theft, adultery, and so forth. Much the same connexion that there is between the A, B, C and fine literature. But I believe that the misconception—it is all but universal—arises in great measure from our looking at the matter through social spectacles. We think that a man who does evil to *us* and to his neighbours must be very evil. So he is, from a social standpoint; but can't you realize that Evil in its essence is a lonely thing, a passion of the solitary, individual soul? Really, the average murderer, *quâ* murderer, is not by any means a sinner in the true sense of the word. He is simply a wild beast that we have to get rid of to save our own necks from his knife. I should class him rather with tigers than with sinners."

"It seems a little strange."

"I think not. The murderer murders not from positive qualities, but from negative ones; he lacks something which non-murderers possess. Evil, of course, is wholly positive—only it is on the wrong side. You may believe me that sin in its proper sense is very rare; it is probable that there have been far fewer sinners than saints. Yes, your standpoint is all very well for practical, social purposes; we are naturally inclined to think that a person who is very disagreeable to us must be a very great sinner! It is very disagreeable to have one's pocket picked, and we pronounce the thief to be a very great sinner. In truth, he is merely an undeveloped man. He cannot be a saint, of course; but he may be, and often is, an infinitely better creature than thousands who have never broken a single commandment. He is a great nuisance to *us*, I admit, and we very properly lock him up if we catch him; but between his troublesome and unsocial action and evil—Oh, the connexion is of the weakest."

It was getting very late. The man who had brought Cotgrave had probably heard all this before, since he assisted with a bland and judicious smile, but Cotgrave began to think that his "lunatic" was turning into a sage.

"Do you know," he said, "you interest me immensely? You think, then, that we do not understand the real nature of evil?"

"No, I don't think we do. We over-estimate it and we under-estimate it. We take the very numerous infractions of our social 'bye-laws'—the very necessary and very proper regulations which keep the human company together—and we get frightened at the prevalence of 'sin' and 'evil.' But this is really nonsense. Take theft, for example. Have you any *horror* at the thought of Robin Hood, of the Highland caterans of the seventeenth century, of the moss-troopers, of the company promoters of our day?

"Then, on the other hand, we underrate evil. We attach such an enormous importance to the 'sin' of meddling with our pockets (and our wives) that we have quite forgotten the awfulness of real sin."

"And what is sin?" said Cotgrave.

"I think I must reply to your question by another. What would your feelings be, seriously, if your cat or your dog began to talk to you, and to dispute with you in human accents? You would be overwhelmed with horror. I am sure of it. And if the roses in your garden sang a weird song, you would go mad. And suppose the stones in the road began to swell and grow before your eyes, and if the pebble that you noticed at night had shot out stony blossoms in the morning? Well, these examples may give you some notion of what sin really is."

"Look here," said the third man, hitherto placid, "you two seem pretty well wound up. But I'm going home. I've missed my tram, and I shall have to walk."

Ambrose and Cotgrave seemed to settle down more profoundly when the other had gone out into the early misty morning and the pale light of the lamps.

"You astonish me," said Cotgrave. "I had never thought of that. If that is really so, one must turn everything upside down. Then the essence of sin really is—"

"In the taking of heaven by storm, it seems to me," said Ambrose. "It appears to me that it is simply an attempt to penetrate into another and higher sphere in a forbidden manner. You can understand why it is so rare. There are few, indeed, who wish to penetrate into other spheres, higher or lower, in ways allowed or forbidden. Men, in the mass, are amply content with life as they find it. Therefore there are few saints, and sinners (in the proper sense) are fewer still, and men of genius, who partake sometimes of each character, are rare also. Yes; on the whole, it is, perhaps, harder to be a great sinner than a great saint."

"There is something profoundly unnatural about sin? Is that what you mean?"

"Exactly. Holiness requires as great, or almost as great, an effort; but holiness works on lines that *were* natural once; it is an effort to recover the ecstasy that was before the Fall. But sin is an effort to gain the ecstasy and the knowledge that pertain alone to angels, and in making this effort man becomes a demon. I told you that the mere murderer is not *therefore* a sinner; that is true, but the sinner is sometimes a murderer. Gilles de Raiz is an instance. So you see that while the good and the evil are unnatural to man as he now is—to man the social, civilized being—evil is unnatural in a much deeper sense than good. The saint endeavours to recover a gift which he has lost; the sinner tries to obtain something which was never his. In brief, he repeats the Fall."

"But are you a Catholic?" said Cotgrave.

"Yes; I am a member of the persecuted Anglican Church."

"Then, how about those texts which seem to reckon as sin that which you would set down as a mere trivial dereliction?"

"Yes; but in one place the word "sorcerers" comes in the same sentence, doesn't it? That seems to me to give the key-note. Consider: can you imagine for a moment that a false statement which saves an innocent man's life is a sin? No; very good, then, it is not the mere liar who is excluded by those words; it is, above all, the 'sorcerers' who use the material life, who use the failings incidental to material life as instruments to obtain their infinitely wicked ends. And let me tell you this: our higher senses are so blunted, we are so drenched with materialism, that we should probably fail to recognize real wickedness if we encountered it."

"But shouldn't we experience a certain horror—a terror such as you hinted we would experience if a rose tree sang—in the mere presence of an evil man?"

"We should if we were natural: children and women feel this horror you speak of, even animals experience it. But with most of us convention and civilization and education have blinded and deafened and obscured the natural reason. No, sometimes we may recognize evil by its hatred of the good—one doesn't need much penetration to guess at the influence which dictated, quite unconsciously, the 'Blackwood' review of Keats—but this is purely incidental; and, as a rule, I suspect that the Hierarchs of Tophet pass quite unnoticed, or, perhaps, in certain cases, as good but mistaken men."

"But you used the word 'unconscious' just now, of Keats' reviewers. Is wickedness ever unconscious?"

"Always. It must be so. It is like holiness and genius in this as in other points; it is a certain rapture or ecstasy of the soul; a transcendent effort to surpass the ordinary bounds. So, surpassing these, it surpasses also the understanding, the faculty that takes note of that which comes before it. No, a man may be infinitely and horribly wicked and never suspect it. But I tell you, evil in this, its certain and true sense, is rare, and I think it is growing rarer."

"I am trying to get hold of it all," said Cotgrave. "From what you say, I gather that the true evil differs generically from that which we call evil?"

"Quite so. There is, no doubt, an analogy between the two; a resemblance such as enables us to use, quite legitimately, such terms as the 'foot of the mountain' and the 'leg of the table.' And, sometimes, of course, the two speak, as it were, in the same language. The rough miner, or 'puddler,' the untrained, undeveloped 'tiger-man,' heated by a quart or two above his usual measure, comes home and kicks his irritating and injudicious wife to death. He is a murderer. And Gilles de Raiz was a murderer. But you see the gulf that separates the two? The 'word,' if I may so speak, is accidentally the same in each case, but the 'meaning' is utterly different. It is flagrant 'Hobson Jobson' to confuse the two, or rather, it is as if one supposed that Juggernaut and the Argonauts had something to do etymologically with one another. And no doubt the same weak likeness, or analogy, runs between all the 'social' sins and the real spiritual sins, and in some cases, perhaps, the lesser may be 'schoolmasters' to lead one on to the greater—from the shadow to the reality. If you are anything of a Theologian, you will see the importance of all this."

"I am sorry to say," remarked Cotgrave, "that I have devoted very little of my time to theology. Indeed, I have often wondered on what grounds theologians have claimed the title of Science of Sciences for their favourite study; since the 'theological' books I have looked into have always seemed to me to be concerned with feeble and obvious pieties, or with the kings of Israel and Judah. I do not care to hear about those kings."

Ambrose grinned.

"We must try to avoid theological discussion," he said. "I perceive that you would be a bitter disputant. But perhaps the 'dates of the kings' have as much to do with theology as the hobnails of the murderous puddler with evil."

"Then, to return to our main subject, you think that sin is an esoteric, occult thing?"

"Yes. It is the infernal miracle as holiness is the supernal. Now and then it is raised to such a pitch that we entirely fail to suspect its existence; it is like the note of the great pedal pipes of the organ, which is so deep that we cannot hear it. In other cases it may lead to the lunatic asylum, or to still stranger issues. But you must never confuse it with mere social misdoing. Remember how the Apostle, speaking of the 'other side,' distinguishes between 'charitable' actions and charity. And as one may give all one's goods to the poor, and yet lack charity; so, remember, one may avoid every crime and yet be a sinner."

"Your psychology is very strange to me," said Cotgrave, "but I confess I like it, and I suppose that one might fairly deduce from your premisses the conclusion that the real sinner might very possibly strike the observer as a harmless personage enough?"

"Certainly; because the true evil has nothing to do with social life or social laws, or if it has, only incidentally and accidentally. It is a lonely passion of the soul—or a passion of the lonely soul—whichever you like. If, by chance, we understand it, and grasp its full significance, then, indeed, it will fill us with horror and with awe. But this emotion is widely distinguished from the fear and the disgust with which we regard the ordinary criminal, since this latter is largely or entirely founded on the regard which we have for our own skins or purses. We hate a murderer, because we know that we should hate to be murdered, or to have any one that we like murdered. So, on the 'other side,' we venerate the saints, but we don't 'like' them as we like our friends. Can you persuade yourself that you would have 'enjoyed' St. Paul's company? Do you think that you and I would have 'got on' with Sir Galahad?

"So with the sinners, as with the saints. If you met a very evil man, and recognized his evil; he would, no doubt, fill you with horror and awe; but there is no reason why you should 'dislike' him. On the contrary, it is quite possible that if you could succeed in putting the sin out of your mind you might find the sinner capital company, and in a little while you might have to reason yourself back into horror. Still, how awful it is. If the roses and the lilies suddenly sang on this coming morning; if the furniture began to move in procession, as in De Maupassant's tale!"

"I am glad you have come back to that comparison," said Cotgrave, "because I wanted to ask you what it is that corresponds in humanity to these imaginary feats of inanimate things. In a word—what is sin? You have given me, I know, an abstract definition, but I should like a concrete example."

"I told you it was very rare," said Ambrose, who appeared willing to avoid the giving of a direct answer. "The materialism of the age, which has done a good deal to suppress sanctity, has done perhaps more to suppress evil. We find the earth so very comfortable that we have no inclination either for ascents or descents. It would seem as if the scholar who decided to 'specialize' in Tophet, would be reduced to purely antiquarian researches. No paleontologist could show you a *live* pterodactyl."

"And yet you, I think, have 'specialized,' and I believe that your researches have descended to our modern times."

"You are really interested, I see. Well, I confess, that I have dabbled a little, and if you like I can show you something that bears on the very curious subject we have been discussing."

Ambrose took a candle and went away to a far, dim corner of the room. Cotgrave saw him open a venerable bureau that stood there, and from some secret recess he drew out a parcel, and came back to the window where they had been sitting.

Ambrose undid a wrapping of paper, and produced a green pocket-book.

"You will take care of it?" he said. "Don't leave it lying about. It is one of the choicer pieces in my collection, and I should be very sorry if it were lost."

He fondled the faded binding.

"I knew the girl who wrote this," he said. "When you read it, you will see how it illustrates the talk we have had to-night. There is a sequel, too, but I won't talk of that."

"There was an odd article in one of the reviews some months ago," he began again, with the air of a man who changes the subject. "It was written by a doctor—Dr. Coryn, I think, was the name. He says that a lady, watching her little girl playing at the drawing-room window, suddenly saw the heavy sash give way and fall on the child's fingers. The lady fainted, I think, but at any rate the doctor was summoned, and when he had dressed the child's wounded and maimed fingers he was summoned to the mother. She was groaning with pain, and it was found that three fingers of her hand, corresponding with those that had been injured on the child's hand, were swollen and inflamed, and later, in the doctor's language, purulent sloughing set in."

Ambrose still handled delicately the green volume.

"Well, here it is," he said at last, parting with difficulty, it seemed, from his treasure.

"You will bring it back as soon as you have read it," he said, as they went out into the hall, into the old garden, faint with the odour of white lilies.

There was a broad red band in the east as Cotgrave turned to go, and from the high ground where he stood he saw that awful spectacle of London in a dream.

The Green Book

The morocco binding of the book was faded, and the colour had grown faint, but there were no stains nor bruises nor marks of usage. The book looked as if it had been bought "on a visit to London" some seventy or eighty years ago, and had somehow been forgotten and suffered to lie away out of sight. There was an old, delicate, lingering odour about it, such an odour as sometimes haunts an ancient piece of furniture for a century or more. The end-papers, inside the binding, were oddly decorated with coloured patterns and faded gold. It looked small, but the paper was fine, and there were many leaves, closely covered with minute, painfully formed characters.

I found this book (the manuscript began) in a drawer in the old bureau that stands on the landing. It was a very rainy day and I could not go out, so in the afternoon I got a candle and rummaged in the bureau. Nearly all the drawers were full of old dresses, but one of the small ones looked empty, and I found this book hidden right at the back. I wanted a book like this, so I took it to write in. It is full of secrets. I have a great many other books of secrets I have written, hidden in a safe place, and I am going to write here many of the old secrets and some new ones; but there are some I shall not put down at all. I must not write down the real names of the days and months which I found out a year ago, nor the way to make the Aklo letters, or the Chian language, or the great beautiful Circles, nor the Mao Games, nor the chief songs. I may write something about all these things but not the way to do them, for peculiar reasons. And I must not say who the Nymphs are, or the Dôls, or Jeelo, or what voolas mean. All these are most secret secrets, and I am glad when I remember what they are, and how many wonderful languages I know, but there are some things that I call the secrets of the secrets of the secrets that I dare not think of unless I am quite alone, and then I shut my eyes, and put my hands over them and whisper the word, and the Alala comes. I only do this at night in my room or in certain woods that I know, but I must not describe them, as they are secret woods. Then there are the Ceremonies, which are all of them important, but some are more delightful than others—there are the White Ceremonies, and the Green Ceremonies, and the Scarlet Ceremonies. The Scarlet Ceremonies are the best, but there is only one place where they can be performed properly, though there is a very nice imitation which I have done in other places. Besides these, I have the dances, and the Comedy, and I have done the Comedy sometimes when the others were looking, and they didn't understand anything about it. I was very little when I first knew about these things.

When I was very small, and mother was alive, I can remember remembering things before that, only it has all got confused. But I remember when I was five or six I heard them talking about me when they thought I was not noticing. They were saying how queer I was a year or two before, and how nurse had called my mother to come and listen to me talking all to myself, and I was saying words that nobody could understand. I was speaking the Xu language, but I only remember a very few of the words, as it was about the little white faces that used to look at me when I was lying in my cradle. They used to talk to me, and I learnt their language and talked to them in it about some great white place where they lived, where the trees and the grass were all white, and there were white hills as high up as the moon, and a cold wind. I have often dreamed of it afterwards, but the faces went away when I was very little. But a wonderful thing happened when I was about five. My nurse was carrying me on her shoulder; there was a field of yellow corn, and we went through it, it was very hot. Then we came to a path through a wood, and a tall man came after us, and went with us till we came to a place where there was a deep pool, and it was very dark and shady. Nurse put me down on the soft moss under a tree, and she said: "She can't get to the pond now." So they left me there, and I sat quite still and watched, and out of the water and out of the wood came two wonderful white people, and they began to play and dance and sing. They were a kind of creamy white like the old ivory figure in the drawing-room; one was a beautiful lady with kind dark eyes, and a grave face, and long black hair, and she smiled such a strange sad smile at the other, who laughed and came to her. They played together, and danced round and round the pool, and they sang a song till I fell asleep. Nurse woke me up when she came back, and she was looking something like the lady had looked, so I told her all about it, and asked her why she looked like that. At first she cried, and then she looked very frightened, and turned quite pale. She put me down on the grass and stared at me, and I could see she was shaking all over. Then she said I had been dreaming, but I knew I hadn't. Then she made me promise not to say a word about it to anybody, and if I did I should be thrown into the black pit. I was not frightened at all, though nurse was, and I never forgot about it, because when I shut my eyes and it was quite quiet, and I was all alone, I could see them again, very faint and far away, but very splendid; and little bits of the song they sang came into my head, but I couldn't sing it.

I was thirteen, nearly fourteen, when I had a very singular adventure, so strange that the day on which it happened is always called the White Day. My mother had been dead for more than a year, and in the morning I had lessons, but they let me go out for walks in the afternoon. And this afternoon I walked a new way, and a little brook led me into a new country, but I tore my frock getting through some of the difficult places, as the way was through many bushes, and beneath the low branches of trees, and up thorny thickets on the hills, and by dark woods full of creeping thorns. And it was a long, long way. It seemed as if I was going on for ever and ever, and I had to creep by a place like a tunnel where a brook must have been, but all the water had dried up, and the floor was rocky, and the bushes had grown overhead till they met, so that it was quite dark. And I went on and on through that dark place; it was a long, long way. And I came to a hill that I never saw before. I was in a dismal thicket full of black twisted boughs that tore me as I went through them, and I cried out because I was smarting all over, and then I found that I was climbing, and I went up and up a long way, till at last the thicket stopped and I came out crying just under the top of a big bare place, where there were ugly grey stones lying all about on the grass, and here and there a little twisted, stunted tree came out from under a stone, like a snake. And I went up, right to the top, a long way. I never saw such big ugly stones before; they came out of the earth some of them, and some looked as if they had been rolled to where they were, and they went on and on as far as I could see, a long, long way. I looked out from them and saw the country, but it was strange. It was winter time, and there were black terrible woods hanging from the hills all round; it was like seeing a large room hung with black curtains, and the shape of the trees seemed quite different from any I had ever seen before. I was afraid. Then beyond the woods there were other hills round in a great ring, but I had never seen any of them; it all looked black, and everything had a voor over it. It was all so still and silent, and the sky was heavy and grey and sad, like a wicked voorish dome in Deep Dendo. I went on into the dreadful rocks. There were hundreds and hundreds of them. Some were like horrid-grinning men; I could see their faces as if they would jump at me out of the stone, and catch hold of me, and drag me with them back into the rock, so that I should always be there. And there were other rocks that were like animals, creeping, horrible animals, putting out their tongues, and others were like words that I could not say, and others like dead people lying on the grass. I went on among them, though they frightened me, and my heart was full of wicked songs that they put into it; and I wanted to make faces and twist myself about in the way they did, and I went on and on a long way till at last I liked the rocks, and they didn't frighten me any more. I sang the songs I thought of; songs full of words that must not be spoken or written down. Then I made faces like the faces on the rocks, and I twisted myself about like the twisted ones, and I lay down flat on the ground like the dead ones, and I went up to one that was grinning, and put my arms round him and hugged him. And so I went on and on through the rocks till I came to a round mound in the middle of them. It was higher than a mound, it was nearly as high as our house, and it was like a great basin turned upside down, all smooth and round and green, with one stone, like a post, sticking up at the top. I climbed up the sides, but they were so steep I had to stop or I should have rolled all the way down again, and I should have knocked against the stones at the bottom, and perhaps been killed. But I wanted to get up to the very top of the big round mound, so I lay down flat on my face, and took hold of the grass with my hands and drew myself up, bit by bit, till I was at the top. Then I sat down on the stone in the middle, and looked all round about. I felt I had come such a long, long way, just as if I were a hundred miles from home, or in some other country, or in one of the strange places I had read about in the "Tales of the Genie" and the "Arabian Nights," or as if I had gone across the sea, far away, for years and I had found another world that nobody had ever seen or heard of before, or as if I had somehow flown through the sky and fallen on one of the stars I had read about where everything is dead and cold and grey, and there is no air, and the wind doesn't blow. I sat on the stone and looked all round and down and round about me. It was just as if I was sitting on a tower in the middle of a great empty town, because I could see nothing all around but the grey rocks on the ground. I couldn't make out their shapes any more, but I could see them on and on for a long way, and I looked at them, and they seemed as if they had been arranged into patterns, and shapes, and figures. I knew they couldn't be, because I had seen a lot of them coming right out of the earth, joined to the deep rocks below, so I looked again, but still I saw nothing but circles, and small circles inside big ones, and pyramids, and domes, and spires, and they seemed all to go round and round the place where I was sitting, and the more I looked, the more I saw great big rings of rocks, getting bigger and bigger, and I stared so long that it felt as if they were all moving and turning, like a great wheel, and I was turning, too, in the middle. I got quite dizzy and queer in the head, and everything began to be hazy and not clear, and I saw little sparks of blue light, and the stones looked as if they were springing and dancing and twisting as they went round and round and round. I was frightened again, and I cried out loud, and jumped up from the stone I was sitting on, and fell down. When I got up I was so glad they all looked still, and I sat down on the top and slid down the mound, and went on again. I danced as I went in the peculiar way the rocks had danced when I got giddy, and I was so glad I could do it quite well, and I danced and danced along, and sang extraordinary songs that came into my head. At last I came to the edge of that great flat hill, and there were no more rocks, and the way went again through a dark thicket in a hollow. It was just as bad as the other one I went through climbing up, but I didn't mind this one, because I was so glad I had seen those singular dances and could imitate them. I went down, creeping through the bushes, and a tall nettle stung me on my leg, and made me burn, but I didn't mind it, and I tingled with the boughs and the thorns, but I only laughed and sang. Then I got out of the thicket into a close valley, a little secret place like a dark passage that nobody ever knows of, because it was so narrow and deep and the woods were so thick round it. There is a steep bank with trees hanging over it, and there the ferns keep green all through the winter, when they are dead and brown upon the hill, and the ferns there have a sweet, rich smell like what oozes out of fir trees. There was a little stream of water running down this valley, so small that I could easily step across it. I drank the water with my hand, and it tasted like bright, yellow wine, and it sparkled and bubbled as it ran down over beautiful red and yellow and green stones, so that it seemed alive and all colours at once. I drank it, and I drank more with my hand, but I couldn't drink enough, so I lay down and bent my head and sucked the water up with my lips. It tasted much better, drinking it that way, and a ripple would come up to my mouth and give me a kiss, and I laughed, and drank again, and pretended there was a nymph, like the one in the old picture at home, who lived in the water and was kissing me. So I bent low down to the water, and put my lips softly to it, and whispered to the nymph that I would come again. I felt sure it could not be common water, I was so glad when I got up and went on; and I danced again and went up and up the valley, under hanging hills. And when I came to the top, the ground rose up in front of me, tall and steep as a wall, and there was nothing but the green wall and the sky. I thought of "for ever and for ever, world without end, Amen"; and I thought I must have really found the end of the world, because it was like the end of everything, as if there could be nothing at all beyond, except the kingdom of Voor, where the light goes when it is put out, and the water goes when the sun takes it away. I began to think of all the long, long way I had journeyed, how I had found a brook and followed it, and followed it on, and gone through bushes and thorny thickets, and dark woods full of creeping thorns. Then I had crept up a tunnel under trees, and climbed a thicket, and seen all the grey rocks, and sat in the middle of them when they turned round, and then I had gone on through the grey rocks and come down the hill through the stinging thicket and up the dark valley, all a long, long way. I wondered how I should get home again, if I could ever find the way, and if my home was there any more, or if it were turned and everybody in it into grey rocks, as in the "Arabian Nights." So I sat down on the grass and thought what I should do next. I was tired, and my feet were hot with walking, and as I looked about I saw there was a wonderful well just under the high, steep wall of grass. All the ground round it was covered with bright, green, dripping moss; there was every kind of moss there, moss like beautiful little ferns, and like palms and fir trees, and it was all green as jewellery, and drops of water hung on it like diamonds. And in the middle was the great well, deep and shining and beautiful, so clear that it looked as if I could touch the red sand at the bottom, but it was far below. I stood by it and looked in, as if I were looking in a glass. At the bottom of the well, in the middle of it, the red grains of sand were moving and stirring all the time, and I saw how the water bubbled up, but at the top it was quite smooth, and full and brimming. It was a great well, large like a bath, and with the shining, glittering green moss about it, it looked like a great white jewel, with green jewels all round. My feet were so hot and tired that I took off my boots and stockings, and let my feet down into the water, and the water was soft and cold, and when I got up I wasn't tired any more, and I felt I must go on, farther and farther, and see what was on the other side of the wall. I climbed up it very slowly, going sideways all the time, and when I got to the top and looked over, I was in the queerest country I had seen, stranger even than the hill of the grey rocks. It looked as if earth-children had been playing there with their spades, as it was all hills and hollows, and castles and walls made of earth and covered with grass. There were two mounds like big beehives, round and great and solemn, and then hollow basins, and then a steep mounting wall like the ones I saw once by the seaside where the big guns and the soldiers were. I nearly fell into one of the round hollows, it went away from under my feet so suddenly, and I ran fast down the side and stood at the bottom and looked up. It was strange and solemn to look up. There was nothing but the grey, heavy sky and the sides of the hollow; everything else had gone away, and the hollow was the whole world, and I thought that at night it must be full of ghosts and moving shadows and pale things when the moon shone down to the bottom at the dead of the night, and the wind wailed up above. It was so strange and solemn and lonely, like a hollow temple of dead heathen gods. It reminded me of a tale my nurse had told me when I was quite little; it was the same nurse that took me into the wood where I saw the beautiful white people. And I remembered how nurse had told me the story one winter night, when the wind was beating the trees against the wall, and crying and moaning in the nursery chimney. She said there was, somewhere or other, a hollow pit, just like the one I was standing in, everybody was afraid to go into it or near it, it was such a bad place. But once upon a time there was a poor girl who said she would go into the hollow pit, and everybody tried to stop her, but she would go. And she went down into the pit and came back laughing, and said there was nothing there at all, except green grass and red stones, and white stones and yellow flowers. And soon after people saw she had most beautiful emerald earrings, and they asked how she got them, as she and her mother were quite poor. But she laughed, and said her ear-rings were not made of emeralds at all, but only of green grass. Then, one day, she wore on her breast the reddest ruby that any one had ever seen, and it was as big as a hen's egg, and glowed and sparkled like a hot burning coal of fire. And they asked how she got it, as she and her mother were quite poor. But she laughed, and said it was not a ruby at all, but only a red stone. Then one day she wore round her neck the loveliest necklace that any one had ever seen, much finer than the queen's finest, and it was made of great bright diamonds, hundreds of them, and they shone like all the stars on a night in June. So they asked her how she got it, as she and her mother were quite poor. But she laughed, and said they were not diamonds at all, but only white stones. And one day she went to the Court, and she wore on her head a crown of pure angel-gold, so nurse said, and it shone like the sun, and it was much more splendid than the crown the king was wearing himself, and in her ears she wore the emeralds, and the big ruby was the brooch on her breast, and the great diamond necklace was sparkling on her neck. And the king and queen thought she was some great princess from a long way off, and got down from their thrones and went to meet her, but somebody told the king and queen who she was, and that she was quite poor. So the king asked why she wore a gold crown, and how she got it, as she and her mother were so poor. And she laughed, and said it wasn't a gold crown at all, but only some yellow flowers she had put in her hair. And the king thought it was very strange, and said she should stay at the Court, and they would see what would happen next. And she was so lovely that everybody said that her eyes were greener than the emeralds, that her lips were redder than the ruby, that her skin was whiter than the diamonds, and that her hair was brighter than the golden crown. So the king's son said he would marry her, and the king said he might. And the bishop married them, and there was a great supper, and afterwards the king's son went to his wife's room. But just when he had his hand on the door, he saw a tall, black man, with a dreadful face, standing in front of the door, and a voice said—

Venture not upon your life, This is mine own wedded wife.

Then the king's son fell down on the ground in a fit. And they came and tried to get into the room, but they couldn't, and they hacked at the door with hatchets, but the wood had turned hard as iron, and at last everybody ran away, they were so frightened at the screaming and laughing and shrieking and crying that came out of the room. But next day they went in, and found there was nothing in the room but thick black smoke, because the black man had come and taken her away. And on the bed there were two knots of faded grass and a red stone, and some white stones, and some faded yellow flowers. I remembered this tale of nurse's while I was standing at the bottom of the deep hollow; it was so strange and solitary there, and I felt afraid. I could not see any stones or flowers, but I was afraid of bringing them away without knowing, and I thought I would do a charm that came into my head to keep the black man away. So I stood right in the very middle of the hollow, and I made sure that I had none of those things on me, and then I walked round the place, and touched my eyes, and my lips, and my hair in a peculiar manner, and whispered some queer words that nurse taught me to keep bad things away. Then I felt safe and climbed up out of the hollow, and went on through all those mounds and hollows and walls, till I came to the end, which was high above all the rest, and I could see that all the different shapes of the earth were arranged in patterns, something like the grey rocks, only the pattern was different. It was getting late, and the air was indistinct, but it looked from where I was standing something like two great figures of people lying on the grass. And I went on, and at last I found a certain wood, which is too secret to be described, and nobody knows of the passage into it, which I found out in a very curious manner, by seeing some little animal run into the wood through it. So I went after the animal by a very narrow dark way, under thorns and bushes, and it was almost dark when I came to a kind of open place in the middle. And there I saw the most wonderful sight I have ever seen, but it was only for a minute, as I ran away directly, and crept out of the wood by the passage I had come by, and ran and ran as fast as ever I could, because I was afraid, what I had seen was so wonderful and so strange and beautiful. But I wanted to get home and think of it, and I did not know what might not happen if I stayed by the wood. I was hot all over and trembling, and my heart was beating, and strange cries that I could not help came from me as I ran from the wood. I was glad that a great white moon came up from over a round hill and showed me the way, so I went back through the mounds and hollows and down the close valley, and up through the thicket over the place of the grey rocks, and so at last I got home again. My father was busy in his study, and the servants had not told about my not coming home, though they were frightened, and wondered what they ought to do, so I told them I had lost my way, but I did not let them find out the real way I had been. I went to bed and lay awake all through the night, thinking of what I had seen. When I came out of the narrow way, and it looked all shining, though the air was dark, it seemed so certain, and all the way home I was quite sure that I had seen it, and I wanted to be alone in my room, and be glad over it all to myself, and shut my eyes and pretend it was there, and do all the things I would have done if I had not been so afraid. But when I shut my eyes the sight would not come, and I began to think about my adventures all over again, and I remembered how dusky and queer it was at the end, and I was afraid it must be all a mistake, because it seemed impossible it could happen. It seemed like one of nurse's tales, which I didn't really believe in, though I was frightened at the bottom of the hollow; and the stories she told me when I was little came back into my head, and I wondered whether it was really there what I thought I had seen, or whether any of her tales could have happened a long time ago. It was so queer; I lay awake there in my room at the back of the house, and the moon was shining on the other side towards the river, so the bright light did not fall upon the wall. And the house was quite still. I had heard my father come upstairs, and just after the clock struck twelve, and after the house was still and empty, as if there was nobody alive in it. And though it was all dark and indistinct in my room, a pale glimmering kind of light shone in through the white blind, and once I got up and looked out, and there was a great black shadow of the house covering the garden, looking like a prison where men are hanged; and then beyond it was all white; and the wood shone white with black gulfs between the trees. It was still and clear, and there were no clouds on the sky. I wanted to think of what I had seen but I couldn't, and I began to think of all the tales that nurse had told me so long ago that I thought I had forgotten, but they all came back, and mixed up with the thickets and the grey rocks and the hollows in the earth and the secret wood, till I hardly knew what was new and what was old, or whether it was not all dreaming. And then I remembered that hot summer afternoon, so long ago, when nurse left me by myself in the shade, and the white people came out of the water and out of the wood, and played, and danced, and sang, and I began to fancy that nurse told me about something like it before I saw them, only I couldn't recollect exactly what she told me. Then I wondered whether she had been the white lady, as I remembered she was just as white and beautiful, and had the same dark eyes and black hair; and sometimes she smiled and looked like the lady had looked, when she was telling me some of her stories, beginning with "Once on a time," or "In the time of the fairies." But I thought she couldn't be the lady, as she seemed to have gone a different way into the wood, and I didn't think the man who came after us could be the other, or I couldn't have seen that wonderful secret in the secret wood. I thought of the moon: but it was afterwards when I was in the middle of the wild land, where the earth was made into the shape of great figures, and it was all walls, and mysterious hollows, and smooth round mounds, that I saw the great white moon come up over a round hill. I was wondering about all these things, till at last I got quite frightened, because I was afraid something had happened to me, and I remembered nurse's tale of the poor girl who went into the hollow pit, and was carried away at last by the black man. I knew I had gone into a hollow pit too, and perhaps it was the same, and I had done something dreadful. So I did the charm over again, and touched my eyes and my lips and my hair in a peculiar manner, and said the old words from the fairy language, so that I might be sure I had not been carried away. I tried again to see the secret wood, and to creep up the passage and see what I had seen there, but somehow I couldn't, and I kept on thinking of nurse's stories. There was one I remembered about a young man who once upon a time went hunting, and all the day he and his hounds hunted everywhere, and they crossed the rivers and went into all the woods, and went round the marshes, but they couldn't find anything at all, and they hunted all day till the sun sank down and began to set behind the mountain. And the young man was angry because he couldn't find anything, and he was going to turn back, when just as the sun touched the mountain, he saw come out of a brake in front of him a beautiful white stag. And he cheered to his hounds, but they whined and would not follow, and he cheered to his horse, but it shivered and stood stock still, and the young man jumped off the horse and left the hounds and began to follow the white stag all alone. And soon it was quite dark, and the sky was black, without a single star shining in it, and the stag went away into the darkness. And though the man had brought his gun with him he never shot at the stag, because he wanted to catch it, and he was afraid he would lose it in the night. But he never lost it once, though the sky was so black and the air was so dark, and the stag went on and on till the young man didn't know a bit where he was. And they went through enormous woods where the air was full of whispers and a pale, dead light came out from the rotten trunks that were lying on the ground, and just as the man thought he had lost the stag, he would see it all white and shining in front of him, and he would run fast to catch it, but the stag always ran faster, so he did not catch it. And they went through the enormous woods, and they swam across rivers, and they waded through black marshes where the ground bubbled, and the air was full of will-o'-the-wisps, and the stag fled away down into rocky narrow valleys, where the air was like the smell of a vault, and the man went after it. And they went over the great mountains and the man heard the wind come down from the sky, and the stag went on and the man went after. At last the sun rose and the young man found he was in a country that he had never seen before; it was a beautiful valley with a bright stream running through it, and a great, big round hill in the middle. And the stag went down the valley, towards the hill, and it seemed to be getting tired and went slower and slower, and though the man was tired, too, he began to run faster, and he was sure he would catch the stag at last. But just as they got to the bottom of the hill, and the man stretched out his hand to catch the stag, it vanished into the earth, and the man began to cry; he was so sorry that he had lost it after all his long hunting. But as he was crying he saw there was a door in the hill, just in front of him, and he went in, and it was quite dark, but he went on, as he thought he would find the white stag. And all of a sudden it got light, and there was the sky, and the sun shining, and birds singing in the trees, and there was a beautiful fountain. And by the fountain a lovely lady was sitting, who was the queen of the fairies, and she told the man that she had changed herself into a stag to bring him there because she loved him so much. Then she brought out a great gold cup, covered with jewels, from her fairy palace, and she offered him wine in the cup to drink. And he drank, and the more he drank the more he longed to drink, because the wine was enchanted. So he kissed the lovely lady, and she became his wife, and he stayed all that day and all that night in the hill where she lived, and when he woke he found he was lying on the ground, close to where he had seen the stag first, and his horse was there and his hounds were there waiting, and he looked up, and the sun sank behind the mountain. And he went home and lived a long time, but he would never kiss any other lady because he had kissed the queen of the fairies, and he would never drink common wine any more, because he had drunk enchanted wine. And sometimes nurse told me tales that she had heard from her great-grandmother, who was very old, and lived in a cottage on the mountain all alone, and most of these tales were about a hill where people used to meet at night long ago, and they used to play all sorts of strange games and do queer things that nurse told me of, but I couldn't understand, and now, she said, everybody but her great-grandmother had forgotten all about it, and nobody knew where the hill was, not even her great-grandmother. But she told me one very strange story about the hill, and I trembled when I remembered it. She said that people always went there in summer, when it was very hot, and they had to dance a good deal. It would be all dark at first, and there were trees there, which made it much darker, and people would come, one by one, from all directions, by a secret path which nobody else knew, and two persons would keep the gate, and every one as they came up had to give a very curious sign, which nurse showed me as well as she could, but she said she couldn't show me properly. And all kinds of people would come; there would be gentle folks and village folks, and some old people and boys and girls, and quite small children, who sat and watched. And it would all be dark as they came in, except in one corner where some one was burning something that smelt strong and sweet, and made them laugh, and there one would see a glaring of coals, and the smoke mounting up red. So they would all come in, and when the last had come there was no door any more, so that no one else could get in, even if they knew there was anything beyond. And once a gentleman who was a stranger and had ridden a long way, lost his path at night, and his horse took him into the very middle of the wild country, where everything was upside down, and there were dreadful marshes and great stones everywhere, and holes underfoot, and the trees looked like gibbet-posts, because they had great black arms that stretched out across the way. And this strange gentleman was very frightened, and his horse began to shiver all over, and at last it stopped and wouldn't go any farther, and the gentleman got down and tried to lead the horse, but it wouldn't move, and it was all covered with a sweat, like death. So the gentleman went on all alone, going farther and farther into the wild country, till at last he came to a dark place, where he heard shouting and singing and crying, like nothing he had ever heard before. It all sounded quite close to him, but he couldn't get in, and so he began to call, and while he was calling, something came behind him, and in a minute his mouth and arms and legs were all bound up, and he fell into a swoon. And when he came to himself, he was lying by the roadside, just where he had first lost his way, under a blasted oak with a black trunk, and his horse was tied beside him. So he rode on to the town and told the people there what had happened, and some of them were amazed; but others knew. So when once everybody had come, there was no door at all for anybody else to pass in by. And when they were all inside, round in a ring, touching each other, some one began to sing in the darkness, and some one else would make a noise like thunder with a thing they had on purpose, and on still nights people would hear the thundering noise far, far away beyond the wild land, and some of them, who thought they knew what it was, used to make a sign on their breasts when they woke up in their beds at dead of night and heard that terrible deep noise, like thunder on the mountains. And the noise and the singing would go on and on for a long time, and the people who were in a ring swayed a little to and fro; and the song was in an old, old language that nobody knows now, and the tune was queer. Nurse said her great-grandmother had known some one who remembered a little of it, when she was quite a little girl, and nurse tried to sing some of it to me, and it was so strange a tune that I turned all cold and my flesh crept as if I had put my hand on something dead. Sometimes it was a man that sang and sometimes it was a woman, and sometimes the one who sang it did it so well that two or three of the people who were there fell to the ground shrieking and tearing with their hands. The singing went on, and the people in the ring kept swaying to and fro for a long time, and at last the moon would rise over a place they called the Tole Deol, and came up and showed them swinging and swaying from side to side, with the sweet thick smoke curling up from the burning coals, and floating in circles all around them. Then they had their supper. A boy and a girl brought it to them; the boy carried a great cup of wine, and the girl carried a cake of bread, and they passed the bread and the wine round and round, but they tasted quite different from common bread and common wine, and changed everybody that tasted them. Then they all rose up and danced, and secret things were brought out of some hiding place, and they played extraordinary games, and danced round and round and round in the moonlight, and sometimes people would suddenly disappear and never be heard of afterwards, and nobody knew what had happened to them. And they drank more of that curious wine, and they made images and worshipped them, and nurse showed me how the images were made one day when we were out for a walk, and we passed by a place where there was a lot of wet clay. So nurse asked me if I would like to know what those things were like that they made on the hill, and I said yes. Then she asked me if I would promise never to tell a living soul a word about it, and if I did I was to be thrown into the black pit with the dead people, and I said I wouldn't tell anybody, and she said the same thing again and again, and I promised. So she took my wooden spade and dug a big lump of clay and put it in my tin bucket, and told me to say if any one met us that I was going to make pies when I went home. Then we went on a little way till we came to a little brake growing right down into the road, and nurse stopped, and looked up the road and down it, and then peeped through the hedge into the field on the other side, and then she said, "Quick!" and we ran into the brake, and crept in and out among the bushes till we had gone a good way from the road. Then we sat down under a bush, and I wanted so much to know what nurse was going to make with the clay, but before she would begin she made me promise again not to say a word about it, and she went again and peeped through the bushes on every side, though the lane was so small and deep that hardly anybody ever went there. So we sat down, and nurse took the clay out of the bucket, and began to knead it with her hands, and do queer things with it, and turn it about. And she hid it under a big dock-leaf for a minute or two and then she brought it out again, and then she stood up and sat down, and walked round the clay in a peculiar manner, and all the time she was softly singing a sort of rhyme, and her face got very red. Then she sat down again, and took the clay in her hands and began to shape it into a doll, but not like the dolls I have at home, and she made the queerest doll I had ever seen, all out of the wet clay, and hid it under a bush to get dry and hard, and all the time she was making it she was singing these rhymes to herself, and her face got redder and redder. So we left the doll there, hidden away in the bushes where nobody would ever find it. And a few days later we went the same walk, and when we came to that narrow, dark part of the lane where the brake runs down to the bank, nurse made me promise all over again, and she looked about, just as she had done before, and we crept into the bushes till we got to the green place where the little clay man was hidden. I remember it all so well, though I was only eight, and it is eight years ago now as I am writing it down, but the sky was a deep violet blue, and in the middle of the brake where we were sitting there was a great elder tree covered with blossoms, and on the other side there was a clump of meadowsweet, and when I think of that day the smell of the meadowsweet and elder blossom seems to fill the room, and if I shut my eyes I can see the glaring blue sky, with little clouds very white floating across it, and nurse who went away long ago sitting opposite me and looking like the beautiful white lady in the wood. So we sat down and nurse took out the clay doll from the secret place where she had hidden it, and she said we must "pay our respects," and she would show me what to do, and I must watch her all the time. So she did all sorts of queer things with the little clay man, and I noticed she was all streaming with perspiration, though we had walked so slowly, and then she told me to "pay my respects," and I did everything she did because I liked her, and it was such an odd game. And she said that if one loved very much, the clay man was very good, if one did certain things with it, and if one hated very much, it was just as good, only one had to do different things, and we played with it a long time, and pretended all sorts of things. Nurse said her great-grandmother had told her all about these images, but what we did was no harm at all, only a game. But she told me a story about these images that frightened me very much, and that was what I remembered that night when I was lying awake in my room in the pale, empty darkness, thinking of what I had seen and the secret wood. Nurse said there was once a young lady of the high gentry, who lived in a great castle. And she was so beautiful that all the gentlemen wanted to marry her, because she was the loveliest lady that anybody had ever seen, and she was kind to everybody, and everybody thought she was very good. But though she was polite to all the gentlemen who wished to marry her, she put them off, and said she couldn't make up her mind, and she wasn't sure she wanted to marry anybody at all. And her father, who was a very great lord, was angry, though he was so fond of her, and he asked her why she wouldn't choose a bachelor out of all the handsome young men who came to the castle. But she only said she didn't love any of them very much, and she must wait, and if they pestered her, she said she would go and be a nun in a nunnery. So all the gentlemen said they would go away and wait for a year and a day, and when a year and a day were gone, they would come back again and ask her to say which one she would marry. So the day was appointed and they all went away; and the lady had promised that in a year and a day it would be her wedding day with one of them. But the truth was, that she was the queen of the people who danced on the hill on summer nights, and on the proper nights she would lock the door of her room, and she and her maid would steal out of the castle by a secret passage that only they knew of, and go away up to the hill in the wild land. And she knew more of the secret things than any one else, and more than any one knew before or after, because she would not tell anybody the most secret secrets. She knew how to do all the awful things, how to destroy young men, and how to put a curse on people, and other things that I could not understand. And her real name was the Lady Avelin, but the dancing people called her Cassap, which meant somebody very wise, in the old language. And she was whiter than any of them and taller, and her eyes shone in the dark like burning rubies; and she could sing songs that none of the others could sing, and when she sang they all fell down on their faces and worshipped her. And she could do what they called shib-show, which was a very wonderful enchantment. She would tell the great lord, her father, that she wanted to go into the woods to gather flowers, so he let her go, and she and her maid went into the woods where nobody came, and the maid would keep watch. Then the lady would lie down under the trees and begin to sing a particular song, and she stretched out her arms, and from every part of the wood great serpents would come, hissing and gliding in and out among the trees, and shooting out their forked tongues as they crawled up to the lady. And they all came to her, and twisted round her, round her body, and her arms, and her neck, till she was covered with writhing serpents, and there was only her head to be seen. And she whispered to them, and she sang to them, and they writhed round and round, faster and faster, till she told them to go. And they all went away directly, back to their holes, and on the lady's breast there would be a most curious, beautiful stone, shaped something like an egg, and coloured dark blue and yellow, and red, and green, marked like a serpent's scales. It was called a glame stone, and with it one could do all sorts of wonderful things, and nurse said her great-grandmother had seen a glame stone with her own eyes, and it was for all the world shiny and scaly like a snake. And the lady could do a lot of other things as well, but she was quite fixed that she would not be married. And there were a great many gentlemen who wanted to marry her, but there were five of them who were chief, and their names were Sir Simon, Sir John, Sir Oliver, Sir Richard, and Sir Rowland. All the others believed she spoke the truth, and that she would choose one of them to be her man when a year and a day was done; it was only Sir Simon, who was very crafty, who thought she was deceiving them all, and he vowed he would watch and try if he could find out anything. And though he was very wise he was very young, and he had a smooth, soft face like a girl's, and he pretended, as the rest did, that he would not come to the castle for a year and a day, and he said he was going away beyond the sea to foreign parts. But he really only went a very little way, and came back dressed like a servant girl, and so he got a place in the castle to wash the dishes. And he waited and watched, and he listened and said nothing, and he hid in dark places, and woke up at night and looked out, and he heard things and he saw things that he thought were very strange. And he was so sly that he told the girl that waited on the lady that he was really a young man, and that he had dressed up as a girl because he loved her so very much and wanted to be in the same house with her, and the girl was so pleased that she told him many things, and he was more than ever certain that the Lady Avelin was deceiving him and the others. And he was so clever, and told the servant so many lies, that one night he managed to hide in the Lady Avelin's room behind the curtains. And he stayed quite still and never moved, and at last the lady came. And she bent down under the bed, and raised up a stone, and there was a hollow place underneath, and out of it she took a waxen image, just like the clay one that I and nurse had made in the brake. And all the time her eyes were burning like rubies. And she took the little wax doll up in her arms and held it to her breast, and she whispered and she murmured, and she took it up and she laid it down again, and she held it high, and she held it low, and she laid it down again. And she said, "Happy is he that begat the bishop, that ordered the clerk, that married the man, that had the wife, that fashioned the hive, that harboured the bee, that gathered the wax that my own true love was made of." And she brought out of an aumbry a great golden bowl, and she brought out of a closet a great jar of wine, and she poured some of the wine into the bowl, and she laid her mannikin very gently in the wine, and washed it in the wine all over. Then she went to a cupboard and took a small round cake and laid it on the image's mouth, and then she bore it softly and covered it up. And Sir Simon, who was watching all the time, though he was terribly frightened, saw the lady bend down and stretch out her arms and whisper and sing, and then Sir Simon saw beside her a handsome young man, who kissed her on the lips. And they drank wine out of the golden bowl together, and they ate the cake together. But when the sun rose there was only the little wax doll, and the lady hid it again under the bed in the hollow place. So Sir Simon knew quite well what the lady was, and he waited and he watched, till the time she had said was nearly over, and in a week the year and a day would be done. And one night, when he was watching behind the curtains in her room, he saw her making more wax dolls. And she made five, and hid them away. And the next night she took one out, and held it up, and filled the golden bowl with water, and took the doll by the neck and held it under the water. Then she said—

Sir Dickon, Sir Dickon, your day is done, You shall be drowned in the water wan.

And the next day news came to the castle that Sir Richard had been drowned at the ford. And at night she took another doll and tied a violet cord round its neck and hung it up on a nail. Then she said—

Sir Rowland, your life has ended its span, High on a tree I see you hang.

And the next day news came to the castle that Sir Rowland had been hanged by robbers in the wood. And at night she took another doll, and drove her bodkin right into its heart. Then she said—

Sir Noll, Sir Noll, so cease your life, Your heart pierced with the knife.

And the next day news came to the castle that Sir Oliver had fought in a tavern, and a stranger had stabbed him to the heart. And at night she took another doll, and held it to a fire of charcoal till it was melted. Then she said—

Sir John, return, and turn to clay, In fire of fever you waste away.

And the next day news came to the castle that Sir John had died in a burning fever. So then Sir Simon went out of the castle and mounted his horse and rode away to the bishop and told him everything. And the bishop sent his men, and they took the Lady Avelin, and everything she had done was found out. So on the day after the year and a day, when she was to have been married, they carried her through the town in her smock, and they tied her to a great stake in the market-place, and burned her alive before the bishop with her wax image hung round her neck. And people said the wax man screamed in the burning of the flames. And I thought of this story again and again as I was lying awake in my bed, and I seemed to see the Lady Avelin in the market-place, with the yellow flames eating up her beautiful white body. And I thought of it so much that I seemed to get into the story myself, and I fancied I was the lady, and that they were coming to take me to be burnt with fire, with all the people in the town looking at me. And I wondered whether she cared, after all the strange things she had done, and whether it hurt very much to be burned at the stake. I tried again and again to forget nurse's stories, and to remember the secret I had seen that afternoon, and what was in the secret wood, but I could only see the dark and a glimmering in the dark, and then it went away, and I only saw myself running, and then a great moon came up white over a dark round hill. Then all the old stories came back again, and the queer rhymes that nurse used to sing to me; and there was one beginning "Halsy cumsy Helen musty," that she used to sing very softly when she wanted me to go to sleep. And I began to sing it to myself inside of my head, and I went to sleep.

The next morning I was very tired and sleepy, and could hardly do my lessons, and I was very glad when they were over and I had had my dinner, as I wanted to go out and be alone. It was a warm day, and I went to a nice turfy hill by the river, and sat down on my mother's old shawl that I had brought with me on purpose. The sky was grey, like the day before, but there was a kind of white gleam behind it, and from where I was sitting I could look down on the town, and it was all still and quiet and white, like a picture. I remembered that it was on that hill that nurse taught me to play an old game called "Troy Town," in which one had to dance, and wind in and out on a pattern in the grass, and then when one had danced and turned long enough the other person asks you questions, and you can't help answering whether you want to or not, and whatever you are told to do you feel you have to do it. Nurse said there used to be a lot of games like that that some people knew of, and there was one by which people could be turned into anything you liked, and an old man her great-grandmother had seen had known a girl who had been turned into a large snake. And there was another very ancient game of dancing and winding and turning, by which you could take a person out of himself and hide him away as long as you liked, and his body went walking about quite empty, without any sense in it. But I came to that hill because I wanted to think of what had happened the day before, and of the secret of the wood. From the place where I was sitting I could see beyond the town, into the opening I had found, where a little brook had led me into an unknown country. And I pretended I was following the brook over again, and I went all the way in my mind, and at last I found the wood, and crept into it under the bushes, and then in the dusk I saw something that made me feel as if I were filled with fire, as if I wanted to dance and sing and fly up into the air, because I was changed and wonderful. But what I saw was not changed at all, and had not grown old, and I wondered again and again how such things could happen, and whether nurse's stories were really true, because in the daytime in the open air everything seemed quite different from what it was at night, when I was frightened, and thought I was to be burned alive. I once told my father one of her little tales, which was about a ghost, and asked him if it was true, and he told me it was not true at all, and that only common, ignorant people believed in such rubbish. He was very angry with nurse for telling me the story, and scolded her, and after that I promised her I would never whisper a word of what she told me, and if I did I should be bitten by the great black snake that lived in the pool in the wood. And all alone on the hill I wondered what was true. I had seen something very amazing and very lovely, and I knew a story, and if I had really seen it, and not made it up out of the dark, and the black bough, and the bright shining that was mounting up to the sky from over the great round hill, but had really seen it in truth, then there were all kinds of wonderful and lovely and terrible things to think of, so I longed and trembled, and I burned and got cold. And I looked down on the town, so quiet and still, like a little white picture, and I thought over and over if it could be true. I was a long time before I could make up my mind to anything; there was such a strange fluttering at my heart that seemed to whisper to me all the time that I had not made it up out of my head, and yet it seemed quite impossible, and I knew my father and everybody would say it was dreadful rubbish. I never dreamed of telling him or anybody else a word about it, because I knew it would be of no use, and I should only get laughed at or scolded, so for a long time I was very quiet, and went about thinking and wondering; and at night I used to dream of amazing things, and sometimes I woke up in the early morning and held out my arms with a cry. And I was frightened, too, because there were dangers, and some awful thing would happen to me, unless I took great care, if the story were true. These old tales were always in my head, night and morning, and I went over them and told them to myself over and over again, and went for walks in the places where nurse had told them to me; and when I sat in the nursery by the fire in the evenings I used to fancy nurse was sitting in the other chair, and telling me some wonderful story in a low voice, for fear anybody should be listening. But she used to like best to tell me about things when we were right out in the country, far from the house, because she said she was telling me such secrets, and walls have ears. And if it was something more than ever secret, we had to hide in brakes or woods; and I used to think it was such fun creeping along a hedge, and going very softly, and then we would get behind the bushes or run into the wood all of a sudden, when we were sure that none was watching us; so we knew that we had our secrets quite all to ourselves, and nobody else at all knew anything about them. Now and then, when we had hidden ourselves as I have described, she used to show me all sorts of odd things. One day, I remember, we were in a hazel brake, overlooking the brook, and we were so snug and warm, as though it was April; the sun was quite hot, and the leaves were just coming out. Nurse said she would show me something funny that would make me laugh, and then she showed me, as she said, how one could turn a whole house upside down, without anybody being able to find out, and the pots and pans would jump about, and the china would be broken, and the chairs would tumble over of themselves. I tried it one day in the kitchen, and I found I could do it quite well, and a whole row of plates on the dresser fell off it, and cook's little work-table tilted up and turned right over "before her eyes," as she said, but she was so frightened and turned so white that I didn't do it again, as I liked her. And afterwards, in the hazel copse, when she had shown me how to make things tumble about, she showed me how to make rapping noises, and I learnt how to do that, too. Then she taught me rhymes to say on certain occasions, and peculiar marks to make on other occasions, and other things that her great-grandmother had taught her when she was a little girl herself. And these were all the things I was thinking about in those days after the strange walk when I thought I had seen a great secret, and I wished nurse were there for me to ask her about it, but she had gone away more than two years before, and nobody seemed to know what had become of her, or where she had gone. But I shall always remember those days if I live to be quite old, because all the time I felt so strange, wondering and doubting, and feeling quite sure at one time, and making up my mind, and then I would feel quite sure that such things couldn't happen really, and it began all over again. But I took great care not to do certain things that might be very dangerous. So I waited and wondered for a long time, and though I was not sure at all, I never dared to try to find out. But one day I became sure that all that nurse said was quite true, and I was all alone when I found it out. I trembled all over with joy and terror, and as fast as I could I ran into one of the old brakes where we used to go—it was the one by the lane, where nurse made the little clay man—and I ran into it, and I crept into it; and when I came to the place where the elder was, I covered up my face with my hands and lay down flat on the grass, and I stayed there for two hours without moving, whispering to myself delicious, terrible things, and saying some words over and over again. It was all true and wonderful and splendid, and when I remembered the story I knew and thought of what I had really seen, I got hot and I got cold, and the air seemed full of scent, and flowers, and singing. And first I wanted to make a little clay man, like the one nurse had made so long ago, and I had to invent plans and stratagems, and to look about, and to think of things beforehand, because nobody must dream of anything that I was doing or going to do, and I was too old to carry clay about in a tin bucket. At last I thought of a plan, and I brought the wet clay to the brake, and did everything that nurse had done, only I made a much finer image than the one she had made; and when it was finished I did everything that I could imagine and much more than she did, because it was the likeness of something far better. And a few days later, when I had done my lessons early, I went for the second time by the way of the little brook that had led me into a strange country. And I followed the brook, and went through the bushes, and beneath the low branches of trees, and up thorny thickets on the hill, and by dark woods full of creeping thorns, a long, long way. Then I crept through the dark tunnel where the brook had been and the ground was stony, till at last I came to the thicket that climbed up the hill, and though the leaves were coming out upon the trees, everything looked almost as black as it was on the first day that I went there. And the thicket was just the same, and I went up slowly till I came out on the big bare hill, and began to walk among the wonderful rocks. I saw the terrible voor again on everything, for though the sky was brighter, the ring of wild hills all around was still dark, and the hanging woods looked dark and dreadful, and the strange rocks were as grey as ever; and when I looked down on them from the great mound, sitting on the stone, I saw all their amazing circles and rounds within rounds, and I had to sit quite still and watch them as they began to turn about me, and each stone danced in its place, and they seemed to go round and round in a great whirl, as if one were in the middle of all the stars and heard them rushing through the air. So I went down among the rocks to dance with them and to sing extraordinary songs; and I went down through the other thicket, and drank from the bright stream in the close and secret valley, putting my lips down to the bubbling water; and then I went on till I came to the deep, brimming well among the glittering moss, and I sat down. I looked before me into the secret darkness of the valley, and behind me was the great high wall of grass, and all around me there were the hanging woods that made the valley such a secret place. I knew there was nobody here at all besides myself, and that no one could see me. So I took off my boots and stockings, and let my feet down into the water, saying the words that I knew. And it was not cold at all, as I expected, but warm and very pleasant, and when my feet were in it I felt as if they were in silk, or as if the nymph were kissing them. So when I had done, I said the other words and made the signs, and then I dried my feet with a towel I had brought on purpose, and put on my stockings and boots. Then I climbed up the steep wall, and went into the place where there are the hollows, and the two beautiful mounds, and the round ridges of land, and all the strange shapes. I did not go down into the hollow this time, but I turned at the end, and made out the figures quite plainly, as it was lighter, and I had remembered the story I had quite forgotten before, and in the story the two figures are called Adam and Eve, and only those who know the story understand what they mean. So I went on and on till I came to the secret wood which must not be described, and I crept into it by the way I had found. And when I had gone about halfway I stopped, and turned round, and got ready, and I bound the handkerchief tightly round my eyes, and made quite sure that I could not see at all, not a twig, nor the end of a leaf, nor the light of the sky, as it was an old red silk handkerchief with large yellow spots, that went round twice and covered my eyes, so that I could see nothing. Then I began to go on, step by step, very slowly. My heart beat faster and faster, and something rose in my throat that choked me and made me want to cry out, but I shut my lips, and went on. Boughs caught in my hair as I went, and great thorns tore me; but I went on to the end of the path. Then I stopped, and held out my arms and bowed, and I went round the first time, feeling with my hands, and there was nothing. I went round the second time, feeling with my hands, and there was nothing. Then I went round the third time, feeling with my hands, and the story was all true, and I wished that the years were gone by, and that I had not so long a time to wait before I was happy for ever and ever.

Nurse must have been a prophet like those we read of in the Bible. Everything that she said began to come true, and since then other things that she told me of have happened. That was how I came to know that her stories were true and that I had not made up the secret myself out of my own head. But there was another thing that happened that day. I went a second time to the secret place. It was at the deep brimming well, and when I was standing on the moss I bent over and looked in, and then I knew who the white lady was that I had seen come out of the water in the wood long ago when I was quite little. And I trembled all over, because that told me other things. Then I remembered how sometime after I had seen the white people in the wood, nurse asked me more about them, and I told her all over again, and she listened, and said nothing for a long, long time, and at last she said,

"You will see her again." So I understood what had happened and what was to happen. And I understood about the nymphs; how I might meet them in all kinds of places, and they would always help me, and I must always look for them, and find them in all sorts of strange shapes and appearances. And without the nymphs I could never have found the secret, and without them none of the other things could happen. Nurse had told me all about them long ago, but she called them by another name, and I did not know what she meant, or what her tales of them were about, only that they were very queer. And there were two kinds, the bright and the dark, and both were very lovely and very wonderful, and some people saw only one kind, and some only the other, but some saw them both. But usually the dark appeared first, and the bright ones came afterwards, and there were extraordinary tales about them. It was a day or two after I had come home from the secret place that I first really knew the nymphs. Nurse had shown me how to call them, and I had tried, but I did not know what she meant, and so I thought it was all nonsense. But I made up my mind I would try again, so I went to the wood where the pool was, where I saw the white people, and I tried again. The dark nymph, Alanna, came, and she turned the pool of water into a pool of fire . . .

Epilogue

"That's a very queer story," said Cotgrave, handing back the green book to the recluse, Ambrose. "I see the drift of a good deal, but there are many things that I do not grasp at all. On the last page, for example, what does she mean by 'nymphs'?"

"Well, I think there are references throughout the manuscript to certain 'processes' which have been handed down by tradition from age to age. Some of these processes are just beginning to come within the purview of science, which has arrived at them—or rather at the steps which lead to them—by quite different paths. I have interpreted the reference to 'nymphs' as a reference to one of these processes."

"And you believe that there are such things?"

"Oh, I think so. Yes, I believe I could give you convincing evidence on that point. I am afraid you have neglected the study of alchemy? It is a pity, for the symbolism, at all events, is very beautiful, and moreover if you were acquainted with certain books on the subject, I could recall to your mind phrases which might explain a good deal in the manuscript that you have been reading."

"Yes; but I want to know whether you seriously think that there is any foundation of fact beneath these fancies. Is it not all a department of poetry; a curious dream with which man has indulged himself?"

"I can only say that it is no doubt better for the great mass of people to dismiss it all as a dream. But if you ask my veritable belief—that goes quite the other way. No; I should not say belief, but rather knowledge. I may tell you that I have known cases in which men have stumbled quite by accident on certain of these 'processes,' and have been astonished by wholly unexpected results. In the cases I am thinking of there could have been no possibility of 'suggestion' or sub-conscious action of any kind. One might as well suppose a schoolboy 'suggesting' the existence of Æschylus to himself, while he plods mechanically through the declensions.

"But you have noticed the obscurity," Ambrose went on, "and in this particular case it must have been dictated by instinct, since the writer never thought that her manuscripts would fall into other hands. But the practice is universal, and for most excellent reasons. Powerful and sovereign medicines, which are, of necessity, virulent poisons also, are kept in a locked cabinet. The child may find the key by chance, and drink herself dead; but in most cases the search is educational, and the phials contain precious elixirs for him who has patiently fashioned the key for himself."

"You do not care to go into details?"

"No, frankly, I do not. No, you must remain unconvinced. But you saw how the manuscript illustrates the talk we had last week?"

"Is this girl still alive?"

"No. I was one of those who found her. I knew the father well; he was a lawyer, and had always left her very much to herself. He thought of nothing but deeds and leases, and the news came to him as an awful surprise. She was missing one morning; I suppose it was about a year after she had written what you have read. The servants were called, and they told things, and put the only natural interpretation on them—a perfectly erroneous one.

"They discovered that green book somewhere in her room, and I found her in the place that she described with so much dread, lying on the ground before the image."

"It was an image?"

"Yes, it was hidden by the thorns and the thick undergrowth that had surrounded it. It was a wild, lonely country; but you know what it was like by her description, though of course you will understand that the colours have been heightened. A child's imagination always makes the heights higher and the depths deeper than they really are; and she had, unfortunately for herself, something more than imagination. One might say, perhaps, that the picture in her mind which she succeeded in a measure in putting into words, was the scene as it would have appeared to an imaginative artist. But it is a strange, desolate land."

"And she was dead?"

"Yes. She had poisoned herself—in time. No; there was not a word to be said against her in the ordinary sense. You may recollect a story I told you the other night about a lady who saw her child's fingers crushed by a window?"

"And what was this statue?"

"Well, it was of Roman workmanship, of a stone that with the centuries had not blackened, but had become white and luminous. The thicket had grown up about it and concealed it, and in the Middle Ages the followers of a very old tradition had known how to use it for their own purposes. In fact it had been incorporated into the monstrous mythology of the Sabbath. You will have noted that those to whom a sight of that shining whiteness had been vouchsafed by chance, or rather, perhaps, by apparent chance, were required to blindfold themselves on their second approach. That is very significant."

"And is it there still?"

"I sent for tools, and we hammered it into dust and fragments."

"The persistence of tradition never surprises me," Ambrose went on after a pause. "I could name many an English parish where such traditions as that girl had listened to in her childhood are still existent in occult but unabated vigour. No, for me, it is the 'story' not the 'sequel,' which is strange and awful, for I have always believed that wonder is of the soul."

THE SEA LURE

by Dion Fortune

Born Violet Mary Firth, Dion Fortune (1890-1946) is known amongst occultists as a brilliant magician and esoteric scholar. Like Machen and Crowley, she was an adept of the Hermetic Order of the Golden Dawn, and penned the classic modern textbook of Hermetic magic, *The Mystical Qabalah* (1935). Her direct and indirect influence on the revival of magic and the evolution of the hermetic thought in the twentieth century is incalculable.

She was also a marvelous and lucid novelist whose mastery of the psychological works of Jung and Freud lifted the arts of Western Esotericism out of the pit of mediaeval superstition. "The Sea Lure," taken from her greater collection *The Secrets of Doctor Taverner*, is one of a dozen stories that tell of supernatural disorders and the doctor's unconventional methods of treatment. In the introduction to the collection, she wrote:

> It may not unreasonably be asked what motive anyone could have for securing a hearing for such histories as are set forth in these tales, beyond the not unreasonable interest in the royalties of horrors; I would ask readers, however, to credit me with another motive that the purely commercial. I was one of the earliest students of psychoanalysis in this country, and I found, in the course of my studies, that the ends of a number of threads were put into my hands, but that the threads disappeared into the darkness that surrounded the small circle of light thrown by exact scientific knowledge. It was following these threads out into the darkness of the Unknown that I came upon the experiences and cases, which, turned into fiction, are set down in these pages.

The Sea Lure

"Do you know anything about stigmata?" said my *vis-à-vis*. It was a very unexpected question to have shot at one under the circumstances. I had been unable to evade an invitation to spend the evening with an old fellow-student who since the war had held the uninspiring post of medical officer at a poor law institution, a post for which I should say he was admirably fitted, and I now found myself facing him across a not very elegant supper table in his quarters in a great fortress of dingy red brick which looked out for miles over the grey wastes of sordidness which are South London.

I was so taken by surprise that he had to repeat his question before I answered it.

"Do you know anything about stigmata? Hysterical stigmata?" he said again. "I have seen simulated tumours," I said, "they are fairly common, but I have never seen actual flesh wounds, such as the saints were supposed to have had."

"What do you attribute them to?" asked my companion.

"Auto-suggestion," I replied. "Imagination so vivid that it actually affects the tissues of the body."

"I have got a case in one of my wards that I should like to show you," he said. "A most curious case. I think it is hysterical stigmata, I cannot account for it any other way. A girl was brought in here a couple of days ago suffering from a gunshot wound in the shoulder. She came here to have the bullet removed, but would give no account as to how she came by the injury. We admitted her, but couldn't see any bullet, which was rather puzzling. She was in a condition of semi-stupor, which we naturally attributed to loss of blood, and so we kept her here. Of course there is nothing odd in all that, save our failure to locate the bullet, but then such things happen even with the best apparatus, and ours is a long way from being that. But here is the queer part of the case.

"I was sitting quietly up here last night between 11 and 12 when I heard a shriek, of course there is nothing odd about that either, in this district. But in a minute or two they rang up on the house telephone to say that I was wanted in the wards, and I went down to find this girl with *another* bullet wound. No one had heard a shot fired, all the windows were intact, there was a nurse not 10 feet from her. When we X-rayed her we again failed to find the bullet, yet there was a clean hole drilled in her shoulder, and, oddest of all, it never bled a drop. What do you make of it?"

"If you are certain there is no external agency at work, then the only hypothesis is an internal one. Is she an hysterical type?"

"Distinctly. Looks as if she came out of one of Burne-Jones's pictures. Moreover, she has been in a sort of stupor each night for an hour or more at a time. It was while in this state that she developed the second wound. Would you care to come down and have a look at her? I should like to have your opinion. I know you have gone in for psychoanalysis and all sorts of things that are beyond my ken."

I accompanied him to the wards, and there we found in one of the rough infirmary beds a girl who, lying on the coarse pillow, with closed eyes and parted lips, looked exactly like the *Beata Beatrix* of Rossetti's vision, save that honey-coloured hair flowed over the pillow like sea-weed. When she opened her eyes at our presence, they were green as sea-water seen from a rock.

All was quiet in the ward, for infirmary patients are settled for the night at an early hour, and my friend signed to the nurse to put screens round the bed that we might examine our case without disturbing them. It was as he had said, two obvious bullet wounds, one more recent than the other, and from their position and proximity, I judged that they have been inflicted with intention to disable, but not to kill. In fact she had been very neatly "winged" by an expert marksman. It was only the circumstances of the second shot that gave the case any interest except a criminal one.

I sat down on a chair at the bedside, and began to talk to her, seeking to win her confidence. She gazed back at me dreamily with her strange sea-green eyes and answered my questions readily enough. She seemed curiously detached, curiously indifferent to our opinion of her; as if she lived in a far-away world of her own, about which she was quite willing to talk to any one who was interested.

"Do you dream much?" I said, making the usual opening.

This seemed to touch a subject of interest.

"Oh, yes," she replied, "I dream a tremendous lot. I always have dreamt, ever since I can remember. I think my dreams are the realest part of my life—and the best part," she added with a smile, "so why shouldn't I?"

"Your dreams seem to have led you into danger recently," I answered, drawing a bow at a venture.

She looked at me sharply, as if to see how much I knew, and then said thoughtfully: "Yes, I mustn't go there again. But I expect I shall, all the same," she added with an elfish smile.

"Can you go where you choose in your dreams?" I asked.

"Sometimes," she replied, and was about to say more, when she caught sight of my companion's bewildered face and the words died on her lips. I saw that she was what Taverner would have called "One of Us," and my interest was roused. I pitied the refined, artistic-looking girl in these sordid surroundings, her great shining eyes looking out like those of a caged creature behind bars; and I said: "What is your work?"

"Shop girl," she replied; a smile curling the corners of her lips. "Drapery, to be precise." Her words and manner were so at variance with her description of herself, that I was still further intrigued.

"Where are you going when you come out of here?" I enquired.

She looked wearily out into the distance, the little smile still hovering about her mouth. "Back into my dreams, I expect," she replied. "I don't suppose I shall find anywhere else to go."

I knew well Taverner's generosity with necessitous cases, especially if they were of "his own kind," and I felt sure that he would be interested both in the personality of the girl and in her peculiar injuries, and I said:

"How would you like to go down to a convalescent home at Hindhead when you leave here?" She gazed at me in silence for a moment with her strange gleaming eyes.

"Hindhead?" she asked. "What sort of a place is that?"

"It is moorland," I replied. "Heather and pine, you know, very bracing."

"Oh, if it could only be the sea!' she exclaimed wistfully. "A rocky coast, miles from anywhere, where the Atlantic rollers come in and the seabirds are flying and calling. If it could only be the sea I should get right! The moors are not my place, it is the sea I need, it is life to me."

She paused abruptly, as if she feared to have said too much, and then she added: "Please don't think that I am ungrateful, a rest and change would be a great help. Yes, I should be very thankful for a letter for the nursing home—" Her voice trailed into silence and her eyes, looking more like deep-sea water than ever, gazed unseeing into a distance where I have no doubt the gulls were flying and calling and the Atlantic rollers coming in from the West.

"She has gone off again," said my host. "It is apparently her regular time for going into a state of coma."

As we watched her, she took a deep inspiration, and then all breathing ceased. It ceased for so long, although the pulse continued vigorously, that I was just on the point of suggesting artificial respiration, when with a profound exhalation, the lungs took up their work with deep rhythmical gasps. Now if you observe a person's respiration closely, you will invariably found that you yourself begin to breathe with the same rhythm. It was a very peculiar rhythm which I found myself assuming, and yet it was not unfamiliar. I had breathed with that rhythm before, and I searched my subconscious mind for the due. Suddenly I found it. It was the respiration of breathing in rough water. No doubt the cessation of breathing represented the dive. The girl was dreaming of her sea.

So absorbed was I in the problem that I would have sat up all night in the hope of finding some evidence of the mysterious assailant, but my host touched my sleeve. "We had better be moving," he said. "Matron, you know." And I followed him out of the darkened ward.

"What do you make of it?" he enquired eagerly as soon as we were out in the corridor.

"I think as you do," I answered; "that we are dealing with a case of stigmata, but it will require more plumbing than I could give it this evening, and I should like to keep in touch with her if you are willing."

He was only too willing; seeing himself in print in the *Lancet* and possessed of that dubious type of glory which comes to the owners of curios. It was a blessed break in the monotony of his routine, and he naturally welcomed it.

Now that which is to follow will doubtless be set down as the grossest kind of coincidence, and as several such coincidences have been reported in these chronicles, I do not suppose I have much reputation for veracity anyway. But Taverner always held that some coincidences, especially those which might be conceived to serve the purpose of an intelligent Providence, were not as fortuitous as they appeared to be, but were due to causes which operated invisibly upon the subtler planes of existence, and whose effects alone were seen in our material world; and that those of us who are in touch with the unseen, as he was, and as I, to a lesser degree on account of my association with him in his work, had also come to be, might get ourselves into the hidden currents of that realm, and thereby be brought in touch with those engaged in similar pursuits. I had too often watched Taverner picking up people apparently at random and arriving at the psychological moment apparently by chance, to doubt the operation of some such laws as he described, though I neither understand their workings nor recognize them at the time; it is only in perspective that one sees the Unseen Hand.

Therefore it was that when, on my return to Hindhead, Taverner requested me to undertake a certain task, I concluded that my plans with regard to the study of the stigmata case must be set aside, and banished the matter from my mind.

"Rhodes," he said, "I want you to undertake a piece of work for me. I would go myself, but it is extremely difficult for me to get away, and you know enough of my methods by now, combined with your native common sense (in which I have much more faith than in many people's psychism) to be able to report the matter, and possibly deal with it under my instruction."

He handed me a letter. It was inscribed, "Care G.H. Frater," and began without any further preamble: "That of which you warned me has occurred. I have indeed got in out of my depth, and unless you can pull me out I shall be a drowned man, literally as well as metaphorically. I cannot get away from here and come to you; can you possibly come to me?" And a quotation from Virgil, which seemed to have little bearing on the subject, closed the appeal. Scenting adventure, I readily acceded to Taverner's request. It was a long journey I had to undertake, and when the train came to rest at its terminus in the grey twilight of a winter afternoon, I could smell the keen salt tang of the wind that drove straight in from the West. To me there is always something thrilling in arriving at a seaside place and getting the first glimpse of the sea, and my mind reverted to that other solitary soul who had loved blue water, the girl with the Rossetti face, who lay in the rough infirmary bed in the dreary desert of South London.

She was vividly present to my mind as I entered the musty four-wheeler, which was all that the station could produce in the off-season, and drove through deserted and wind-swept streets on to the sea-front. The line of breakers showed grey through the gathering darkness as we left the asphalt and boarding houses behind us and followed the coast road out into the alluvial flats beyond the town. Presently the road began to wind upwards towards the cliffs, and I could hear the horse wheezing with the ascent, till a hail from the darkness put a stop to our progress; a figure clad in an Inverness cape appeared in the light of the carriage lamps, and a voice, which had that indefinable something which Oxford always gives a man, greeted me by name and invited me to alight.

Although I could see no sign of a habitation, I did as I was bidden, and the cabman, manoeuvring his vehicle, departed into the windy darkness and left me alone with my invisible host. He possessed himself of my bag, and we set off straight for the edge of the cliff, so far as

I could make out, leaning up against the force of the gale. An invisible surf crashed and roared below us, and it seemed to me that drowning was the order of the day for both of us.

Presently, however, I felt a path under my feet. "Keep close to the rock," shouted my guide. (Next day I knew why.) And we dipped over the edge of the cliff and began to descend its face. We continued in this way for what seemed to me an immense distance, I learnt later it was about a quarter of a mile, and then, to my amazement, I heard the click of a latch. It was too dark to see anything, but warm air smote my face, and I knew that I was under cover. I heard my host fumbling with a box of matches, and as the light flared, I saw that I was in a good-sized room, apparently hewn out of the cliff face, and a most comfortable apartment. Book-lined, warmly curtained, Persian rugs on the smooth stone of the floor, and a fire of drift wood burning on the open hearth, which the toe of my companion's boot soon stirred to a blaze. The amazing contrast to my gloomy and perilous arrival took my breath away.

My host smiled. "I am afraid," he said, "that you were making up your mind to be murdered. I ought to have explained to you the nature of my habitation. I am so used to it myself, that it does not seem to me that it may appear strange to others. It is an old smuggler's lair that I have adapted to my use, and being made of the living rock, it has peculiar advantages for the work on which I am engaged."

We sat down to the meal that was already upon the table, and I had an opportunity to study the appearance of my host. Whether he was an elderly man who had preserved his youth, or a young man prematurely aged, I could not tell, but the maturity of his mind was such that I inclined to the former hypothesis, for a wide experience of men and things must have gone to the ripening of such a nature as his.

His face had something of the lawyer about it, but his hands were those of an artist. It was a combination I had often seen before in Taverner's friends, for the intellectual who has a touch of the mystic generally ends in occultism. His hair was nearly white, in strange contrast to his wind-tanned face and dark sparkling eyes. His figure was spare and athletic, and well above middle height, but his movements had not the ease of youth, but rather the measured dignity of a man who is accustomed to public appearances.

It was an interesting and impressive personality, but he showed none of the signs of distress that his letter had led me to expect. After-dinner pipes soon led to confidences, and after sitting for a while in the warm fire-lit silence, my host seemed to gather his resolution together, and after crossing and uncrossing his legs several times uneasily, finally said:

"Well, doctor, this visit is on business, not pleasure, so we may as well 'Cut the cackle and come to the 'osses.' I suppose I appear to you to be sane enough at the present moment?" I bowed my assent.

"At 11 o'clock you will have the pleasure of seeing me go off my head."

"Will you tell me what you are experiencing?" I said.

"You are not one of us," he replied (I had probably failed to acknowledge some sign), "but you must be in Taverner's confidence or he would not have sent you. I am going to speak freely to you. You are willing to admit, I presume, that there is more in heaven and earth than you are taught in the medical schools?"

"No one can look life honestly in the face without admitting that," I replied. "I have respect for the unseen, though I don't pretend to understand it."

"Good man" was the reply. "You will be more use to me than a brother occultist who might encourage me in my delusions. I want facts, not fantasies. Once I am certain that I am deluded, I can pull myself together; it is the uncertainty that is baffling me."

He looked at his watch; paused, and then with an effort plunged *in medias res*.

"I have been studying the elemental forces: I suppose you know what that means? The semi-intelligent entities behind the potencies of nature. We divide them into four classes—earth, air, fire and water. Now I am of the earth, earthy."

I raised my eyebrows in query, for his appearance belied the description he gave of himself. He smiled. "I did not say of the flesh, fleshly. That is quite a different matter. But in my horoscope I have five planets in earth signs, and consequently my nature is bound up with the formal side of things. Now in order to counteract this state of affairs I set myself to get in touch with the fluidic side of nature, elemental water. I have succeeded in doing so." He paused and packed the tobacco in his pipe with a nervous gesture. "But not only have I got in touch with the water elementals, but they have got in touch with me. One in particular.' The pipe again required attention.

"It was a most extraordinary, exhilarating experience. Everything I lacked seemed to be added to me. I was complete, vital, in circuit with the cosmic forces. In fact, I got everything I had sought in marriage and failed to find. But, and here's the rub, the creature that called me was in the water, and it was in the water that I had to meet her. Round this headland the tides run like fury, no swimmer could hold his own against them, even in calm weather; but by night, and in a storm, which is the time she generally comes, it would be certain death; but she calls me, and she *wills* me to go to her, and one of these nights I shall do so. That is my trouble."

He stopped, but I could see by the working of his face that there was more to come so I kept silence. He bent down and took from the side of the hearth an object which he handed to me. It was a small crucible, and had evidently been used to melt down silver.

"You will laugh when I tell you what I used that for. To make silver bullets—silver bullets to shoot with." He hid his face in his hands. 'Oh, my God, I tried to murder her!' The flood-gates of emotion were open, and I could see his shoulders heave to the tide of it.

"I could see her as she swam in the moonlight, and as her shoulder rose to the stroke, I shot her in the round white curve of it, white as foam against the black water. And she vanished. Then I thought I had killed the thing I loved. I would have given heaven and earth to bring her back and to swim out there to her in the tide-race and drown with her. I was like a madman, I wandered on the shore for days, I could neither eat nor sleep. And then she came again, and I knew that it was my life or hers, and I, being of the earth, clung to the life of form, and I shot her again. And now I am in torment. I love her, I long for her, I call to her in the unseen, and when she comes to me, I wait for her with a rifle."

He came to an abrupt stop and remained rigid, gazing into the heart of the dying fire, his empty pipe in his hand. I glanced surreptitiously at my watch, and saw that the hands were pointing to 11. His hour was upon him.

He rose, and crossing the room, drew back the draperies at the far end and revealed a casement window. Flinging it open, he seated himself on the sill and gazed fixedly into the darkness without. Moving softly I took my place behind him, where I could see what was happening outside, and be ready to seize hold of him if necessary.

For a while we waited; the clouds hurried over the moon sometimes, letting its radiance pour out in a silver flood, but more often hiding its face and leaving us in the roaring, crashing darkness of that surf-beaten coast.

It was indeed a "magic casement opening on the foam of perilous seas in faery lands forlorn." I shall never forget that vigil.

Nothing but heaving waters as far as eye could see, all flecked with foam in the moonlight where the reefs were hidden by the flood tide, which swirled below us like a mill-race. My companion's fine-cut features had the boldness and immobility of the statue of a Roman emperor, silhouetted against the silver background of the water.

He never stirred, he might have been carven in stone, till I saw a quiver run through him and knew that he had found that for which he waited. I strained my eyes to see what it was that had caught his attention, and sure enough, right out in the track of the moonlight, something was swimming. Coming steadily towards us through the reefs, the white shoulder lifting to the stroke just as he had described it, nearer, nearer, where no living soul could have swum in that wild tide-race, till, not 30 yards from the base of the cliffs, I could descry a woman's form with the hair streaming out like seaweed.

The man at the window leant right out stretching forth his arms to the swimmer, and I, fearing that he would overbalance, put mine gently round him and drew him back into the room.

He seemed oblivious of my presence, and yielded to the pressure as if asleep, and I lowered him gently to the floor where he lay motionless in a trance. I stooped to feel his pulse, and as I counted the slow beats, I heard a sound that made me hold my breath and listen. It seemed as if the sea had risen and filled the room, and yet not the material sea, but its ghost; shadowy impalpable sea-water flowed in waves to the very ceiling, and the seacreatures looked in from without.

Then I saw the form of a woman at the window. Shining with its own luminosity, it was clearly visible in the green gloom that was like the bottom of the sea. The hair floated out like seaweed, the shoulders gleamed like marble, the face was that of a *Beata Beatrix* awakened from her dream, and the eyes were like sea-water seen from a rock, and there, sure enough, were the marks where the silver bullets had wounded her.

We looked into each other's eyes, and I am convinced she saw me as clearly as I saw her, and that she knew me, for the same faint smile that I had seen before hovered on her lips. I spoke as one addressing a sentient creature.

"Do not try to take him in this way," I said, "or you will kill him. Trust me, I will make things right. I will explain everything."

She looked at me with those strange sea-green eyes of hers, as if piercing my very soul; apparently satisfied, she withdrew, and the shadowy seawater flowed after till the room was emptied.

I came to myself to find the quizzical eyes of my host fixed on me as he sat in his chair smoking his pipe.

"Physician, heal thyself!" he said.

I rose stiffly from my seat and subsided into a chair, lighting a cigarette with numbed fingers. A few whiffs of the soothing smoke steadied my nerves and enabled me to think.

"Well, doctor," came the voice of my host in gentle raillery, "what is your diagnosis?"

I paused, for I realized the critical nature of that which I was about to do. "If I were to tell you that last night I was at the bedside of that girl we saw swimming out there, and that she had two bullet wounds in her shoulder, what would you say?"

He leant forward, his lips parted, but no sound came from them. "If I told you that the bullet-wounds arose spontaneously without any external agency, and that the doctor considered them to be hysterical stigmata, how would you explain it?"

"By Jove," he exclaimed, "it sounds like a case of repercussion! I came across several instances of it when I was studying the Scottish State Papers relating to the witch trials in the sixteenth century. It was a thing often related of the witches, that they could project the astral double out of the physical body and so appear at a distance. I had something of that kind at the back of my mind when I made the silver bullets. Old country-folk believe that it is only with silver bullets that you can shoot a witch. Lead has no effect on them. But you mean to tell me that you have actually seen—seen in the flesh—the woman whose astral body it was we saw out there in the water? Good Lord, doctor, I am indeed out of my depth! I don't believe I ever thought in my heart that the things I was studying were real, I thought they were just states of consciousness."

"But aren't states of consciousness real?"

"Yes, of course they are, on their own plane, that is the whole teaching of occult science. But I always thought they were entirely subjective, experiences of the imagination. It never occurred to me that anyone else could share them."

"You—we both—seem to have shared in this girl's dreams, for she escapes from her dreary reality by imagining herself swimming in the sea."

"Tell me about her—What is she like? Where did you meet her?"

"Before I answer that question, will you first tell me your motive for asking it? Do you want to be rid of her? Because if so, I can probably persuade her to leave you alone."

"I want to make her acquaintance," came the reluctant reply. "I was pretty badly bitten once, and haven't spoken to a woman for years, but this—seems to be different. Yes, I would like to make her acquaintance. Tell me, who is she? what is she? what is her name? what are her people like?"

"She is, as you have seen, of very unusual appearance. Many people would not consider her beautiful, others would rave about her. She is somewhere in the twenties. Intelligent, refined, her voice is that of an educated woman. Her name I do not know, for she was lying in an infirmary bed, and was therefore just a number. Nor do I know what her people are. I don't fancy she has any, for I gathered she was entirely destitute. She is a shop girl by trade—drapery, to be precise."

During this recital my host's face had changed in an indefinable way. The cheeks had fallen in, the eyes had lost their brilliancy and become sunken, and a network of lines sprang up all over the skin. He had suddenly become worn and old, the burntout cinder of a man. I was at a loss to account for this appalling change till his words gave me the clue.

"I think," he said in a voice that had lost all resonance, "that I had better let the matter drop. A shop girl, you say? No, it would be most unsuitable, most unwise. It never does to marry outside one's own class. I—er—No, we will say no more about the matter. I must pull myself together. Now that I understand the condition I am sure I have the willpower to return to the normal. In fact I feel that you have cured me already. I am sure that I shall never have a return of my dream, its power over me is broken. If you will give me your companionship for just a few more days till I feel that my health is quite re-established I shall be all right. But we will not refer to the matter again; I beg of you, doctor, not to refer to it, for I wish to banish the whole experience from my mind."

Looking at him as he crouched in his chair, the broken, devitalized wreck of the man whose fine presence I had admired, it seemed to me that the remedy was worse than the disease. He had, by an effort of his trained will, broken the subtle magnetic rapport that bound him to the girl, and with the breaking of it, the source of his vitality had gone.

"But look here," I protested, "are you sure that you are doing the right thing? The girl may be quite all right in herself, even if she has to work for a living. If she means all this to you, surely you are throwing away something big."

For answer he rose, and going silently out of the room, closed the door behind him, and I knew that argument was useless. He was bound within his limitations and unable to escape out of them into the freedom which is life. Of the earth, earthy. I wrote a full account of these transactions to Taverner, and then settled down to await his instructions as to future procedure.

The situation was somewhat strained. My host looked like a man whose life had fallen about his ears. Day by day, almost hour by hour, he seemed to age. He sat in his rock-hewn room, refusing to move, and it was with the greatest difficulty that I succeeded in coaxing him out daily for a walk on the smooth hard sands that stretched for miles when the tide receded. When the water was up he would not go near it; he seemed to have a horror of the sea.

Two days passed in this way, with no word from Taverner, till on our return from our morning walk, we found that a slip of paper had been pushed under the door of our cavern. It was the ordinary post office intimation to say that a telegram had been brought in our absence, and now awaited me at the post office. Not sorry for a break in our routine, though a little uneasy about my patient, I immediately set off on the three-mile walk to the town to get my telegram. I went up the perilous path cut out of the face of the rock, and then along the cliff road, for though it was possible to walk into town on the sands, the tide was coming in, and it was doubtful if I would be able to round the headland before the undercliff was awash, at any rate my host thought it was too risky for a stranger to attempt it.

As I went up over the turf of the headland, a thrill ran through me like wine to a starving man. Th e air was full of dancing golden motes; the turf, the rock, the sea, were alive with a vast life and I could feel their slow breathing. And I thought of the man I had left in the dwelling in the cliff face, the man who had come so far in his quest of the larger life, but who dared not take the final step.

At the post office of that desolate and forsaken watering-place I duly received my telegram.

"Am sending stigmata case. She arrives 4.15. Arrange lodgings and meet her. Taverner." I gave a whistle that brought the postmaster and his entire staff to the front counter, and taking counsel with them, I obtained certain addresses whither I repaired, and fi nally succeeded in arranging suitable accommodation. What the upshot would be could not imagine, but at any rate it was out of my hands now.

At the appointed time I presented myself at the station and soon picked out my protégée from the scanty handful of arrivals. She looked very tired with the journey; frail, forlorn, and shabby. What with the fume of the engine and the frowst of the cab, there was no smell of the sea to revive her, and I could hardly get a word out of her during the drive to the lodgings, but as she disembarked from the crazy vehicle, a rush of salt-laden wind struck her in the face, and below us, in the dusk, we heard the crash-rush of the waves on the pebbles. The effect was magical. The girl flung up her head like a startled horse, and vitality seemed to flow into her, and when I presented her to her landlady, there was little to indicate the convalescent I had represented her to be.

When I returned to the rock-hewn eyrie of my host, his courtesy forbade him to question me as to the cause of my long absence, and indeed, I doubt if he felt any interest, for he seemed to have sunk into himself so completely that his grip on life was gone. I could hardly rouse him sufficiently to make him take the evening paper I had brought from the town; it lay on his knee unread while he gazed into the driftwood fire with unseeing eyes.

The following day the tide had not receded sufficiently for a morning walk, so it was not till the afternoon that we went for our constitutional. We had left it rather late, and on our way back in the early winter twilight we had to ford several gathering pools. We swung along over the sand barefoot, boots slung over our shoulders and trousers rolled to the knee, for it was one of those mild days that often come in January—when out on the edge of the incoming surf we saw a figure.

"Good Lord!" said my companion. "Who in the world is the fool out there? He will be cut off by the tide and won't be able to get out of the bay by now. He will have to come up by the cliff path. I had better warn him." And he let out a halloo.

But the wind was blowing towards us, and the figure, out there in the noise of the surf, did not hear. My companion went striding over the sand towards the solitary wader, but I, who had somewhat better eyes than he had, did not elect to accompany him, for I had seen long hair blown out like seaweed and the flying folds of a skirt.

I saw him walk into the ankle-deep water that creamed over the flat sands, forerunner of the advancing line of breakers. He called again to the wader, who turned but did not come towards him, but instead held out her hand with a strange welcoming gesture. Slowly, as if fascinated by that summoning hand, he advanced into the water, till he was within touch of her. The first of the advancing waves smote her knees and ran past her in yeasty foam. The next smote her hip; the tide was rising fast with the wind behind it. A shower of over-carried spray hit him in the face. Still the girl would not move, and the waves were mounting up perilously behind her. It was not until he caught the outstretched hand that she yielded and let him draw her ashore.

They came towards me over the sand, still hand in hand, for they had forgotten to loosen their fingers, and I saw that the life had come back to his face and that his eyes sparkled with the brilliancy of fire. I drew back into the shadow of a rock, and oblivious of me, they passed up the steep path to the cliff dwelling. A glow of firelight shone out as he opened the door to admit her, and I saw her wet hair streaming over her shoulders like seaweed and his profile was like the rock-cut statue of a Roman emperor.

Above this eruptive cadaver, the head, tumultuous, enormous, encircled by a disordered crown of thorns, hung down lifeless. One lacklustre eye half opened as a shudder of terror or of sorrow traversed the expiring figure. The face was furrowed, the brow seamed, the cheeks blanched; all the drooping features wept, while the mouth, unnerved, its under jaw racked by tetanic contractions, laughed atrociously.

FROM *LA BAS* BY J K HUYSMANS

FURTHER READING

Many of the stories in this collection were first published in pamphlets, journals, or what would have been considered "zines" of their day. The following is our attempt to track the first publications, or at least some of the earliest ones containing the author's works. We realize there may be discrepancies, as so many editions of the stories ran and were included in collections not unlike the one you are holding in your hands. This book is meant as an homage to such collections, and we hope that it inspires you to seek out more stories by the authors or thumb through the original collections.

Sir Edward Bulwer Lytton's "The House and the Brain" had an alternate title of "The Haunters and the Haunted" and was published in *The Haunters and the Haunted: Ghost Stories and Tales of the Supernatural*, and edited by Ernest Rhys, London: Daniel O'Connor, 1921.

Montague Rhodes James' "Casting the Runes" was published in *More Ghost Stories of Antiquary*, London: Edward Arnold. 1911.

Mary Wilkens Freeman's "Luella Miller" was published in *The Wind in the Rose-Bush and Other Stories of the Supernatural*. New York: Doubleday, Page & Company. 1903.

Ambrose Bierce's "An Inhabitant of Carcosa" was first published in the *San Francisco News Letter and California Advertiser*. San Francisco. 1886.

Ralph Adams Cram's "No. 252 Rue M. le Prince" was first published in *Black Spirits & White: A Book of Ghost Stories*. Chicago: Stone and Kimball, 1895.

Aleister Crowley's "The Testament of Magdalen Blair" was first published in *The Equinox: Vol. 1, No. 9* by in London, 1913.

Robert W. Chamber's "The Messenger" was published in *Famous Modern Ghost Stories, selected with an introduction by Dorothy Scarborough, PhD*. G.P. New York and London: Putnam's Sons. 1921.

Sir Arthur Conan Doyle's "The Ring of Thoth" was published as part of the collection *The Captain of the Pole Star and Other Tales*. London: Lonngman's, Green, and Co. 1890.

Bram Stoker's "The Dream of Red Hands" was published in *The Sketch: A Journal of Art and Actuality*. Ingram Brothers. London. 1894, and then as part of the collection *Dracula's Guest*. Ireland: George Routledge and Sons. 1914.

Edgar Allan Poe's "Ligeia" was published in *The American Museum* in 1838, Baltimore. It was republished, revised, and edited throughout Poe's life. This version appeared first in *Famous Modern Ghost Stories* and selected with an introduction by Dorothy Scarborough, PhD. G.P. New York and London: Putnam's Sons. 1921.

Frank Belkamp Long's *At the Home of Poe* was first published in *The United Amateur, Volume XVI, No. 4*. Georgetown, IL: United Amateur Press Association. 1916.

Howard Phillips Lovecraft's *The Alchemist* was first published in *The United Amateur, Volume XVI, No. 4*. Georgetown, IL: United Amateur Press Association. 1916.

Joseph Sheridan Le Fanu's "Dickon the Devil" was published in numerous collections. It appeared first in *London Society*, Christmas Number, 1872, and later in *Madam Crowl's Ghost and other Tales of Mystery*, collected and edited by M.R. James, London: G. Bell & Sons Limited, 1923.

Arthur Machen's "The White People" published in *The House of Souls*, London: Grant Richards Ltd. 1906.

Dion Fortune's "The Sea Lure" was first published as part of *The Secrets of Dr. Taverner*, London: Society of the Inner Light. 1922.

ABOUT THE EDITOR

Lon Milo DuQuette is a bestselling author and lecturer on such topics as magick, tarot, and the Western Mystery Traditions. He is currently U.S. Deputy Grand Master of Ordo Templi Orientis and is on the faculty of the Omega Institute and the Maybe Logic Academy. Among his many books, he is the author of *My Life with Spirits*, *Understanding Aleister Crowley's Thoth Tarot*, *Enochian Vision Magick*, and *Tarot of Ceremonial Magick*. He is also the curator for the Magical Antiquarian Curiosity Shoppe series of e-books, which includes Robert Chamber's *The King in Yellow* and Sir Edward Bulwer-Lytton's *Zanoni*. He lives in Costa Mesa, CA with his beautiful wife Constance. Visit Lon online at: *www.facebook.com/lonmilo*.

To Our Readers

Weiser Books, an imprint of Red Wheel/Weiser, publishes books across the entire spectrum of occult, esoteric, speculative, and New Age subjects. Our mission is to publish quality books that will make a difference in people's lives without advocating any one particular path or field of study. We value the integrity, originality, and depth of knowledge of our authors.

Our readers are our most important resource, and we appreciate your input, suggestions, and ideas about what you would like to see published.

Visit our website at *www.redwheelweiser.com* to learn about our upcoming books and free downloads, and be sure to go to *www.redwheelweiser.com/newsletter* to sign up for newsletters and exclusive offers.

You can also contact us at *info@rwwbooks.com* or at

Red Wheel/Weiser, llc
665 Third Street, Suite 400
San Francisco, CA 94107